Wind Castle

by

Brian Hammar

Rosstrum Publishing
Nashua, NH

Also by Brian Hammar

Anastasia's Quest for Wind Castle
The Fall of Wind Castle
Cold Facts
A Time to Stop
There Was A Man

Short Stories

Fishermen's Justice
Shoes
Spin
A Warm Place
Adjutant
Vigilante
Treacherous Care
One Good Soul
Frothgarde

Also available from Rosstrum Publishing

Non-Fiction

Fast Track for Caregivers
366 Tips for a Successful Job Search
How to Improve your Interviewing Skills
States Have Rights
Journey of a Beam: A 9-11 Pictorial Remembrance
The Happy Heart Cookbook
The Teacher Within the Coach
The Dave Maynard Spin (Also in Large Print)

Fiction

Lawless in Brazil
Dr. Lawless, I Presume
Timberline
Pursuit
Missing
Death in Cedar Canyon
Emotions In Motion (poetry)
Fishermen's Justice (short story)
Tapping In To Murder

Visit *www.rosstrumpublishing.com* for details

ACKNOWLEDGMENTS

The author would like to acknowledge the support of his family during his years of writing. His wife Mary (Betty) and his children, Christine and Jennifer, were his inspiration and motivation for the many hours he spent before a word processor. This story would not have been possible without their understanding and encouragement.

The author would also like to acknowledge the tremendous support he received from the Tyngsborough Writers Group. This group of dedicated writers was founded and sustained for many years by Mike Johnson and his sister, Karen. Specifically, the author would like to acknowledge the contributions made by Mike Johnson, Rick Cooper, Karen Johnson, Dale Phillips, Joe Ross, Peter Spring, Bernie Ziegner, and the many other TWG members throughout the years. He would also like to thank the staff of the Tyngsborough Public Library in Tyngsborough, Massachusetts, who supported the Tyngsborough Writers Group for so long.

Finally, the author would like to acknowledge the contribution of his nephew, Christopher Hammar, a fine graphic artist responsible for the cover artwork for the Wind Castle series.

DEDICATION

To Betty, Christine, and Jennifer.

Rosstrum Publishing
A division of The Border Company LLC
8 Strawberry Bank Rd., Unit 20
Nashua, NH 03062-2763
www.rosstrumpublishing.com
rosstrumpublishing@gmail.com

ISBN no.: 978-1-62570-044-5 Large print
978-1-47750-857-2 Regular print

e-book available from iTunes and Smashwords

Manufactured in the United States of America
First large print printing August 2018

2 4 6 8 10 9 7 5 3 1

Wind Castle

TABLE OF CONTENTS

.

O_{NE}

Making Ready

A STRING OF BELLS hit the door to the outfitter's store. George Severe pushed it open and stepped over the wood threshold into the warm room. After he removed his hat and opened his jacket to the warmth, he walked past the hot stove to the counter where the clerk and several others had stopped their conversations.

George looked down to the average-sized man and extended his hand. "Hello! My name's George Severe. I'm supposed to meet an A. J. Strummond here."

The clerk answered, "Glad to meet ya, Mr. Severe. We was just talkin' about you. I'd be Tom Franklin, owner of this store. It's surely nice to meet the man who just about doubled my sales for this time of year."

"Well, as much as I'd like to take the credit, I didn't make the arrangements."

"No matter. I'm sure I can give ya anything ya need

and for less money than you'd spend in Durango."

"I don't doubt it." George placed his gloves and hat on the counter and looked toward the other men standing nearby.

"I'm Stan Maszewski." The heavy dark man extended his hand. "Mark Waxman sent me to help you with your monitoring equipment. Strummond should be here soon."

George shook his hand as the bells on the door clanged. George and Stan turned to see the new patron. "Speak of the devil," the clerk said. "Looks like half your bunch got here OK, Annie."

George looked at Stan and said quietly, "Annie?"

"Strummond," Stan answered. "Our guide."

George found it difficult to believe that A. J. Strummond was a woman. She walked into the outfitter's wearing clothes that best resembled those of an old-time prospector. Her stringy, knotted hair was short – just covering her ears below her dusty hat. And her face was weathered. Even her voice did not reveal her true sex. "That'll do for now," she said to the clerk, "if one of them be this Severe character."

George was ashamed to be thinking how ugly she appeared – even if she were a *man,* she would have been ugly. "That's me." He tried imagining her without the decrepit clothing as he stepped toward her from the counter, but he could see no potential for beauty in the huddled form that loosened her heavy wool scarf.

She introduced herself to George and some of the other members of the party. Her voice was crusty and she spoke abruptly. When one of the party questioned her suitability to serve as their guide, both she and the clerk assured them there were few in Colorado who knew the area better than she and it was well-known that she possessed the talent, endurance, and determination needed to lead their expedition. George thought she must have gained her endurance and determination from years of ugliness.

"Now the feller who hired me figgered you need the best. And by the looks of some of you, I'd say he's right. There's been plenty of snow and wind this winter and if you'd like to take on that mountain with someone who don't know shit, then I'd be plenty glad to go back to my nice warm cabin," she said, looking at George.

Stan interrupted, "You're just what we need, Annie. Can we call you *Annie*?"

"Course ya can. And so can you, Blondie," she said to George. "Lord, they're sure makin' 'em big back east these days. Well, what do ya say?"

"Mark's given me nothing but the best since I started working for him," George said. "And I'm not about to second guess his choices."

She was quick to organize the group, instructing them to collect their supplies and carry them across the street to a hangar at a small airfield. She advised them that two helicopters would take them up the mountainside as high as practical below the clouds. They were to take their first measurements and hike the remaining distance to the summit where they would collect more data. Two radios would be provided that could be used in the event of an emergency or to call for the helicopters when finished. She suggested they might be on the mountain for three or four days but expressed a willingness to remain longer if necessary.

"One of you wait here for the stragglers while the others

get packin'. I'll take Severe here over to the hangar and go over the route."

"I'll go with you," Stan interjected.

George responded to Annie's inquiring glance, "He's in charge of all the instruments."

"Suit yourself, Mister." She looked back at the others and said, "The rest of ya, get movin'. These two'll meet you at the lodge when we're done. Eat your fill and get plenty o' rest. Some of you greenhorns are gonna need it. The air's mighty thin up there and it's gonna be a chore for ya ta keep up."

George and Stan met the other members of the party in the dining room at the lodge. The others had ordered their supper and one of the men offered them two of the three remaining seats while asking the whereabouts of their guide. George explained that she would meet them at the airport in the morning and he reached for a menu.

It was a paper menu – typed daily by the owner of the lodge. It offered chicken-fried steak or pork chops with chili, pan-fried potatoes, and carrots. He hailed the waitress and asked for the steak if it came with gravy. She assured him that *everything* came with gravy, ". . . and plenty of biscuits to sop it up with. You won't need the menu. This group's big enough, I'll just keep bringin' on the food 'til ya stop eatin'." She filled his cup with coffee brewed to loosen the most obstinate bowels.

George pushed the coffee aside since he preferred water or *tonic* – his term for soda pop, which did not escape significant razzing. The more experienced coffee drinkers knew that particular brew could be dangerous and they limited their consumption.

"So where ya from?" one of George's tablemates asked.

"Connecticut."

"Coe-NEC-tee-cut," a cowboy said from across the table. "Ain't that that puny State somewheres in the northeast?"

"You're thinking of Rhode Island. Connecticut is right next door."

"Hell, there ain't no place back east big enough worth callin' a State."

"What do ya say ya tell us what it is we're goin' after up on the mountain?" another diner asked.

George answered, "We're going up to study a cloud that's decided to park itself up there."

"Why do ya wanna do that?"

"I'm a meteorologist."

"What's so special about this cloud?"

"It seems to go anywhere it wants to."

"Hell, all clouds do that!" the cowboy added. "Send over some of them spuds," he asked another.

"That's true, but this one doesn't follow all the rules."

A bearded man chewing on a gravy-soaked biscuit entered the conversation for the first time. "How d' ya mean?"

"It doesn't move along with any weather system. You can predict where most storms will go, but not this one. It'll move along in a predictable pattern and then turn suddenly for no reason at all.

"A cloud this big should be dropping all kinds of snow or rain but the only thing it's dropped so far is a mercenary named Jack LaRoche and his horse." George noticed several heads rise, including that of Stan Maszewski, who had not been participating in the conversation. "Did you know Jack

LaRoche, Stan?"

"A little. He was a pretty nasty fellow. Mark's been after him for a long time." Stan quickly ended his participation by stuffing some food into his mouth.

George continued addressing the others. "LaRoche was found half-buried in a Tennessee swamp by a farmer who said he saw him fall from the sky."

"Probably fell from a plane or somethin'. What makes you think this cloud has anything to do with it?" the bearded man asked.

"Because of the way it behaves. At first, I thought it was just a quirk of a storm cloud. But then I met an American Indian on my vacation who told me about his father, Cloud Walker, who got lost in a cloud at Harney Peak in South Dakota. Two years later, he showed up in New Mexico. Cloud Walker had no memory of where he'd been all that time until later when he started telling people he'd been in some strange land with all kinds of peculiar creatures and things."

"Just another drunken Injun on a two year binge, that's all," said the diner sitting beside the cowboy.

"I know it's hard to believe, but there's more."

"Bull shit," the cowboy said while shaking his head.

"No, really. Listen! A pilot sees an island floating off the coast of Florida that's not recorded on any maps or charts. LaRoche escapes from prison and disappears in the foggy mountains of Montana. Then reappears in a Tennessee swamp! It all fits. There's something flying around up there."

"You're really full of it. Ya know that?" the cowboy responded. "What do you take us for anyways – a bunch of yokels?"

George smiled hesitantly. "Well, if I'm wrong, at least we'll get some good weather data."

The cowboy took his napkin from his lap and threw it on his plate while addressing the man beside him. "This guy is full of shit . . . or he's crazy." He looked back at George and said, "Look, if I want to hear bedtime stories, I'll go somewheres else. C'mon, Charlie." The cowboy and his friend left the table. The rest of the party did the same shortly afterward.

As George was about to enter his room, he saw Stan hailing the cowboy in the corridor. To be less conspicuous, George stepped into his room and listened to their conversation from behind his door.

"Listen to me, cowboy. You'd better improve your attitude if you're going to be a part of this group."

"What are you talking about?"

"You know what I'm talking about. Don't mess with Severe."

"I didn't mess with him. He messed with me."

"I don't care how it looks to you. You just go along with anything he says. Got it?"

"Hey! Nobody makes a fool out of me."

George heard some shuffling as Stan continued, "Look. My boss is paying you good money for this. Probably more money than you'll see in the next three months. If you want to blow your biggest payday for the year then go ahead and open your trap once more. Now, do you got it?"

"Yeah, I got it."

George heard some more shuffling as he closed his

door tightly. Then he heard some footsteps that stopped outside his door before moving along.

George stepped away from the door wondering what had transpired. He found a local weekly newspaper and read it while resting on his bed. Later, he looked up at the rafters near the ceiling and thought about the next day. He saw the expedition landing on the side of the mountain and he planned the sequence of measurements and tests. Suddenly, he felt a bitter chill — a foreboding that gripped his spine, tore him from his thoughts, and jerked him upright. He tried shaking it. Then his stomach weakened. It wasn't the gravy. It wasn't the water. It wasn't anything he had eaten. He was being torn by a presentiment of impending doom.

He walked across the wood floor and checked the heater. It was warm. There was no cold air leaking into the room from the window. He paced nervously with his arms crossed before his chest.

He stopped. One hand clutched his coat while the other hand remained huddled to his chest. Then he relaxed slightly, draped the coat over his shoulders, and paced again. Finally, he sat on the edge of his bed. A twisted expression distorted his face. He knew the feeling all too well. And he knew something bad always followed.

George considered canceling the trip up the mountain. Despite his long search, he hoped the cloud would be gone in the morning. He would do anything to rid himself of the terrible feeling.

Slowly, the fear subsided, but a touch of chill remained — as if to remind him of the experience. He walked out of his room and down the stairs to the telephone in the lobby.

It was after midnight on the east coast. George knew that once asleep, his wife was deaf to anything except the cries and giggles of their daughter. As he expected, the phone rang eight times before he heard some fumbling on the line. "Janey? Janey? Are you there? C'mon Janey! Wake up and talk to me."

He knew she was still half-asleep when she finally spoke, "Hello."

"Janey, it's George. I'm sorry I called so late. We're going up in the morning." She didn't respond after his pause. "Are you still there?"

"Yes," Jane mumbled.

"I just wanted to talk to you before we go. It might be a few days before I'm near a phone again. How's Anastasia doing?"

"She's fine . . . sleeping."

"That's good. She's doing a lot better . . . finally letting us get some sleep too. Janey!" There was a long pause. "I'm sorry about the way I left."

"Yeah . . . well, when are you coming home?"

"Our guide says three or four days on the mountain. I don't know. I should be home in time for the party."

"You'd better. It's her first birthday and her father should be here."

George was silent for a moment before he added, "Hey, Janey! You'd never guess. Our guide is a woman!"

"What's wrong with that?"

"Oh, nothing, but I've got to tell you," he lowered his voice to a whisper. "she is ug-ly. I thought she was a guy at first!" George was quiet again. He wanted to hear her voice – not his.

Jane asked, "George? Is something wrong? You're not one for chitchat."

"No. . . . I just had a little trouble getting to sleep . . . excited about the trip tomorrow, I guess."

"Are you sure that's all?"

"Of course! Everything's been going fine. With any luck, we'll be home real soon. I'll call you when we get down from the hill. OK?"

"OK. Be careful."

"I will. . . . I love you, Jane."

"Love ya, Georgie."

"Give Anastasia a big smooch from Papa."

"Later. She's sleeping."

"Good night, Jane." George spoke her name just to hear it again.

"Good night." The phone hummed.

George thought Jane might forget much of their conversation and he smiled, thinking how difficult it always was to get Jane moving after waking her. He walked slowly to his room, chilled, almost tearful, and concerned that he may not see his wife and daughter for a long time – if ever. He changed and slid under the blankets of his bed.

Somehow, he found sleep between his tossing fits.

*T*wo

Expedition

THE FIRST FAINT LIGHT of day caught George awake. The chill had gone but his impalpable fear remained. He tried shaking the feeling as he rose from his bed and gathered his toiletries for the short walk down the hall to the communal shower room. The hot water quickly filled the room with steam. He stood, nearly sleeping under the comforting spray, greedily absorbing the warmth. He did not leave the shower until other lodgers arrived. He found some vacant mirror space and shaved. Then he returned to his room and dressed for breakfast.

Like the previous night, the morning meal was served family style. Bowls of scrambled eggs and hot oatmeal, a platter of hot cakes, and two pots of gut-rending coffee flanked a large platter of ham, bacon, and sausage. George looked at the coffee and thought there must be an asphalt plant nearby that could make better use of it.

He was first to sit at the table and he feared the food would cool before the others arrived. However, no sooner had he served himself, than people drifted to the table – some half sleeping, some spry and anxious to begin the trek. They enjoyed a hearty meal and light conversation before their departure for the airport.

When the nine men arrived at the hangar, Annie was checking the straps that would secure their cargo in the helicopters. She greeted them inside the hangar and instructed the group on procedures necessary for a safe trek to the summit. Her tone clearly conveyed her insistence that each member of the party follow her instructions without question or hesitation. After her lecture, they loaded and boarded the helicopters for the flight to the higher slopes.

During the noisy trip Annie called out to George, "You're not very talkative this mornin', Blondie. Did you rest up like I tol' ya?"

"More or less."

"That's some answer, Greenhorn."

George didn't respond.

"Well, something's botherin' ya. Come on! Spit it out."

"Nothing really . . . just a bad feeling."

"Well, shake it off, Sonny. You can tell me about it later. I can't hear much over the chopper anyways."

The cloud had remained in its position – hovering, or moored, at the peak of the mountain. The helicopters rested on a flat area while the party unloaded the equipment. Annie directed the party in the needs of a temporary camp while George examined the instruments.

A cooking fire was readied for the afternoon meal.

After eating, George surveyed the equipment and supplies with Annie – pressure sensors, temperature gauges, weather balloons, cylinders containing helium gas, sonic measurement devices, laser devices . . . all the latest technological gadgets needed for a thorough examination of the cloud mass and the surrounding atmosphere. He explained the purpose of each device and the measurements he wanted.

George heard the shuffling of snowshoes behind him. Stan Maszewski was hardly recognizable in his hooded parka. All the party looked the same – except Annie who wore a bright orange snowsuit.

"You don't have to do all of this yourself," Stan said. "You don't think the department would have given you all this stuff without sending along someone who knows how to use it – do you?"

"Of course not," George answered.

The two men assembled and activated some of the instruments. Two balloons were released. One climbed slowly, then, according to the ground instruments, stopped shortly after entering the cloud. The other rose quickly into the cloud, was lost for a moment, then the instrument it carried fell from the bottom of the cloud with the tattered balloon streaming behind.

"The balloon must have torn," Stan said.

"Or something tore it." George watched as Stan examined the instrument. "Any damage?"

"I'd say so."

"Can you fix it?"

"I'll try at the next stop."

The instrument carried by the first balloon transmitted measurements to a recorder at the camp. While George and Stan continued their work, Annie and the others packed the supplies and equipment for the hike to the summit. The signals from the balloon were strong and clear. A few other instruments measured conditions on the ground while the recorder continued plotting information.

George was reluctant to discuss his theory about the cloud again. So, without any comment about the data he collected, he suggested they pack the remaining equipment and begin the climb. He quietly scuffled on his snowshoes along the slopes behind Annie.

"You wanna tell me what worried ya this mornin'?" Annie asked.

"Just a bad feeling I had about the trip," he huffed as he spoke.

"What kind o' bad feelin'?"

"Like something is going to happen."

"You get those feelings often?"

"No, but when I do, there's usually a reason. It kind of runs in the family."

"How say?"

"My mother was the same way. If it wasn't for her, our whole family would've been wiped out in a hurricane."

"That a fact?"

"When I was just a kid, I'd gone out to the yard to watch a storm. The wind was really blowing and my little sister came out to tell me to get back inside, but I didn't listen to her.

"Well, it wasn't long before my father had me by the arm dragging me down to the basement with my mother and sister. It was pretty scary down there, listening to the surf hammering the seawall.

"All of a sudden, my mother shivered and she cried out, 'We've got to get out of here!' and sent me and my sister upstairs. We just about got to the top of the stairs when a wall of water crashed through the glass doors in the basement, taking my parents and the stairs along with it. My father managed to save himself but he couldn't find my mother in time.

"I don't understand how she knew to get out of there and I don't understand why I get the same feelings sometimes. But it happens. And when it does, I get a little nervous."

"Well, I don't never mess with Providence, Blondie. But I don't usually get myself in a fix I can't get out of either. So, you stick by me and I expect everything'll be fine."

"You can bet I will – if I can keep up with you." George was amazed at her endurance. He was quickly exhausted – as were many of the party. His pack seemed heavier and heavier. Yet Annie pressed ahead at the same steady pace – stopping only to prod her charges.

The group stopped to remove their snowshoes and don their ice cleats as the terrain changed. There were a few areas where they were forced to use their ice axes or set pitons and ropes to climb steep slopes. Generally, Annie circumvented the most hazardous areas.

George and Stan kept pace with Annie throughout the climb but, despite Annie's efforts to ease the struggle, several men faltered and fell back. They usually closed the distance when Annie stopped to change equipment. When the men were permitted a rest, it was difficult to get them moving again.

They camped on comparably level ground a half-day's climb from the peak. After the campsite was established,

George and Stan collected data. Annie joined them.

"You two keep up pretty good," she said. "We already lost near half a day and we're gonna lose more tomorrow if we can't keep them mules movin'." She paused for a moment but neither man spoke. "One of you is gonna have ta take up the rear tomorrow and crack the whip a bit or we'll be spendin' a week up here."

"I'll do it," George said.

"No, not you. You know what it is you're lookin' for. I need ya at the point."

"I guess that leaves me." Stan brushed some snow from one of the instruments as he spoke.

"You guessed right, Fella."

Stan smiled. "OK, I volunteer."

"That's awfully good o' ya," she said as he tied the instrument to an inflated balloon. "And try and get them ta help each other out while yer at it!" She turned to George. "Some bunch you got here. They ain't much concerned about their buddies."

"Most of us met for the first time at the outfitter's in town." Thinking he had to add more to the explanation, he said, "Some of them are local types but I'm pretty sure a lot of them are in the kind of business where they don't *want* to make friends."

"What *kind* of business?" she asked. As George tried to find a way of ducking her question, she added, "Never mind. It ain't nothin' ta me anyways. My job is to get them up this hill and I suppose it don't matter whether you're all best friends or worst enemies. But I'll tell ya one thing, if we get into any trouble along the way, you'd better work together."

"I think we will. I didn't pick these men, but I have to believe my boss knew what he was doing. After all, he picked you, too!"

"Well, that's the best thing he could've done, Sonny. You got the best in these parts. Not that I'm braggin', mind you."

"I don't doubt it one bit."

George heard Annie calling everyone. The tent was still dark. It seemed to be at least an hour before sunrise. He looked at his watch and realized it *was* time to prepare for the climb. He dressed and left the tent. The visibility was poor – not because of wind-blown snow, but because they were enveloped in a heavy fog.

George removed the charts from the recorders and stored them for future study while breakfast was prepared. Annie packed her tent before most had finished eating. When she packed things from under the diners they got the message and gulped the last of their food.

The sky above and the cold rocky peak were totally obscured. Nine men and one crusty old woman formed a line and resumed their climb. Annie and George led with Stan trailing the group. They started without wearing their snow-shoes but were forced to don them after the first hour. Visibility had improved at first but the ceiling pressed down upon them as they climbed. As the slower members of the group lagged, despite Stan's prodding, it became difficult to see them from the point. George noticed Annie's frustration with the slow pace. The group finally tightened its ranks just before lunch.

During the break, George and Stan prepared a balloon for launch. The valve on the bottle of helium had frozen and Stan searched a pack for another cylinder. He removed a first aid kit, some signal flares and a flare gun, radio parts, and candy bars, which he spread over the snow. He found the helium container and handed it to George. The other climbers heated their stoves and dug into their packs for coffee and dehydrated stew.

The air was extremely cold and George struggled to tie the instrument to the balloon lanyard. The balloon and its cargo disappeared soon after release but, before Stan could tune the receiver, the instrument fell to the ground. When George shuffled to where the instrument had fallen, he discovered no lanyard or balloon fragments. It was obvious to him, as it was to Stan, that he had failed to fasten the instrument securely. The balloon was probably still climbing. They abandoned their efforts and had something to eat.

The two men sat next to Annie, hoping to hear her estimate to the top. She said, "We've lost a lot o' time but we could reach the peak by mid-afternoon — if there ain't no more delays. She looked at Stan when she made her point.

"I'll push harder," Stan said. "What are we going to do when we get there, George?"

"I'm not really sure yet."

"Well, you must have *something* in mind — take more measurements, send up some more balloons, what?"

"I really can't say just yet. The first thing will be to explore the cloud to see if we can get past an edge and take measurements above."

"You may find out that you can't *get* around it. It may be higher than the peak."

"I don't think so. Remember the altitude readout from the

balloon?"

"I'm not sure *any* of those measurements can be trusted."

"Maybe so. We'll see when we get there."

When all had eaten, Annie asked George to join her while she walked ahead to survey the path. She had seen a shadow in the mist and suspected it might be an obstruction. George donned his snowshoes and pack while she walked toward the rest of the group.

"George and me are gonna take a look-see up ahead," she said to them. "Finish packin' up and do whatever duties ya need to do. And don't nobody go wanderin' off alone. We don't want to lose anyone in this soup or down some crevasse." She looked around. A few of the men nodded as she looked their way. She walked back to George with her pack on one shoulder and strapped her snowshoes to her boots.

George noticed two of the party sorting through some of the supplies Stan had left on the snow. One of them, who George recognized as the cowboy irritated by his story about the cloud, was brandishing the flare gun and suggesting to his friend that they might be able to get a look at the peak. As Annie passed them, she said, "Let's go, boys. Get that stuff packed away."

George looked back at Stan. "You might want to give the cowboy and his friend a little kick."

Stan set down the instrument, which had fallen from the balloon and stood in place. "I'll get them moving." Before George and Annie left, he jibed George for his carelessness in securing the instrument to the balloon.

"George, you really beat the shit out of this thing. Don't worry though, I might be able to salvage it."

George smiled.

Annie broke a path toward the shadow in the mist and George followed. He noticed that she was walking over some trails that had already been broken. As he stepped closer to her, he thought he saw some unusually large footprints ahead of them.

"Annie! Do you see what you're walking on?"

"I don't see nothin'. And neither do you."

"But this could be important!"

"Not important enough." She continued treading over the impressions.

"Annie! Wait a minute!" George stepped in front of her. "Listen. When I was tracking a storm near the Himalayas in Tibet, I learned that there were a lot of sightings of something called Yeti – a great big thing they call an abominable snowman. These tracks could be the same thing!"

"Sasquatch."

"What?"

"We call 'em Sasquatch – Bigfoot. But there ain't no such thing."

"No such thing? What are you standing on?"

"I'm standin' on NOTHIN'. NOTHIN'! Do you understand me, Blondie?"

"No, I don't."

"People are always playin' gags like this. Makin' phony footprints to get people goin'."

"Way up here?"

"Ya never know. Look, I don't want to see a bunch of reporters up here gettin' theirselves killed chasin' after some-thin' that don't exist. And if it *does* exist, it's probably best left alone."

"But . . ."

"But nothin'. Let's get goin'."

Annie hiked toward the shadow before them. George could do little but follow. As they trudged through the snow, the shadow took form. Just as Annie expected, a rocky ledge projected from the side of the mountain. They would have to climb straight up a snow-filled ravine toward the peak or descend and pass below the ledge, hoping to find a gentler slope beyond. They followed the rock wall down a steep slope for a few minutes, searching for the base of the cliff.

They stopped and stood quietly in the snow facing the rock wall. Annie said. "Can't see any relief this way. Let's go up and test the grade ta see if this bunch can hack it." They had climbed a few feet above the place where they first encountered the ledge. George puffed. He reached to the ledge with his arm extending over his head. Annie rested her pack against the rock and said, "OK, take a minute an' catch yer breath."

George heard a slight thump – a mild concussion coming from the direction of the party. He was looking at Annie at the time. He could barely see the side of her face in the hood of her snowsuit but he had no trouble distinguishing it when it turned pale white despite a rosy, weather-beaten cheek. The change was so sudden, and it came just after he heard that weak, muffled concussion. He looked toward the expedition and saw the red tail trailing from the flare just as he heard a distant cry in the fog, "No!"

It all happen so quickly yet so slowly that every part of the event seemed to have its own story – the thump, Annie's sudden change in composure, the sight of the rising flare with an accompanying *pffffdth* sound, that distant desperate cry, and finally, the premature explosion of the flare a few hundred feet overhead. Then silence . . . for a moment. A brief moment that seemed like a thousand years. Annie looked toward the mountain peak. George followed her glance then looked back toward the rest area.

Then it began – a quiet, barely perceptible rumble.

It seemed to stop.

A thin, sharp crack was followed by another rumble, but this time it didn't stop. It was heavier than the first. Stronger. Struggling for manifestation.

"Against the wall," Annie screamed to George. "And hold on with all you got."

"Why? What's going on?" George saw the urgency in Annie's expression and he hugged the ledge, waiting for an answer.

"Avalanche!" she yelled. That word was all the explanation George needed to understand the danger. "Our only chance is the wall. Maybe it'll slow things down enough so we don't get swept away. Runnin' sure won't do us no good."

The rumble spread across the hidden mountain peak. It was no longer a small tremor. The snow moved under George's feet. The mountain shook as the drifted snow was loosed from its slopes. His eyes flashed terror to Annie.

"Hold on!" she yelled. "Or yer gonna die."

George hugged the ledge and closed his eyes, gritting his teeth.

The mountain continued shaking and the snow was moving. George thought he heard someone calling. He looked behind him and saw a figure appear out of the mist. It was Stan, trying to run toward them but sinking to his thighs with every step because he was not wearing his snowshoes. George could hardly make out his cries. "Take cover!" Stan yelled. "Avalanche!" Trees rolled along the slope with the snow – strong trees, bowled over without resistance. Then Stan was gone.

George pressed his brows to his cheeks and wished with all his imagination that he were someplace else. As he hugged the ledge, he wished he were home with Jane and Anastasia. What was he doing on a sinking mountain with a crusty old woman? What ever compelled him to want to climb to that silly cloud? He could have waited until the cloud stopped at a less treacherous place. He could be home right now – talking with Jane and playing with his daughter.

He opened his eyes. Visibility was poor. Frozen powder rose into the mist of the cloud. He turned his head away from the ledge. Waves of snow rolled and slid just a few feet away from him. The rumble swelled, stretching to engulf him. *Oh Janey, I'm dying*. He hugged the ledge again and tried blocking out the scene.

Squinting, he saw the snow pull away from Annie's feet. She slid down to George. As her foot crashed into his shin, she struggled for a grip on the rock wall. Though he could not hear her, he saw the word *Tarnation* on her lips as she rolled and finally found a handhold before the next wave of snow plowed into her and pushed her against George and the wall. George nearly fell but caught himself and gave Annie the extra support she needed to right herself.

Rocks tumbled down from the ledge toward the two

struggling climbers and they ducked against the wall. The snow shifted below them but they held their positions by lifting their feet as the snow passed. Their snowshoes were still lashed to their boots and they did not sink into the loose snow.

After an acute change in the feel and sound of the rumbling, George watched Annie lean back to look up at the wall. No sooner had she raised her head than she caught a large falling boulder on her chest. It knocked her from the ledge and she rolled down the slope with the snow. George nearly lost his grip as he tried to catch her. He was sure she was lost when he couldn't reach her so he clung to the wall to save himself.

One of his snowshoes was torn from his boot. It dangled loosely from the strap around his ankle. For a brief time, he managed to continue stepping over the snow as it passed him. His proximity to the ledge saved him from the savage flow. But as the avalanche grew more intense, his safety became less assured.

The mountain was mightier than he. A large flow of snow and ice crashed into the ledge and swept him from its face. He tumbled helplessly — buried, disinterred, and buried again. Gray sky and ledge and white snow and dark snow flashed before his eyes as he tumbled. He struggled but could not resist. He was lost and could not be saved.

Something caught his arm and dragged above him then tumbled over him. Then he felt the dragging at his shoulders and it tumbled over him again. It was Annie. Somehow she must have saved herself and now she was trying to save him. But she couldn't. They tumbled together uncontrollably past the bottom of the ledge. George found some comfort in thinking he would not die alone. Someone was with him. The moment of comfort carried thoughts of home. *Janey.*

THREE

Sasquatch

SILENCE, DARKNESS, and suffocating cold pressed upon George. When he tried moving, he felt only confinement and pain. He was not sure he was conscious. Perhaps he was dreaming. Something was missing. A feeling. That awesome sense of impending doom. Rumbling. *The rumbling stopped! I can't move! I can't see! Open your eyes, stupid.* But he couldn't. *I need some rest. . . . I need some . . . sleep.*

Something warm brushed at his face. The pressure around his chest eased. He smelled a breeze and breathed freely again. There was a sound of snow crunching under nearby footsteps. His arms were free and someone was stretching them – tugging to extricate his lower body. The tugging stopped and there was digging at his sides. Then more tugging and more digging. *One more pull should do it. Kick!*

He was free – but upside down. As the blood rushed to his head, he opened his eyes. The snow was too bright. That large inverted ledge seemed familiar. Some shadows moved about. The figures looked like people, but some were incredibly large. The smaller figures seemed to have difficulty walking and they were frequently assisted by the larger figures. Two were squatting over something nearby. His legs slid to one side as he tried to roll and right his view. *That's better.* The two figures were squatting over someone lying in the snow. One of the large figures looked in his direction and rose to approach him. George's vision faded. A private gray storm enveloped him. The figure was just a shadow as it took his hand and stroked his cheek and forehead. His curiosity could not sustain his consciousness. He needed rest. It was getting cold. A gray tunnel closed about the indistinguishable face examining him.

George dreamed he was being carried. He was certain he had dreamed it. He leaned his head away from the warm, musty fur coat and tried desperately to open his eyes. He thought he was moving and the picture that came to him confirmed it. The hillside seemed to bounce. A large figure ahead was carrying something or *someone* – maybe the same person he had seen stretched out on the snow.

He tried holding his eyes open but could not focus on anything. He believed he was cradled in the arms of some strong and enormous person. The air grew warmer and he heard the sounds of someone treading through grass and brush. His senses spun as he was lowered to the ground. Something at his back kept him from reclining completely.

George opened his eyes for a moment – long enough to recognize the form lying on the dirt a short distance away.

Annie? You're alive? He fought against clouding vision. A figure attended her. Another stood over George, then squatted by his legs and removed his shoes. His feet were pressed flatly to the earth. A tingling sensation, like a weak electric shock, ran up his legs. His head rolled back over the obstacle that kept him from reclining and he slept. In his sleep he heard a bell – just one ring with a resonance that emanated from the ground.

Helicopters hovered over the lower slope of the mountain where the devastation had ended. A small advance rescue party descended by cable to the mountainside. Four men formed two teams and began climbing over the debris toward the peak, searching for survivors. Ben Kniep and Josh Windale climbed together, debating the value of their effort.

"Damned tourists," Ben complained. "They do this all the time. They come up here and get themselves hurt or killed and then expect us to clean up. Amateurs, every one of them."

"Annie's no amateur," Josh answered.

"Yeah, well I still don't understand how she got suckered into bringin' these turkeys up here in the first place."

"She said something about owin' some feller back east."

"Oh yeah? Well, this ought to teach her to get mixed up with amateurs – if she's still kickin' that is." Ben huffed as he climbed past an uprooted tree.

"She's too ornery to croak up here. Hell, remember the time that bear got her? She lived to track him down out of plain meanness."

"She wasn't mean – just a little rough around the edges, and a damned sucker for amateurs."

"Don't say *wasn't*. I haven't written her off yet."

"I don't want to either, but sometimes you just gotta face the facts. Look at this mess! If anyone lived through this, it's a miracle – a damned miracle."

As they continued their climb a mist of fog from the cloud enveloped the two men. Ben gave his position at lead to Josh. Breaking trail was difficult and he suggested they swap positions every thousand feet or so. Josh had not been at lead very long when he saw something moving in the fog ahead.

"Holy shit!" Josh cried. "Look at that."

Ben peered through the fog. "What the . . . it's a damned Bigfoot!"

"Look! Over there. Another one!"

Ben said, "They seem to be searching the snow."

"Maybe one of 'em got buried. Quick! Call the others."

"No way! The fewer people who know about this, the better," Ben said.

"What do you mean? This is great! Do you know what a story about these things could get us?"

"Nothin' but trouble. That's what."

The sound of a bell echoed from above. They looked at the sky and then back toward the two creatures. The creatures discontinued their search and moved quickly toward the summit. Josh turned to Ben and said, "Let's follow them." He moved ahead of his partner.

Ben grabbed Josh's backpack. "Listen to me. You're not going anywhere. I don't want a bunch of damned idiots climbing all over these mountains. Besides, you saw how big those things are! Why, I'll bet you they could pull your arm right off before you'd even guess how much it's gonna hurt."

Josh pulled away and looked up the mountainside. "Now look what you've done. I've lost them in the fog. Come on! We can follow their tracks."

"You don't listen too good, do you? Get this out of your head before I throw you off this mountain."

"Up yours." Josh turned his back and tried walking away but Ben grabbed his pack again and wrestled him to the ground.

"Now, you listen to me because I'm only gonna say it once. I'll tell you what we're gonna do and you'll go along unless you want me to tell a certain Fat Danny who knocked up his sister."

Josh's resistance melted at Ben's threat. "All right. What do you want?"

Ben smiled and relaxed his grip. "We're gonna pack down any trace of their tracks and we're not gonna say nothin' about what we saw to nobody. Understand?"

"Yeah, I understand." Josh pulled his elbow away and Ben stood to brush the snow from his snowsuit. Ben offered Josh his hand, but Josh raised himself unassisted.

While Josh and Ben covered the tracks the other rescue team reported finding a body. Ben and Josh moved toward the other two to assist. Once the man had been completely disinterred, it was time to set up camp for the night.

The fog had dissipated by morning and the cloud was gone. The sun was bright and, before the advance rescue party was able to break camp, several helicopters dropped other rescuers on the slopes with supplies and equipment.

While watching an evening news program at her Connecticut home, Jane Severe heard about an avalanche in the Rocky Mountains near Durango, Colorado. She immediately called George's office hoping for some assurance that her husband was not in danger. His secretary, Mary, was no help at first, but called her back on the following day to report that George was among those who had been on the mountain when the avalanche occurred. Jane frantically arranged to have Anastasia remain with her mother while she flew to the site of the tragedy.

A short time after having thought he heard the sound of a bell in his sleep, George awoke to see two strange beasts attending to Annie. He strained to study the beasts while watching for Annie's reaction to their examination. She seemed unresponsive. The sky grew darker. The beasts stood and looked through the trees toward some sounds in the distance. One of them dragged Annie into some nearby brush and returned to sweep the path. The other approached George and, since his eyes were open, pressed its furry hand to his mouth pleading for silence. He then dragged George into some brush and returned to the clearing after pressing George's feet to the ground.

George's senses spun when he was moved. He forced himself to remain conscious. Some other figures entered the clearing and argued with the first two. His vision continued spinning and fading. He could not resist much longer. The first creatures were apparently chased from the area. Not wanting to be abandoned, he tried lifting himself but his sight went black.

He woke under a bright hazy canopy of light that diffused through the trees and brush. He was fully reclined and he felt like he had recovered from whatever injuries caused him so much pain earlier. He raised his head and shoulders, then rose to a sitting position. He examined the straps from his pack after they fell from his shoulders to his lap. Something had singed them. He looked behind him for any evidence of the pack. There was nothing but a pile of white powder. His shoes were missing, too. Then he remembered Annie and crawled to the nearby brush, searching for her. He found her unconscious. Her breathing was shallow but that was better than *not* breathing.

George looked for a way to raise her legs in case she was suffering from shock. While still on his knees, he twisted her around and rested her legs on the branches of a bush. Beyond that, he could do nothing. If he was going to save her, he needed help.

He searched the area, hoping to find those creatures who had helped him. He removed his overalls and parka. As he stood and looked around, he felt that strange tingling again at the bottoms of his bare feet. The sensation did not harm him. In fact, it made him feel *better*. With each step came greater confidence.

He walked across the clearing and found a path that ran in two directions. Choosing the left path, he traveled fifty paces only to see the haze grow more dense – foggy. He wanted to be able to *see* where he was going, so he returned to the clearing and followed the path in the opposite direction. Visibility improved and he noticed strange combinations of plants. Cacti grew beside ferns. Roses flourished a few feet from swamp weeds. The various species did not seem to rely upon any particular soil conditions or moisture content. They all flourished – everywhere. It was as if all had been planted in a garden except that there were no orderly rows or clusters of any particular variety.

He heard some mumbling sounds ahead of him. Two strange creatures, similar to those who had assisted him, spotted him as they approached from a bend in the path. They were approximately eight feet tall and of muscular build, covered with matted brown hair from their heads to their feet. Their faces seemed human and the hair on their faces resembled beards. But their arms were heavier and longer than would be expected. He was sure they could crush him with little effort. He froze in place – torn between his fear of the large creatures and his need for their help.

The two stopped. One turned around and mumbled while pointing toward George. A short, round, bearded man with curly black hair stepped from behind the creatures and approached George. He mumbled something to George that *sounded* familiar but the language was foreign to him.

George muttered, "We . . . we need help! Over here!" He moved to lead them to Annie. One of the creatures took his arm. He twisted free, but stumbled in the bushes along the path. As he looked down to regain his footing, he saw the feet of the creature next to his own. *Bigfoot?*

The man and the other creature flanked him. The man spoke to the creature, "Release him, Scragg. He speaks the language of our friend." He pulled the creature's hand from George's arm. "Please forgive him. We were not sure who we would find here, but your language tells me you could be a friend."

George looked at the plump little man and the two

creatures. "Who . . .?"

"Forgive me," he said. "I am Telemachus. My large friend here is Tmron and this is the son of his father's sister, Scragg. How are you called?"

"George. George Severe." Telemachus was about to say something but George added, "We need help. My friend is hurt." He pulled at the man's arm to lead him to Annie.

Telemachus followed George and knelt beside Annie. He touched her face and neck. "He is very bad."

"She! Her name is Annie."

"*She* is very bad indeed." He looked at one of the creatures. "Tmron, we must take her back to the village." Telemachus stood and stepped aside while the Sasquatch carefully lifted Annie. The group formed a line with Telemachus leading.

They walked together along the path in the direction from which the strangers had come. In a short time they walked out of the forest and, under a brightly overcast sky, George saw a gold gleam accentuating a small village sitting a short distance away on a grassy plain. The settlement was comprised of an odd assortment of adobe or stone huts and buildings. The gleam emanated from the dome on one of the buildings. George saw activity near the village but it was still too distant for him to clearly see the residents.

As the five approached the village, some children ran to meet them. They were of several races and two were similar to the Sasquatch. None took notice of George. They all seemed hopeful that the short round man and the two creatures might be bearing something of interest to them. They talked to the three while looking at what Tmron was holding. One young

Sasquatch ran back to the village. The remaining youngsters walked beside the travelers. They eventually noticed George and grew more cautious. They passed some of the adobe huts and approached the tall stone building with the bright gold dome. A poor semblance of an eagle was perched on the dome. At least, it *looked* like an eagle. George doubted his impression when he thought he saw it move. He fell behind his escorts while watching the figure. It wasn't an eagle. Its head and back were feathered like an eagle but it was much larger and had four legs. It's lower body more closely resembled a lion. George's chin dropped as he realized it was a Griffin – and it *did* move.

Another movement in the sky, just below the cloud line, distracted him. Something was flying toward the village. He realized it was a winged horse just as Scragg grabbed his arm and quickly pulled him into a hut. He was held against a wall with a large hairy hand covering his mouth. All were quiet. Tmron, still holding Annie in his arms, peeked out a window. George heard a rush of air outside and a back-flapping of wings followed by hoof beats. Some barely audible inquiries were made nearby. Then he heard a quick gallop that was suddenly silent and the Sasquatch withdrew his hand from George's mouth.

George was puzzled. He was filled with questions but would not ask them until he felt secure.

Telemachus stepped inside and motioned to Scragg and Tmron. Scragg took George's arm and led him to another building. George was offered a stone seat at a stone table. He placed his cold weather gear on a small table and sat, watching Tmron place Annie on something that looked like a solid stone bed. George was impressed by Tmron's gentle nature. The Sasquatch carefully twisted Annie on the stone and pressed her feet to the dirt floor. Telemachus walked to some shelves carved in the stone wall and returned to the table with a handful of grain and dried fruits, which he offered to George.

At that moment, George realized he was *not* hungry. By his estimate, he had been in this strange place for nearly two days yet he felt no hunger. He had just hiked several miles and felt no fatigue. *Why?* He refused the food.

Telemachus uttered some words to Scragg who then left the building. He ate some of the food and again offered some to George. Again, George refused it. The man grew angry. He took George's hand and filled it with food. "You must eat." Then he pushed George's hand toward his face.

George placed some of the grain into his mouth and chewed. He was very surprised at the flavor – sweet and not dry at all. He tried some of the fruit, which was equally tasty. He saw that Telemachus' anger had subsided.

Scragg, a short elderly woman, and three men entered the room. The woman immediately attended to Annie. The others sat around the table conversing. The two Sasquatch did not talk often, but they *did* talk. Their voices were surprisingly gentle. Some of the words seemed familiar but George could not understand the conversation. The foreign language did not bother him since he was more interested in Annie's condition, until he heard the name *Jack LaRoche* – the name of the convict who had disappeared in the foggy Montana mountains only to reappear in a Tennessee marsh after falling from the sky.

The sudden raising of his head silenced the conversation.

George became self-conscious as the group stared at him. Nervously, he felt now was the time to speak – and to learn some answers.

"What do you know about Jack LaRoche?" he asked.

*F*OUR

New Friends

DURING THE FIRST two days of the search, seven bodies were dug out of the snow and transported to a local hospital for identification. The rescuers moved toward the ledge where George and Annie were lost. While resting near a camp stove, one searcher reported that he had seen some large footprints at the base of the ledge. Josh raised his head when he heard it. Ben kept his head down and nudged Josh's side with his elbow. The men continued drinking coffee as the conversation shifted to the probability of finding the remaining three victims – alive or otherwise. As the discussion continued, Ben disappeared.

Coffee grounds were dumped on the snow and the rescuers resumed their search. The party found Ben at the base of the ledge. The man who reported the large footprints stated that this was the area where he had seen them. Ben denied seeing anything and suggested the other man had an overactive imagination.

Jane paced the hallways of the hospital and the rescue command post. She had seen each of the seven recovered bodies but none were familiar. Then, Mark Waxman, the secretive man who hired George after he had left the National Weather Service, appeared and confirmed that the seven bodies belonged to men who were assigned to George's expedition. Later that day, Stan Maszewski's body was found.

George felt self-conscious as his hosts responded to his recognition of Jack LaRoche's name.

Telemachus asked, "Are you a friend of Jack LaRoche?" George looked at the man dumbly for a moment, encouraging him to continue. "You seem to have knowledge of Jack LaRoche. Are you a friend?"

"I never met him. I've only heard his name." George was afraid to affiliate himself with the mercenary but he was also reluctant to dissociate himself since he did not know his hosts' feelings toward the man.

"Perhaps you can give us news of him," a tall red-haired man asked. "He was lost to us a short time ago."

"I am sorry," Telemachus interrupted. "I have not intro-duced everybody. This outspoken one is Gideon." George and Gideon exchanged nods. Something about Gideon's look made George shiver. Telemachus placed his hand on the shoulder of another man, thinner and slightly taller than himself. "This is my brother, Thaddaeus, and this is Norris." George nodded to the man of average height and build first. Then he greeted Thaddaeus.

Telemachus continued, "You have met Tmron and Scragg and that is Elke attending to your friend. Now, do you have news of Jack LaRoche?"

"When was he lost?" George asked.

"You would say a few months ago."

"If we're talking about the same man, he was killed when he fell from the sky to a farm in Tennessee. You wouldn't happen to know anything about that, would you?"

His hosts were silent and George felt that he should have withheld that last question but he was hoping for some confirmation that he was, in fact, atop the strange cloud. He looked at each of his hosts for some response but found no revelations in their eyes.

"Forgive us," Telemachus stated. "We had hoped that perhaps Jack LaRoche might still be among us. But it is clear now that he must have ridden beyond the edges."

"What edges?"

"The edges of the Land, of course! Where the fog hides its limits. A dangerous place to be without the Ferryman's guidance."

"What Ferryman?"

"He is suzerain of our Land and the only one who knows where the lands meet. Without his guidance," Telemachus added, "anyone who ventures to the edges risks his life."

"Can't you explore the edges and map them?"

Telemachus smiled and slapped George on the back saying, "Now you sound like Jack LaRoche."

Gideon said, "Aye! Such talk came from Jack LaRoche when he helped us in our struggles to be free of the Ferryman."

Telemachus added, "The Ferryman is an evil tyrant and the words of our friend inspired us to stand and oppose him."

George wondered if Jack LaRoche could actually have done some good for these people. The thought seemed contrary to everything he had heard and read about the man. Under the circumstances, he did not want to alienate his hosts. Their opinion of LaRoche was sufficiently high that any *truth* he added might not be well received. And why berate a man who might have performed one good act before he died? Maybe this Ferryman is a tyrant.

Hoping to change the subject, George thought back to his arrival in the village and asked, "Why did you hide us from that flying horse when we first arrived?"

Telemachus answered, "The Ferryman sent a dispatch to find you. We believe he would like to keep your secrets from us."

"What secrets?"

"You must be from the land beyond – the land of Jack LaRoche. He knew many secrets that were helpful in our struggle to be free."

"But, I don't know any secrets!"

"Surely, you do," Gideon said. "They may not be secrets to you, but they are to us. Jack LaRoche often told us that everyone in his land knew the things he taught us. And he was surprised such knowledge was new to us. We invite you to remain with us. We will shelter you from the Ferryman. In return, we ask only that you teach us the ways of your land. Teach us about independence and democracy, and cap-i-tal-ism. Those were the things Jack LaRoche was teaching us."

"I suppose I can help in some of those matters."

The four men and the two Sasquatch smiled at George's acceptance. Annie's nurse was preoccupied with her patient. Telemachus slapped George's back again. "Your friend can rest here tonight, or as long it takes to heal her. Gideon will find another place for you. The light will be gone soon."

The tall red-haired man escorted George to a small stone hut.

Except for token efforts, the search for the last two bodies was discontinued a few days after Stan's body was found. Jane appealed to Mark to use his influence and force the local mountaineers to resume their search. Mark promised he would have a military search party on the mountain within a day and they would search for another week. The only hope lay in the fact that the guide was also missing and it was quite possible that she and George found refuge.

Jane remained in Colorado for the week of the search but then returned home after only a few supplies had been found. She cried each night in her bed with her baby daughter, Anastasia, and gradually became angry. She plagued Mark Waxman with phone calls to keep him from quitting the search. Mark agreed to send patrols through spring. The fact that George's salary continued told Jane that Mark was willing to sustain the belief that George might still be alive – though that possibility seemed less likely as the weeks passed. Whenever Mark suggested there was no reason for hope, Jane reminded him of his promise to withhold judgment until spring. She refused to accept the possibility that her husband might be dead – unless she could see his body with her own eyes.

Phillip Gravely had been corresponding with George since telling him about the strange disappearances of Phillip's father, Cloud Walker. Phillip was a Sioux Indian who lived at the Pine Ridge Reservation in South Dakota and worked outside the reservation wherever there was a call for construction workers. He was aware George was close to finding the unusual cloud but he did not know about the avalanche until, after calling for George, he heard of the tragedy from Jane. He suggested there might be hope, since George and the guide were not found. It was all he could offer during that phone call. Later, he called again and reminded her that his father had been found two years after his first disappearance. He asked Jane if he could visit her.

Jane agreed and Phillip immediately borrowed some money and a friend's pickup truck. He arrived at the Severe's Connecticut home late one afternoon just as Jane returned from work. They walked into the house together. Jane's tall slender form was as much a contrast to his large solid frame as her light skin and blonde hair were to his dark chiseled face and black hair. She wore a business suit and he wore a denim jacket over jeans and a plaid shirt. Jane's high heels raised her head slightly above his. Her mother met them at the kitchen door.

"Ma, this is Phillip Gravely," Jane said. "He's a friend of George's from South Dakota. George told you about him after our trip out west, remember?"

"How do you do?" her mother responded.

Jane and Phillip removed their coats and the three sat around the kitchen table.

"Did you have a good trip?" Jane asked.

"I don't rightly take much pleasure in drivin'."

"Really? George and I *loved* motor trips. The countryside is so beautiful."

"Well, I suppose it goes against my heritage, but I don't notice the countryside on a trip. Driving's too much work. I'd rather be hammerin' nails buildin' things than drivin' around, stuck in some old rust bucket on a highway."

Anastasia's cries broke the awkward silence that followed and Jane rushed to greet her daughter. Phillip asked to use the bathroom.

"Of course," her mother answered. "Out that door and down the hall."

Phillip walked out of the kitchen. When the door closed behind him, Jane's mother asked her if she was sure she wanted this strange man in her house. "I don't think I'd be as trusting as you, Dear," she added.

"He and George have been writing for a long time. They developed a very close friendship. Besides, he might be able to tell us something about George's disappearance."

"Do you really think there's hope, Dear?"

"I *have* to, Ma." Jane's eyes welled with tears. She sniffled and wiped each cheek with the back of her wrist. "I may have to offer him a place to sleep for a couple of nights. Will you stay with me?"

"Of course. I'll call your father. It won't kill him to take care of himself while I'm gone."

When Phillip returned, Jane cooked some food. "I'm sorry, it's kind of slapped together. I can send out for something later if you're still hungry."

"This will be fine, Mrs. Severe."

"Jane, please."

"Jane. . . . It's funny. I know George so well, but you and me only talked a couple o' times and, even though George wrote a lot about you, I still feel like a stranger."

"Don't be silly. George told me just as much about you. We spent quite a few evenings sitting together on the couch reading your letters." She paused and her eyes watered again. "Excuse me." She stood and took some tissues from a box on the counter and used them to dry her eyes and clear her nose.

"Don't you worry none, Jane. There's always hope as long as they ain't found nothin'," Phillip said.

Jane nodded. After eating, Jane took Anastasia and led Phillip into the living room. He stood beside Jane and reached down to stroke the baby's head with his rough, dark hand. Then he sat in a chair opposite the couch. "She's a beautiful baby, Mrs. Severe." Jane cast an admonishing look and he corrected himself, "Jane."

"She's been a joy from the moment she was born." Jane smiled at her baby as she finished the sentence as if she were addressing the child.

Both were quiet for a few moments until Jane raised her head. Phillip spoke slowly, "Jane! Can you talk about how George got lost?"

"He's not lost. George is still alive."

"You're right. I didn't mean . . ."

Jane told him all she remembered – including the strange phone call from George the night before the expedition left for the upper slopes of the mountain.

Phillip asked, "Did anyone say they seen anything unusual?"

Jane answered, "Like what?"

"You were with George when I told him about the first time my father disappeared. Do you remember what I said?"

"I'm sorry. At the time, I wasn't very interested."

Phillip repeated his story. When he told her about the tales his father told of the strange land with the unusual creatures, she seemed curious but she did not interrupt him. He completed his father's story and asked, "Did anything I say ring a bell?"

"No. . . . I don't know." She seemed nervous and frustrated.

"Take your time."

"A bell! Someone said he heard a bell."

"Who?"

"I . . . think it was one of the first rescuers to get there."

"And?"

"They went up before the weather broke."

"You mean the cloud was still there?"

"I *think* so!"

"Don't you know? I thought you said you was there!"

"I was, but not in the beginning. I just heard that they couldn't send many people up there until the weather broke. But I remember the talk about the bell because the guy who said it mentioned that he was afraid the mountain would let go again."

"Anythin' else?"

"I don't know."

"You sort of perked up a mite when I said my father thought he saw some unusual creatures."

"It *seemed* familiar. Oh, I don't know if I'm remembering what I heard or what George told me before he left."

"Jane, try to think. Did anybody say anythin' about seein' any strange creatures?"

"Not *creatures* exactly. Footprints! Big footprints. That's right. Someone said he found some big footprints."

Jane stopped for a moment. The two were quiet.

Phillip raised his head from his thoughts and whispered, "Sasquatch."

"What?"

"Sasquatch. Bigfoot. You *must* have heard of it! A large hairy creature that sort o' looks like an ape."

"Big hairy ape!" An expression of recognition was on her face. "Two men were fighting about a big hairy ape. I heard them through a vent in the ladies' room. One of them threatened the other and told him to keep his mouth shut. Do you think there's a connection?"

"More than that, Jane. *I* think there's hope that George is still alive. I'd bet a week's pay he's been rescued by one of them Sasquatches."

"Why would that guy want to keep it a secret?"

"I don't know. There's a lot of funny people around who all got reasons for doin' what they do."

"If George was rescued, where is he now?"

Phillip looked into Jane's eyes and said, "On the cloud! Where else?"

"I don't believe it."

"Why not? Look. George was chasin' a cloud that was

flyin' around on its own. My father disappeared in a cloud – twice! And he ain't been back again. Maybe it ain't really a cloud!"

"Why go up? Why didn't this Bigfoot character just bring George to the rescue party or leave him where they could find him?"

"I don't know. Course if I were one of 'em, I wouldn't stick around neither. Might end up in a freak show somewheres. Maybe George was hurt and the creature didn't want to leave him alone. I don't know. But that would explain why George and that guide ain't been found. Wouldn't it?"

"I suppose it would. It's so hard to believe though." She hesitated as she looked at Phillip. Her eyes moved from his face to his hands and to the work boots on his feet. "If what you say is true, how do we find these creatures and the cloud? And how do we get to George?"

"Maybe we can't. But my father *did* return once. And George managed to find the cloud and track it to Colorado. There *must* be a way."

FIVE

A Stranger in the Land

GIDEON LEFT GEORGE at the stone hut and warned him to remain there to avoid detection by the Ferryman's couriers. The earlier conversation with the villagers whirled through George's mind as he sat on a warm stone chair.

Shadows dressed the walls of the buildings across the way. As they climbed the buildings, the light in the room dimmed and George felt exhausted. The stone bed looked less inviting than the dirt floor. He thought he might use his parka and overalls as pillows but he could not remember where he had left them. He reclined on the bed. Like the chair, it was unexpectedly warm and quite comfortable. He looked at the ceiling briefly before closing his eyes.

Jane and Anastasia reached out to him in his dreams. He imagined himself watching them from a distance, yet he was able to hear the child's giggles as Jane tickled her. Jane turned toward him and said, "Don't forget to be home in time for

Anastasia's birthday!" Then she turned back and wiggled the baby's toes. A joyful tear rolled down his cheek and there was a comfortable smile on his lips.

George awoke to bright sunlight that splashed into his hut from the window-like opening. He walked to the opening and watched shadows across the way shrink from the same walls they had climbed the previous night. He considered the significance of the evening and morning light coming from the same place. He *had* to be on the cloud. The shadows, yesterday's talk about *edges*, and his knowledge about Jack LaRoche's plummet should be sufficient to convince anybody.

At the sound of footsteps, he moved away from the window. A frail young woman meekly entered, carrying a clay pot filled with fruit, which she placed on a flat stone table.

"Sir? I was told to deliver this fruit," she said.

George stared at her for a moment, thinking she might be pretty if she were to wash her face and clean her knotted blonde hair. He became aware of his silence and answered, "I'm not really hungry." Yet, he hadn't eaten anything except the snack forced on him the previous day.

"Oh, but you must eat something or you will have troubles."

"What kind of troubles?"

The woman was nervous. "You must eat or it will be said that I did not serve you well."

George took a banana from the pot.

She smiled. "I am called Tamara. If there is anything you wish, ask anyone to find me and I will come immediately. Do you wish anything before I leave?"

"Can you tell me if my friend is getting better?"

"I heard she is no better than when she arrived, but no worse either. Elke is a good healer and she knows well how to use the Land. Is there something else, sir?"

"No, Tamara. That's a pretty name. My name is George."

"Yes, sir. I will remember. I will serve you well." She bowed and quickly left.

George's thoughts drifted back to the question of why he was not hungry. Gideon arrived and interrupted, "Good day! I see you have your fruit," he said. "Is Tamara suitable to you?"

"Yes. What is her position in the village?"

"She is a Spoil. You can do with her as you wish."

"A *Spoil?*"

"Yes. I give her to you." Gideon must have seen George's reluctance. He added, "Do not be concerned. I have other Spoils."

Telemachus walked into the hut. He looked at Gideon with a hard stare. "Trying to steal some secrets, Gideon?" His stare melted to a sly smile.

"No! I simply offered Tamara to our guest, but he seems reluctant to accept her."

"Most men would place great value on such a gift, George Severe."

George answered cautiously, "I do value the gift. However, I have never required a servant." He saw that they were concerned or insulted. "Nevertheless, I am sure I can put her to good use." Just as quickly, their expressions changed. "Why do you call her a Spoil?"

Telemachus answered, "Now I understand! You thought she was inferior – like spoiled fruit! This is not true, I assure you. The term was taught to us by your friend, Jack LaRoche.

She is one of the *Spoils of war* taken from a nearby village. Taking Spoils is so much easier than farming our own fruits or laboring with our own hands."

"And much more enjoyable as well." The red-haired man smiled at his friend as if sharing a secret.

George searched for a way to redirect their conversation. "I'd like to see how my friend is doing. I'd also like a tour of your village. Would one of you show me around?"

"It would be a pleasure to us," Telemachus answered. "But, if you will approve, Tmron will meet us here soon. When he arrives, we will all walk together."

George asked something more specific. "Did Tmron rescue me from the avalanche?"

"Avalanche? I know nothing of this. You should ask Tmron."

The three men were quiet. Gideon tore the peel from an orange. Telemachus reached for some fruit and looked at George. "You should eat."

"Thank you," George answered, "I'm not hungry."

"We do not eat because we are hungry. You should do as we do or you will lose your freedom to pass beyond the edges."

"I don't understand."

"Telemachus could not have said it more clearly," Gideon said. "You will not be hungry here. But, unless you eat from time to time, you may never be able to leave the Land."

"I still don't understand. I must have been here a couple days by now, and I'm not hungry. Why is that?"

Telemachus answered, "Because the Land feeds you."

"How?"

Tmron interrupted their conversation as he came into

the hut. The entrance was small for him and he had to crouch and squeeze through.

"Ah, Tmron! You are late, my friend," Telemachus said.

"Yes, I am. Upset you it does?" Tmron snapped.

Telemachus cowered, "No . . . my friend. Shall we show our village to our new friend?"

"Ready I am," Tmron answered.

"Gideon, could you send for Tamara? Our guest will need fresh water and she can carry it, as well as anything else we need as we walk." Gideon left the hut. "Tmron, George Severe has a question for you."

George said, "I wondered if you were the one who rescued me from the avalanche."

"What you are saying I do not know," Tmron answered.

"The avalanche! When was the first time you saw me?"

"When near the edges with Scragg and Telemachus we found you."

"But, I thought . . ."

Gideon returned with Tamara and reported that George's friend was still unconscious. The group walked out of the hut to the main way. Tamara carried a clay bucket and some woven sacks. They crossed the way and passed between two buildings to a garden, which spread along the back of the row of buildings. George was amazed at the variety of colors in the garden. He did not expect it in a land where the sun was so hard to find through the clouds. The limbs of the fruit trees hung low with the weight of their bounty. Tamara picked some of the fruit and placed it in one of the sacks, which she then hung over her shoulder.

Tmron said, "Much of the village, as well as beasts and

birds from the Opens and near the edges, this garden serves."

Tamara moved ahead of them. George asked, "What are the Opens?"

Telemachus answered, "The Opens are the lands between the edges and the hills."

"And what's beyond the hills?"

"There are many hills. Venturing beyond them would take you to the valley castle where the Ferryman wields his power and guides the Land."

As Telemachus finished his description, George heard water trickling. He looked ahead but could not see the source. The sound grew stronger as they walked closer to where he had last seen Tamara. Suddenly, the sound stopped. He was just about to peek through the brush when Tamara stepped out of the bushes onto the path and nearly collided with him.

"Your pardon, sir." She hurried to find her excuses. "I was just fetching some water and I didn't see you coming. If you will approve, sir, I will take back the water and fruit and return quickly to serve you."

Gideon answered for George, "Go, woman. And be quick." As Tamara squeezed past the men on the path, Gideon added quietly, "You must be firm with Spoils or they get lazy. When that happens, they become useless – even after beating."

Tmron snorted, "Bother with them I do not know why we do. More trouble than service they give."

"If you take the time to train them well," Telemachus answered, "they can do much more than serve. Some of them will give great pleasure in their feeble attempts to gain preferred treatment. Jack LaRoche took his pleasure with many Spoils –

regardless of their willingness. In fact, I think he found greater satisfaction if they were unwilling."

Tmron snorted again.

George thought Telemachus' latest description of LaRoche sounded more in character.

They stepped through the brush and stood in a clearing that contained a small pool of water. The bank was wet from the water's edge to a small cluster of rocks. George thought it was strange that there would be such wetness at one place. He remembered the sound of trickling water and wondered if Tamara had been rinsing the clay bucket along the shore.

Tmron led the way around the pool and through more bushes where they were able to look out over the Opens toward the distant hills. The crests of the hills were hidden in the haze. Timid sunbeams stretched through the cloud and spotted the plains and foothills. George admired the land until Telemachus and Gideon directed him back to the way in the village.

Tamara's hurried return caught George's attention as they stepped out from between two buildings. While watching her approach, he saw the backside of a horse entering one of the huts and, further up the way, on its gilded perch, the Griffin stretched its wings.

Telemachus led the tour down the way toward a small park near the center of the village. The path was dark beneath a dense blanket of leaves spreading from the park trees. They walked through the park and crossed another way to a large building. Gideon told Tamara to wait outside. George looked apologetically at the woman who seemed undisturbed by her exclusion.

"This is our Meeting Place," Telemachus said.

George was quick to realize they had entered a tavern. They passed several stone tables en route to a small service bar. Telemachus asked for four drafts of wine. The scrawny keeper served them and George noticed that Telemachus offered no remittance. Telemachus grasped two of the clay mugs and nodded to Gideon to take the others. They walked to a nearby table, followed by George and Tmron. The small rock chairs were obviously uncomfortable to Tmron who was an imposing figure even when seated.

George looked about the large room. Two other guests were talking at another table. There were no others. He examined the construction of the building. The room must have once been several smaller rooms. He traced the locations of the former walls along the outer walls and across the rock ceiling. He guessed the change had occurred recently since the depressions in the dirt floor had not yet filled in along the outer wall.

Tmron answered his interest saying, "Our Meeting Place this became when Jack LaRoche was among us. Many things he taught us here."

"Drink your wine," Telemachus said to George. "You will need its water."

George sipped at the awkward clay mug. He was surprised by the sweet, sparkling taste. The wine was easily swallowed, but its potency became instantly obvious. George knew he would not be able to walk back to his hut if he were to empty the mug. The Sasquatch, on the other hand, had consumed his serving before George lowered his mug to the table.

Telemachus and Gideon each took large swallows before Telemachus resumed the discussion. He told George about the village layout and encouraged him to sip the wine.

Eventually, Tmron, who had nothing more to drink, suggested, "Understand your words our friend does not. Leave we must."

Telemachus and Gideon looked closely at their guest and agreed. They helped George up from the seat and pointed him toward the entrance. As he looked back to be sure his hosts were following, he collided with someone and fell to the floor. While rolling on the floor, he heard some conversation above him but could not understand the language. He rolled to his hands and knees and felt some strong hands reaching under his arms to help him.

"Aristeides offers his apology, George Severe," Telemachus said. "He did not see you."

The first thing George saw was the floor, which smelled like a stable. He reached up to the assisting hands and followed the hooves and legs of a horse with his eyes as he was lifted upward. The chest of the horse slowly became that of a man. He looked up to the man's face and surveyed his body downward again. The skin was dark and tough and it slowly changed to the shiny coat of a horse. He looked again into Aristeides' eyes. His proximity to the Centaur and the effects of the wine were more than his conscious mind could endure.

George slept on the warm, soft rock bed in his assigned hut. He dreamed of Jane and forgot he was in a faraway land with no bridge to his own except his dreams. He felt the comfort of her warm body next to him on their couch as they smiled at Anastasia playing on the floor. He felt the comfort and he lived the dream. But he could not feel the substance of his wife in his arms. Slowly, his vision faded.

George struggled to open his eyes but saw only a distorted view of the rock ceiling above and an unfocused figure to one side. With a soft, sympathetic voice, the figure asked, "Are you better, sir?"

He recognized the voice. His tongue stuck to his palate as he tried speaking. "Tamara?" he groaned. "How . . ."

"Be easy, sir. I will pour some water."

His sight slowly returned. He watched her dip a clay mug into the clay bucket and return to his side. She lifted his head and cradled it in her arm while placing the mug at his lips. The water was the greatest gift he had ever received. It disjoined his tongue and palate, eased his breathing, and cleared his vision. He looked up at Tamara. She smiled and lowered his head. Then she placed the cup on the nearby table.

"You will recover soon," she said. "I will find fresh fruit, sir."

George remained on his back and explored the room with his eyes. Light entered the room through the window and the passage. He remembered the hut, the walk to the garden and down the way to the park, and the tavern. And he remembered the wine. His recollections since then were distorted – suspended between reality and dreams. Although he wrestled with that distorted time, he was unable to distinguish any of the events that might have brought him back to his hut.

He raised his knees and looked at the ceiling. Soon, he found himself intrigued by its construction. He could not determine whether it was monolithic or sectional. The joints often disappeared or blended into the rock structure. The ceiling was flat and logic dictated that some sort of bracing would be needed to prevent the rock from falling. Yet it remained suspended from one wall to the next.

"I have returned, sir," Tamara called as she entered the hut carrying a clay bucket filled with various fresh fruits. She placed it on the table and approached George. "Have you tried to rise?" George shook his head. "Well then, now would be a good time. Do you think so?"

George agreed and raised his head and back. Tamara offered her arm at his back. When he was seated, he swung his legs off the bed. He jumped at the tingling sensation at his feet when they touched the dirt floor. Tamara noticed that he lifted his feet in reaction to the sensation.

"You are very strange to this Land. Gideon told me to see that you did not forget to eat. Why should you have to be told such a thing? And you are sensitive to the forces of the earth and wine." She hesitated before asking, "Where is your home?"

"Connecticut."

"I do not know that village. It is below, somewhere?"

"Below?"

"Yes. Beyond the edges and below."

"Tamara? Have you been below before?"

"Yes. I have gone below many times, but I have never seen Con-ne-tut. Is it a good village?"

"It's a State, . . . much bigger than a village. And yes, it is good."

"A State . . . as good as the villages in this Land?"

"*I* think so." George thought for a moment. "Because it's my home. A person's home is always better than any other place. Isn't it?"

Tamara looked down. Her whisper was barely audible, "Yes, it is."

George cursed his callousness. Hoping her spirits would improve if she talked about her home he asked, "Where is your home?"

Tamara brushed a tear from her cheek. "I am sorry, sir. I did not intend to behave in this way." She set back her shoulders, raised her head, and smiled. "I was raised in Hap Saad, which is the last village before the foothills if you travel across the Opens from this end of the garden."

"Tell me about Hap Saad."

"I cannot. . . . My village is lost to me."

"Why do you say that?"

"Because I was taken so long ago and no one has come for me."

"Why were you taken?"

"Many in this village came to ours. They said they were in search of Spoils. They call me a Spoil. I suppose a Spoil is a servant. But they took other things as well, and they too are called Spoils yet they do not serve."

"Were you at war?"

"Yes, we must have been at war."

"*Must* have been? That's not usually something anyone would have doubts about." George heard someone approaching the entrance.

"George Severe? About you are?" Tmron's shaggy head peeked into the room as he stooped to enter the hut. "Ah!

Recovered you have. Our wine you did not receive very well. Surprised we were so fuddled you became." He looked at Tamara after he sat at the table and dismissed her saying, "For you we will call when needed you are."

Tamara looked at George. George wanted to tell Tmron that she had been given to *him* and *he* would dismiss her when *he* chose. But he did not have the courage. She looked back at Tmron, bowed her head, turned, and left the hut.

George was left alone with his large furry host. While Tmron took some fruit, George watched the entrance quietly – not knowing what to say and ashamed he did not speak his mind when Tmron dismissed Tamara. Eventually, he asked, "What was in that wine?"

The Sasquatch drooled juice and small pieces of the succulent fruit as he spoke. "In the wine? Only wine it was – from grapes grown near the edges and on the hillsides it was made."

"I'm not much of a drinker, but that was the strongest wine I've ever had. I knew it was trouble from the first sip. It didn't seem to bother you – or Telemachus and Gideon."

"Not much of another cup would they have tasted before as well as you they would have slept. As well as my kind none of these villagers can hold wine." Tmron threw the remnants of the fruit he was eating on the dirt floor. "Of course, foolish enough they were not into Aristeides to walk either. A solid sort he is. Lucky you were, easily angered he was not, or walk over you he might have."

"Aristeides?" George tried to think back to the collision. Details flashed in his memory. "Was he a . . . Centaur?"

"If a Centaur is a man somehow contrived in union

with a horse, then that he is."

"Tmron!" George hesitated, trying to judge whether the creature would be receptive to questions about the Land and its inhabitants. He began by asking, "Was this village at war with Tamara's village?"

Tmron tossed an apple core to the floor. "Of course! You we told a Spoil of war she is."

"How long were you at war?"

"What do you mean?"

"How long were you fighting before it ended? What caused the war?"

"No fighting there was before. To the village for a war we went and home with the Spoils came. Jack LaRoche said improve our standard of living it would. Say you could the need for Spoils was the cause of the war."

George was encouraged by Tmron's willingness to discuss matters. "Were there any wars before Jack LaRoche came to you?"

The Sasquatch thought for a moment. George wondered if he was becoming reluctant but the creature responded with a sincere answer. "I do not *think* wars there were. Not any in *my* memory. Why these questions do you ask?"

"I want to know about this Land – what the people are like, whether or not it's safe to walk the streets at night. I'd like to learn as much as I can about your Land."

"About the Land I can tell you. But I do not understand how talk of wars can teach it." George did not answer for a moment. The Sasquatch continued, "Such questions Jack LaRoche asked, too. And much from him we did learn."

Telemachus announced himself and walked into the

hut. "I brought someone you will want to meet." He turned back to the door and encouraged the visitor to come forward. A Centaur stooped and walked into the room accompanied by a musty odor stronger than Tmron's. George's mouth hung open as Telemachus made the introduction. "This is Aristeides. He came between you and the passage at the Meeting Place." Telemachus laughed as he spoke. "Aristeides, this is George Severe from the land of Jack LaRoche."

"Ah! You must be one of the strangers the Ferryman has been calling." The Centaur's voice was as strong as the beast appeared.

"The Ferryman has been calling for *me*?" George asked. "Why? How?"

"All right, Aristeides," Telemachus interrupted, "there is no need to be telling our guest such things. You asked to meet him and so you have. Now, if you'll be on your way, we have things to talk about."

The Centaur passed a scornful glance at Telemachus before accepting his dismissal. As he turned about, he allowed his hind hoof to land on Telemachus' foot. "Excuse me," he said without looking back as Telemachus suppressed a yelp.

After Aristeides ducked through the passage, Telemachus uttered painfully, "Spiteful sort those are. I never should have agreed to bring him here." He sat at the table and massaged his foot, examining it as his hands worked it. Then he placed the foot flat on the dirt floor.

George remained fascinated by the visit from the Centaur. He sat speechless at the table while Telemachus reached for a piece of fruit. Tmron admonished him. "What you deserved you received. And lucky you are worse you did not get. Better you should know than to treat one of them that way."

Telemachus waved away the Sasquatch's comments. George regained his composure and asked, "What did he mean when he said the Ferryman had been calling me?"

Telemachus waved away that question as well. But Tmron answered, "Call to us the Ferryman can – sometimes. Not too long ago, times there were when all the time hear him calling we could. But hear him call for you I did not. In the village are many who hear still. If please you it will, what they have heard I will ask."

"Yes, it would please me," George answered.

"Don't let this silly talk distract you, George Severe. It is but a trick the Ferryman uses to brainwash you." Telemachus said, "You must not open your mind to him. That is how he controls. If we are to win our independence, we must close our minds to his thoughts."

"Are you saying the Ferryman can communicate by thought?"

Tmron answered, "At one time what he wanted us to know we knew. Yes."

"Telepathy. Does he know what we're doing?"

"We do not think so," Telemachus responded. "We cannot be sure about the times when our minds were open to him but we are confident he does not hear us now.

"But we have spoken too much these last lights. We want to learn about your land and customs. Tell us about your village and how you came to our Land."

George told them about his family and his interest in weather. He did not tell them how he tracked the cloud. Instead he told them he was on an expedition and accidentally came upon their Land after being trapped in an avalanche. He answered questions about his life and the political structure of his land. Eventually, George said, "I don't know why, but I'm awfully tired. Do you mind talking later?"

Telemachus complained, "We still have much to learn from you."

"I could use a nap."

"You may still be suffering from the wine. As you wish, we will continue another time."

S*IX*

Awakening

HIS GUESTS HAD LEFT. George sat on the edge of his warm rock bed, looking at the floor where they had dropped the fruit remnants. Everything except the seeds had deteriorated to white dust. He stood and walked to where the wastes had been, stooped down, and touched the powder with his fingers. After some consideration of the seeds, he stood and returned to sit on the bed.

The decomposition of the fruit waste raised some concern that the tingling sensation in his feet might be harmful. He raised one foot to the opposite knee and examined the sole. The tingling ceased as soon his foot left the dirt floor. He set it down again and alternately raised and lowered each foot and both feet at once to test the sensation. Weariness crept up on him and he lowered his head to the stone.

George rose suddenly at the sounds of a woman yelling and screaming. He ran out of the hut and looked down the way toward the noise. A Sasquatch ran out of the hut where Annie was kept. A clay pot followed the giant, striking him on the back. George recognized Tmron and ran toward the commotion. Tmron jumped to avoid another projectile. The screaming came from inside the hut.

"Annie?" George called as another clay pot flew out of the passage. "Are you OK?"

"Is that you, Blondie? Watch yerself! There's one of them overgrowed monkeys out there."

"It's all right, Annie. . . ."

"If that don't beat all. I never thought I'd see one of them. Thought sure all them tracks I seen was someone playin' tricks."

"Annie, it's OK! Will you stop throwing things and let me come inside?"

"All right, Sonny. But you be careful out there."

"There's nothing to worry about. They're friendly," George said as he walked through the passage.

Annie continued babbling. "Ain't nothin' else ta throw anyways. Be careful now. He might still be out there!"

"He *is* still out there and I told you he's friendly."

Annie was crouched on the bed, ready to jump. She rested back on her feet when George entered the room. "Be careful o' that floor, Sonny. There's somethin' awful strange 'bout that too!"

"Relax, Annie. OK?"

"I *am* relaxed!" she snapped.

"Good. That's good. Now just sit there for a minute."

George held his hands before him to hold her in place. He looked back at the entrance and called, "Tmron? Come on in."

Tmron ducked through the passage slowly. As he straightened up, Annie stood on the bed with her back to the wall and yelled, "Ahhhgh. Get away. Get away." She looked for something to throw and Tmron started ducking back through the entrance.

George stood between them with one hand raised toward each and said, "Stop it."

Annie and Tmron held their places. Elke, the nurse who first attended to Annie, came into the hut. "What is happening here?" She looked at Tmron and George. "Sit down, you two. She finally awakens after being nearly dead these days and you two get her all upset." Several hurried steps placed her beside the bed, looking up at Annie. "So, you are finally among us. How do you feel?"

"Ain't nothin' wrong with me a shot o' whiskey and a good bear rifle wouldn't fix."

"Sit down and tell me what you are saying."

"The whiskey's fer me. The gun's ta put one b'twixt the eyes o' that gorilla over there."

George interrupted, "Annie, he's a friend . . . and he knows what you're saying."

Annie pressed tighter against the wall. Elke turned to George and Tmron and said, "It will be better if you both leave until she can rest some more."

"I don't need no rest," Annie insisted.

Elke left the side of the bed and marshaled the two through the passage. "Thank you for watching her while I was away, Tmron. I'm sorry I did not return more quickly." She looked at George and said, "I will see to her needs and then I will come to you and tell you how she has healed."

Elke walked into George's hut without announcing her-self. "I hope you will excuse me for saying so, but I have always been one to speak my thoughts. Your friend is one of the most stubborn women I have ever met."

"Will she be all right?"

"I think so. She is very strong and she is healing. She refuses to place her feet on the ground so all the healing will have to come from within."

George wanted her to explain but she quickly added, "She absolutely refused to step off the bed without shoes. I gave her a pair I use when I go below. Then, she insisted I show her which path had taken you here. We will move her into your hut next light. She has tired me. Now that I have told you about your friend, I will return to my home and sleep. I asked your Spoil, Tamara, to stay with her this night." Elke turned away and walked out of the hut.

George wanted to check on Annie before retiring to his warm stone bed but found no sign of her or Tamara at her hut. He remembered Elke told him that Annie had asked how they had come into the village. The dreadful thought occurred to him that Annie might try to find her way back to the mountain. If she went too close to the edges, she would suffer the same fate as Jack LaRoche. He had to find her.

He stole through the village. The sky was dark but the path was clear and he followed it to the trees that marked the beginning of the edges. Many paths extended into the mist and he could not remember passing them when he first walked out of the fog and trees. Unable to navigate, he rested below a large oak until morning.

With daylight to guide his steps, he followed each path and surveyed each clearing in vain. He was ready to abandon his efforts when, just before nightfall, he heard a rustling sound coming from the thick undergrowth along the path before him. He stepped off the path and waited. He peered through some low branches and saw a woman walking along the path – searching. She appeared distressed. Her hair was disheveled and her face and arms were bruised, swollen, and cut. It was not Annie. "Tamara?"

"Sir? Oh, sir! Please forgive my intrusion, but I was told to find you. You must come back to the village. You are too near the edges!"

George stepped out of the bushes. "Tamara! What happened to you? Who did this?"

"I was punished, sir . . . because you and your friend were gone. I only left her for a short time to fetch some fresh water!"

"Tamara, I'm sorry." He went to stroke her hair to offer comfort but held back.

"Forgive me, sir. I did not mean to say you were at fault. I am to blame. You were my charge and I lost you. But sir, I beg you, do come back with me now. I have been told to find you and return with you to the village or . . . You must come!"

"Tamara, I don't understand. Who did this?"

She did not answer. George saw that his questions caused her more pain. Nevertheless, he pressed her for an answer. Tears trickled down her cheeks. "George Severe," she pleaded, "life is not what it once was. Things have changed. Please return. I will serve you well."

The pain in her face was too great for him to deny her. "I'll go back with you, Tamara. But not right now. I have to find Annie!"

Her beaten face expressed relief. She was silent for a moment as she gazed at the ground. Then she sniffed and asked. "Have you eaten today, sir? Did you drink water?"

George thought for a moment. He could not understand why he was never hungry or thirsty. He did not think about it long before she admonished him.

"Sir, you must eat and drink or you will never be able to go to the lands beyond the edges. Come. We will find water and fruit, or perhaps some sweetroot."

"How come I never get hungry here?"

"I cannot say. I just know that you must eat or you must remain here forever." She turned away and led him along the path to a small creek.

She dug in the ground below the red leaves of a bush and pulled some bulbous roots from the dirt. George watched her collect four round rocks of equal size. She set three in a triangular cluster on the ground by the bank of the creek. As she placed the fourth rock atop the other three, a small stream of water jumped from the creek and splashed over the top rock.

Dumbfounded, George watched her wash the roots in the water flow. She drank from the flow and stepped aside, offering him a chance to drink. He cautiously approached the fountain and sipped the water. Then, he sat back and asked, "How did you do that?"

"What?" she asked.

"The water! How did you make it jump up like that?"

"I have always fetched water that way. That is how *everybody* fetches water – almost everybody."

"But . . . how? Show me how you did it."

"I only placed the rocks, sir." She reached to the pile of rocks and removed the top piece. The water stopped instantly. She explained as he looked on in amazement, "I arrange the three base rocks and place the crown on top like this." As the rock was nested atop the other three, the water leapt from the creek again.

"Can *anyone* do that? I mean . . . can I try it?"

"Of course!" Tamara removed the crown and placed it in his hands.

George timorously held the rock – hefted it. He expected it to burn or move at his touch, but it did not.

"When the crown is in place, the water will come."

He looked inquisitively at Tamara who, with a nod of her head, encouraged him to place the rock on the other three. Instantly, the water jumped from the cool creek and splashed over his arm, which crossed its path to the pile of rocks. He shook the water from his arm and sat back to watch the water flow.

Tamara smiled. "You seem amused by this, sir – like a child at play."

"I like to study things. Always have." He touched the pile of stones. "It must be some kind of magnetic distortion. Does it work only with certain *types* of rock, or certain sizes?"

"No, but they all must be the same size – all large, or all small. Larger stones draw larger streams, and," she pointed to the pile of stones, "they must be stacked in that way – three together at the base, and one at the crown."

George watched the fountain. He reached into the flow and the water splashed around his hand trying to reach its goal. "It's like magic. I can't see any physical explanation for it."

"It is the nature of the Land. Sir? We must return soon. I beg you, sir, eat some sweetroot and I will help you find your friend. Then we can return to the village."

"OK." George bit into one of the bulbs she handed him. The root was like a potato in texture but its flavor was as sweet as fruit.

After ingesting two of the delectable roots, he stood to resume the search for Annie. Tamara displaced the rocks and followed. The sky darkened but George thought some movement would ease Tamara's anxiety. "We can walk until it is too dark to see the path," he said. "Then we'll rest and try again in morning. OK?"

"As you wish, sir."

The two walked along the path until George could no longer see beyond the bushes by his side. They rested at a grassy knoll by the side of the path. Neither said much during the night. George was preoccupied with the wonders he had discovered and Tamara quickly fell asleep.

George looked at the shadow of Tamara's form and thought of Jane. He wanted to be with her so much that he thought for a moment of finding comfort with Tamara. But Tamara was not Jane – and never could be. He needed Jane. And his need for her was a fact that reminded him of his home and his intention to return. He thought about the avalanche that brought him to this Land. Then, a horrible thought occurred to him. *Jane must be frantic! She must think I'm dead.* He fell asleep determined to find a way to let her know he was alive.

SEVEN

Hearing the Call

SOMETHING COLD sniffed at George's face. Half awake, he was about to brush it away with his hand but he opened his eyes before moving. He was startled as he looked up to the raised chin of a small crocodile – or, what *looked* like a crocodile. George screamed. The animal rolled its head back and caught its tail with its teeth to form a ball with its body. Then it used its legs – more than four as George could tell – to propel itself, rolling on its underside until it collided with Tamara's legs as she rushed toward George. After the collision, Tamara reached down to comfort the animal. "What is wrong?" she asked the animal – and George.

"What is that? George asked. "It scared the hell out of me!"

"It is a Rollabee," Tamara answered. "And I think you scared *him* just as much as he scared you!"

"What's a Rollabee?"

"It is a rare beast which seems to have been bred by two

different kinds of animals," she answered. She stretched out the creature to demonstrate. "You see?"

It was a reptile of some sort with leather-like skin at the bottom and the fur of a mammal on its back. George rose and walked to Tamara. He leaned over to touch the Rollabee and the animal curled next to Tamara. After he pet the animal for a moment, it relaxed. "There, fella," George said. "I didn't mean to scare you!"

The creature entertained them for a short time before it looked down the path behind them and rolled away through the underbrush. George laughed at the queer rolling motion. Then he looked down the path and thought he saw something moving. "Who's there?" He listened and watched. "Annie?"

"Blondie?" Annie stepped into view and squinted in George's direction. "Tarnation! Was that you makin' all that racket?"

"We had an unexpected visitor, that's all. Where have you been?"

"Been? I been lookin' to find our way back down the mountain! Where do ya think?" As she stood before George, she looked at Tamara. "What happened to you? Did you do this, Sonny?"

"Of course not! It was somebody at the village and she won't say who."

"I didn't think you were that sort. Woulda throwed me some if you was. I fancy myself a pretty good judge."

"Annie, you shouldn't be walking around here all by your-self."

"Don't worry, Sonny. I'd o' come back for ya – as soon as

I found a way back."

"That's not the point. This place is dangerous. They tell me we're pretty near the edges. You could fall off."

"I ain't about to fall off no mountain."

"We're on the cloud, Annie. Your mountain isn't anywhere near us."

"Get out," Annie smirked.

"Annie, we're stuck on this cloud and there's no way off it – at least none that I know of yet."

" B-u-l-l-shit."

Tamara said, "He speaks truly. Only the Ferryman can show you the way to the land below."

"Annie, think about it. You just came from the village. Have you ever seen that village on your mountain?"

Annie didn't answer.

George said, "Tell her, Tamara."

Tamara didn't answer either. She seemed to be listening to something. He strained and thought he heard it – a faint voice far away – but he could not understand what was said. "What is it?"

"The Ferryman calls for the stranger in the Land. I haven't listened for him since I was taken. I believe *you* are the stranger he seeks!"

"But why? How does he know I'm here? And how does he call? I couldn't make out anything. Did you, Annie?"

"Nothin'."

"He knows everything about the Land," Tamara said. "You have to listen for him if you are to hear him. For so long, I have worked so hard that I did not listen."

George, Annie, and Tamara walked down the nearly deserted main way. Before reaching George's hut, they met Tmron.

"That you have returned, I am pleased," Tmron said.

Annie kept a distance between her and the Sasquatch. George said, "Thank you. Where is everyone?"

"To gather more Spoils they have gone."

"Why didn't you go with them?"

Tmron shrugged his shoulders.

The four entered George's hut – Tmron with the usual difficulty. Tmron and George sat at the table and Tamara excused herself. Annie remained standing near the entrance.

"When will the villagers return?" George asked.

"Next light," Tmron answered. "Far the village is not, but to watch first the village Jack LaRoche taught us, and for a time and place of weakness to plan our approach."

"You don't seem pleased about the things LaRoche taught you."

"Many things he taught us – some good things. But improvements they have not brought – only Spoils." The Sasquatch glanced at Annie.

George said, "Annie, will you sit down? You're perfectly safe."

"I'll be the judge o' that."

"Suit yourself." George looked back at Tmron. "You were saying?"

"Many Spoils we have taken. But troubles they have brought as well as benefit. More huts we must build to house them and unharvested our gardens stand because from other villages so much is taken."

Annie moved and sat on a stone bed. George asked, "Tmron? You never did any of this before Jack LaRoche came?"

"No. What I have been telling this is. These things Jack LaRoche taught us."

"Didn't anybody question him?"

"Some at first there were, but with his thunder he crushed them."

"His thunder?"

"A weapon he had like thunder it sounded. Those who were by his thunder struck, lost to the Land were they."

Annie mumbled, "I'd like ta get my hands on that!"

George could hardly make it out and he spoke quickly, hoping the comment would go past the Sasquatch. "Tmron, I have to tell you what I know about Jack LaRoche." Tmron nodded for him to continue. "Jack LaRoche was an evil man and a criminal in my land. He was a mercenary – someone who fights for money or simply because he likes to fight."

George told Tmron all he knew about Jack LaRoche. When he finished, the Sasquatch scratched his head and said, "To speak of this where Telemachus and his friends can hear, wise it might not be. Important to them Jack LaRoche is. Leaders in this village they became because his friends they were. If trying to take their power they thought you were, to harm you might come."

"You're their friend. Why do you tell *me* this?"

"Yes, their friend I am. But as before I have said, improve our living I am not sure we have by following the teachings of Jack LaRoche. What you have told me I will consider. And with others I will discuss it. With the changes Scragg is very satisfied but one to follow others he has always been. But, to him I will talk to see if know he might about such teachings how Telemachus might feel.

"While away you were, some other friends about the Ferryman's callings I asked." The new subject was particularly interesting to George since Tamara had told him of the call while they were near the edges. Tmron continued, "Many calls there have been as well as a few visits from messengers. About a stranger they asked. No doubt there is that to see you the Ferryman is anxious."

"Why is that?"

"Know I do not. For the same reason Telemachus wants you to remain here it could be. He believes power you have – like Jack LaRoche."

"Why are you so concerned about Telemachus' opinions? He can't be a threat to you!"

"As I told you, a friend he is. Threatened by him I am not. But consider one must that, though puny his kind is, many more of *his* kind in this Land there are than mine."

George and Tmron continued discussing their ideas while Annie sat quietly listening. Evening fell before their conversation ended. Tmron stood to leave the hut and George was left alone with Annie.

Annie stood by the bed. "We gotta get outta here,

Blondie."

"Where would we go?"

"Back!"

"I told you, there *is* no back. Besides, I'm not ready to leave yet. There's a lot to learn about this Land."

"Well, we can't stay here. I don't like that big ape and, from what I seen done to your girlfriend, I ain't figurin' I'm gonna like any of his friends either."

"I think Tmron's OK. He's got enough doubt about LaRoche to earn my trust. You should try to get to know him. He's very intelligent and receptive to new ideas. Just think about what an opportunity it is to study a creature like him! The others might come around too, if we can get them to forget about LaRoche."

"You got more faith in 'em than I do, Sonny."

George smiled. "One of my character flaws. I tend to think the best of people – even when they don't deserve it."

"Well, I don't need to be hit over the head. If they cross me once, I'm gone."

"If they let you leave."

"What ya mean by that?"

"I don't know. It's just that sometimes I feel more like a prisoner than a guest."

"Well, let me tell you, Sonny. If I wanna be gone, I'll be gone. And when the time comes, you can be gone too, or ya can stay. It's up ta you."

George walked to his rock bed, exhausted from his recent exploration. None of the day's activities and conversations kept him from sleeping. He was lost almost immediately after he reclined.

Tamara returned in the morning with fresh water and fruit. Annie ate most of the fruit in less time than it took George to nibble through one banana.

The raucous crowd of conquerors stumbled down the main way of the village. Telemachus and his followers had elected to consume several skins of choice, very potent wine that they had taken from the other village. It had been an easy victory and there was no need to delay their celebration. All the captives were burdened with booty and the female captives had obviously been abused.

The villagers who had remained behind came out of their huts to assist the captives and the conquerors. George, Annie, and Tamara attended to the injured and abused captives but the new Spoils were more fearful of them than they were of their injuries. Tmron saw them trying to help and suggested their time and effort would be better used in getting the victors to their beds, leaving the captives to mend themselves. They worked together carrying the men and women of their village to their huts where they were set comfortably to sleep. The sky was black and the village silent before they found their own beds.

George and Annie slept as well as the drunkards, but rose to consciousness when the morning light penetrated the overcast sky. The village remained quiet – drunkards sleeping, local residents cautious not to disturb them, and captives too fearful to speak.

As George and Annie walked along the way, George noticed several areas where white powder and decaying fruits and supplies littered the path. "See this? All this waste just dissolves whenever it sits on the ground – except the seeds. But I still don't understand why I can walk on it without hurting my feet!"

"I felt that ground before. You won't see me walkin' on it without a good pair o' shoes – not that these loaners are anywheres near as good as my climbin' boots."

"You were pretty hungry this morning, weren't you?"

"So?"

"*I* wasn't! I haven't been since I got here."

"What's yer point, Sonny?"

"You wear shoes and you're hungry. I don't and I'm not."

"And?"

I don't know *and*. And I don't know *how* or *why*, but I sure do want to find out."

"Ya seem ta want ta spend an awful lot o' yer time findin' out stuff."

"I suppose. I've always been curious about things. My wife, Jane, said I was obsessed about this cloud."

George thought about the Ferryman – wondering if he could teach him about this strange Land and wondering if he was a fair man or a dictator as Telemachus described him.

"Penny for yer thoughts, Blondie." Annie said.

George raised his hand to quiet her. He thought he heard someone mumbling. He strained to listen until, finally . . .

Find the stranger in the Land. We must speak together.

Eight

The Village Grows

ANNIE FOLLOWED George into the Meeting Place. "I jes hope yer not goin' dizzy on me, Sonny. Hearin' voices that ain't there ain't normal. Hey! This ain't half bad! They got some decent grub here?"

"I don't know. I've only had the wine."

"Sissy drink. I could go for a good belt o' somethin' a little stronger." Annie pushed her way in front of George as they approached the bar. "You got any whiskey?"

The scrawny keeper looked up at George and back down at Annie. "We have wine and water."

"What . . ."

"Two waters, please," George said.

"Speak for yerself, Sonny. If wine's all ya got, hit me with a double."

"Annie, that's pretty strong wine. Maybe you should try it first."

"I don't need no greenhorn tellin' me how to do my drinkin'."

George looked at the keeper. "One water and one wine, please."

"Stubborn as a mule, ain't ya, Sonny?"

"Look who's talking! And stop calling me *Sonny*. My name's George." George led her to one of the stone tables.

"Gettin' touchy, ain't ya? First ya hears voices and now yer gettin' all sensitive on me." Annie took the clay mug of wine George had placed on the table. She raised it to her lips as if she were about to chug it in one swallow.

"Easy, Annie. I'm not kidding. That's really strong." Annie took a short draw from the mug. "I'll give ya this much, Sonny. It's got a kick like good whiskey, but it tastes like sodie pop."

"Ah! George Severe." A voice called from the entrance to the Meeting Place. George and Annie turned as Telemachus led his friends to George's table. "We feared you might have left us, but here you sit. And you're friend is up and about."

"Annie," George said, "this is Telemachus and Gideon and Norris."

Telemachus said, "We will sit together." He looked at two people sitting at the next table and they immediately stood and abandoned their seats. Telemachus sat with Annie and George while the other two took the abandoned seats.

"Why did you run off?" Telemachus asked.

"I was looking for Annie. I was afraid she might have gone too close to the edges."

Annie lowered her empty clay mug to the table and said, "I told you before, George, I don't need no lookin' after."

"Oh, she is a wild one," Telemachus said. "Or is it the wine that speaks for her?"

"That itty bit o' wine ain't gonna bother me none."

"Well then, you will drink some more." Telemachus raised his hand and called to the keeper. "More wine for all of us."

George interrupted, "Annie . . ." Annie cast a deadly glance at George and he held his complaint. "Suit yourself."

"So," Telemachus said, "you found your way back to the village."

"Tamara found us."

"Ah yes. I heard she returned."

"What happened to Tamara when we left? She didn't look well when she found us."

"She was supposed to be serving you. But, instead, she lost you. Gideon had to punish her. We will understand if you wish to have another Spoil to serve you, but I think she has learned her lesson."

George pretended he was indignant at the fact that Gideon had exercised the right of punishment of *his* servant. "She is adequate for my needs. But if I am to train her to my ways, it will be necessary for *me* to be the one to discipline her." George looked at Annie intermittently as he spoke, hoping she would stay out of the conversation.

Telemachus smiled and answered, "Forgive us, George Severe. We meant no intrusion."

The keeper delivered their drinks and Gideon spoke to Telemachus. "Now that our new friend has returned, maybe he will begin to share his secrets with us."

"Perhaps he can, Gideon. I was about to suggest it myself."

"I told you before, I don't have any secrets," George answered.

"We will be happy if you tell us about your world," Telemachus said.

"Why? You seem to be pretty successful already. You've just defeated another village and brought back more Spoils. Nothing I could say would improve on that."

"We will have to manage our new Spoils somehow," Telemachus said. "First, we will build new huts for them. They claim to have no stone craftsmen among them."

Gideon interrupted, "They *must* have craftsmen. They are just stubborn. Let them sleep in the rain, or thrash a few of them and we will find the craftsmen we need."

"They are well-beaten now, Gideon. We will begin to build the huts with our own craftsmen and some of the other Spoils. We will call upon the new Spoils when they recover." Telemachus turned to George. "Perhaps our two new friends can help."

"Of course," George answered. He ignored Annie's look of concern. "We'd love to help you."

Annie reached in front of George and asked, "You drinkin' this, Sonny?"

George ignored the stern look Annie passed and said, "No, but that doesn't mean you should . . ." Before he finished speaking, she had raised his mug. Telemachus and Norris smiled, but Gideon just watched as Annie drank.

Annie lowered the mug to the table and said, "Well, seein' as how you volunteered us to workin', we'd best get at it."

Telemachus said, "Gideon will take you to the new huts. Won't you, Gideon?"

"Yes." Gideon grunted and stood.

"Well, lead on, Red. C'mon, Blondie!" Annie followed Gideon to the door. Her gait was just as steady and aggressive as always.

George followed, expecting to have to pick her up off the floor at any moment.

With Tamara's help, George persuaded the new Spoils to work with the village craftsmen and he suggested that the craftsmen would be better used if they concentrated on the construction of the huts while the unskilled workers collected the building materials. Everyone seemed intrigued by his idea. Gideon ordered the craftsmen and other workers to carry out his instructions. George was amazed that his suggestion could have been so impressive.

After the day's work was done, Annie and George retired to George's hut, which they now shared. George sat on his warm stone bed while Annie sat at hers and removed the borrowed shoes.

"My dogs is killin' me," she said.

"I'm surprised that's not all that's killing you."

"How ya say?"

"Annie, you had three mugs of that wine. Just one, and I was on the floor!"

"You don't drink much, do ya, Sonny?"

"No, but I'm twice your size."

"Size don't matter as much as what yer used to. I been drinkin' men under the table most o' my life."

"I wouldn't leave your shoes on the floor like that."

"Yeah. I keep forgettin'. Thanks." Annie placed her shoes on the bed. "Oh, by the way. What was all that about in the Tavern? And why did you go and volunteer us for all that work?"

"You mean the stuff about Tamara?"

"That and ever'thin' else."

"I just thought she might be better off if I made it sound like I wanted to be the one who hit her if she needed it. I'd never actually do it!"

"I know that, Sonny. So why go soundin' like ya would?"

"They seem to respect LaRoche and I thought that's what he might have said. I wanted to get them to leave her alone without making it look like I disapproved."

"I ain't so sure actin' like ya *do* approve is the right way ta go about it. That Telemachus feller probably ain't no worse than any o' them windbags in Washington. But that red-headed one, Gideon . . . he's a snake *and* a weasel all in one. I'd be watchin' my back when he's around if I was you. I still don't—"

"Look, Annie. I want to be able to trust these people but I'm not as naive as you think. I'll watch my back, but I want to give them a chance, too. I still don't know if we're prisoners or guests here. Right now, it looks like we have something they want – those secrets they think we have about our land. I don't know many of the things LaRoche knew about. So, I volunteered to help build the huts. If they get tired of waiting for answers, I'd like to be on their good side. Besides, it gives me a chance to study this place. Just think about what we learned today!"

"All I learned was how much these shoes hurt. Somewhere's along the line, I'm gonna make me a decent pair o' boots."

"Didn't you pay attention today? Didn't you see how the stone behaves?"

"What d'ya mean?"

"It's *alive*, Annie! Oh, I can't believe you didn't see it. The rock is alive – that's why it sticks to itself! It's like cutting your finger. If you hold the skin together, it heals. The cut fuses together just like the stones do here."

"How did ya figger that?"

"By watching and asking questions. You saw them putting the stones together. Did you see them using any mortar or glue?"

"No, but I seen plenty o' dry stone walls and the like before."

"So have I. But this is different. The stones stick to each

other because they grow together. I'll bet tomorrow you can't knock down any one of the walls we built today."

The Meeting Place was crowded with village workers. Telemachus made room for George and Annie at his table. "Gideon has told me about your ideas for speeding our work. I knew you held secrets."

George answered, "If those are the kinds of secrets you're looking for, I'll be happy to share them."

George noticed that Annie was sitting next to Tmron. He was glad to see she was no longer afraid of him. Then he realized she was also sitting opposite Gideon. That made him wonder if she was actually warming up to Tmron or just keeping an eye on Gideon.

Telemachus offered George and Annie some fruit. "Take something to eat and tell us more of your secrets."

George said, "Well, I do have another idea for building the huts."

"Speak it!"

"Yesterday, I noticed that the workers had to hold each ceiling stone in place until the stones fused together and I thought it would be easier if they just made a platform to hold them in place."

"How would they make such a platform?"

"We could use wood from trees cut into boards, or limbs lashed together. Then we could use some heavier pieces for braces between the platform and the ground and load the platform with the stones for the ceiling. When the stones are bonded, all we have to do is knock the heavy braces out from under the platform and reuse the pieces on the next hut."

Tmron interrupted, "But the wood will break apart when it touches the ground . . . unless you know a way of keeping the trees alive after you move them."

"The stone is alive, right? Just put a stone between the supports and the ground. The wood should last long enough for the stones to bond."

"It sounds like a good idea," Telemachus said. "I don't really understand how it will save time, but I know your last idea proved itself worthy. Indeed! Your secrets will be most helpful. Try your plan."

The village had no technology for cutting trees into boards. As a result, George suggested less mature trees be lashed together to establish the platform. George and Gideon went to the new huts to discuss his idea with the craftsmen. Annie went with Thaddaeus and two of the captives to gather the trees.

Annie and George stripped the small trees and lashed them together. They set the forms with high, rounded crowns at the centers to cause greater pressure at the joints as the braces settled. Much like an arch, the stones would be held together until they fused.

After the craftsmen had placed their stones over several of the forms, George removed the first brace and the wood platform sagged. He pushed up on the form to check for the weight of the stones. It was clear there was no weight resting on the platform. He carefully kicked away each brace until the platform fell to the ground inside the hut, leaving the ceiling suspended. The craftsmen and the workers cheered and hailed George for his ingenuity.

Annie kicked off her second shoe and reclined on her warm stone bed. "You was pretty proud o' yerself today."

George took a similar position on his own bed and answered, "I wouldn't say I was overly proud, but I was pretty happy about the way things worked out. Why?"

"That Gideon feller weren't none too pleased. I'm warnin' ya, Sonny. Don't cross that weasel."

"How did I cross him?"

"Yer hornin' in on his territory. You keep comin' up with all these great ideas and next thing ya know, Telemachus will be gettin' all his advice from you and Gideon's gonna start to feelin' left out. That's when ya kin expect a knife in yer back or whatever these folks use to do in each other."

"That's a little extreme, isn't it?"

"Depends on how ya look at it, Sonny. Depends on how ya look at it." Annie pulled her hands from behind her head and rolled to her side, leaning her head on her hand. "Let me ask ya somethin' else."

"Go ahead."

"Yesterday ya said I should try ta learn somethin' about this place. Well, I did and I'm not so sure I like it much."

George assumed the same posture. "What did you learn?"

"It has to do with them trees we cut down. Thaddaeus

and them others was real particular about which trees was picked. They always pulled a leaf from the tree first and inspected it real careful like. When I asked about it they said they was lookin' fer blood. I figgered they was talkin' about sap but that weren't so. Thaddaeus said they was makin' sure they didn't do no harm to no wood nymph. They was really lookin' for blood."

George sat on the edge of his bed. "Wood nymphs? Tell me more."

"He said there wasn't many of 'em around but the consequences for killin' one was pretty serious. Sure enough, they did find one that started to bleed. They was making all sorts o' apologies to the tree. Imagine – apologizin' to a tree! One o' them Spoils made a mud paste and stuck it on the branch to stop the bleedin'. After a few minutes, they washed the mud away and a new sprout was already a growin'."

"That's incredible! Do you think you could find this tree again?"

"Could, if I wanted. But I don't want to."

"Why not?"

"Listen, Sonny. You're the scientist in this group. If you wanna study this place, have at it. But I ain't inter'sted. Findin' me a way back home is all I have a mind for. And I ain't interested in goin' back and findin' no bleedin' tree. That thing give me the willies."

N<small>INE</small>

Sneaking Away

TMRON LED GEORGE and Annie to a corner table in the Meeting Place. "We must claim a table early or stand. As the sky darkens, it will be difficult to move about in the crowd."

George asked, "How do you know it's going to rain?"

"Can't ya feel it in the air, Sonny?" Annie said.

"Yes, and I can tell by the change in the overcast. If I had my instruments, I could confirm what I see. But, somehow it seems like there's another reason for knowing it will rain . . . like it's *supposed* to rain."

"What you say is true," Tmron answered. "There is a sense of it in the air. Weak the clouds have been of late and the soil is dry. The Land needs the water so rain it will. The darkness we saw across the Opens will soon cover the sky and the rain will fall."

The three enjoyed some wine and conversation while the crowd in the Meeting Place grew and the sconces were lighted. As much of the afternoon passed, George was pleased to realize the wine was not affecting him as it had previously. Although his cup was nearly empty, he was fully coherent. "Is this the same wine I had before?"

"It is. Slow to drink you have been Suffer you will not."

Annie said, "It's like I said b'fore, Sonny. It's what yer used to. You've had a few drinks since you been here and yer startin' ta get used to it."

"Maybe you're right."

"Course I'm right."

A crash of thunder hushed the Meeting Place for a moment. George lowered his empty mug to the table and said, "I think I'm going to call it a day." Tmron seemed confused as George stood. "I'm going back to my hut."

"I, too, to my hut will go," Tmron said. "But first, find friends we must to take our seats so that have them we may on our return."

"Oh, I don't think I'll be back tonight," George said.

"A place tomorrow we will need." Tmron called to Scragg and offered his chair.

Annie chugged the last of her third mug of wine and stood. Two people joined Scragg at the table as George, Annie, and Tmron squeezed their way to the entrance.

The street was dark. A flash of lightning stopped them in their tracks and drew all their faces to the sky. "At a good time we left," Tmron said.

"Yer right, big feller. Won't be long 'fore it'll be pourin' cats an' dogs," Annie said.

George smiled. Annie was warming up to Tmron. They continued walking. George watched the sky with each new flash. He noticed the bright reflection from the gold-domed building. The Griffin was not at its perch. The flashing became more frequent as they walked down the way. The stroboscopic effect of the lightning gave all movement an eerie appearance. Suddenly, George saw an awesome figure in the sky. In the next flash it had flown by them.

"What in tarnation was that?" Annie asked.

Yet another flash and George saw the Griffin sitting on the gold dome.

"The bird of the golden dome, in the storms it likes to fly," Tmron answered.

As Tmron left their company for his shelter, Annie went into the hut. George remained in the middle of the way, watching the Griffin and the sky until the rain fell. After the first few drops gently struck his face, he was drenched with a sudden downpour. The rain was cold and hard, like sleet. Though his feet were warm, George shivered from the cold on his back and shoulders. He ran into his hut.

"What in blazes was ya doin' out there, Sonny? Don't ya got 'nough sense ta get out o' the rain?" Annie asked.

"I was studying the Griffin. It's a remarkable bird . . . or, whatever."

"There ya go studyin' stuff agin. I wish you'd think a mite more 'bout findin' a way home."

"I will, eventually. Please be patient with me. After two years of chasing this cloud, I don't want to pack up and head home just yet. I may never get another chance like this. *You* may never get another chance. I can't believe you're not even half as excited about this place as I am!"

"Sure, some of these things is interestin' enough. But I'm a guide, not no scientist. I got better things ta do."

"Just stick with me for a while longer, OK?"

"Don't worry, Sonny. I brung ya here, I'll bring ya back."

The chills dissipated as George sat at the table, sipping water and nibbling fruit. It was late. He was tired from his work and the long discussions at the Meeting Place. He went to his warm rock bed and slept.

"George! George!" *Was that Jane?* "Come on, we're going to be late for dinner at my mother's." *It was Jane.* "Dad hasn't seen the baby for a while and the visit will do us all some good. Let's go, George." George shifted his head from side to side, trying to awaken to see his wife. He thought he saw himself sleeping on the couch in his living room. As his picture of himself grew more clear, he took his place in the dream and looked through half-closed eyes to the doorway where someone stood, holding something.

"Come on, George." The demand was clear – and so was the figure standing in the doorway. Jane was dressed in warm clothing holding Anastasia who was reaching out of her snug bundle to Jane's face. "Do you want me to go without you?"

George mumbled and tried turning over. A sudden crack

of thunder drew his attention back to the doorway where Jane had been standing but, in her place stood a young boy. He assumed the boy's place and looked down through a door to see his mother being dragged away from the basement stairs. He saw his father struggling toward her. Someone tugged at George's sleeve. It must be his little sister. The turbulent waters churning and crashing in the basement wrenched his parents from his view. More tugging at his sleeve. Another violent crack of thunder.

George awoke and lurched upright on his bed causing as much fright in the woman who tugged at his arm. The room was dark and the flashing and noise outside the hut held George in a stupor for another moment. Someone whispered, touching him, trying to comfort him. Eventually, the panic subsided and he looked around.

"Sir? Oh, sir! I am so sorry, sir. I did not mean to frighten you." Tamara's whispers soothed him and he recovered his faculties. "Here, drink some water."

"Thank you," he said as he noticed Annie asleep on her bed. He sipped the water and paused for a moment before he whispered, "I didn't mean to scare you, either. I was dreaming and the noise from the thunder must have upset me." He looked at Tamara. "You're soaking wet! What are you doing here at this time of night?"

"Sir! You seem like a good man." Tamara hesitated. "Sir . . . I am leaving and I ask that you not report my absence until it becomes necessary."

"In this storm? Are you crazy?"

"It is the only way to escape without detection."

"But where will you go? Surely the villagers will come looking for you! And if they catch you, they'll beat the heck out of you."

"I *have* to go. Somebody must tell the Ferryman what is happening here. We have discussed it at length and now, I must go."

"Who are *we*? And why tell the Ferryman? I hear he might be just the same as Telemachus and his buddies. Besides, he probably knows anyway."

"All the Spoils have discussed this. I have volunteered with two others to ask the Ferryman for help. We must go now so we are not followed. We need the time to make our way to the castle before we can be caught. No one will follow us in the storm. And these storms often last many days."

George remained quiet. He was concerned for her safety and hoped to think of a suitable argument that would convince the woman to remain. "Maybe things will get better here!"

Tamara lowered her face and shook her head.

"Maybe I'll be able to convince Telemachus and the others to stop raiding other villages and let the Spoils go home. Tmron seems to be coming around. With some more time, if I stay on his good side, maybe Telemachus will realize that Jack LaRoche was wrong."

Tamara stood silent.

"You really *have* to do this?

"You won't report my absence, will you, sir?"

George looked into her hopeful eyes and answered, "Of course not. But are you sure you know what you're doing?"

"It is the only way."

"Are you sure no one from your village or theirs hasn't already tried to go to the Ferryman?"

"We are not sure about the last village, but it has been a long time since the war on my village. We would have heard something by now."

"I hope you're right about him. Do you need anything for your trip?"

"Only your silence . . . as long as you can . . . and your best wishes."

"You have both." George stood for a moment, gazing through the darkness into her eyes. He wanted to embrace her but his dream of Jane was too fresh in his mind. He knew it was silly to consider such an embrace a compromise of his love for Jane but he wanted his wife so desperately that he could not offer himself to anyone else then – even if only in friendship.

Tamara leaned forward and hugged him. "I *knew* you would understand. There were those among the Spoils who thought I should not tell you." She released him and stepped back. "Thank you." She turned and left, looking back briefly as she passed through the entry.

George returned to his bed. There was so much on his mind – his dream of Jane, his dream of his mother, and Tamara's escape.

Annie said quietly, "We shoulda gone with her, Sonny." She rolled over, facing the wall of the stone hut.

One more thing to think about. He was certain he would not get back to sleep, but the warm magic of the stone bed relaxed him. He turned only twice before he was sleeping again. He slept comfortably and late, despite the crashing of thunder and the splashing wind blowing through the hut.

George and Annie forced their way through a less boisterous crowd in the Meeting Place. Most of the patrons were involved in games of various sorts – card games, board games, thumb wrestling, arm wrestling, and others. George saw Tmron waiting for a mug of wine at the same corner table. Annie called for some wine as she followed George to Tmron's table.

Tmron told George and Annie the storm would likely continue for a few days and little work was ever done during such a storm. "Quickly the time will pass if a game we play."

"I'm willing," George said as he looked at Annie.

"Ain't got nothin' better ta do," she said.

Tmron told them about a board game that used round colored stones as moving pieces. He signaled to the keeper and a board was delivered to the table with a clay pot filled with twenty-one pebbles. Tmron took the pebbles and set them in notches on the slate board. He demonstrated the method of play. Annie and George understood the game after just a few moves. "Sorta like Chinese Checkers," Annie said.

As the game continued, George's thoughts drifted. He examined the playing pieces. Annie tried to get him to pay attention. "You still with us, Sonny? Your move."

"Sorry." George moved a stone. "I was just looking at this game. We're playing with stone pieces on a stone board and the pebbles were kept in a clay pot. Seems like they should stick together."

"There ya go studyin' stuff agin. Why can't ya just play the game?"

"It looks like they're painted or coated with some sort of waxy material."

"You keep this up, Sonny and maybe I won't pass up the next chance ta . . ." Annie looked at Tmron and at the next table.

Tmron interceded, "With wax paints the pebbles *are* coated. Apart the wax keeps the pieces and, on the ground wax does not fall to dust." During the explanation, Tmron landed on one of George's pieces and sent it back to the beginning.

Although George was not pleased that he was forced to start anew with a piece so advanced in play, he was very pleased with the friendly smile he saw on his opponent's face. He had indeed found a friend in this strange Land.

For two more days George, Annie, Tmron, and others occupied the Meeting Place and played games. The storm ended abruptly, but no sun shown through the overcast. Much to George's surprise, the village did not remain wet very long. He expected to be walking in mud for several days, but the ground was firm throughout. The tingling sensation through his feet and up his legs seemed stronger. The ponds and streams had swollen but not to the extent they should have after such intense rainfall. The Land seemed to have absorbed the water like a sponge and George thought the storm might have ended by design simply because the Land was satisfied.

"George Severe?" The sound of Telemachus' voice drew George from his work. He looked up from his position sitting on a low rock and saw the village leader with Gideon standing behind. Telemachus continued, "I would like to ask you when you last saw Tamara."

George dropped the tool he was using and the stone he was trimming fell off his lap. He looked at Annie to be sure she would support his story. Annie stood back and turned her attention to Gideon. George stood and said, "A few days ago." He brushed the stone dust from his hands. "I sent her to the edges to find some sweetroot I'd seen there."

"There is sweetroot in our garden. Why did you send her to the edges?"

"The sweetroot I tried there was better."

"Did she return?"

"I don't remember."

"It has been said that she has left our village."

"As I understand it, she's been here for a long time. There's no reason to leave. Maybe she's helping the new Spoils!"

Gideon said, "Two of the new Spoils are also missing."

"I don't know anything about that, unless she took them to help her find the sweetroot."

An uncomfortable silence was broken when Telemachus said, "We will find them, I am sure. When we do, they will be punished."

"I think you'll find them in the village and there will be no need for punishment," George said. "If punishment is necessary, leave Tamara to me. She is *my* Spoil."

Gideon stepped forward and said, "She *was* your Spoil, but you have lost her."

"Gideon is right, George Severe. He made a gift to you and it seems you have misplaced it."

"I'm sure she's around somewhere."

Telemachus seemed satisfied with George's responses. "The true reason I have come is to see how well you have built these new huts." He looked at the completed huts and walked over to them, examining them as he walked.

George followed, anxious to hear the leader's comments. Annie walked beside George, but watched over her shoulder where Gideon followed the three. George said, "I didn't build them. Your craftsmen and the Spoils did."

"Yes, but you taught them the secrets. The workmanship is good. These huts should endure. You have done well, George Severe. Your secrets will be of great help to us as I expected from the time we first met."

Telemachus did not provide George with another Spoil. It was the leader's position that George should not have lost Tamara. He told George that she would not have escaped if he had been more responsible with his charge.

With no fruit and water delivered to their hut, George and Annie had to collect their own. If not for Annie's appetite,

George might have forgotten to eat at times. He still did not completely understand why he was never hungry, but he appreciated the need to keep his internal systems in good working order.

He enjoyed fetching his own water since he never tired of watching the fountains he could create with four round stones of equal size. "It ain't natural," was all Annie said about that. During one of his trips to the pond, he saw one of the villagers throw an empty clay pot over a pyramid of stones and then kick them into the water before storming away.

George's and Annie's friendship with Tmron grew as did friendships with many villagers and captives. Occasionally, he heard the hollow calls of the Ferryman – announcing certain events, or calling for someone to find the stranger in the Land. He often kept what he heard to himself – no sense getting Annie thinking he was crazy again.

The captives appeared to have accepted their roles as servants to their conquerors and the village was back to normal – except that the Meeting Place was filled with larger crowds more frequently then ever before. The villagers enjoyed more leisure while the captives performed their chores.

George realized that the physical nature of the village was changing. "Annie, does this place seem different to you?"

"That's a stupid question, Sonny. Course it's different, but I'm gettin' used to it."

"That's not what I mean. Are things different now than they were when we first got here?"

"Seems just as weird as always."

"No. Things are changing. Some of the people can't even get the water to jump out of the creek or the pond anymore, and the waste seems to be taking longer to decay on the ground. It's like the Land . . ."

"The Land what? Don't leave me hangin'!"

"Like the natural order of things has somehow been upset. Like it's . . . sick!"

*T*EN

Catching Unicorns

SHORTLY AFTER the Spoils were housed in their new huts there came a day of clear skies and bright sunlight such as George had not seen since he left for the treacherous slopes in the Rocky Mountains. It was a time to celebrate for the villagers and the captives. The main way bustled with activity, and games were set up in the park near the Meeting Place.

The games included various and sundry competitions in strength and skill – wrestling, lifting, throwing stones at targets, and one interesting game that required the stacking of oddly-shaped stones until the pile toppled. George enjoyed watching the children of the village at play. Although the Sasquatch and Centaur young seemed out of place with their human counterparts, their play was equally amusing.

"Good sun, George Severe," Telemachus said.

"It sure is," George answered. "I thought I might explore the Opens today."

"I have much to do today and I cannot take you there."

"That's OK! I'll go with Annie."

"You are yet strange to the Land to wander about all alone. I see Tmron over there. He will walk with you."

The giant agreed to guide George and Annie. He called to his daughter to tell her he was leaving. The young Sasquatch was clearly not pleased, so Tmron asked, "Would you mind if with us the young female walked?"

"Of course not!" George answered. "I have a daughter, too!"

Tmron called to his daughter, "Come, Fleng." Her grin exposed her large yellow teeth. "Fleng, you should know George Severe. You can speak."

"Good sun, George Severe." Her face beamed with excitement.

"Good sun to you, too!" George answered with a smile.

Fleng followed close to her father – skipping and jumping as they advanced, her long hairy arms swinging about. George called out, "Annie! Do you want to come with us?"

Annie joined the explorers and was introduced to Fleng. "You're Tmron's young un? You're near as big as Blondie here!"

Fleng showed her large teeth again and stretched taller.

As they left the village, George asked, "Why were we

suddenly blessed with such a sunny day?"

"Whenever the Ferryman believes it is safe to reveal the Land such days occur, or when the Land for water is starved."

"The Ferryman can control the cloud?"

Annie said, "Sounds like this Ferryman feller is pretty interestin' – may even be worth studyin'!"

Fleng played as they trekked over the Opens toward a wooded area some distance away. George felt the heat on his head and shoulders. He also felt more than the usual tingle in his legs and a cooling sensation that made him feel as if he were wading in a cool stream of water – until he tread off the soil to the grass. Though the grasses offered comfort to his tender feet, they insulated the refreshing feeling that the soil provided.

As they traveled across the Opens, Fleng danced through the higher grasses and munched on flowers and berries. The wooded oasis stood a much shorter distance away. The lazy motion of the grasses bending to a gentle breeze looked like rolling seas and gave the oasis an island-like appearance. George observed, "Look at all these animals out here – buffalo, lions, and horses, and they don't seem to mind each other, either!"

"Ain't hardly natural," Annie said.

The wooded oasis contained palm trees and coconut trees, which contributed to the island illusion. Much of the plant life was tropical except for a few large pines and some deciduous trees. The sun was falling toward the horizon.

Moisture from the plants evaporated into a fine mist — almost a fog. The explorers pushed aside wide-leafed branches as they walked. Arboreal animals such as monkeys, squirrels, koala bears, and birds watched with curiosity as the strangers infiltrated the small forest. The ground was cool and spongy. Moss, humus, and white powder pressed against their ankles as they walked. The jungle flowers frequently distracted Fleng. George was surprised to find a cluster of daisies, which should never have grown in a place so sheltered from sunlight. They saw a clearing with a small pond at one side.

George stood by the pond, watching Fleng play by the water's edge. Annie sat on a stone and removed her shoes. "These dad-blamed shoes is gonna be the death o' me. I'm gonna make me some decent boots jes as soon as we get back to the village."

Tmron said, "Soon back we should walk. Here you can wait while George Severe to the other side of the wood I take."

"Now jes a darn minute! I ain't gonna fall back 'cause of a few bitty blisters. I'm right behind ya."

"Very well," Tmron said. "Fleng, stay here and play you can. Far away we will not be."

The three trekked through the jungle growth to some other clearings and finally to the opposite side. The hills were pink from the setting sun. Annie asked, "What's over them hills?"

"More hills, some valleys, and the home of the Ferryman," Tmron answered.

Annie nudged George as she spoke, "Looky that place jes o'er the foothills where there ain't no trees. Looks like some sorta canyon or wash."

George wasn't sure why the area interested Annie but the nudge told him to go along. "Very nice."

Tmron said, "Setting the sun is and in the wood the mist grows heavy. Return to the pond we should to find Fleng and leave."

They walked into the blackness of the plants and trees. The mist was cooling and condensing. It splashed in their faces as they pushed the branches and leaves aside. They heard Fleng humming and talking. George smiled, "I can't wait to hear Anastasia talking to flowers and imaginary friends."

The clearing at the pond let the little remaining daylight illuminate the shore. George saw Fleng sitting near a ledge petting the neck of an animal, which had rested its head in her lap. He signaled to Annie and Tmron to be quiet. George saw a white tail swing up from the brush and he realized it must be a horse. He saw the young Sasquatch stroking from poll to withers. Annie stepped closer for a better view. George released a branch he was holding. The beast raised its head and looked directly at George, then squarely at Annie.

Suddenly, George realized they were looking into the eyes of a Unicorn. He stumbled as he tried for a better view. Tmron stepped forward. The Unicorn nonchalantly rose to its feet before walking through the mist, into the brush. Fleng stood and watched it leave. She turned and saw her father. "Away you chased her just when good friends we became!"

Tmron answered sympathetically, "To scare your friend we did not want, but return we must. The sun has fallen and the end of the feast you do not want to miss, do you?"

"That was a Unicorn!" George said. "Did you see that, Annie?"

"Yeah, I seen it. It acted like it knew me. Danged critter give me the willies."

Tmron explained, "Only a few remain. Very unusual it is to see one come so close to anyone. Fleng has done well. It may be as it has been said, that to purity and innocence such as is found in young females these animals are attracted."

They left the wooded island and stood under the most clear, most beautiful twilight sky George had ever seen. "This is great! I'd almost forgotten how peaceful the evening sky can be."

"The heart it does move," Tmron answered. "But go back we should now. Finished are the village games and the feasting will end at midnight, when together we sit and to stories we listen while eating sweet cakes." Tmron led the way toward the village.

George looked around and asked, "How do you know which way to go? The stars move so randomly!"

Tmron explained, "The path you must *sense*. Most of those who remember the ways of the Land can do it. Our lore you have learned well, George Severe. And in such a short time. Keep it true. Many have lost it in our village."

"What do you mean?"

"If it is not practiced lore can be lost. Since much of our work the Spoils do, some among us cannot call upon the water as easily as once they could. Lost the lore completely some have."

"I thought so. Annie, that's what I meant before – about things being different."

"Looks like you was right, Sonny – for once," Annie answered.

George asked, "Have you lost the lore, Tmron?"

"Lose the lore I will not," Tmron answered with stubbornness and pride. "My children as well will always know it."

They arrived at the village center and found places to sit on the grass where they watched as a storyteller completed his tale. The crowd laughed and cheered when he finished. George could not understand the language of the speaker, but somehow, he knew what was said. He enjoyed watching the faces of those who cheered.

Norris presented the next tale in George's language. He told an adventurous tale about an encounter with a Dragon that he claimed to have been twice the size of the largest building in the village. The eyes of the young listeners grew wide with excitement when he described his battle with the Dragon, which he claimed to have subdued and subsequently befriended.

Another storyteller took the center of the circle and sang her tale. George quietly asked Tmron, "Do you think Norris' story is true?"

"Possibly, some parts are true. Likely, many parts are not."

Annie said, "I lean toward yer last thought, big feller."

"Now Annie," George said, "if there are Unicorns around

here, there could just as well be Dragons."

Just as he spoke the words, Tmron looked at him in alarm. Telemachus stood behind George and asked, "Where *was* this fine animal you describe?"

Gaining some sense of Tmron's concern, George told Telemachus, "The Unicorn ran away when it saw us. It's probably a long way off by now."

George's suggestion did not discourage Telemachus. "Unicorns are rarely seen. I would like to find it."

George spoke to Tmron as they walked back to their homes after the celebration ended. "I suppose I shouldn't have said anything about the Unicorn."

Tmron answered, "Of things which are rare it is not usually wise to speak to a man of such greed. He may want to possess it. Fear not, however. If true to its ancestry the beast is, it will not be easily captured."

As they reached Tmron's hut, he and his daughter bade good moon to George and Annie. George and Annie continued walking.

"Why so quiet, Sonny?"

"I hope Telemachus doesn't go chasing that Unicorn."

"Who's ta say, Sonny. If it worries ya so much, next time keep yer trap shut."

Most in the village slept late after their long celebration. George was helping Annie stitch the heavy soles to her new boots when Telemachus interrupted. "George Severe! Delay your chores. I have an opportunity for you!"

George placed an awl on the stone table. "Hello, Telemachus! What's up?"

"I am going to find the Unicorn. Come along and show me where you saw it."

"I'm quite exhausted from yesterday's trip. You should have no trouble finding it, if it's still around."

"I can promise you some great sport! There is no one I know who has captured one of these beasts – let alone take its magic horn."

George was overcome by concern for the animal. "You can't do that!"

"I do what I choose, George Severe."

"I mean, won't that hurt it?"

"No! Animals have no sense to their horns. Some even shed them occasionally. We will have some fun and I will have a prize by nightfall. Come along! Your little friend, too!"

George spoke over Annie's combative mumbling. "No. I'm too tired and I'd just as soon you leave the animal in peace."

"There are times, George Severe, that I think you do not compare well to Jack LaRoche."

"People are different in my land as they are in yours."

"Remain if you wish. There are other ways of finding the animal."

George wrestled with a foreboding feeling. He walked with Annie. She was breaking in her new boots. During their walk, George saw Tmron walking from hut to hut along the main way.

"Hello, Tmron! Are you looking for something?"

"My young female I seek. You have seen her about?"

"No, but we'll help you look."

As the three walked together, George told the Sasquatch about Telemachus' plan to take the Unicorn's horn. Tmron seemed concerned by this. When they reached Scragg's hut, they learned that Fleng had been there but Scragg had asked her if she wanted to go to see the Unicorn again.

Tmron was obviously angered by the news. After they left Scragg's hut, George asked, "What's wrong, Tmron? Won't she be safe with Scragg?"

"Without my approval Scragg should not have taken her."

"I know what you mean. I'd worry about my daughter, too, if someone took her without asking."

"Fear for her I do not with Scragg about. For the Unicorn I fear."

"Why?"

"To lure the animal to a place of attack Telemachus will use Fleng. I must follow them and with my young one return."

"But they left a long time ago!"

"Try I must."

"We'll go with you. OK, Annie?"

"Course."

"No. Too short of stride you are. Slow my progress you will. Alone I must go."

The foreboding feeling remained with George as Tmron left the village. During that day and throughout the night, he could not shake the feeling. He paced in his hut until Annie complained, "Will you sit still, Sonny? You're gettin' yerself all worked up over nothin'."

"Not really, Annie. I've got one of those bad feelings again."

"Damn. How bad?"

"Really bad."

"Double damn. Well, ain't nothin' *you* can do. No sense turnin' yer stomach inside out."

George took to his bed where he slept fitfully through the night. His nervousness continued through the next morning. Annie accompanied him to the end of the way where he continued pacing while looking across the Opens.

Eventually, Annie spotted two men and two Sasquatch in the distance. They waited at the end of the way and saw that one Sasquatch was limping and the other was carrying something. Neither of the men seemed to be walking in good stride. George soon recognized that Tmron was carrying Fleng. The men were Telemachus and his brother, Thaddaeus. Both were bloodied and Thaddaeus was crouched as if he were injured near the stomach.

George and Annie walked out to them to offer their assistance. George asked Tmron, "Is she all right?"

"Recover her senses she will. Rest she must. To my hut I will take her and return. To their huts take these. Then find Elke and ask her help."

Tmron continued walking and left the others to George and Annie. George saw that Telemachus held a long helical horn stained with blood. The leader's face was pale with shock, as was his brother's. The fur on Scragg's leg was soaked with blood and torn from a wound. George looked to the Sasquatch since he seemed most able to answer. "What happened? Where are the others?"

Scragg answered, "To the Land the others are lost. Gored by the very horn which Telemachus holds I was. Gored by another was Thaddaeus and I fear he will not recover, for the Land offers no strength to him. To his family he should be taken for comfort and whatever relief to his pain they may give. Help him Elke will not. Return to *my* family I will and we will soon leave this unlucky village."

The Sasquatch walked away leaving George standing before the two men. George and Annie helped Thaddaeus to his hut. Telemachus followed, then excused himself. "I must go and clean myself and this magic horn which cost us so dearly," he said with a pale blank expression. "Something so painfully earned is surely a prize to be valued."

George remained with Thaddaeus who rested in his hut attended by his wife. Annie sought Elke. When Elke arrived, she examined Thaddaeus and tried to dress his wound. His face was white from shock and loss of blood. George and Annie stood to one side of the hut with Thaddaeus' family, ready to offer their assistance. Tmron ducked into the hut. George asked, "What happened out there?"

Tmron said, "Tell you I can what Scragg and Fleng described when I found them. Telemachus and Thaddaeus called upon Scragg and Norris and Alexander and Ivan to help capture the Unicorn. Invite Fleng Telemachus asked Scragg so she might visit her friend. In fact, to use her to entrap the beast he wanted. He knew the Unicorn to her would go again. To watch over the affairs of the village Gideon was left behind.

"When at the wooded area they arrived, the sky was growing dark. To the pond Fleng led them. Alone they left her, and in the wood beyond the clearing they concealed themselves. Eventually, to Fleng the Unicorns came just as Telemachus planned."

George interrupted, "Unicorns? You mean there were more than one?"

"A mare and her colt. With Fleng they played for a time and by the shore to rest they lay before Telemachus called for the attack. The mare rose immediately and ran. But a tight circle Telemachus had formed and there was no escape.

"Near Fleng the colt remained until the hunters closed on the mare. Then to escape he ran. Thaddaeus tried to block his path but too fast was his horn. The colt gored him and to the ground threw him. Then it trampled over his chest and into the brush it ran where Scragg to catch him waited.

"In Scragg's hands the colt would have been if Fleng had not interfered. Between Scragg and the colt she ran and pleaded with Scragg to let him pass. Aside Scragg stood and told Fleng to go after him to protect the young beast and to keep him from returning. Fleng left, and the battle to capture the mare continued.

"When on the mare Scragg closed with the others, onto her back Telemachus jumped. To shake him she tried but he held fast. Alexander must have thought the beast was slowed by Telemachus for closer he went, reaching for her head. Then, more swiftly than Scragg could see, Alexander lay disemboweled near the pond and no longer was Telemachus on the animal's back.

"Some distance away Fleng and the smaller beast waited. Fleng said that whenever the colt cried out, the mare returned his cries as if she were telling him to stay away from the battle."

George said, "Fleng must have been frightened."

Annie answered, "Scared half out o' her wits I'd say, Sonny. Big as she is, she's still jes a kid."

"Indeed, she said she was frightened – but more for her friend than herself," Tmron said as Thaddaeus groaned and trembled.

Elke called to Thaddaeus' wife to help. The two women calmed his spasms and Tmron continued the story. "Ivan and Norris chased the mare and Scragg a position took her flight to stop. Scragg held the Unicorn to the clearing. Telemachus recovered and stood beside Scragg as Ivan took hold of the beast's tail and Norris to her side leapt. His footing Ivan lost. But he did not release his hold of the tail. Dearly this refusal cost him because in the head the beast kicked him squarely. Scragg said that despite all the other yelling and crying, Ivan's skull he heard crack at the blow.

"Without Ivan dragging behind her, the Unicorn turned on Norris and with two slashes of her horn dispatched him. The first tore Norris' arm and the second pierced right through his neck. All who remained to deny the animal her well-earned freedom were Telemachus and Scragg.

"Quick Scragg was to block the animal's escape until she lowered her head and charged. As she was about to strike Scragg, her horn Telemachus grasped and deflected the attack so that only the wound you saw Scragg received. At the same time, a powerful kick to the animal's side Scragg threw. A hideous scream she cried out as she abruptly turned the cause of her pain to attack. The horn Telemachus held firm and away it broke from her skull.

"Her cries of agony Scragg and Fleng said were too horrendous to describe. Profusely the Unicorn bled where the horn was broken. She jumped about wildly as from her cries her terror poured and from her broken skull her life poured. In the last of her wild fury, Telemachus she knocked to the ground and Scragg she pushed into the pond. Only a few steps from the pond, to her knees she fell, crying. The cries were answered by the small Unicorn but close to her Fleng held him.

"Bloodcurdling cries the injured beast continued as she tried to stand. Her head she tossed to protect herself from anyone who might be nearby. Telemachus recovered and stood safely away from the Unicorn as out of the pond Scragg waded. The Unicorn offered one last terrible shriek and to the Land was lost.

"The last call I heard as I came to the wood. Fleng I found holding the crying colt and I told her to release him. To the clearing he ran as Scragg and Telemachus approached us bearing Thaddaeus."

Thaddaeus coughed blood as Tmron finished the story.

George stood quietly. He had never heard a story of such horror and he did not know how to respond. George stepped toward Thaddaeus. Discarding his revulsion at his wound, he stood beside the injured hunter. Finally, he asked, "Was Telemachus satisfied with the quest?"

"There was no joy in the victory." Thaddaeus cringed with the pain of speaking. "In all the teachings of Jack LaRoche, he never told us of such consequences as we have suffered." He coughed again. More blood passed through his lips and ran down his cheeks. George let him rest with his family around him. All the visitors, save Elke, left the hut. Everyone knew Thaddaeus would probably not live through the night.

As George and Annie entered their hut, Annie said, "'Bout them terrible feelin's o' yorn."

"What about them?"

"Looks like they was right agin!"

George nodded.

Eleven

Haunting

AS EXPECTED, Thaddaeus did not live long. George sat alone at a stone table in the Meeting Place, lamenting over having told Telemachus about the Unicorn. A clay mug of wine was his only companion in the crowded room. He sat until the sky was black and his wine had been slowly consumed. Then he walked back toward his hut.

As he walked along the main way, he was alarmed by a terrifying scream that came from the hut where Telemachus lived. He entered and saw Telemachus' wife holding her husband as he crouched at the corner of his bed with a dreadful expression on his face. George asked, "What's wrong?"

"I do not know," she answered. "He was sleeping well after turning all night. Then, he suddenly cried out. He said a

Unicorn was chasing him, trying to soak him with blood." As she spoke, Telemachus became less anxious.

"Can I help?" George asked.

"He is better now. He needs to rest."

". . . then I came back here," George said to Annie in their hut. "On my way, I bumped into Gideon. He said he heard the cry and was concerned about Telemachus."

"Sounds ta me like he's got a screw loose, Sonny. I seen it before. It can happen to anyone."

"Maybe this is a good time to persuade him to go back to the old ways."

"I wouldn't count on it, Sonny. If he's near as looney as you say, he ain't gonna know what yer sayin' half the time."

"Maybe he'll feel better tomorrow."

"Maybe . . . maybe not."

George greeted Telemachus' wife as he and Annie approached the hut. "Did Telemachus sleep better last night?"

"He did not sleep well, but he seems less disturbed."

A voice called from inside the hut, "Who is out there?" George and Annie followed Telemachus' wife inside. George thought Telemachus had aged considerably in the last two days. Not only had his complexion whitened, but so had his hair. "Are you all right?" he asked.

"Why should I not be?"

"You seemed troubled when you returned from your hunt and last night—"

"Last night was only a dream. Something to be forgotten. Jack LaRoche would not let such things bother him."

"Why do you always bring up Jack LaRoche? Don't you see that his ways are not good for you?"

Telemachus looked surprised. "Jack LaRoche taught us many wonderful things. Without his help, we would not have Spoils to work for us. Since we followed his ways, we have grown in strength and power. We have built many new huts for the Spoils we have taken. So many huts have not been built at one time since the village was first settled. And —"

"Telemachus—" George interrupted.

". . . all the time we now have—," the leader continued.

"Telemachus! Listen to me!" Telemachus was quiet. "Let me tell you about Jack LaRoche." George paused for a moment to be sure he held Telemachus' attention. "In my land, Jack LaRoche was a criminal, an evil man who killed other people for reward and for the pleasure or excitement of doing it. He was not the kind of person who should be the model for your village. Think back, Telemachus. Think of how it was before he came. Weren't you happier? Do you really enjoy raiding villages and killing Unicorns?"

For the first time since Telemachus returned, George saw a hint of color in his face. "George Severe! Are you saying that the hunt was of no value? I took it's horn! It is a prize of great value – very rare. It is magic, and with it's help, I will rule this Land in the place of the Ferryman."

"How do you know it's magic? And why do you want to rule this Land? Is the Ferryman so bad?"

"The Ferryman is a tyrant." Telemachus' face was tight with conviction.

"That's LaRoche talking. *I* haven't seen any evidence of the Ferryman's tyranny. What has he done that's so bad? Can you name *anything*?"

"Jack LaRoche told us how the Ferryman oppresses our rights. He must be conquered. I have heard enough of your foul words." He turned to his wife and demanded, "Woman, fetch me my horn. I am going to the Meeting Place where I will hear better conversation."

"But I cannot!" his wife exclaimed. "You gave it to Gideon last night in your rage. You said you feared it's magic."

"Enough," he barked. "I will have it back." He stormed out of the hut.

Telemachus' wife stood on the brink of tears. She pleaded, "George Severe! You must follow him and protect him from harm."

After George and Annie left the hut, Annie pulled back George's arm. "We ought ta stay out of this, Sonny."

George stopped and turned around. "You know I can't do that."

"Don't say I didn't warn ya."

"Go back to the hut, if you want. I won't stay long."

"Nothin' doin'. You'll be needin' someone watchin' yer back."

George and Annie walked into the Meeting Place. Gideon sat at a table brandishing the horn. Telemachus stood before him and bellowed, "You hold my horn, Gideon. I want it back."

Gideon answered, "Of course you can have it back." He handed the horn to Telemachus. "I knew you would want it, once you thought more about it. You were quite unhappy with it last night. Do sit with me and have some wine."

Telemachus sat and George approached the table. Annie stood a few steps behind him as he asked, "Do you feel better, now that you have the horn?"

Telemachus looked at him with squinted eyes and said, "You are not welcome here, George Severe."

When George hesitated, Gideon added, "Telemachus is upset right now. A little wine will ease his troubles. Perhaps it is best that you leave. Things will be better later."

George turned. As he walked away, he heard Telemachus mumble, "Things will *not* be better later." George almost heard the gesture Gideon used to quiet the leader. He continued walking away, followed by Annie.

"I tol' ya there'd be no talkin' to 'im," Annie said as they walked onto the main way.

George held up his hand to quiet her, then pointed to several Sasquatch walking toward the opposite end of the village. The limp of one told him Scragg was among them. Another group of Sasquatch walked out of a hut. "Where are you all going, Tmron?" he asked.

"Back to our own kind," Tmron answered. "Scragg is true – unlucky this village is."

"Why not stay and try to change things?" George stopped walking, hoping to detain the Sasquatch long enough to consider his proposition.

"Before I have told you, fighting these people we do not want. Many more of them than us there are."

"I don't mean to fight them physically. I mean *politically*. Talk to the other villagers and tell them the ways of LaRoche and Telemachus are no good."

"Listen to me they will not. One of their kind I am not. To you they might listen."

George thought for a moment. Then he said, "I'm an outsider." He frowned. "I don't think they'd listen to me either." He rubbed his forehead. Then he lifted his frown to a hopeful expression and said, "Maybe Gideon could help us! He's well-known. Maybe they'd listen to *him*."

"Lead Gideon does not. Waste your time in this village you will. Corrupted they are. To Scragg's village you should follow me. Or another village of your own kind you should seek. Like these people you are not – unless you remain."

"No. I can't go yet. I have to try to persuade them to change." George's expression was not very hopeful – more one of resignation to a hopeless task. "I hope you find what you're looking for. Maybe we'll meet again."

"Perhaps." Tmron stood quietly for a moment looking at George then turned to join his family.

"Jes don't know when ta give up, do ya, Sonny?"

"One more try, Annie. That's all I ask."

Annie folded her arms.

"I mean it. If it doesn't work, we'll go looking for the Ferryman."

George turned to walk between two huts and into the

garden. He walked beyond the fruit trees and the pool of water and looked out over the Opens in the direction Tmron had taken. Soon, he saw his friend pass the limits of the village with his family, following the other Sasquatch. In the distance he could still make out the form of Scragg, limping along. And off to one side, though it was difficult to ascertain, he saw two Unicorns. "Look! A large one and a small one."

Annie said, "Wonder what they're up to."

"They're watching the Sasquatch."

Evening approached and Gideon announced himself as he entered George's hut. "George Severe, I would like to speak."

Gideon walked to the table as he spoke and sat before George answered, "Gideon . . . of course. I was just telling Annie, *I* should be talking with *you*!"

"Very curious. I wanted to tell you not to take the words of my friend to your heart. Telemachus is grieved, almost maddened, by his recent hunt."

George was quiet for a moment as he thought about a suitable approach to Gideon. "Why do you suppose he's so upset?"

"Because he is weak. He did not learn enough from Jack LaRoche."

"Are you sure it's not because he realizes how wrong LaRoche's ways might be and he's just unable to return to the old ways?"

"Why would he think such a thing?"

"Because Jack LaRoche was an evil man. The lives of others meant nothing to him. You were much better off before he came." George watched Gideon as he told him this, but the villager was very good at keeping expression from his face.

"Why are you saying this?"

George was encouraged by Gideon's interest. "You have to persuade Telemachus to stop following LaRoche's ways."

"He will not hear such advice."

"Then talk to the people yourself. You have to return to the old ways. It's the only way you can live peacefully again."

"But what of the Spoils? The villagers will not want to labor again."

"They will, if they realize what they're losing – if they take the time to see what's going on around here."

"I could not tell them this."

"You're well-known in the village. You *could* do it!" George waited after he spoke.

"Telemachus would never allow it. He would put me away with the Spoils if I stirred the people."

"You said yourself that he's near madness. People won't follow someone like that very long. *You* could take his place as leader!" For the first time, he saw a reaction in Gideon's eyes.

"I have no interest in leadership." Gideon was lying and George saw it. "I could not speak of Jack LaRoche's works in your land." Gideon was silent. George was disappointed. Then Gideon added, "But *you* knew about him. *You* could tell the people about his evil ways, and you know the secrets of his world, too. *You* could be leader!"

"No, I couldn't be your leader. You need someone who knows *this* Land – someone from *this* village." He saw a glint of satisfaction in Gideon's eyes. George was sure the villager was testing him to see if he had any aspirations for power. He continued, "But I wouldn't mind telling what I know about LaRoche."

"Perhaps I can arrange something. I will give some thought to this matter. We will talk next light." Gideon stood and walked out of the hut.

"Crackin' a deal with that snake ain't likely to put you on top, Sonny," Annie said.

"I don't need to be on top. I just need to see things get back to normal around here."

"I keep tellin' ya, Sonny, with that one ya got —"

"Gotta watch my back. I won't forget."

"Well, there's another thing you ought ta remember. Sooner or later, we gotta get out o' here and head on home."

George grew weary. He wanted to sleep but the events of the day and Annie's last reminder pressed upon his mind. He reclined on his warm rock bed but could not close his eyes – until he thought of Jane. The thought of her took his apprehensions away and slowed his breathing. His eyelids drooped and the monolithic ceiling faded into darkness.

He did not dream, though his thoughts of Jane had him thinking he *would*. Instead, he slept peacefully – a peace inspired by the simple thought of the woman he loved so much yet abandoned to pursue his obsession.

In the morning, he thought about his adventure and the events that brought him to this place. He felt remorse for having been so preoccupied with his research. Suddenly, his thoughts were interrupted by a man's scream. He jumped to the entrance of the hut and looked out.

"What is it, Sonny?"

"Telemachus is running out of the garden. Something must have scared him."

"Wanna check him out?"

"Nah. Gideon's on his way to help him. Let's see what's in the garden."

George and Annie walked between two buildings. "Look!" George said.

"What ya see?"

"Just some bushes moving. I couldn't make out anything."

"Well, looky here," Annie said as she bent to one knee and pointed to some tracks on the ground. "Looks like one o' them Unicorn critters."

TWELVE

Exiled

"GIDEON TOLD ME he might be able to set up an assembly of the villagers, where I could tell them all about Jack LaRoche."

"You think that's a good idea, Sonny?"

"They have to be told, Annie. I've been planting the ideas for quite a while but nobody seems to want to take a stand."

"Does Telemachus know about this meetin'?"

"I don't know."

Annie shook her head. "What else did Red tell ya?"

"Not much. I did most of the talking."

"How ya mean?"

"He asked me what I was going to say—"

"An' you tol' 'im?"

"Of course! I have to hold his trust if I'm going to pull this off."

Annie shook her head again. "Remind me to sit in on any poker game you're in, Sonny."

"Why?"

"Ya keep showin' yer hand! Should be some easy winnin's."

"It's not that simple, Annie. If I didn't tell him what I'm going to say, he might not have gone along."

"Maybe you're right. But we'd better be prepared if'n things go bad."

"I'm listening."

"We might have ta get outta here real quick. You said you'd go to the Ferryman if this doesn't work, right?"

George nodded.

"If they turn on us, we might have ta split up. First thing's ta get outta the village. We can meet at that wash at the foothills I showed ya. Ya can see it as soon as ya get outside the village – looks like a scar on the side o' the hill. Whoever gets there first waits two days for the other. Then we go o'er the top to the Ferryman. Got it?"

"I don't like splitting up. I'm not about to leave you behind."

"Don't worry about me, Sonny. I tol' ya before, if I wanna be gone, I'll be gone. Besides, more likely I'll be at the wash long afore *you*."

George and Annie walked through the crowd of villagers gathered in the square outside the Meeting Place. As they approached the steps George turned to Annie and said, "Telemachus is here!"

"Not a good start, Sonny. Are ya sure ya wanna go through with it?"

George stopped walking and looked at Annie.

"Just thought I'd ask," she said. "Go on. I'm gonna find me a place where I can watch things."

"Thanks."

All the people watched Telemachus. George stepped toward him and saw Gideon at the front of the crowd.

Telemachus spoke as if he were introducing George. "My friends, George Severe would like to speak with you this day. He would like to talk to you about the path we have chosen – a path of prosperity, a comfortable path, a path of strength and leadership."

George was concerned about the tone of the introduction.

"He is going to tell you about our good friend, Jack LaRoche. He will tell you that Jack LaRoche was an evil man in his land. He will try to convince you that the ways of Jack LaRoche will corrupt us.

"As he speaks to you, I ask that you consider the question, 'What harm has come to us since Jack LaRoche taught us his secrets?' When you ask this question, you will realize how much *good* has come. Until Jack LaRoche came here, we were forced to labor ourselves if we needed anything. Now we are served by the Spoils.

"George Severe will tell you it is wrong to take Spoils. He will tell you that we were happier when we were without the

Spoils. Yet he was not here then and cannot know of our lives before he came.

"He will try to tell you that the Land rebels against us by withholding its power from us. In fact, it is the way of the Land to know our needs. If the Land does not serve us as it did before, it is because it knows the Spoils will serve us in its stead.

"He will tell you that I am an unworthy leader. Yet it is *I* who took him to our village when he was found wandering dangerously close to the edges. I gave him my trust and he will betray me by conspiring to take the leadership of our village for himself. If *I*, who rescued him cannot trust him, how can *you* put your trust in him?"

George looked at the faces of the crowd as Telemachus spoke and thought this was not going well for him.

"He will tell you that I have brought bad luck upon us because of the hunt for the Unicorn. Yet is it not true that no other has ever come so close to a Unicorn? The hunt brought great fortune for we now have possession of this magic horn. With this horn, we can lead the Land and have all our desires. We will never again need to labor for ourselves."

George saw Gideon nudging those around him into a cheer.

"He will tell you that you must return to the old ways, that we must work for ourselves, that we must not take Spoils, that Jack LaRoche was evil, that *I* am evil, that I am *mad . . .*"

George thought the glaze over Telemachus' eyes should have made that point clear.

". . . that this horn has no meaning after having cost us so dearly – my own brother was lost in the quest for its magic. He will tell you to follow *him* and return to the old ways. But he does not tell you it is only power for himself he seeks. He will think nothing of leading you to drudgery to satisfy his lust for power."

Gideon led the crowd in protest.

"Very well, George Severe, you can speak now." He turned back to the crowd after addressing George. "Hear what he says, but ask yourselves if you should trust someone who is strange to the Land, or if you would be better to trust one of your own. Speak, George Severe. Speak!"

George looked contemptuously at Telemachus, then nervously at the agitated crowd of listeners. He looked at Gideon. Gideon had betrayed him and told Telemachus every detail of his planned address. He could not find Annie in the crowd. He wanted to fix on at least one friendly face as he spoke. "My friends, I am not here to take power from anyone."

"Oh? Then what are you here for?" A familiar voice from the crowd taunted him but he did not see who spoke. His eyes fell upon Gideon, standing stoically before the crowd.

"I am here to warn you that you are pursuing a course which can only lead to despair. Telemachus found that despair himself after he killed the Unicorn—"

"What do you know of the hunt? You were not there!" This time the heckler spoke long enough for George to see him. Gideon cracked a sly smile as George looked into his eyes.

"Tmron told me what had happened—"

"Tmron is not here and you are a stranger."

The crowd murmured and grumbled.

"He told me the hunt was nothing less than murder."

"Were those *his* words or *yours*, George Severe?"

"That's not *exactly* what he said, but—"

"Exactly what we thought. *You* are the one who lies. *You* are the one we cannot trust."

The crowd cried out its support for Gideon's words; "Aye!" "Hear, hear!" "So it is!"

George panicked. Some of the people were angry. As others heckled and jeered him, he felt physically threatened. He did not know how to deal with such a crowd. Certainly he could not win their allegiance with his marginal speaking skills. Nonetheless he tried. "But, I spoke with Tmron before . . . before Thaddaeus died! He told me what happened."

"Liar! Liar!" After Gideon spoke the word twice, the throng joined in a chant, "Liar! Liar! Liar! . . ."

Couched in the din, a voice called out, "Liar, begone! Begone, stranger!" It sounded like Annie and came from behind Gideon. He saw Gideon begin to yell, "Kil—" and fall forward, gasping for breath. Annie stood over Gideon and nodded to George as she stepped back and disappeared into the crowd. Their voices grew louder.

Telemachus yelled over the noise of the crowd to George, "We do not need you here anymore. We do not *want* you here anymore. Liar, begone! Begone, stranger!"

The crowd joined in, "Liar, begone! Stranger, begone! Liar, begone! Stranger, begone . . ."

George was intimidated and could not speak above the noise. Some of the people shook their fists and advanced toward him. His stubbornness kept him from running. Though none could hear his words, he said, "If you will not hear the truth, then you will have to live with your *own* lies."

Seeing only deaf ears, he turned and tried to walk toward his hut, but the crowd quickly blocked his path. He turned again and was pushed out of the village by the angry crowd. As he left the main way and stepped into the Opens, the villagers stopped.

George turned back and said, "I won't go without my friend. Annie? Where are you?"

A muffled voice called out from the crowd, "You're on yer own, Sonny. I ain't goin' nowheres."

Telemachus said, "You see? Even the little ugly one from your own land will not stand with you. Consider yourself fortunate you still breathe, George Severe."

Telemachus and the villagers turned away. Only one remained, watching him . . . Gideon, standing gingerly, holding his back. He wore the expression of a proud conqueror that dared George to challenge him in the future. Gideon turned and left George standing in the Opens.

George suddenly felt cold and alone as he looked back at the village while the people disappeared between the buildings. Even the Griffin, perched atop its golden dome had its back turned to him. He finally believed that he could not save this village from the influence of Jack LaRoche. He thought of

Annie's plan to meet at the foothills and he remembered Tamara's flight to find the Ferryman.

George headed for the scar on the hillside. Annie had said the scar might be a canyon or wash. It could also be a steep cliff or a ledge where trees could not grow. The cloud blanketed the hilltops and pressed down toward the scar.

As he walked, his loneliness spurred thoughts of Jane and Anastasia. He walked toward his destination without seeing anything around him. The picture of the scar in the hillside was clear to his eyes, but he did not see past his thoughts of home. It disturbed him that he did not know how long he had been gone. He thought about how much he had learned since coming here but none of it seemed important anymore. He was ostracized from the only society he knew in the Land. The most important people left to him were his wife and child, and he imagined seeing them, as clearly as if they stood before him.

However, his steps toward his family brought him no closer. He knew his legs were moving because he felt the high grasses brush his worn trousers, but his wife and daughter remained out of reach. They were waiting for him, wanting him, needing him. They looked at him anxiously, encouraging him to step more quickly. Before long he was running, stretching his arms toward them, but he was unable to close the distance between them. He did not stop running until he stepped into a shallow brook and fell to its opposite bank.

George awoke at break of day and scanned the Opens, finding nothing of his earlier illusion. Another day passed before he stood at the foot of the hill that bore the scar. The scar was indeed a steep rocky slope, which could not support the growth of many trees. Those whose seeds unluckily fell at some craggy ledge struggled in their growth to cling to the rocky precipice. George found a comfortable resting place where he would wait two days for Annie.

During his rest, he heard the sound of a bell but could not find the source. The ground itself seemed to ring. He kept vigil over the Opens, hoping to see Annie approaching. His loneliness grew but he dispelled concerns of never returning to his real home by recalling the stories about Phillip Gravely's father, Cloud Walker.

George was not certain that the Ferryman would help him return. He knew nothing about the man. He had heard the Ferryman's thoughts a few times – but not recently, not since after Tamara left the village. *Tamara* had faith in the Ferryman. She did not accept the words Telemachus took from Jack LaRoche. If there were enough people in the village who thought like Tamara, maybe they *could* be saved from Jack LaRoche's poison.

The second day of rest brought no sign of Annie. Despite Annie's assurance that she could take care of herself, George decided he would return to the village to be sure Telemachus and Gideon had not held her.

As he crossed the Opens, he came upon a deserted village. There was evidence of a hurried or forced departure – broken clay pots and mugs, some of which had fused their broken pieces together; piles of white dust along the ways and in some of the huts; and a few stray dogs. George believed it was one of the villages raided by Telemachus.

He walked through the village and continued his trek toward a shining object in the distance – the golden dome where the Griffin perched. Shortly after leaving the abandoned village, he came upon three huts made from peat or clay, different in construction from those of the villages. He approached one of the huts and called inside the high, wide entrance. A Sasquatch stepped out of the hut and walked toward George in an unfriendly manner. George was about to retreat when he heard a voice at the entrance of one of the other huts.

"Mrudg! A friend he is."

George turned to see Tmron standing with arms akimbo. George looked back at the larger Sasquatch threatening him and said, "It's nice to see you again, Tmron, but I am not sure your friend appreciates visitors."

"Mrudg! George Severe you should know. A threat he is not."

The large Sasquatch stepped back and let his broad shoulders drop to a less menacing posture. After George saw him relax, he took his eyes off the aggressor and spoke directly to his friend.

"Tmron! I'm glad to see you again!" he said. As he spoke, Mrudg returned to his hut.

"Why are you here, George Severe? Tame Telemachus and his friends you were to do!"

"You were right. They wouldn't listen to me. I was forced

to leave the village. Now I'm going back for Annie."

"Your sudden departure is known. That you continue to breathe is good fortune. That you should go there I would not counsel. Unnecessary it is. Last light through this village your friend came."

"Annie was here? Where is she now?"

"To the Ferryman over the hills she has headed."

"I waited for two days but she never showed up at the place we arranged. If I get started right away, maybe I can catch up with her."

"Darkness approaches. With us you can rest. Next light your friend you can seek."

George agreed to remain at the Sasquatch village for the evening. Tmron told him that Annie said she thought they had a better chance of getting away from the village separately. By rejecting George when he was exiled, she felt comfortable that the village leaders would not watch her too closely. And so it was, since she made good her escape. She reported that not much had changed in the troubled village as a result of George's exile.

"I can't believe they still listen to Telemachus," George said. "He was practically over the edge when I left. How can people follow someone who is so obviously deranged?"

"Unusual it is not with your sort. Raving he continues. The village support Gideon sustains. You I told trust not Gideon. A worm he is. The decay of others he consumes. Then stand he will upon their bones and the memories of their deeds to his advantage he will use. If in failure Telemachus is lost, a new path Gideon will promise. If successful Telemachus passes, credit by his counsel Gideon will take. Either way, very soon the leadership of the village Gideon will claim."

"Why do you say that?"

"Lost to the Land Telemachus will be. The Unicorn or the dead Unicorn's spirit the cause. Certain of this I am – for so taken was Scragg from us."

George's eyes were wide with concern as he asked, "What happened to Scragg?"

"See we did not. Gone we know. And two Unicorns watching his hut were seen before and not after. The ghost of the Unicorn he killed Telemachus fears. A ghost it may be – or vengeful living Unicorns. The village Telemachus has not left since your exile. To the gardens he will not venture for fear of a Unicorn. If for him the surviving Unicorns are waiting, tire and steal into the village they will some evening. Complete their vengeance they will. If chasing him is a ghost, his own life he will take."

"Is he really that bad?"

"I believe it. Only time can answer."

"Is . . ." George did not want to ask, but he did. "Is Fleng all right?"

"Less often she cries. Strong she is."

"Do you think she's in danger?"

"Opportunities there have been for haunting but none have occurred."

"Good." George sighed his relief for the young Sasquatch.

George awoke eager to follow Annie's path. He asked Tmron, "Can you turn me in the right direction?"

"To start it would help. Later, your steps your thoughts must guide."

"Are you trying to say that all I have to do is *think* about a place and I'll get there?"

Tmron smiled at George's disbelief. "It is much as you say. But more there is. Your path you must *sense* as well. That you will be there you must *feel*. And that you be there you must *desire*. All these things you must do or stray you will."

"Do I have to be familiar with a place before I can find my way?"

"Easier it would be. Necessary it is not." Tmron suggested a test. He told George to close his eyes while he spun him around to disorient him. Then he stopped him and told him to keep his eyes closed and imagine the village, his wish to be there, his being in the village, and some idea about the path he might take to get there from his present position. When he had done this, the Sasquatch told him to turn toward the village and take a few steps in that direction with his eyes closed. George did as he was instructed. Then he opened his eyes and saw that he had, in fact, stepped toward the gleam of the Griffin's roost.

Tmron suggested he think about the edges where George was first discovered. George was not familiar with the path from his present location and he could not choose a direction.

156 | WIND CASTLE

Tmron said, "What the path *should* be like you must think."

"I'm trying. . . . Wait! . . . There!" He turned and took three steps.

"Good." The Sasquatch smiled at his student's success. "Learning our ways, you are quick. The path to the Ferryman and your friend you shall find. Some of the things along the path I will tell you, but of your goal you must not lose sight, or wander you will."

"I'll try to remember that. Thank you, Tmron."

THIRTEEN

Frothgarde

GEORGE FOUND IT difficult to concentrate on his destination. He kept thinking about other places. He remembered Tmron's warning that distractions could cause him to wander. So, he combined the use of landmarks and the techniques Tmron had taught him. Before noon on the next day, George had climbed into the clouds. He was surprised he could see clearly through the light mist along the slopes. The dense cloud coalesced near the treetops and did not intrude on the ground.

In the foggy hills, time lost all meaning. George knew he wanted to find Annie and reach the Ferryman as soon as practical, but his interests in the varieties of plants and animals consumed much of his time. Days of wandering seemed like only one afternoon. George rested against a hard, scratchy mound one evening, gazing to the milky sky. A brief thought of Jane made him realize his need to move along and he resolved to rise early the next day and resume his trek.

He was about to drift into sleep when he heard some groaning coming from the scratchy mound behind him. He listened but could not distinguish the sound. He *thought* it was groaning. But it also sounded like a pulse of blood coursing through a person's veins. Whatever it was, it kept him from sleeping.

Suddenly, the mound pulled away and he was left lying flat on the ground, wondering what had happened. *You humans make me itch!*

"What?" George sat up and tried to find the source of the words. He stood and saw something moving behind him. The milky clouds did little to illuminate the dark forest. "Who's there?"

You are so noisy, too! Who is there. Who is asking?

"Who are you? I'm George Severe – a stranger to this Land. Why won't you show yourself? I won't harm you!"

Ha ha! Few humans raise fear in me. George thought he was not *hearing* the words. The conversation seemed to be taking place in his mind. He heard only his own words. *You can call me Frothgarde.*

"I can't see you!" George squinted. All he distinguished was a large dark mass a short distance away.

Because he did not actually *hear* the words, he did not know which part of the slowly moving mass to address – until he saw something that might have been the head of the large creature. It was high on the moving mass and as the mass slowly approached him, two fiery eyes pierced the evening mist. George looked into the eyes with his head tipped back and asked, "Frothgarde?"

That is what I am called. The name was given to me many years ago. I think I will keep the name. The form took shape. It was very large and walked on four legs. Its head moved across its form and changed height as the creature stepped forward, leading George to the conclusion that it had a long neck. Its face finally came into view. It was covered with leather-like scales and had a frightful, yet unthreatening appearance.

The animal walked into view and George saw its large body and the odd wings folded and resting on its back. "You're a . . . you're a . . . D-D-D- . . ."

Dragon.

"Your lips didn't move! You *do* have lips, don't you?"

Why must you speak in riddles? What are you asking?

"How are you talking to me? I can't see you speaking. And I don't think I hear you either – unless my ears are all blocked up."

I do not speak the way you speak. You understand my thoughts.

"Telepathy? Like the Ferryman? Can you hear mine?"

Oh, so many questions. I should have let you itch me. Oh, well, what is done is done. No, I cannot hear your thoughts. You are not skilled at projecting them – though I sense you have the ability.

"Forgive my curiosity. A Dragon is a mythical beast to me

and, although I've seen a lot of mythical beasts since I came to this Land and I once heard a tale about a Dragon, I didn't expect to actually *meet* one."

I am no beast. *And I am not a* myth. *How long have you been here?* George was about to answer but the Dragon continued, *What other so-called mythical beasts you have seen since you came to this Land?* George tried answering again but Frothgarde added, *How do you like being asked so many questions at one time?*

"I'll slow down." George turned as he spoke and sat on a nearby rock. He told Frothgarde a little about himself and how he came to be in the strange Land. "I'm on my way to see the Ferryman."

Ah yes. A respectable example of your species. There are few of your kind who earn my forbearance. The Ferryman is one.

"You know the Ferryman?" George stood. "Do you know how I can find him?"

If you came from the troubled Opens, you are heading in the right direction.

"The troubled Opens? You know about the raids on the villages?"

Yes.

"Well, isn't anybody going to *do* something about them?"

I am not concerned about human wars and battles. Let them slay each other.

"How can you say that?" George turned and plopped back down on the rock in frustration. "If they fight among themselves, it won't be long before they fight the likes of you. I was told the Land was peaceful until recently. If the raids continue, they'll spread all over and there will be no peace at all. The whole Land could be lost."

I suppose you speak truly, but I am old and tired. I have no desire to fight your knights again.

"Knights? You've fought Knights? How old are you?"

I am sleepy, Human. We can speak at next light – if you do not run off. The Dragon lowered its large body to the ground and rested its head near its front legs. *Think not to harm me for I will know if you have malicious thoughts.*

The Dragon closed its eyes. Seeing the size of the beast and now familiar with its shape, George wondered how he could have leaned against its tail without seeing it.

"Very well, we'll talk in the morning, Dragon."

Address me as Frothgarde, Human.

"If you'll call me George."

As you wish. Now leave me to my rest.

George rose early, pleased to see that Frothgarde had not left. The beast did not appear to be strong and healthy. George had always imagined Dragons as having moist, shining scales accentuating their muscular forms, and their wings would be large and firm. However, Frothgarde appeared worn – like an old stuffed animal, molting from generations of use and years in the attic.

He walked along its side to examine the wings more closely. As he moved he continued to watch the head. He saw the lower eyelid of one eye slowly drop to reveal a dark brown glazed eye. He smiled as Frothgarde closed the eye. "You can rise now!" he said. "I saw you peeking!"

The Dragon responded. *I see you found the courage to remain through the night.* Frothgarde unsteadily rose to his feet and expelled a breath of exhaustion after finding his balance. Then he continued, *Most of your kind would have stolen away as soon as I closed my eyes.*

"Is that so?" George answered. "That's not what Norris told me. He said he met a Dragon and immediately conquered and tamed him. And I have read many tales of battles with Dragons during the middle ages."

I knew of a man by such a name. When he first saw me, the color to his face was lost. When he realized I did not give chase, he had the audacity to challenge me.

"What do *you* say happened next?"

I had to decide whether I should dispatch him or offer friendship. I chose to offer friendship. But it seems he is now inclined to contrive tales which bear no resemblance to the truth – much like the tales you must have read, which probably came from the journals of knights who sought accolades from their less worthy admirers.

George felt the courage Norris must have felt after discovering the Dragon did not chase him. "You have an interesting perception of events," he said. "Norris was one of the first people I met when I came here. Why should I believe your account any more than his?"

I have no interest in impressing others with tales of

glory – though I have many from my younger days. What I could tell you about . . . oh, what a bother! I care not what you choose to believe.

The two were silent in voice and thought for a few moments. Then George asked, "Will you tell me how to find the Ferryman?"

How would you know whether I am truthful? You have already chosen not to believe my account of my meeting with your friend.

"That's not so! I simply posed the question." George paused. Hoping to placate the Dragon with his own offer of friendship, he suggested, "If I knew you better, I might believe you!"

Why should I care? Your kind do not offer much to Dragons.

"It can't hurt to try, can it? Why don't you tell me about yourself – how you came to this Land, where you came from, how long you've been here? You will only lose the time of telling, and you may find in me a better friend than you found in Norris."

Frothgarde slowly set down his hindquarters while he stretched his long neck and pushed his scaly face into George's where he peered into his eyes. Then he raised his head and sighed, *Very well. I suppose my time is no great cost to me. I have lived for a long, long time – almost longer than I can remember, though my memory fails me at times. I am somewhat tired as well as old. If I did not use my time with you, I would probably just lie down and waste the light. Where do I begin? I know! I will tell you how I came to live in this Land:*

As a young hatchling I gamboled through the countryside, free of any concerns about where and when I would find my next meal. After all, there were plenty of mice and rabbits about. I did not threaten any humans, but I soon learned that they were not pleased to find Dragons roaming their fields and forests. Whenever any of their kept animals were missing, they blamed Dragons. Although I must admit, there were times I enjoyed their chickens and dogs and cats. Later, when I was older, I enjoyed a cow every now and then, but I did not consider such behavior cause to be hunted.

As I grew, I came to realize that my kind would always be at odds with humans. Certainly, my own nature would not change, and I did not expect that of humans to change. Eventually, I found my way to the western channel and, after roaming its shores for a number of years . . . Ahh, there were some wonderful fish along those shores – tasty and plentiful. I truly enjoyed diving upon their schools and emerging from the sea with a full belly.

Well, I was telling that, after I roamed the shores for some years, I crossed the channel to a large island with bountiful game and a comfortable climate. I could have been quite content to remain there for the rest of my years – which would see several generations of humans pass. But yours is a persistent and abrasive sort which refused to accept my kind. Humans were so greedy with their cows and goats. And they had so many! What did it matter that I occasionally enjoyed a few tender treats?

Since the hunting was good in the forests, I tried to stay away from the farms. But in later years, the humans became possessive of certain wild animals too! Dragons became impatient with the farmers and their kings and knights, and chose to eat what pleased them. We really had no choice. The humans were unwilling to leave us to the forests or the hills, so we decided to live our lives without regard for them.

Knights rose to protect villages from Dragons – not that protection was needed, at first. We never fed on humans. Even when they attacked us, we did not eat them. Human meat is stringy and it bears an unpleasant odor. The knights were more pests than threats until they worked together. Several knights together were capable of capturing a Dragon and slaying him – it is difficult to fly away when you have been awakened by the puncture of a spear in your side.

Many Dragons were lost to this practice. As our population decreased, we were not seen as frequently in the countryside. Consequently, the farmers did not complain as much to their kings and the kings did not send their armies to attack us as often. Another thing, which contributed to our survival, was the behavior of humankind. The knights no longer found glory in slaughtering Dragons in the company of a horde of other

166 | **WIND CASTLE**

knights.

Knights competed among themselves in combat and in deeds. Their numbers dwindled as they fought each other and foolishly challenged Dragons individually. The armor, which protected them from each other, hindered them when fighting Dragons. They were not able to move quickly and those of us who could blow fire cooked them in their metal ovens. Their horses were quite tasty when eaten that way. Although individual knights were occasionally successful, they were usually not much more than sporting diversions.

There was one knight, however, who proved himself more formidable than most. He did not slay many Dragons, but he did much to keep peace with them. He was called Arthur and he eventually became king of much of the island.

George interrupted, "You knew King Arthur?"
Do not pester me, Human!
"George."
If you want to learn, George, do not interrupt.
George nodded, "Sorry."

I was mature in years when first I met him. I had recently feasted on some sheep and was resting near a cave when I opened my eye to see a young man – not much more than a boy. He rode a farm horse and neither of them wore armor. He carried a stick in one hand that he had split several times at its end and he called out to me as he approached. He warned me to stop feeding on the local livestock. I thought, This little imp cannot deter me from eating what I choose. Much to my surprise, he understood my thoughts!

"If you do not restrain yourself, Dragon, I shall have to use force," said he. Ha, thought I. Even having just eaten my fill, I could crush an imp such as you with little effort. One burst of fire is all I will need to dispatch you.

These thoughts too, he understood, and he responded by challenging me to attempt my boast. So I raised my head and puffed some warm air toward him – not to do him any real harm, just to make him leave. But the rascal and his unimpressive horse swiftly stepped aside.

Unencumbered by heavy armor, he approached more closely before I was able to rise and attack in earnest. Hindered by the walls and vault of the cave and the imp's proximity to me, I could not discharge my fire accurately. He kept taunting me and he struck me often with his stick. Though I am well-protected, I felt the sting of each blow.

I decided to fall upon him and crush him, but each time I tried, his horse withdrew quickly and I fell to the ground causing no harm to either of them. Then, as if his life's quest was to torment me, he rode the horse around me and struck my nose while I was still on the ground. I dare say I can still feel the sting. Each time he struck, I rose angrily and blew fire indiscriminately. I singed my tail more than once.

I do not know why I did not flee. He was not well-armed. I could easily have trampled him and flown away to a place where I could digest my meal in peace. At the time, however, that thought had not occurred to me. Go away, imp, thought I. Why must you pester me?

He did not answer. But I knew he heard my thoughts. He charged again and struck my foot. I tried to grab him in my talons. Repeatedly, he evaded my grasp. He rode beside and around my legs so that I obstructed my own attempts to capture him. I wondered if he would ever tire. He was relentless in his charging and his horse seemed to know exactly when to retreat. I thought, Why do you keep hitting me with that stick? You will never kill me with that! Again, he did not answer and I became irritated by the pleased expression he bore.

He battled me all day and into the night. My fires were nearly exhausted. I was nearly exhausted. I thought the imp and his plow horse were tiring but they pressed on. His attacks were less frequent and less severe during the night. I, however, was equally less resistant. Every attempt to communicate with him was rejected. I thought he would withdraw if I promised not to eat him. He was not moved by my offer of mercy. But then, why should he have been? He was winning! My offer must have told him that, and he renewed his attacks.

As the sun rose, I realized that I would not see another day if I did not deal with the imp. I did not know

*what to offer him and he seemed to ignore any sugges-
tion I made. My fire was gone. My only remaining weapons
were my talons and teeth but they, too, were no help to
me since I did not have the strength to use them. I
begged him to take my life and release me from pain and
misery, but he offered no fatal blow.*

*Why was he doing this? He could have destroyed me
any time he wished. I thought he enjoyed the battle and
the infliction of pain. Although the look on his face
showed satisfaction in the course the battle was taking, it
seemed he felt some of the pain of each strike. I
finally fell to the ground. My strength was gone. I hardly
held my head from crashing to the rocks outside the cave.*

*The imp dismounted and led his horse to a nearby
stream where the wretched beast drank and then reclined
on the bank. The youth walked with difficulty as he
approached me. As a last act of defiance, I raised my
head and bared my teeth. Then I stretched my neck
toward him, hoping he had not the ability to move aside. If
I could fall upon him and crush him in my teeth, I was
certain I would recover. But he was swifter than I, and
he struck my face and nose as my head fell to the dust
beside the rocks.*

*You have beaten me, imp, thought I. Why do you not
take your prize? Destroy me. I waited for the final blow but
he only stood over my head and looked into my eyes.
He displayed a strength I had never seen in a human. It
seemed a divine strength. I thought the gods must have*

been protecting this man. No wonder I could not defeat him. Surely he would torment me until I expired. It was as if he wanted me to die of my own accord. I thought, I can offer you no further sport, imp. What is it you want from me?

He smiled and relaxed. He was quiet for a moment as he dropped his stick to the ground by my nose. Then he sat before me and finally spoke. "I seek a boon."

A boon? But, when you first approached me, you told me to stop eating! A Dragon must eat to live. If your boon is that I fast until I die slowly of starvation, I would rather you kill me now.

He answered, "I expect no such thing. What are you called?" I was confused by his question and I responded with the term Dragon. "Your name," said he. "What is your name?" Although I had traveled at length, I had never communicated with humans and I did not know how much they liked to name things. I told him I had no name. "Then, I shall give you one," said he. And he sat wearily and thought for a moment. Then he tightened his fist and pointed his finger at me, saying, "Henceforth, you shall be called Frothgarde and you shall answer to that name when addressed."

Frothgarde? And by what name are you called, imp?

"Most call me Arthur, although I answered to other names as a child."

As a child? You are hardly more than that now! Shall I address you with the name you spoke or one from your childhood?

He told me to use the name Arthur. I have accepted the name you have given me, I thought. Is that your boon?

He smiled and suggested I was foolish if I thought he had fought me for a day and a night for nothing but the privilege of naming me. "The boon I ask is that you leave this place and disturb the villagers and farmers no longer. Your life is spared if you will hide yourself in the northern hills and forests and prey only upon wildlife, leaving no evidence of your hunt for men to find. If you meet any person, you must run and hide yourself or, if necessary, leave the area. If a knight should see you and challenge you, you must not fight. You must flee and leave him unharmed. You must give these instructions to any of your kind that you meet. If you do these things, I give you your life and your freedom. If you lie to escape me and return to your past ways, I shall hunt you down and beat you with my stick until you writhe in pain and beg again for death."

Not that I would ever have broken my given word, his last statement convinced me that I should accept his terms. I saw in his face, and observed during our battle, that he was a man of conviction and would never abandon a quest. He accepted my pledge and discarded his stick. He then, with great difficulty, rolled to a position from which he could raise himself, and he walked to his horse and coaxed it to its feet. He removed the saddle and bridle and left the beast to drink and graze as it pleased.

He walked back toward the cave and reclined nearby. For two days we rested while discussing our respective histories and plans. He asked me to teach him how I passed my thoughts to him. We worked at that for a short time, and he was learning but became discouraged when I told him his talent would be of little use among humans since it would be difficult to find any who were willing to open their minds to his thoughts. The fact that few knights ever reported a conversation with a Dragon was sufficient to substantiate my statement. After that, we parted – he to his world of knights and kings, and I to the northern hills and forests.

I wandered for many years all over that part of the island and sometimes across the channel until, one foggy night, I found my way to this Land. I do not know from whence it came nor how it came to be in my path, but I do know that it moves about and that I do not need to hunt here. I expect that I will breathe my last in these hills. And now you know how I came to be here.

Frothgarde quietly rested from the telling of his tale as George remembered the questions he had been holding back while listening. "You said you knew King Arthur. Do you mean to tell me you're fifteen hundred years old?"

I knew King Arthur. My years in his land and this, I do not know. There seems to be no measure of time here. In Arthur's land, I counted the years by the changes in seasons. But in this

Land, the seasons sometimes change more quickly than I can blink my eyes. Despite such an inconvenience, this Land has been good to me. I have no need to hunt because I am never hungry. Men do not challenge me very often – except for an occasional upstart such as your friend Norris. Yes, my life here is comfortable – most comfortable. The Dragon yawned. As he exhaled, he blew warm, smoky air over George's head. *This tale has tired me. I must rest.* His eyes were nearly closed as he reclined and lowered his head.

"But, I have more questions!" George did not want to forget the questions he had held while Frothgarde told his story. "Don't sleep now!"

I am old. I will answer your questions later . . . if you remain until I awaken. With those last thoughts, Frothgarde closed his eyes and slept.

George did not want to resume his trek without further discussions with the Dragon. But he also did not want to waste any more time. He paced nearby and played in the water of a fountain for a while. He admired the plants and some of the unusual animals in the area. Some berries offered a refreshing treat. As he nibbled the fruit, he recalled the Dragon's comment that he did not have to hunt and he wondered if the Dragon was eating at all. George had been warned, when he first came to the Land, to eat and drink routinely or he would not be able to return to the land below.

Watching the sleeping Dragon had a lethargic effect on George. He soon scattered the rocks that drew the fountain and he fell asleep beside the brook. He dreamed of adventure by a Dragon's side as they roamed the Land. He saw an older Anastasia seated over the Dragon's shoulders with he and Jane looking up to her as she directed the path of their adventure. The Dragon was none other than Frothgarde, though he appeared less venerable. Their path led to a small hill that must have been low among the foothills because he was able to look below the clouds and across the valley to the next hill. A large and a small Unicorn looked in their direction. When George's eyes contacted those of the larger animal, it seemed to nod its head to him before turning and leading the smaller one down the opposite side of the hill. George turned back to see Jane catching Anastasia as she slid off the side of the Dragon. He walked toward them and the image faded. Though he wanted to hold the dream, it slipped away and he saw only darkness.

Half the day was lost to Frothgarde's tale and his nap.

George awoke to the frightening sight of the large face of a Dragon observing him at close range. He quickly crawled away as he lay on his back pushing with his elbows and feet to distance himself from the beast. As Frothgarde raised his head in response to George's panic, George recognized him. "Frothgarde! You frightened me. Don't ever do that."

Don't ever do what?

"Sneak up on me like that."

I do not sneak.

After George recovered his composure, he enjoyed a lengthy exchange with the Dragon – during which he became convinced Frothgarde spoke truthfully. He learned that the

Dragon nearly died shortly after his arrival from some sort of intestinal infection that developed after he stopped hunting. Frothgarde credited the Ferryman of that time and the Land's healing power for saving his life. As a result of his affliction, however, Frothgarde could never again live in his own land. If he were to remain there for an extended time, he would likely starve to death.

The Dragon's physical deterioration gave evidence of his age. George was not surprised by Frothgarde's confession that he could no longer fly or blow fire. The tissue, which comprised his wings, seemed to have rotted and George thought the joints might be arthritic because Frothgarde seemed pained whenever he stretched them. The possibility of flight seemed doubtful to George even if the wings were healthy, since the Dragon's bulk was more likely to succumb to the persistence of gravity than to levitate.

Despite Frothgarde's diminished physical condition, his mind was sharp. His moments of incoherence were due more to exhaustion than to any impairment of his thought process. His memory was better than the Dragon claimed – very good, considering his years of existence.

George asked Frothgarde to teach him to project his thoughts as he had taught Arthur. The Dragon agreed. The lessons progressed to the point where George was able to project images to the Dragon – though not complete thoughts needed for effective communication. Frothgarde told him he would have to practice. The Dragon received his thoughts because, by nature, he was sensitive to them. Much work would be needed if George expected to be able to pass his thoughts to other people.

George persuaded the Dragon to accompany him along part of his journey to find Annie and the Ferryman. Much of George's time was consumed in studying the marvels of the Land while the Dragon rested. Had George not enjoyed the companionship and communication with the Dragon so much, he would have parted from Frothgarde because of his slow progress. Conscious of his goal, he asked, "How much further to the Ferryman's castle?"

It is yet some distance. . . . Are you eager to be there?

"Well, yes! Why do you question that?"

Your path is not well directed.

"*My* path? I was following you!"

*How odd. Two individuals wandering the countryside –
each thinking the other is leading their way. With such guidance, it is a wonder we have not been lost to the wilderness. If this Land were more vast, perhaps we would be.*

George thought he saw a smile break in the Dragon's craggy face. He smiled, too, and tried to imagine a path to Annie and the Ferryman. Frothgarde complained that the travel was too difficult. He could not move through trees and undergrowth as easily as when he was younger and so, he begged George to go on without him. George promised he would return to learn more from the Dragon and he thanked him for the companionship. After they parted, George looked back to see his friend resting his head and closing his eyes. "Sleep, Frothgarde," he muttered. "Until we meet again, my friend."

George turned and walked through the brush.

FOURTEEN

Cloud Walker

GEORGE HAD BEEN thinking about Annie, trying to imagine a path she might follow to the Ferryman's castle. When he started down a hill, he could see shadows almost twenty feet ahead of his path but, as he continued down the slope, he barely saw beyond his outstretched hands. He feared he was approaching the edges and was about to turn around when he stumbled. He rolled down the slope and through some brush, screaming as he fell. A large tree trunk arrested his fall and stole his consciousness.

George felt something slap him. He opened his eyes but saw only a gray distorted figure moving before his face.

"Tarnation, Sonny! Ya give me another fright."

Annie's weathered face came into view. "Annie?"

"That's right, Sonny."

"How'd you . . ." George tried sitting up but reconsidered when he felt a sharp pain in his back.

"Better set a spell."

"Yeah." He pressed his bare feet flat on the ground and felt an immediate tingle of relief. "How'd you find me?"

"Weren't so hard. Ya make enough noise ta roust the dead."

When George's strength returned, he sat up. There was an eerie sense to the surrounding misty darkness. The ground was warm, but a chill in the air penetrated his bones.

Annie placed her hand on George's shoulder. "We might as well set here 'til mornin'. Findin' any kind o' trail 'round here ain't easy – 'specially in this soup."

"Good idea," George said. "But I doubt the weather will be any better tomorrow. I think we're lost near the edges."

"Speak fer yerself, Sonny. I don't never get lost."

"Really? Well, how come you're not sitting in the Ferryman's castle right now?"

"I could've been! I was jes lookin' fer you, that's all."

"OK, OK. Let's talk about it in the morning."

George dreamed of his wife and daughter. He saw Jane and Anastasia playing on their living room floor. He smiled as he slept and was well-rested when the dim morning light struggled to penetrate the heavy fog. Though the Land adequately nourished him, he ate some berries Annie offered him and drank from some cupped leaves that held puddles of condensed fog.

"I waited for two days, just as we planned," George said. "But I couldn't go on without you. So I went back to find you."

"Weren't no need o' that. I tol' ya, if I wanted to be gone, I'd be gone."

"I guess I should have believed you. Although, if I did, I might not have found you."

"What ya mean by that, Sonny? *I* found *you!*"

"Really? You don't think you're lost?"

"I tol' ya I don't *get* lo—"

"Shhh," George whispered. "I think I hear something."

Something moved through the brush a short distance away. It was coming toward them — quietly but obviously. Annie crouched beside a tree. In the fog-muffled quiet of the hillside, George heard his own heart beating. He wondered if an animal of some sort might be approaching. He had not seen many animals since becoming lost in the fog. The noise continued. He called out, "Is someone there? Hello!"

"Yes! Stay where you are! *I'll* come to *you.*" The voice sounded confident and knowledgeable. "Speak, so I can follow your voice."

"We're over here!"

Annie slapped his leg and whispered, "Why'd ya tell 'im there's two of us?"

George called out, "Who are you? Where did you come from?" George peered through the fog as he spoke.

"I am Iron Bull and I come from the valley in search of a stranger. Are you a stranger to this Land?"

"Yes, I am."

"I thought as much. Otherwise you would never be wandering about in this fog." A form took shape in the mist and a man stepped into view. George smiled immediately and stood to greet him as Iron Bull said, "You know me. Now who are you?"

"I'm George Severe and this is Annie Strummond. We're really glad to see you." Annie stood after George introduced her.

"It is good that I found you. This is not a safe place for anyone unfamiliar with the Land. It is not a good place for *me*, and I have traveled these hills many times."

"We can take care of our own selves, Ol' Man," Annie said.

The man paused for a moment, then said, "If I can rest my old weary bones, I will tell you why I have come."

"Of course!" George said. The two men sat together. Annie remained standing. George looked at the man's dark chiseled face and coarse black hair. He had seen him somewhere before.

"I have been searching for you, George Severe. For the last day, I have followed your trail. If you weren't such a sloppy traveler, I would have lost you in this fog. Fortunately, you left a very clear trail."

"Ain't that the truth," Annie said.

"I thought just the opposite," George said. "Every time I tried to find my way back, I couldn't even find my own footprints."

Iron Bull said, "You must be a city boy."

"I've done my share of camping and hiking."

"Probably have a big tent with a heater and all kinds of fancy equipment."

George looked at Annie, expecting her to add to the man's comment but she seemed satisfied that George knew what she might say. He thought about the man's greeting and asked, "You said you were looking for me. How did you know about me? Are you the Ferryman?"

"No. The Ferryman sent me. He thinks you might be able to help the Land."

George was sure he knew Iron Bull. His appearance, the way he spoke, his posture, and the way he moved were very familiar. "What makes the Ferryman think I can help? For that matter, does he know anything at all about me?"

"He knew you were here from the moment your feet touched the Land. But he learned about you from a woman who found her way to him a short time ago. She is called Tamara."

"Tamara? Annie, she made it! How is she?"

"She was weak and injured when she arrived but she is better now. She was foolish to try to cross the hills when we were taking the rains. She was nearly lost in a mudslide."

George and Iron Bull talked about Tamara and the Ferryman for a while. George confirmed what Tamara had reported concerning the events at the villages across the Opens. As they talked, George wrestled with the familiarity of Iron Bull. He asked the man if they had ever met before and Iron Bull insisted they had not. But the denial did not satisfy

George. He knew this man – as surely as he knew himself.

Annie said, "If you two are done yackin', what do ya say we get out o' here?"

Iron Bull answered, "It would not be wise. Soon, it will be a sun day. We should not move until then."

"Why not?"

"He's right, Annie" George said. "I think we're pretty near the edges. We could fall over!"

"Poppycock! Jes go up that there hill."

"Please, Annie. Let's just wait awhile."

Annie sat down and folded her arms mumbling, "Mule-headed . . ."

The sky grew brighter as the fog slowly burned away. The white mist melted to reveal lush green trees and a brilliant blue sky above. Iron Bull invited George and Annie to follow him down the hill. The slope increased quickly to become a vertical cliff, which could have claimed a disoriented traveler from three sides. George looked down the cliff and out over a deep blue sea spotted with islands of ice. He shrunk back, clutching at the nearest bush as he fell to the ground. Annie remained standing but seemed to have lost her ability to speak.

Iron Bull said, "You now can see why it is so dangerous to travel in these parts. No one ever travels the edges without guidance from the Ferryman or knowledge of the Land."

Annie mumbled, "I got yer point, Ol' Man."

George sat up, fully recovered. He looked at Iron Bull. Iron Bull looked back at him. George continued his penetrating gaze. Then he remembered. "Cloud Walker!" he exclaimed.

"You're Cloud Walker – Thomas Iron Bull Gravely, Phillip Gravely's father!"

The rescuer's face tightened at the name but relaxed and developed a smile when he heard his son's. "Yes, I have been called Cloud Walker. You know my son?"

George was thrilled with the confirmation. "Yes! If it wasn't for his encouragement, I wouldn't be here today. His story about you rekindled my interest in this cloud."

The old Sioux Indian asked, "How is it that you know my son? You are not from the Dakotas."

"You're right. I'm from Connecticut. I met Phillip while I was out West, climbing in the Black Hills. He was sitting by a fire at Harney Peak, waiting for you to return."

"He waits for me? He should know better. He was aware of my wish to return here. I can take care of myself."

"I don't think he was worried about that. He was worried that you might have met with some trouble."

Iron Bull frowned and said, "They are better off with me gone. I brought shame to them many times when I told people about my first adventure to this Land." The old man paused for a moment. "Oh they stood by me good enough – like any family would. Phillip listened, but I did not think he believed any of my stories."

"Well, he believes you now. At least, he believes you've walked among the clouds. Even though that name was given to you maliciously, I think he takes pride in it."

"Phillip *liked* the name *Cloud Walker*? That surprises me. It caused him much grief at the time. It was not the only name they had for me, but it was the one that stuck. It spread like a prairie fire in the Badlands."

As the old man sat quietly, George said, "Phillip and the rest of your family love you very much and they miss you terribly. They were upset by your last disappearance and they pray to see you again."

"Upset? They should not have been. I told them I was going to find this Land again."

"Yes, but I don't think they were convinced this Land existed then. I think Phillip believed you. He often went to the mountain to light a signal fire so you could find your way back. I'd been following this cloud for quite a while and I suppose my interest in the cloud might have bolstered his belief in your stories. He helped me with my research. He wanted to prove to your friends that you weren't crazy."

Iron Bull said, "I am sad and happy at the same time. I miss my family and it is a wonderful feeling for a father to know his son is proud of him and will do so much to defend him.

"Me and Phillip have done much together. I have always had high hopes for him. I thought, when I was much younger, that taking a white name and naming my children the same would make their lives much easier. I sent them to school and told them to learn the white history, but none of my children ever wanted to go away from our home to better themselves. They all remained close to our home – and opportunities in the area were few. But we were happy.

"I am happy here, too, but it is different. I miss the happiness of my family. When I came to this Land, I shed my white name and the name my people used to mock me. Phillip has done well. He has made proud his father. If he can take pride in the name given to me, I should share his pride and bear the name *Cloud Walker.*" Cloud Walker paused for a moment.

George watched him quietly and leaned back on his elbows. He looked around and drank in the beauty of the Land and the sea and icebergs below. He felt joy all around him – in the reflections of an old man, in the strange Land, and in the bright sun, so unusual there. George asked, "How did you know today would be a sun day?"

"The Ferryman told me."

"How did *he* know?"

"I did not question him. I think he just *knows*. He says things will be, and they happen. Maybe he *makes* them happen."

Annie interrupted, "If you two are through yammerin' like it's old home week, I'd like ta get on out o' here!"

Cloud Walker answered, "We will walk much of the day. If you can't keep up with an old Indian, we may walk another day."

"Ain't many I can't keep up with, Ol' Man. Lead on!"

George added, "I'm right behind you."

They walked away from the edges – first climbing, then descending, but each climb was longer than the preceding descent. George admired the beauty of the forest and he often looked back toward the sea until the trees hid it from view.

As they climbed over the top of a hill, George noticed an unusual distortion to the trees just below the opposite ridge. "What's that?"

Cloud Walker answered, "It is a *Slanted Forest*."

"I'd like to get a closer look!"

Annie interrupted, "There ya go with yer studyin' again. You don't never learn."

George frowned.

Cloud Walker said, "It is along our path."

As they descended the hill, they lost sight of the Slanted Forest. The climb up the opposite hill offered nothing unusual until they approached an area where the trees were bent and unnatural. George rested on the slope for a moment while he examined one of the trees. It grew straight to half its height where it curved away from the hillside and then grew straight again. Further up the slope were many trees that grew perpendicular to the slope until they reached a place overhead where they curved and climbed vertically.

Annie and Cloud Walker remained standing, each leaning against a tree, waiting for George. George stood to examine the higher trees and Cloud Walker said, "Walk carefully."

"Why?" George asked.

"You will see as we climb."

George watched Cloud Walker as he grasped trees and slowly moved forward. He followed carefully but did not realize why he should be holding onto the trees.

Annie was less cautious. "Tarnation. If we crawl along at this pace, it'll be near next century afore we get out o' here."

She moved ahead and soon fell forward, rolling a short distance uphill.

George leaned forward to assist her. He suddenly felt very dizzy and felt himself falling but he could not tell where he would fall. At one moment, he thought he was falling forward and at the next, he was sure he would fall down the hill. Struggling to find security, he leaned forward and reached for a tree. He fell uphill and rolled into the trunk of one of the slanted trees. He was winded and shocked.

Cloud Walker smiled and slowly moved toward them. As George lay helpless on the hillside, he saw Cloud Walker's posture change. Gradually, his guide walked up the slope, standing perpendicular to it. George's eyes grew wide as he looked at the Native American standing over him at the same angle as the slanted trees. Cloud Walker offered his hand. He accepted it and slowly stood beside him where he continued feeling dizzy until his eyes set themselves on the nearby trees and away from those on the lower slope. Slowly, he released his grip and stood unassisted. "This is really weird!"

"What are ya grinnin' at?" Annie refused the Indian's help. Righting herself with the aid of a tree, she complained, "Danged place. Don't nothin' work right 'round here?"

George asked Cloud Walker, "What causes this?"

Cloud Walker answered, "I don't know. It just is!" George bent over and picked up a pebble. When he let it drop, it fell at his feet. He took another and threw it up in the air. It, too, fell at his feet. Then he took another and threw it higher still. Though he threw it straight overhead and away from the slope, it soon curved toward true vertical and, when it fell, it followed its upward path – first it fell straight, then it curved toward him.

"What in tarnation are ya doin' now, Sonny?" Annie said.

"I'm just testing something."

"Ain't no need to test nothin'. Clear as can be, this place ain't natural."

George tried rolling a stone on the ground. Within the Slanted Forest, it rolled like any other rock on flat ground, slowing as it moved away. Once it passed the boundary of the Slanted Forest, it accelerated and rolled down the hillside.

"Enough's enough," Annie said. "Let's get packin'!"

Throughout the Slanted Forest, the growth of the plants and the travelers' posture followed the contour of the Land. It was as if the Land was flat and somehow their eyes were distorting its image. They rested near the top of the ridge beside a small brook. George found four rocks of equal size and assembled them as necessary to draw a fountain. But the water did not leap as he expected.

Cloud Walker said, "The water will not leap to the stones here."

George wanted to question his guide but decided to accept his words unchallenged. He leaned over the brook and pulled some water to his face with cupped hands.

Annie said, "Finally, one thing back ta normal." She stretched out at the edge of the brook next to Cloud Walker and drew water to her face. Then she tried to stand, grasping a nearby tree for assistance. Suddenly, she beat the tree and kicked it.

George thought her hand was stuck to the tree. Finally, she was free and she fell into the small brook. George reached to help her. "What happened?"

"Danged tree was grabbin' me and wouldn't let go."

"What?"

"Don't look at me like that, Sonny! I'm tellin' ya, it grabbed my hand."

Cloud Walker touched the tree. "It is warm where she touched it. I think it lives. In this Land they are called wood nymphs."

"Annie! Didn't you see one of those back at the village?"

"Yeah, I seen one."

Cloud Walker said, "There is a strange connection between the wood nymphs. Did you harm the one you saw? Maybe this one knows about it and wanted to hurt you!"

"I didn't do no harm to it. I'd jes as soon stay away from 'em."

"I don't understand," Cloud Walker said. "I've never heard of them behaving this way."

"I don't much care," Annie said. "Let's jes get out o' here. This place give me the willies."

They resumed their trek and left the Slanted Forest with the same difficulty they experienced when entering it. They stood at the top of the ridge and looked across a valley to another hill. Cloud Walker said, "Beyond that hill, our journey will end. If we hurry, we can get there by sunset."

George's heart skipped with excitement. His wandering would be over and he could rest, and learn about the Land

and the Ferryman, and talk to Tamara again.

Annie disturbed his thoughts by saying, "Good! Then maybe we can get back home and away from this fersaken place."

George sucked in a deep breath of air and stepped off the ridge while looking back at Cloud Walker saying, "Well! What are we waiting for? Last one down is a rotten egg!"

"Go easy, my friend," Cloud Walker said. "It is better if you don't risk getting hurt. And you won't save much time if you get so tired that you have to rest."

"Best pace yerself, Sonny," Annie added.

They descended the ridge at a strong and steady pace. The trees were thin on the hillside and George enjoyed looking out over the lower hills as they walked. The sky was filled with various birds and George saw many arboreal animals in the trees as well as some animals that he would not have expected to see in trees. At one time a winged horse flew across the sky, bearing a rider whose hair stretched out behind her in the breeze. He felt he could call out to her and she would hear. Annie mumbled a curse.

Soon, the trees and undergrowth became more dense and the sky was nearly obscured. Small patches of the bright blue sky struggled through the treetops and then were hidden when light breezes moved the branches. George continued wondering at the presence of bright flowers along the darker regions of their path.

They were joined in their travels by a wolf that followed closely as would a household pet. The Indian was not concerned but Annie seemed somewhat nervous about the size of the animal. The wolf offered no threatening movements or expressions however, and Annie and George gradually became accustomed to its presence.

Eventually, they came upon a large cat, which Annie identified as a mountain lion. George thought the wolf and the lion might not enjoy each other's company. He was surprised to see the big cat run and jump toward the wolf until it landed on its back and slid down its side. The wolf responded by rolling over and jumping over the cat. They played and wrestled while the travelers watched. When the animals tired of their play, they wandered off together.

There were several such encounters as the three crossed the lower hills. Annie and George lagged behind as they climbed the last high hill. George was first to catch up with Cloud Walker. The Indian said, "Your friend is not as strong as she speaks. And she called me an old man."

"It's a long hike, and she refuses to take off her boots."

"She is stubborn. She needs a man to control her, but she is so ugly, I think few men would choose her."

"She's got her faults, but there's a lot more good about her."

"I wonder if the wood nymphs see her good or her stubbornness. There is something very strange between them."

Annie huffed closer to the men and Cloud Walker said, "Why do you wear your boots? You would not tire so much if you pressed your feet to the ground."

"This ground ain't natural. I ain't takin' off these boots fer no reason, Ol' Man."

     "You would feel better, Woman."

     "Don't you worry none 'bout how I feel. Jes lead on."

FIFTEEN

Land's Heart

ANNIE, GEORGE, and Cloud Walker climbed through the thinning forest. Cloud Walker pointed to a pass. "That shortcut ahead should get us to the castle before sunset." The pass developed into a colorful chasm. Sunlight splashed onto one of its high walls, while the other was hidden from view. The red tint to the ledges was highlighted with shadows and clusters of plant life. They entered the pass. The opposite wall was lost in dark shadows, which gradually encroached on the path at the bottom.

Eagles flew overhead, gliding and playing with each other. Goats walked along ledges. Small streams tumbled down the edifice and disappeared.

George said, "This has got to be one of the most gorgeous places I've ever seen."

"Sure is a sight," Annie said.

They trekked along the pass and the shadows climbed the pink wall. George noticed a spire stretching into view at the end of the pass. He scurried ahead and saw more spires, the top of a wall and soon, the entire castle. He stopped. When Annie and Cloud Walker caught up with him, he said, "Would you look at that?" The castle reflected the same pink color, which had splashed on the chasm wall.

Cloud Walker said, "That is *Wind Castle*. It is the home of the Ferryman . . . and many others who are his friends or who serve him and the Land."

"It's very ahh . . . romantic! Kind of like a dream castle." George looked beyond the castle at nothing, yet at everything – everything he had left behind. He wished Jane and Anastasia stood beside him.

Annie brought him out of his thoughts. "'Nuff gawkin', Sonny. Let's get on down there."

Cloud Walker said, "The Ferryman is eager to meet you. Come."

The sky grew hazy during their descent. The result was a subdued brightness in the sky. The shadows from the hills climbed the castle walls. When the sun was gone, only a few stars pierced the thickening canopy and they, too, were soon consumed by the cloud.

The castle, however, never disappeared from view. It always retained just enough contrast to the Land and the sky to remain visible. The night pressed and they came closer to the castle. Small areas of light emanated from different parts of its towers and walls.

They walked through a gate and along a way that passed through a village. Cloud Walker said, "Most of the people have retired for the night."

They approached a stone walkway. George said, "That looks like a bridge."

Cloud Walker nodded.

"But it doesn't seem to serve any purpose! See? The Land is level on both sides."

Cloud Walker shrugged. He stepped onto the bridge and its walls glowed. Annie stepped back and George hesitated until Cloud Walker said, "Don't worry! It's only Torch Stone." They passed through a gatehouse with walls, which, like the bridge, illuminated as they approached and extinguished when they entered the Middle Bailey.

George said, "These lights are amazing, and this castle . . . Look, Annie! No doors at the gate."

They continued inward. Again, the walls glowed as they approached. George examined a stone, which cast some of the light. He touched it with a curious hand. Its glow intensified, then faded when he withdrew his hand. The stone had the appearance and texture of quartz but it felt warm – much like any other stone in the Land.

"Will you stop messin' with them walls, Sonny?" Annie asked. "They ain't natural."

George walked along the passageway. "Look! No portcullis . . . at either end! No doors. No arrow loops in the walls. And no murder holes overhead! It's a clear passage all the way to the Inner Bailey!"

"Jes keep walkin'," Annie said. "I'm ready ta sack out. My dogs is killin' me an' you're fartin' around with yer studyin' again."

Cloud Walker led them across the courtyard to the Great Hall. "Please rest here while I ask if the Ferryman is about."

George and Annie sat at a stone table, which illuminated when they took their places. Annie leaned away from the table and mumbled, "Cursed place."

George suddenly noticed a figure standing beside their table. It was a man dressed in a loose robe. The man bore a frail yet regal appearance and he said, "I am sorry if I startled you. Welcome to Wind Castle, strangers. I am Alden."

"How do you do? I'm George Severe and this is Annie Strummond." George stood and offered his hand, which the man received gracefully. When he shook Annie's hand, he held it for a moment and embraced it with his other hand until Annie pulled it away. George said, "This is a pretty nice castle." He signaled Annie to be quiet. She wiggled her fingers and clenched her jaw.

"Yes, it is a very warm place." The tone of Alden's voice was relaxing.

Cloud Walker returned. The Indian's expression changed as he approached the table. George offered an introduction. "Cloud Walker! This is Alden. Have you—"

Cloud Walker interrupted and addressed the man respectfully, "Ferryman! I was just looking for you."

"Welcome back, Iron Bull – or is it *Cloud Walker*?"

"George has told me of the pride my son took in the name given to me by my people and I have decided to share his pride."

"Cloud Walker is a good name – certainly worthy of one who has explored so much of this Land."

Cloud Walker smiled.

"I have been wanting to meet George Severe for quite some time and, when I sensed his approach, I decided to come to the hall. I was pleasantly surprised to find Annie Strummond here, too. You have done well, Cloud Walker."

George said, "I didn't know you were the Ferryman."

"How could you? Cloud Walker, could you find an empty room for Annie? I will find a place for George."

"Yes, Ferryman."

"Oh, and see if you can find Tamara. She will know how to attend to Annie's needs."

"Ain't nothin' I need 'cept a place ta lay down."

The Ferryman smiled. "Very well. We will meet next light."

Cloud Walker left the table and Alden invited George to follow him to a private room. It was a small room with a stone table and chairs and a stone cot. Alden said, "Consider this your home. Rest now and we will talk next light."

"But I just got here! I have a lot of questions to ask you."

"Forgive me. I must return to my work. We will talk later."

After the Ferryman left him, George walked over to the

stone cot and sat on its edge. He felt its soft warmth and reclined. He gazed for a moment at the ceiling and felt himself drifting to sleep. The glow from one of the wall panels dimmed as his eyes closed.

The morning came much too soon. George did not want to leave the comfort of his bed, but he sensed someone in his room. He opened his eyes, turned his head toward the table, and saw a woman sitting next to a clay bowl filled with fresh fruit. Her smooth, long, blonde hair was clear to him but his eyes could not distinguish her face. He sat up and rubbed his eyes. "Tamara?"

"Welcome to Wind Castle, George Severe. We have been worried about you." She was more beautiful than he had remembered.

"I'm glad to see you again," George said. "You look good. Life in this castle has done you well." She blushed. Then he asked, "Why were you worried about me?"

"I did not know if you would be blamed when I ran away. We heard you were exiled from the village. Then we heard nothing about you for a very long time! The Ferryman assured me you still lived but he did not know where you went and he did not want to call to you because he did not want Telemachus or the others to know I found my way to the castle and told him about you. So, he sent Iron Bull to search for you."

"Cloud Walker."

"Your pardon, sir?"

"Cloud Walker. He likes the name, *Cloud Walker.* Why are you still here? Are you a *servant* in the castle?

Tamara smiled and answered, "No. There are no servants here! I do things here because I *want* to. And so it is with all who live at Wind Castle."

George stood up and walked to the table. He sat across from his guest. "Would you show me around this place?"

"I think the Ferryman would like to do that himself. Eat and drink. Then, I shall take you to him."

"I'm not really that hungry." He stood. "Let's get going."

Tamara admonished him. "Sir? Must you still be reminded to eat?"

George smiled and sat down again. He reached for a banana. "No, I've been pretty good about that. I'll have one piece of fruit and half a cup of water if you'll join me."

"That would please me, sir."

"And stop calling me *sir.*"

The two sat for a few minutes, quietly eating and drinking. George looked at her, studied her features and mannerisms – so much of her reminded him of Jane. Tamara kept her gaze on the orange she was pulling apart.

"Blondie! You in there?" Annie leaned into George's room.

"Yes. Come in."

"Well, who ya got here?" Annie squinted and tilted her head toward Tamara. "That you, Dearie? That Injun said ya made it."

"Yes," Tamara said.

"So what 're you two up to?" Annie plopped onto one of

the stone chairs and reached for an apple.

George answered, "We were just about to go see the Ferryman."

"Well, don't let me hold ya up. Sooner we find a way out o' here, the better." Annie stood and chomped into her apple.

Tamara led George and Annie through the doorway and down some stairs to the courtyard. She dropped the orange peels and they immediately began disintegrating. She led them up another set of stairs and stopped at the entrance to a small room. "Ferryman, I have brought the strangers."

There was no answer. "He is not here," Tamara said. "We will go to the Heart." She led George and Annie back toward the stairs.

George rushed to walk beside her and asked, "What's the Heart?"

"It is the center of the Land. Without it, the Land would not exist. The Ferryman spends most of his time there."

"Why?"

"Such is his duty to the Land!"

George and Annie followed her down the stairs, across the courtyard, and into the Great Hall. The hall was filled with people working or talking. They crossed the hall to a stairway that led to a balcony. Tamara led them through a door, into a long and narrow room with three openings in the wall opposite the doorway.

The Ferryman greeted them, "I trust you rested well, George Severe and Annie Strummond."

George said, "Better than I have in a long time."

"He has asked to tour Wind Castle," Tamara said. "I am willing to guide them, but I thought you would prefer to do it."

"Indeed I would," the Ferryman answered. "You are thoughtful Tamara. Leave them in my charge. I have only a few tasks to complete and then we can begin. Please sit here."

George and Annie sat on stone chairs and Tamara said, "I will find you later in the day."

George nodded, his interest clearly set on the Ferryman's activities.

Annie said, "I jes as soon tag along with you, Dearie, if ya don't mind. I got me a feelin' I ain't gonna be much inter'sted in what these two is gonna be talkin' about."

George did not notice their departure. He watched the Ferryman performing his duties and studied the room. A red glow poured from the window-like openings into the room. George ached to stand and look through the windows. "What's in there?"

"Stand and watch, if you wish," the Ferryman said.

"Thank you."

The Ferryman placed his hands over stones that were nestled along each sill. He seemed to have a method and pattern to touching the stones. George sensed a response from each stone as the Ferryman touched it. The round stones remained in their places but the cylindrical stones sunk into the sills or extended at the Ferryman's beckoning.

George leaned toward the closest window. Bright pink light splashed over stone walls in the chamber. More windows dressed the opposite wall.

The Ferryman spoke, "Step forward if you wish, but try not to touch anything."

George leaned into the window.

"You can lean on the sides. The balance stones are only on the shelf."

George placed one hand on the side and looked deep into a large stone chamber. There was no floor. The glow emanated from the round chamber wall. At the center, where a floor might have been, was a dense cloud. "What is it?"

"It is the Heart of the Land – the life source. Without it, this Land would crumble and fall below."

"What are you doing with those stones?"

"The stones control the energy from the Heart. They direct the flow of life forces and control the path the Land follows – much like the helm of a ship."

"What's at the bottom?" George asked.

The Ferryman smiled. "Your curiosity is refreshing. Let me demonstrate." He walked to the far window and twisted a stone. George heard a whoosh of air, which intensified as the stone turned. "Observe!"

George looked at the bottom of the chamber and saw the earth passing below them. He saw rivers and buildings, roads, farms, and trees. "It's amazing! We're just floating over everything – like we're in a balloon! But . . . it's so heavy! How does it fly?"

"There is no simple answer. I will explain it to you in time . . . if you remain with us."

George withdrew from the window and looked at the Ferryman. He wanted to make it clear that he had every intention of returning to his own land and his family – as soon as he learned everything he wanted to know.

The Ferryman twisted the stone and the sound of rushing air dissipated. George looked down again and the cloud covered the viewing port. The Ferryman adjusted a few more stones. "That will suffice. Now, I will show you more of Wind Castle."

They walked along the hallway to the stairs, down through another hall and to the Inner Bailey where the Ferryman stopped and turned, stretching his arm toward the walls and towers of the castle. George turned. He saw several men clinging to one of the walls high above the ground.

George asked, "What are they doing?"

"The stone grows constantly and must be chipped away to maintain the shape and utility of the castle."

"How do they keep from falling?"

"They cut footholds in the wall but the castle assists them in their balance. It is almost impossible for them to fall."

George continued looking around. "There are merlons – places for archers to hide along the parapet?"

"Not for archers. That was long ago. We have no archers. The merlons gradually grew together until all the embrasures were filled with new stone. We have trimmed away some of the stone for the pleasure of looking over the village and foothills."

"The whole castle is without fortifications. Don't you need

protection?"

"Protection?"

"What if some other village revolts? Or, what if somebody decides they want to lead the Land in your place? You have no protection! Even the gates are gone!"

"The people of the Land know there is no reason to war. There have been a few instances when some grew restless but they always returned to reason — until the arrival of Jack LaRoche, the stranger who came before you. The troubles he has caused have persisted much longer than any I can remember. I hope it is not your intention to follow his example."

"So, you have doubts about me! Don't worry; I would hardly follow someone like him. He was a criminal."

They walked across the courtyard. George looked at all the people and the other creatures. "There aren't many children here . . . compared to the last village I was at."

"That is good. Even a few lead me to worry."

George thought the Ferryman's response strange but he chose not to press him for an explanation.

The Ferryman directed George to one of the gate towers where they entered through a doorway and climbed the circular stairs to the parapet then down some outer stairs and along the top of the wall.

They looked over the village and below the cloud to see a small island in the middle of a swamp. The Ferryman asked, "See the small hill beyond the village?"

George nodded.

"Please do not consider this request too strange, but I

am curious to know what your small friend feels about that place."

"Annie? What do you mean?"

"I would like to know if she is . . . drawn to it."

"Even if she is, she wouldn't tell anybody. She's been harping about getting back home ever since we got here."

"Perhaps we can go there before she leaves."

"I'll ask her, but I can't promise anything."

Alden nodded. "I must return to the Heart to prepare to settle on the land below."

"We're stopping?"

"Yes, we need water."

"You mean . . . I could go home?"

"Not this time. This mooring is too treacherous for anyone from our Land to go below."

George struggled between disappointment that he could not return and relief that he could remain to continue his studies. "If you don't mind, I'll explore the castle while you're gone."

"As you wish. I will find you again before nightfall."

"You all studied out, Sonny?" Annie asked as George stepped out of the entrance to the gate tower.

"Hello, Annie. Tamara. Did you have a good morning?"

Tamara answered, "We just came from the village. There is talk that we are about to touch the land below."

"Yeah, 'cept we ain't close enough ta climb down our own selves."

"Just as well," George said. "It would be hard to pull myself away right now. There's so much to learn here!"

"Danged fool. I knowed ya wouldn't wanna break loose. I'm tellin' ya Sonny, my patience is wearin' thin."

"What's got you so upset, Annie?"

"Nothin'."

"She was disturbed by the marsh outside the village."

"I ain't disturbed by that swamp. Jes give me the willies is all – like most o' this place." The sound of a bell emanated from the ground and stone around them. "See what I mean?"

Tamara said, "The mooring was successful."

George felt a slight shift in the ground and a moment of dizziness as he heard the winds building. The pennants atop the towers stretched out and clapped in a strong steady breeze.

"There will be no surveyors leaving the Land this time. We will not hear the toll again until it is time to move again."

George asked, "Who are the surveyors and what do they do down there?"

Tamara said, "The surveyors trade with people below. The Sasquatch, and sometimes Centaurs, usually remain near the mooring to insure there is good contact with the ground so the others can find their way back and the Land can take on water."

"How do you know all this?"

"The Ferryman told me. I was not very interested in his teachings. He still teaches Cloud Walker. They talk often. Your friend likes to explore the Land and he always returns with stories that please the Ferryman. I think he has also spoken to the Ancient Counselor."

"Who's the *Ancient Counselor*?"

"Few have seen the Ancient Counselor. I only know that he is old. He is probably the oldest man in the Land. Maybe he is as old as the Land itself!"

"How long has Alden been Ferryman?"

Tamara looked puzzled.

"Alden – didn't he tell you his name?"

"I suppose he did, but I never thought to call him such."

"Well, how long has he been Ferryman?"

"As long as I can remember."

George thought of Frothgarde and the tale of his encounter with Arthur. He wondered if the Ferryman, or the Ancient Counselor, could have been around then. He looked through the castle gates and asked, "Could you show me around the village?"

"If it would please you."

"Annie, do you want to go down there again?"

"No. I'm gonna head back to my room and set a spell." Annie walked across the Inner Bailey toward the stairs that led to her room.

George and Tamara went into the village. Activity was waning and there was little more to see than when George first passed through it. The mountain shadows stretched toward the village and George asked, "Before we go back to the castle, could you show me where Annie got so bothered?"

Tamara led him to the edge of the village. "That lake wasn't here before!" George said.

"When?"

"This morning! I was up on the wall with the Ferryman and there was nothing but a dried out swamp then."

"This is where your friend was disturbed. It was nearly dry then. The Land has been taking water from below."

"That much? We've only been here for a short time and . . . .." George decided to save those questions for the Ferryman. "What about Annie? What disturbed her about this place?"

"She would not say. She looked across the damp earth and quickly turned away."

George looked across the water to the island Alden had pointed out. Something about that island . . . George turned back and they walked toward the castle. George watched workers haul the last of the day's debris from the wall. There must have been a moat below the Bridge-Over-Nothing and it must have since been filled with debris from the walls.

Tamara left George inside the Great Hall. He sat alone, moving his hands across the light of the table. Activity in the hall was waning too, and George grew tired. A voice said, "There are certain stones in this Land which would yield music with such play as yours."

George looked up into the kind, cheerful face of the Ferryman. "I'd like to see those stones sometime. Please sit with me."

The Ferryman sat beside him. "Your curiosity is exciting, George. Did you learn much this day?"

"I saw a great deal. But what I saw only raised more questions."

"Perhaps I can answer some of them."

A hunched man, walking by the table, stopped to offer his assistance. "Can I get something for you, Ferryman?"

"Yes, Peter. A small mug of wine and some grain if you do not mind. And some for George, too."

"No mind at all, Ferryman. I shall return." As he walked toward the kitchen, George looked at him strangely. The man had not spoken English. Yet he understood every word precisely. It was not just a vague understanding of the conversation. He knew every word.

The Ferryman drew his attention. "George."

"Yes?"

"You said you had some questions."

"Well, for one thing, he wasn't speaking English!"

"No. He was not."

"But I understood him! And I never heard his language before!"

"That is not unusual. Everyone can understand what others say in this Land if they have been here long enough. And those who are strange to the Land need only speak their own language and the others will use it in their presence."

"I understood what he said . . . but I know I couldn't repeat it."

"That will come in time. You have learned much in a short time. And your learning is enhanced by your proximity to the Heart."

George hesitated while thinking of his next question. "This table. The light that comes from it. How does it work?"

"It does not *work*. It senses the need for light." The Ferryman smiled. "You have asked something which gives me great joy to tell. There are few things in this Land which one can say he truly discovered. The Torch Stone is one that I can claim. I found it, quite by accident actually, while roaming the hills when I was young.

"I was walking with the carelessness of youth when I fell down a crevasse and uncovered a small slab of the stone. It seemed not unusual at first. But, as I climbed toward the stone slab, it glowed. Many cycles passed after I was appointed Ferryman before I remembered the discovery and decided to use it at Wind Castle. We have been mining the stone and setting it into the walls and tables in the castle."

Peter returned with two mugs of wine and a bowl of nuts, dried fruit, and some grains. He set the mugs and the bowl on the table and walked away.

"It's a remarkable material!" George said.

"Indeed it is. It not only senses your presence, but it also senses your level of consciousness, which makes it ideal for lighting the sleeping quarters. As you approach the stone, it becomes excited, and it dims as you withdraw. It remains excited if you stay close to it – unless you drift toward sleep. Then it drifts to sleep with you. It also rests if there is adequate light nearby."

"Amazing!" George sat quietly, again playing his hands across the illuminated table. "Another question: When you took me up on the wall this morning, I saw no lake in the valley, but now there is one. How did all the water get there so fast? Have you got a dam somewhere?"

"We are moored now. One of the main reasons we moor to the land below is to take water. We discussed this earlier."

"But so much water? What? Do you just suck it up from the earth?"

"Something like that. We normally moor at a large lake or near some snow-covered peaks. It is not unusual for us to bare the mountaintop, if the Land is particularly dry and the cloud nearly exhausted. The Land slakes its thirst rapidly. Most often, within a day or two we have taken enough water to quench the Land and restore the cloud. If there is not sufficient water where we moor, I guide the Land to a rain cloud and the Land drinks from the heavens."

"It's clear enough how water would restore the lakes when it rains, but how exactly does the water get from a lake or mountaintop on the ground to the lakes up here?" George imagined some kind of pumping system but he had seen no machines or mechanical systems since coming to the Land. Perhaps a pyramid of four giant stones?

"Follow me to the Heart and you shall see." The Ferryman rose and walked across the hall to the stairs.

They walked into a noisy room that offered four windows to the Heart. The two middle windows leaned slightly into the Heart chamber. The Ferryman said, "Look through that opening as I do here." He stretched his arms to the sides and leaned forward. George did the same at his window. The turbulence he saw almost caused him to lose his balance. Below him raged a maelstrom of water and vapor. Instead of spinning toward the center, however, everything moved out to the walls of the Heart.

"The water or snow is drawn to the Heart along the bottom of the Land. It is then cast to the walls of the chamber, which absorb it and distribute it throughout the Land. Some moisture is also absorbed directly through the bottom, but that flows only to the adjacent areas."

George's eyes were wide with disbelief and interest. He thought for a moment about the hurricane that had taken his mother's life when he was a child. Then he thought about his interest in weather. He raised his voice so he could be heard without withdrawing from the window and said, "I've never been so close to such a violent storm. Where does the power come from?"

"Power?"

"What makes it happen?"

"It is the nature of the Land. How do storms brew in your land? Why do rivers flow? What changes the ocean tides?"

"You happen to be asking questions I can answer," George yelled. "The sun has a lot to do with our weather. The force of gravity makes the rivers flow. And the moon is responsible for the tides."

"You seem quite sure of your answers."

George stepped back and lowered his voice. "I've studied weather for a long time. As far as tides and rivers are concerned, that's pretty basic knowledge in my land. Both have to do with the laws of gravity – the pull of the moon on the oceans and the earth's pull on the water in the rivers."

"These *laws* of gravity you mentioned – are you able to legislate the nature of your land?" The Ferryman cracked a playful smile.

"Of course not!" George answered very seriously. "They're called laws because they *are* the nature of the land and nothing can defy them."

"Nothing? How do explain the presence of *this* Land? Does this Land obey your laws of gravity?"

"No. It doesn't seem to obey *any* physical laws. That's how I got interested in it in the first place."

The Ferryman smiled. "I was teasing you. I am familiar with the laws of nature in your land. Most do not differ much from the nature and lore here. There are some exceptions, however. A few, you have already discovered. Others, I will teach you if you wish."

"I'd like that very much."

"Good! After we cast away, there is someone I would like you to meet."

"The Ancient Counselor?"

"Ah! You have heard of him. You can learn much from him."

Sixteen

The Ancient Counselor

GEORGE WALKED along the main way of the village, thinking about the time he spent tracking the cloud while forecasting weather in Connecticut. He ambled to the Bridge-Over-Nothing, which led to the castle. The bridge reminded him of the peaceful, yet defenseless nature of the castle.

The people were not unlike the castle. They had lived without conflict for so long, they would never be able to defend themselves against an aggressor. It was the same reason Tamara's village and others fell so easily to the raids of Telemachus and his followers. They could not contend with those who had learned the *secrets* of combat from a ruthless mercenary.

George crossed the bridge and passed through the gateway to the Inner Bailey. He saw Cloud Walker in the hall and joined his friend at a table.

Cloud Walker said, "You seem nervous."

"I'm going to meet the Ancient Counselor." They shared some grain and nuts and drank some thick, foamy mead. "It should be a great chance to learn more about this Land – and the cloud. You've met him before. Is there any special protocol I should know about?"

"What do you mean?"

"Should I bow? Shake his hand? What?"

"Just be patient."

"Why?"

"You will see."

George turned as he heard Annie and the Ferryman approaching. "You ready ta go, Blondie? Time ta meet that Counsel feller."

"I'm ready." George rose and looked at Cloud Walker.

Alden asked, "Do you wish to join us, Cloud Walker?"

"Not today, thank you."

As George followed the Ferryman and Annie across the hall, Alden said, "I ask you as I have asked Annie, to be patient with my friend. He is eager to meet you, but he is quickly exhausted."

The Ferryman led them deep into the castle near the Heart. The floor was bare earth and the sensation at George's feet and legs was very strong. They walked along passages illuminated by Torch Stones. George felt energy in the walls, like static electricity. The stone was warm to his touch and radiated the same force that spread through his legs.

A long passage led to a room illuminated with the red color of the Heart. The Ferryman and George entered the room. Annie peeked inside before following. The Ferryman led them across the room where a cowled figure sat leaning against the wall, facing the Heart chamber. George, Annie, and the Ferryman took positions on stone chairs opposite the figure.

George peered into the hooded cloak, searching for a face. Two eyes reflected the red light as the Ferryman introduced them. "Simon! I would have you know George Severe, a stranger to our Land." George nodded his head respectfully but the figure did not respond. "And this is Annie Strummond." The hood of the cloak moved. "Annie, George, I would have you know Simon, our Ancient Counselor."

All were quiet. George squinted to see the face. Annie mumbled in George's ear, "Not a very talkative sort, is he?" Finally, the Ancient Counselor slowly moved his arm and pulled back the hood. George gasped at the aged appearance of the man. His face was emaciated and his eyes were nearly consumed by his skull. His neck was so thin that George could barely find it in the folds of the cowl.

The head moved as the man drew a labored breath and spoke. "Welcome . . . George . . . Severe." Speaking required great effort by the old man. George noticed that he was twisting his feet in the dirt. He listened intently and wanted to help the man with his words – to finish his sentences for him. He forced himself to be patient. The man cleared his throat. "And especially you, Annie Ssstrummonnnd. We see few strangers in our Land." He struggled with the words and his sentence was slow. "Some come in friendship. But others come with malicious intent. Which are you?"

"We come in friendship," George said. "We mean you no harm."

Simon looked into George's eyes with a soul-penetrating gaze and said, "Yes." He looked at the Ferryman. "I believe he is of a good spirit – just as you concluded, my friend." He closed his eyes and breathed heavily while twisting his feet again.

George looked at the Ferryman to ask if the Ancient Counselor was strong enough to continue. The Ferryman casually raised his hand. Simon slowly opened his eyes – first, one eye half way and then the other. He blinked and nodded, saying, "Yes, a good spirit. You are indeed welcome here, George Severe." He looked at Annie and nodded. The statement made George more comfortable, but he noticed a slight shiver in Annie when Simon looked at her. The man continued, "You have many questions about our Land. Alden, tell them about the Land's beginning and its history. I shall sit here and listen." He paused for a moment. George looked to the Ferryman to begin the tale, but the Ancient Counselor had not finished speaking. The old man coughed. "I shall contribute to the telling if you drift from the truth or if the moment moves me." George thought he saw the man trying to smile. Simon reached for his hood.

The Ferryman helped the Ancient Counselor adjust his cloak and sat beside George and Annie. "I shall tell you how this Land came to be and how it moves at our commands."

"This Land came to be at a time when the world was plagued by many wars. It was a few hundred years after the one called *Christ* began his teachings when a group of sorcerers, tribesmen, priests, kings and emperors from all around the world assembled with the noble intention of quelling the conflict around them through the spoken word or the invention of powerful methods of enforcing the peace of their dreams. They built a large hall where the assembly met and worked. After an attack, which left many great craftsmen murdered, a certain king offered an army for protection until the hall, which became this castle, could be fortified.

"Under the protection of the soldiers, the noble work resumed. There were frequent calamities, which resulted from poorly executed experiments. Alchemists mixed incompatible potions, magicians cast unproven spells, priests performed miracles over which they had no control, engineers built strange contraptions and machines, and even the cooks brewed unusual concoctions intended to enhance the creative talents of the other crafts. It was a rare day indeed when nothing exciting happened.

"So it was when one inventor lost control of his experiment. He had built a large apparatus within the Keep which allowed him to drop a bladder filled with stones on a bowl containing a rocklike metal submerged in a fluid developed by some alchemists."

George asked, "What kind of metal?"

"I do not know. The metal stones started glowing brighter

and brighter until they became fire, although the word *fire* does not clearly describe the condition. It was the only word known by those who saw it that could illustrate the phenomenon.

"The apparatus was consumed and the very stone of the Keep grew warm. The heat pushed observers out of the castle. Smoke spewed through windows and doors as the heat consumed everything which could burn, along with many things which were thought not to burn."

George said, "Uranium . . . or something like it. But, how did they get it to react?"

Annie said, "Will you shush and let 'im get this over with?"

Alden continued, "The ground shook. The towers of the castle swayed back and forth and the people fled in panic. Some of the better runners reached the nearby hills before the earth shook more violently. After the quake, they were pressed to the ground and could not raise themselves. The pressure gradually eased and the strong righted themselves, followed in short time by the weak. The worst seemed past.

"Small groups traveled to other villages to determine the extent of the disaster. As they returned, it became known that the effects were widespread indeed. But the most remarkable reports came from a group who ventured toward the next castle. It was gone – as was the land that led to it. The group reported seeing mountaintops sailing past them. They said they stood at the edge of the Land and saw the plains and rivers in the valleys moving below them.

"These reports unnerved many of the people. One man

calmed them with reason. He told them to cast away their fears; that they stood on a Land that contained ample supplies and sufficient intellectual and spiritual talent to devise a way to stabilize their condition. He eventually became the first Ferryman. They returned to the castle to study the effects of the fire and quake. The Keep had lost its red color by then.

"During the following weeks many strange physical ailments developed. Most of the people closest to the apparatus were afflicted with a disease which had taken the lives of those who had sought and handled the strange metal."

George said, "Radiation poisoning, I'll bet." George held any further comment after catching Annie's elbow in his ribs.

The Ferryman continued, "Survival was greatest among those who farmed or excavated the earth. The Land seemed to provide the necessary resistance to the disease. These same people were found not to hunger as much as those who rarely ventured from their study halls.

"Any part of the study hall and other parts of the castle that could burn had done so. The floors and roof structures remained intact, however. Somehow, the stones and roofing slates had bonded together and held their positions. And the bonding or growing continued over the years until it was necessary to remove stone to prevent the castle from becoming a useless solid mass.

"It was while studying the stone and the castle that the first Ferryman discovered the sensitive ledges at the openings overlooking the chamber in the Keep. After many years of experimentation, he found he could adjust the course the Land followed. Control of the Land improved but its appearance over the inhabited parts of the earth frightened the people below who thought it possessed some great power and would do them harm."

Annie said, "Hey, now there's somethin' that might be int'restin'. You remember this, Sonny."

"What?"

"Later."

George looked at Annie and shrugged to the question on the Ferryman's face.

Alden said, "The Ferryman learned how to develop and control the cloud which now envelops the Land. He used the cloud as a cloak to hide the Land as it drifted through the sky. Much water was needed to sustain the cloud and rainfall alone was insufficient for the needs of the Land. Quite by accident, it was discovered that the Land could draw its water from below if held in position for a period of time. So, the Land travels wherever we wish, undetected."

George said, "But you are not undetected! *I* found you, and I tracked you for quite a while." George felt Annie's elbow again and he scolded, "Stop it," as he continued his discussion with the Ferryman. "I didn't come here by accident, you know. I *wanted* to be here, and all I had to do was watch you and wait until you stopped."

Simon coughed. "We would be . . . honored if you would . . . tell us how you were able to do this."

"Of course."

"Perhaps when . . . next we meet. Alden, please continue."

"While the Ferryman had been learning how to direct the course of the Land and how to raise the cloak, others learned about the nature of the Land. The ability of the stone to grow and the soil's ability to nourish those who tread upon it were early discoveries. It was also learned that lifeless materials quickly decompose when left in contact with the ground. The attraction of water to piled stones was discovered later as was the ability of the Land to maintain it's populations of animals and plants at optimum levels."

George asked, "What do you mean?"

"Somehow the Land is able to anticipate disasters such as wars, and normal life cycles of trees, plants, and animals. We expected the loss of life which occurred after the arrival of Jack LaRoche because there had been many children born to the villages in the area some years ago. We expect some small tragedy here at Wind Castle, too, since there are a few children living in the village now. That is why I become concerned when I see many children about.

"As the years stretched to centuries, the Ferryman could not continue his work and he found an apprentice. Thus began the custom of passing leadership from an Ancient Counselor to a new Ferryman. The Ancient Counselor remains to teach and advise the Ferryman just as Simon has done for me and I shall do for the next Ferryman. Simon would not mind my saying that he has grown weary and now awaits his passing. He has instructed me to begin my search for a new Ferryman. The next Ferryman will be the seventh since the Land was created. He will be trained for many years and be counseled as long as I draw breath."

George asked, "You said the next Ferryman would be the seventh. And you said the Land was created a few hundred years after Christ. How can that be? How old are you? How old is he?"

"Logical questions for someone who has come from your land. Longevity comes with the nourishment provided by the Land – though it seems that Ferrymen endure longer than most. I think it is because of our proximity to the Heart. There are some exceptions, however, such as certain creatures or plants who are traditionally long-lived."

George persisted, "So, if you don't mind my asking, how old *are* you?"

"I do not mind your asking," he answered. "But it is difficult to say exactly, since our years are not the same as yours. Although we can move in any direction, we usually drift with the winds, which generally take us east. We track our positions and correct for the days gained as we circle the earth. I have seen approximately one hundred fifty of your years pass before me."

George's eyes widened. "And him?"

Both looked toward the old man hidden in the hood of his cloak. The Ferryman did not answer. He waited and looked into the dark hood. The Ancient Counselor cleared his throat and slowly answered, "Let it be sufficient . . . to say that I was a young Ferryman before men of the white race . . . colonized your part of the world – even before very many . . . of them came to your continent. Alden was truthful when . . . he told you I am near my passing."

George said, "That's amazing! I mean . . . your age."

The Ferryman continued, "Perhaps you have noticed many strange creatures in the Land. I do not fully understand the reasons, but the Land attracts those animals and other creatures who are driven from the world below. It is a safe haven for them and they know how to find us. It is not unusual to welcome new species when we are moored. Sometimes they are waiting for us as we approach. Many of the creatures who are extinct in your world, thrive here. Along with these new friends, our surveyors have sought and transplanted various forms of vegetation. I do not know of any plant that has not thrived in this Land. The Land provides all the nourishment needed. Even the lack of sunlight caused by the presence of the cloud is compensated through the roots.

"There are many things I could tell you about this Land – far more than you could learn during one visit. But, I can feel that the light is gone and Simon must rest. I am sure he would like to see you again." The Ferryman looked toward the Ancient Counselor. Simon nodded.

George said, "But I have a million questions! I have no reason to doubt your account. Just the fact that this place exists . . ."

"It *is* a fantastic tale," the Ferryman answered. "We should rest and continue our discussion another time."

Before he could speak, George felt Annie's elbow. "All right. I don't mean to impose."

"I will lead you back to the hall."

Simon addressed him slowly, "Alden, please stay for a moment . . . if our guests can find their way without you."

George and Annie left the chamber and walked along the passage. Eventually, they found their way to the Great Hall and walked into the kitchen where George found a clay crock full of mead. He filled two cups and offered one to Annie. They walked to a table in the hall and sat. George played with the mug and moved his hands over the light emanating from the stone tabletop.

"Will you set still, Sonny?"

George sipped some mead. "Annie. What was so important about the cloud that you wanted me to remember?"

"You're a decent feller. How did ya get mixed up with them folks at the lodge?"

"What do you mean?"

"Them that went with us up the mountain. I don't mean the whole bunch. Mostly the feller what did all the talkin' – and watchin'."

"Watching?"

"That Stan somethin' or other. He watched you like a hawk."

"He works for the same guy *I* work for."

"And what do ya know about *him*?"

"Not much. He hired me after the Service let me go."

"Did ya ever wonder why he bankrolled this fool expedition?"

"He's . . . funding my weather research."

"Maybe so. But I done work for them folks before an' I wouldn't exactly say they was humanitarians or such."

"What are you getting at?"

"Don't know exactly. Somethin' 'bout what that Ferryman feller said 'bout the folks below bein' afraid o' what the folks in this Land might do. It got me ta wond'rin' why yer boss is so int'rested. If we ever get outta here, ya might wanna keep what ya know about this place to yerself."

"Did you enjoy your conversation with the Ancient Counselor?"

George heard the words, but he did not respond until he saw Annie looking behind him. He looked up and saw Cloud Walker. "Yes, it was very interesting. Please sit."

Annie slapped the stone chair between her and George. "Park it right here, Ol' Man."

Cloud Walker offered a stern expression to Annie and chose another seat.

"What did *you* think of him?" George asked.

"I think he is an old and wise man. I listen whenever he speaks – even if I do not understand what he says."

"Did you believe his age?"

"I never asked his age. That would be disrespectful."

George frowned and thought the Indian was probably right. "What is it that you did not understand?"

"I do not remember – *because* I didn't understand. But it does not matter if I understand. The old possess wisdom and it is the duty of the young to listen. If understanding does not come immediately, perhaps it will come later in life. That is why it is important to listen. Another reason for listening is to be kind. The old have labored to raise the young and the young have a duty to give them comfort and hear their words before they die. I know the feeling of age and the ridicule the young can cast on the old if their tales are unusual. But I also know the tales can be true."

George thought about Phillip Gravely's story relating the torment Cloud Walker had suffered when he remembered his first visit to the Land. "You are so right, my friend."

"Poppycock," Annie said.

George said, "I thought I might explore outside the castle tomorrow. Will you come along?"

Cloud Walker looked at Annie. "Is *she* going?"

"What's it to ya, Ol' Man?"

"I might want to bring some beeswax along for my ears."

Annie stiffened but George spoke before she could find her words. "Come on, you two. We'll all go and make a morning of it. OK?"

Annie mumbled and Cloud Walker grunted.

"OK! I'll meet you in the morning." George upended his mug and swallowed the last of his mead. They all rose from their seats, and walked out of the hall.

Illumination from the Torch Stones preceded them until they stepped out of the hall to the courtyard. The still air was cool and crisp but the heat from the ground surged up through

George's legs. Snow fell as they approached the stairway that led to George's room. George remained at the foot of the stairs while Annie and Cloud Walker continued up the steps.

The snow reminded George of the winter in Connecticut, which marked the beginning of his interest in the strange cloud . . . and the cascading spring snow near Durango, which peeled him and Annie off the side of the mountain. Connecticut was a better memory – Jane and Anastasia. He missed his daughter's first birthday because of that avalanche. When was it? A week ago? A month ago? *How long have I been here?*

Tamara approached George, Annie, and Cloud Walker as they walked through the gate. "Good light. Are you going to the village?"

George answered, "And a little further, I hope. Do you want to join us?"

"It would please me, George."

The four jaunted through the village and out the gate leading to the valley and surrounding hills. George suggested they follow a path around the outer wall of the village and castle. That took them to the shore of the lake.

George felt the water with his foot, then waded in – ankle deep. He felt strange; wading in a foggy lake while snow slowly fell on his shoulders. He turned around and saw Annie standing rigidly by the shore, looking out at the nearly hidden island. "What's the matter, Annie?"

Annie did not respond.

"Annie?"

230 | WIND CASTLE

She snapped her gaze toward George. "I'm gettin' outta here." She turned and stomped away.

"Annie? Are you OK? Come back!"

Tamara said, "Let her go, George. Something troubles her – something beyond her understanding."

"Do you know what it is?"

"No."

"Cloud Walker?"

"That woman has been a mystery to me since I found you near the edges."

George remembered the Ferryman's interest in Annie's reactions to the island. "Well, somebody knows, and it's time I found out."

Cloud Walker, I ask you to return with your friend.

"What?" George asked.

Tamara said, "It is the Ferryman. He wants us to return."

Cloud Walker said, "He has rarely called to me in this manner. It must be important."

They saw the Ferryman in a corridor and approached him. "I heard your call," Cloud Walker said.

The Ferryman answered, "It is good that you did. I would like to discuss some matters with each of you. We will retire to my room where we can talk comfortably and without interruption."

Alden led the way to his room and invited them to sit at the small table. He poured water into some mugs and offered each a drink. George wondered why they were called back and why only Cloud Walker was addressed. "Troubles have indeed come to the Land. They are the same troubles that came with Jack LaRoche. The people he led continue attacking many of the villages near to them and it is feared that they will not be satisfied with their local conquests. Each raid has become more brutal and deaths have resulted at the plundered villages.

"Tamara, you were one of the first to find us and warn us of the troubles. After your arrival, I decided to wait to see if the aggression would cease. But it is now obvious that it will not end of it's own."

George interrupted, "So, what are you going to do?"

"I have spoken with the Ancient Counselor and we have not yet decided. We would like to know more. I can sense much from the Heart. I feel when lives are lost but I cannot feel other troubles – I should say, I can feel that there is trouble, but not its nature. I feel a sickness. I cannot venture very far from the castle or we will drift uncontrolled and risk collision with high mountains or detection from the land below.

"But someone must go to learn about the troubles and return with an evaluation. George, you are most familiar with the village and their methods. You knew of Jack LaRoche and both you and Cloud Walker know much about the ways of the land below. And Cloud Walker has learned much about this Land. Tamara has lived near the village all her life. You could learn much about these people if you are willing to go there to observe them.

"I do not want you to endanger yourselves. You should

keep yourselves hidden. I can send new reports to you by calling to Cloud Walker. That village is not familiar with his name and it is not as likely that they will hear my calls to him as it is that your names would be heard." He looked at Tamara and George.

"I wouldn't mind checking things out," George responded. He could not believe he spoke the words. He volunteered to go back to the village that ostracized him – might have killed him if Annie had not silenced Gideon.

"If it is your wish, Ferryman, I shall follow," Tamara said.

As the Ferryman's eyes fell upon him, Cloud Walker quickly proclaimed his willingness to accompany his friends.

"Thank you. Now, you must rest. I would like you to leave next light."

The three stood and walked toward the entrance.

"George," Alden said. "Please remain for a moment."

Tamara and Cloud Walker continued, while George returned to his seat.

"Do you have any questions, George?"

"A few."

"Please ask."

"What about Annie? What's happening to her?"

"What do you mean?"

"That island you asked me about. Every time she sees it, she gets all . . . weird."

"That is one answer I cannot give you. She must find her own answers and then she must choose. We cannot help her. Nobody can."

George was glum but understood that further questions on that subject would be fruitless. But there were other questions. "You can send your thoughts to anyone you want?"

"To anyone who will listen."

"Because of the power in the Land?"

"Those who reject the lore of the Land cannot hear me. It is the Heart which helps me send my thoughts, but the lore was taught to me by Simon."

"Can you read the thoughts of others?"

"No . . . unless they are skilled in *sending* their thoughts."

"Why not? I would think that anyone with telepathic ability could send or receive thoughts."

"I have no desire to know the thoughts of others."

"Why not? You'd be able to tell if people were lying to you . . . or plotting against you. It would be an invaluable tool."

"A person's thoughts should remain his own unless freely given."

"I don't understand."

"If I were to know your thoughts, you would soon become fearful and resentful. Eventually, you would realize that your only protection from my invasion of your privacy would be to stop *having* thoughts altogether, or to destroy me. And if such would not be my undoing, surely I would suffer some kind of madness if I knew what everyone was thinking."

"I see. I met a Dragon while trying to find this place, and he taught me some things about passing thoughts. But he didn't say anything about not seeking thoughts against someone's will."

"Perhaps you can develop the things he taught you and we can contact each other when you are away."

"Yes, I'll try that. But I doubt I can master it so soon."

"Of course not! I speak of future adventures. George, before I answer any more questions, I would like to visit the Ancient Counselor with you. Would you be willing to see him now?"

"Sure! He seems a little spooky, but I imagine *I'd* be the same way if I were *that* old." Again George thought after he had spoken. He hoped the Ferryman would not think him disrespectful.

"Yes, the passing of years has its way of changing us all." The Ferryman's tone was cool but not angry.

The men stood and walked to the lower level of the Keep where the Ancient Counselor sat in the same position George had last seen him. The hood of his cloak still covered his face. The Ferryman directed George to sit as he addressed the Ancient Counselor, "George has agreed to travel to the village."

The old man was quiet, but he slowly moved his arm to the hood of his cloak and dropped the hood to his back. Incredibly, he was more emaciated than before. Just as before, he labored to move and speak. He moved his feet in the dirt and struggled to breathe. Each word came painfully and slowly. "It is good . . . but I cannot speak of this now. My time is near its end, and I must tell you how I will pass." He turned his head toward Alden. The Ferryman leaned closer. "All Ancient Counselors meet their end very quickly. The Land sustains us as well as it can, until the very last moment of our lives. Then, even the power of the Land so close to Heart cannot hold us together."

The Ferryman bore a woeful countenance as the Ancient Counselor continued, "Alden, as I expel my last breath, I shall disintegrate in a bright flash and a puff of smoke. My bones will immediately fall to dust." There was a long moment of silence. The Ferryman held his mentor's hand, waiting for him to continue. "I do not fear death, dear friend, for I have lived long, but it is my wish that you be near when the time comes."

"I will be here," the Ferryman answered. "Take comfort, Simon."

"Yes . . . yes, I know." Simon closed his eyes and nodded. The Ancient Counselor moved his feet again and struggled to continue, "You must choose your Ferryman, Alden. We have spoken of this before. You can continue without . . . a counselor and without an apprentice for a time, but the Land would be in danger if . . . something were to happen to you before another has learned to guide it.

"You are fortunate to have two good candidates. We have spoken of them before. Iron Bull . . . *Cloud Walker,* has much to give the Land. He could do well, if he were to choose a life of leadership. But I do not know that he would. George Severe has shown great . . . promise." He slowly turned to George. "You could be a . . . good Ferryman. Though we have not spoken many times, I know much about you – your character, your nature." He spoke each quality with emphasis. Then he whispered, "Your very soul."

George was taken aback. He never imagined being

Ferryman in this strange Land. Suddenly, he wondered what he was doing here. He thought of his own land and his family – Jane, Anastasia. Connecticut is where he belongs. He is just visiting here! He couldn't assume responsibility for the Land! He had *other* responsibilities! But the Ancient Counselor's last words haunted him – *your very soul*. But to become Ferryman? And lead the Land? For the rest of his life? Preposterous!

The Ancient Counselor turned back to the Ferryman. "I would not expect . . . any . . . candidate to accept such a task casually. Beside these two, there are several from this Land who could also serve it well – some not of . . . the human species. You must choose and begin teaching. Make your decision as soon as the troubles in . . . the Land are put aside. It is doubtful that I will be here then. This is why I advise you now. Prepare yourself and . . . prepare your candidates."

The man's speech was labored. He turned one last time to George. "I wish . . . you good fortune on your journey to the troubled village. You can depend on the Land to . . . help you. Hold faith. I see in you, the ability to resolve this . . . conflict. Such is your charge." He leaned against the wall and struggled with his hood.

The Ferryman rose to assist, but George had already stood. He did not know why he stood, but he did. After doing so, he leaned toward the Ancient Counselor and pulled the hood over his head. George looked at Alden but the Ferryman raised his hand to his lips and directed George outside the room.

They walked quietly to the Ferryman's room where Alden

directed George to a seat at the table. When the Ferryman returned with water and grain, he took his place next to George and waited for George to speak.

"What was that all about?" George asked. "I didn't come here to lead this Land! I just wanted to *learn* about it!"

"Do not concern yourself at this time. Nothing will be asked of you that you do not offer freely. My immediate concern is the troubles in the Land and I ask your help. You, Cloud Walker, and Annie know more about the ways of Jack LaRoche than anybody. I will need your counsel when you return."

"I'm not so sure I know all that much about the ways of mercenaries, but I agree we have an advantage over people who know nothing at all about wars. I mean, at least we learned about war in history classes and from books."

Having agreed to spy on Telemachus and the troubled village, George returned to his own room. He wanted to pace out the things he had learned but instead, was drawn to the stone bed where he slept as soon as he lowered his head.

Seventeen

Scouts

EVENING APPROACHED, but the sky grew exceptionally dark over the troubled village. A flash of lightning told George the Land was sailing into a thunderstorm. He could hardly see the golden dome that beaconed the troubled village. The storm would provide the cover they needed to approach undetected. Hopefully, they would find shelter in the village garden before being inundated by heavy rains.

It was a stark contrast to the day they left Wind Castle. Then, the morning air had been saturated with a strong spring fragrance, demanding notice and forbidding sleep. Radiant warmth passed through the cool air, touching anything in its path. It had been a sun day. The castle residents scurried about in preparation for a feast. George told Annie about the trip. After scolding him for being foolish enough to volunteer to spy on

Telemachus and Gideon, she had asked, "Why do you gotta go? Can't he learn as much by sending one of them flyin' horses?"

George answered, "Alden says they can't fly in the cloud and they can't get close enough otherwise without being seen."

"Tarnation, now we gotta go traipsin' about this danged place again."

"You don't have to go!" he told her.

"You ain't ditchin' me that easy, Sonny. No tellin' how much trouble ya can get in without me around."

The trek across the mountains was tedious – not so much because of the difficult terrain as due to the frequent bickering between Annie and Cloud Walker. Tamara did not seem to fit much better with Cloud Walker. He complained to George that women had no place in this work.

After leaving the foothills, they passed the oasis where George, Annie, and Tmron had seen the Unicorn resting with Fleng. George was disturbed by the memory of the slaughter perpetrated by Telemachus and his friends in their quest for power.

Now, they stood in sight of the gold dome, about to sneak into the village. The first gusts of the storm flattened the high grasses. No birds ventured into the sky. Most of the animals hid or lay flat on the ground. Two men and two women leaned into the wind, pushing their way toward the garden. Lightning flashed from cloud to cloud. A deluge of rain fell. Still, they did not falter. They huddled together and helped each other move toward their destination. George thought it was the best effort of cooperation he had seen since leaving Wind Castle. They squinted to see what was ahead of them. Each step was slow and hard-earned.

Suddenly, Cloud Walker yelped and pointed to the sky. George could not hear what the Indian said. He looked to the sky and shrugged. Cloud Walker pressed his cheek next to George's and yelled above the noise of the wind and rain as he pointed to the sky again, "Wakinyjan Tanka. George! There, in the clouds . . . the Great Thunderbird!"

George struggled to see beyond the rain, which spiked his face. Lightning flashed. "Something's up there."

After George spoke, that *something* swooped toward them. Tamara dove for the ground when it passed over her. She stood after another flash of lightning illuminated the sky. She moved close to George to shout what she had seen. "It is the large bird from the village . . . the one that rests on the gold dome."

George asked, "The Griffin?"

"Yes," she answered. "He will not harm us. He often flies in storms."

Cloud Walker touched George's shoulder. George leaned toward Cloud Walker and shouted, "That's a Griffin. You call it a *Thunderbird*?"

"Yes, Thunderbird. The Great Wakinyjan flies above us. If I die today, I will be a happy man for I have seen something none of my people who still live have seen. This is a great day."

George knew the Indian did not hear his explanation and

he wondered if the Griffin and the Wakinyjan Tanka could be one and the same. The creature was not seen in the next flashes of lightning.

The cold, penetrating rain, drove them more quickly to the garden near the village. A dense stand of trees offered shelter from the torrent.

Though it was still early, they were not about to explore the village during the storm. Cloud Walker said he would survey the village from behind the buildings when the rain stopped. Tamara agreed to contact some of her friends among the Spoils.

Annie jumped into their discussion. "And what do ya suppose me and Blondie ought ta do while you're out pokin' about?"

George answered, "We'll go with Tamara. The Spoils might recognize us, but I don't think they'll turn us in to the villagers."

The scouts huddled together in the cold rain. Cloud Walker said, "Something is wrong here. I have never been cold in this Land."

George and Tamara twisted their feet on the soil. George said, "I'm cold, too."

Tamara agreed, "This feeling is not right."

Annie was first to rise in the morning. She awakened the others when she dropped some rotting, withered fruit on their laps. "Better eat while ya can. This place is all picked out or somethin'. That's the best I could find hereabouts."

George looked at the pitiful fruit in his lap and stood to look around. "Nowhere near as bountiful as it was." Leaves and fruit were wilting and falling to the ground. The hardier, more prolific varieties continued growing but were obviously lacking in quality and quantity.

Tamara said, "It is not as it should be."

They found their way to the pond. Tamara collected four rocks and offered them to George. He set three in a triangular pattern and rested the fourth atop the first three. The surface of the pond bubbled weakly, but it did not issue its water to the stones. Sitting beside the stones, Tamara and George looked at each other while Cloud Walker stood over them.

Cloud Walker said, "You're not doing it right." He leaned down to the pile of stones and removed the top rock. The weak bubbling stopped. Then he returned the stone to the pile and the bubbling resumed. He stood and watched the water for a moment. Reaching down again, he squeezed the stones tightly together. He stood again and waited but little more happened. Then he kicked the pile, sending the stones splashing into the water. "They are destroying the Land," he cried. "This must stop! We must tell the Ferryman about this."

Annie said, "I don't know why you're gettin' all fired up. Seems ta me things is jes gettin' back ta normal 'round here. Water ain't supposed ta jump out o' ponds an' cricks. An' it's normal for fruit ta rot after pickin' time is passed."

Tamara said, "It is not normal for this Land. Cloud Walker is right. We must tell the Ferryman."

"First, we have to finish our survey," George said. "Cloud

Walker, do as we planned. Learn as much as you can about the village and we'll try to contact some of the Spoils." George looked at Annie and Tamara. "If we get separated, meet back where we slept. Cloud Walker, we'll see you there around midday. OK?"

Cloud Walker nodded.

"One more thing. If anything goes wrong, we have to get word to Alden. We'll do just as Annie told me last time we were here. If there's trouble, we split up and meet at that scar on the side of the hill across the Opens." George looked at Cloud Walker and Tamara. "You can't miss it. It's a section of exposed ledge with no trees."

Annie said, "An' don't nobody get no ideas 'bout bein' a hero. Whoever gets caught is on his own 'til we get back to that Ferryman feller."

George looked at each of the scouts. "Agreed."

Cloud Walker crouched and walked away while George and Annie followed Tamara toward the huts that were built for the Spoils. As the three walked through the brush, George said, "I'm hungry!"

Annie answered, "Course ya are, Sonny. It's mornin' and ya didn't eat the fruit I gave ya."

"No. I mean I *feel* hungry."

Holding her hand over her stomach, Tamara asked, "Is it a strange sense inside around here?"

"Yes. . . . You've never felt that before, have you?"

"I can remember it once when I was at the land below . . . but never here."

"I haven't felt it in this Land before either," George said.

"Like I tol' ya before – it's mornin' and things 'round here is jes gettin' back ta normal."

"Normal for our world maybe," George said. He looked at Annie's feet. "Or for someone wearing shoes up here. But, no. It doesn't fit here. Alden said he sensed some kind of sickness and I think we've found it."

They ate fruit as they walked. The sounds of babies and young children were heard as they approached the Spoils' end of the garden. George looked at the huts and whispered, "How long have we been gone?"

Nobody answered. Annie and Tamara stared ahead. There were many more huts for the Spoils and the living conditions were worse than they had been. Sewage and other wastes littered the area. George said, "Nothing's dissolving. Too many people? Or just more sickness in the Land?"

Tamara led George and Annie along the huts until she waved at someone. Her friend almost called out to her, but caught herself before she spoke. She looked about, then ducked into the shadows where George and Annie waited.

"Tamara! You live!"

Tamara answered, "Yes, I live."

"We thought you were lost to the Land. It has been so long! Tell me where you have been all this time." Her friend's eyes opened wide when she saw George and Annie. "They must not be seen in the village. Come quickly." She looked around and signaled them to follow.

Inside her hut, Tamara's friend told them about the happenings in the village since their departures. Most interesting to George was the fact that Telemachus had disappeared. "Gideon rules the village now," she said.

Annie said, "I tol' ya Red was a snake, Sonny. Probably done in that other feller jes ta take over."

"I don't think so."

"What ya mean?"

"Telemachus was the last of the Unicorn hunters. Scragg disappeared and the others were killed. That left Telemachus. Tmron told me this might happen."

Tamara's friend said, "I heard Telemachus was of a sickly mind and went out of the village, challenging the Unicorns when all were asleep. Nobody knows what happened. We know only that Gideon holds the Unicorn's horn and leads the village. He pressed many of us to serve with the raiding parties. Some of the Spoils enjoy the raids as much as the villagers. That is the reason you should not be seen here. Spoils who were once Tamara's friends might deliver her and you to Gideon now."

George said, "We shouldn't stay any longer then. We don't want to get you in trouble."

"Do not be concerned about me. I will always be Tamara's friend."

Tamara hugged her. "Thank you."

"All right," Annie said. "Cut the mush an' let's get goin'. It's near midday an' we got more ta see yet."

George, Annie, and Tamara waited at the stand of trees where they planned to meet Cloud Walker. Annie said,

"Never knew no Injun couldn't tell when midday was. We ought ta check it out, Sonny."

They stole through the garden behind the village but found no sign of Cloud Walker. Eventually, they came upon a small clearing that offered an unobstructed view of the Griffin, perched atop the gold dome. George said, "This is as far as we can go. It's getting dark. Any suggestions, Annie?"

"Tarnation, Sonny. We never should've let that ol' coot go off on his own in the first place."

Tamara walked to the back of the nearby huts and peeked down an alley.

George said, "He wanted to do it, and he's the only one of us the villagers wouldn't recognize."

"I 'spect they'd treat strangers no different than they'd treat us."

"He's made it clear more than once during this trip, he'd prefer to be on his own. He's almost as stubborn as someone else I know!"

"Now don't you go comparin'—"

Tamara waved at them from the alley.

Annie asked, "What ya suppose she wants?"

"One way to find out!"

When George and Annie reached Tamara she whispered, "I have found him."

Cloud Walker stood in the middle of the main way, looking up at the Griffin. A villager addressed him from across the way, but Cloud Walker did not respond.

The villager left. George crouched in the alley and waved

to the Indian. "Pssst, over here!"

Cloud Walker slowly moved closer to the alley but, before he could slip away, the villager returned, followed by Gideon and several others. Cloud Walker looked at George and dashed toward him. Gideon followed. Annie and Tamara were already running toward the garden when Cloud Walker passed George. George stood and followed – too late to avoid detection.

Gideon called out behind them, "I see you, George Severe. And you have a new friend."

George and Cloud Walker gained on Annie and Tamara. Aided by the darkening conditions, they put a safe distance between themselves and the pursuing villagers.

"You should not have come back, George Severe. You will not escape me a second time."

Annie and Tamara waited for George and Cloud Walker. They gathered and sucked in enough air to be able to speak. Annie said, "What was ya thinkin' of, Ol' Man? Ya trying ta get us all killed?"

"I was thinking I should offer myself to the great Wakinyjan, woman. But he does not respond to my prayers."

George said, "That doesn't matter now. We've been seen and we have to make sure word gets back to Alden. Let's keep going."

"We got a better chance if'n we split up."

"Annie's right. We'll meet at the foothills like we planned." George looked at Tamara and Cloud Walker. Both nodded.

"Where are you, George Severe? I have sent for light. You

will not escape."

George whispered, "OK, let's go. And be careful!" The scouts scattered into the suffering trees of the garden.

The torches of his pursuers were clearly visible through the failing garden growth. George moved inches at a time while they advanced toward him. It was fortunate they had spread in a wide pattern. It would be easier to evade one or two individuals than a cluster of people. On the other hand, the tactic made it necessary for George to pass through the net.

Gideon's calls were sufficiently loud for George to hear. "I know you are here. It will not be long before I hold you. Why do you delay your fate?"

George heard someone moving through the brush near-by. He hid in a thicket and watched the flickers of distant torches. There was something closer. He squinted. Two figures slowly advanced through the shadows. George stopped breathing as the men approached.

EIGHTEEN

Captive

GEORGE TREMBLED with each thunderous crack of a twig or branch. The men crept through the darkness, closer . . . and closer . . . and closer still. His only hope of avoiding detection was to remain absolutely still and hope they would pass without noticing him. The torchbearers came closer, too. If he had to run, there was only one way to go – right past the two men who were practically standing over him.

One of the men passed. The other was nearly by George when he tripped over George's leg. George tried not to move, but his leg withdrew just enough for the searcher to see that a fallen branch had not upset him. As he reached for George's leg, George rolled away. The other man returned, calling to those with the torches. George scrambled in and out of the clutches of the searcher who had tripped over him. He nearly escaped, but the other man joined the struggle and tackled George.

The two searchers wrestled with George until he realized he could not escape from them and surrendered. They pulled him to his feet as the torchbearers approached. Gideon stepped out of the darkness, into the circle of torches and confronted the captive.

"George Severe! I never thought well of you and it seems I was right. Only a fool would have returned after being sent away." He looked into George's face with a sinister expression. "What purpose have you in spying on our village?"

"I don't know what you're talking about, Gideon. I was just camping here on my way to the edges."

"Really. And your friend?"

"I just met him today. He seemed to be running from something, and I offered to let him stay with me for the night." George knew his words were not very convincing. But he felt a need to delay the continued search for Cloud Walker and the others.

"How many are with you, George Severe?"

George did not answer.

Gideon looked into the dark garden. "How many more of you are out there? I have your leader here! Unless you surrender to us, I will do him harm."

There was no answer and George shuddered as Gideon turned toward him. "You will cause me no concern. Soon you will be lost to the Land." Then he looked at the searchers. "Take him with us. We will seek his friends at the Opens."

The crowd tore past the trees and shrubs as they moved through the garden. Gideon called as they walked, "I have your leader. Come to me and I will not harm him."

Subdued moonlight scattered through the cloud and brushed across the Opens. Anything standing above the grass was cloaked in shadow – cloaked, but clearly distinguishable forms in silhouette. George saw nothing of his friends, but two Unicorns stood a stone's throw away. Gideon's commanding stride halted abruptly. "If his friends have escaped, they have gone another way. If not, we can find them next light." Gideon waved the Unicorn's horn under George's chin. "Perhaps they will be as foolish as George Severe and try to rescue him."

The searchers dragged George through the garden and down the main way to the village Meeting Place. Gideon stood before George and the crowd hushed.

"What should we do with you, George Severe?" Gideon turned and shrugged at his followers.

"Send him to the hunt," one said.

"Stake him in the square," said another.

"Put him with the Spoils," yet another said.

Others offered suggestions until Gideon raised the Unicorn's horn. "You are not well-loved, George Severe. Why is it?"

George did not answer. He stared into Gideon's eyes and struggled to release himself. At Gideon's signal, they released the prisoner and Gideon stepped closer. George returned Gideon's stare until the village leader arched his back and looked away. "I asked why you are not loved." He spoke to the crowd. "Could it be that you brought a plague to our village?" Some in the crowd murmured agreement.

"I didn't—"

Gideon slapped George. He looked at George and held a second stroke. George knew Gideon feared as much as hated him. Gideon said, "It is late. Take him to the Spoils and keep him there until I decide his punishment."

He walked toward the Meeting Place, stopped, and added, "And make sure one of you watches over him." Gideon stepped inside the Meeting Place while a few with torches took George away.

Spoils stood at the entrances to their huts as the villagers delivered George. They stopped at a hut next to the one used by Tamara's friend. One of the villagers said, "I will keep this prisoner bound here until Gideon calls for him."

George glanced at the next hut and noticed Tamara, peeking from behind her friend. He shook his head, almost imperceptibly and she moved back into the shadows.

George followed the villager into the hut and sat on the floor as instructed. He leaned against the back wall and looked out the entrance. As the night wore on, the guard fell asleep with his leg draped over George's ankles. Whenever George moved, the guard stirred.

George could not sleep. He stared outside, trying to keep from disturbing the guard. Long after all were silent, he saw a shadow moving toward the hut. It continued until it rested by one side of the entrance. A sudden loud snore caused the shadow to duck away from the entrance. After the guard rested quietly again, the shadow peeked around the side of the entrance and shot a pebble at George's chest. The motion and size of the shadow told George it must be Tamara.

George was overcome by fear for Tamara's safety and tried to warn her to leave by moving his lips to the words. She did not respond. So, he moved, trying to get her to see his face more clearly. His movement stirred the guard, who rolled over.

George and Tamara froze as they watched the dark form slowly succumb to sleep again. Then George tried to whisper, "Go to Alden! I'll be all right!"

He knew she heard him, but he also saw that she hesitated. He whispered louder, "Go! Now!"

The last word aroused the villager. He sat up and looked at George. Tamara ducked back.

"What is it that you say, Spoil? Has your friend returned for you?"

"Nothing. I must have been dreaming. I often call out in my sleep." George saw the shadow shrink away.

"Perhaps I should look outside."

"Do what you want," George answered, rolling to one side.

The villager rose and left the hut. George peeked over his shoulder. The man looked to each side of the hut before returning. "Your friend is not out there," he said. "Do not hope for escape."

George did not answer. *Alden. Call them back.* Soon, the villager was snoring again, but George could not sleep.

He could have muffled the noise, but he could not

silence his concern for his friends. They *had* to follow their plans and go back to the Ferryman.

After a few hours of watching the noisy darkness, George felt lonely and abandoned. Maybe he should not have sent Tamara away. Maybe he should not have tried communicating with Alden. If Alden does what he asked, George will be left alone in Gideon's grasp. Tamara, Annie, and Cloud Walker had better get word to Alden, and they had better hurry.

George's guard checked the bindings at his wrists and led him to the square outside the Meeting Place. George sat on the ground, thirsty and hungry, too worn to think about his impending session with Gideon. A crowd gathered and the guard sent one of its members into the Meeting Place for Gideon. George searched for sympathetic eyes in the crowd and was surprised to find them – mostly among those who stood quietly behind the others.

Gideon appeared atop the steps at the entrance to the Meeting Place. "Ah, George Severe. It is so kind of you to join us this light. What can I do to make your stay more comfortable?"

George knew Gideon was mocking him but he thought he would ask for something anyway. "I could use some water and food."

"Of course," Gideon responded. "How rude of me not to have offered you something before!" He turned to the villager who was guarding George. "Unbind him and take him to a table inside the Meeting Place."

The guard was dismissed after Gideon sat next to George at the stone table. The Meeting Place had changed since George last sat there. The dirt floor was littered with wasted food and smelled of soured wine. A few of the stone tables were broken.

Gideon ordered, "Some food and water for our guest."

The keeper placed a pot of fruits and grains on the table along with two mugs of water. Gideon pointed to the food. George wanted to consume all he saw ravenously but, instead, casually took one large, soft apple and slowly ate it while Gideon watched. Between bites, he drank some of the water and waited for Gideon to speak. He knew that Gideon was not playing the role of a gracious host without reason. The insidious leader was trying to make him believe he was in no danger. What could he want from George? What made him think George would give it to him?

Gideon watched George and rolled the Unicorn's horn back and forth on the table. George refused to follow its motion. As George finished the apple, Gideon offered another and rolled the horn again. George could no longer resist the distraction and let his eyes follow. "You are attracted to the magic of my horn," Gideon said.

"Not really," George answered, "and I doubt that it has magic."

Gideon wore a stinging smile as he responded, "Oh, be not mistaken, George Severe, it has magic . . . very powerful magic."

"No, it doesn't. That horn has brought you nothing but

256 | WIND CASTLE

trouble since Telemachus brought it into the village." George was confident in his reply and he saw that his confidence and his words angered Gideon.

Gideon grit his teeth and argued, "It is not this horn which has caused so much trouble. It is you, George Severe. You know the secrets of Jack LaRoche and you could have shared them with us. If you did, we could have gained much. Instead we are overpopulated with Spoils and tormented by creatures who are determined to destroy us."

"I told you before that I know no secrets. And you know you were much better off before LaRoche came here."

"You speak falsely. Our real troubles came when you were found near the edges. You should have been left there to fall from the Land to a place where you could do us no harm."

"What harm could I do?"

Gideon said, "Now that you are in my grasp, you can do nothing. So, you might as well confess. Why did you return to our village?"

"I told you, I was on my way to the edges!"

"Why would you go to the edges after all this time?"

"I was trying to find my way back to my own land." As he spoke, thoughts of home flashed in his mind – brief images of a warm embrace from Jane, Anastasia smiling as she tried to run on hands and knees to her father's waiting arms.

He was not given time to dwell on those thoughts before Gideon asked, "Are you not pleased with our Land? Do you not think you have been welcome here? We offered you shelter and friendship. In return, we asked only that you share the secrets known to those from your land, but all you offered was treachery. You tried to tell the people that their leaders were insane and corrupted." He paused before continuing, "I am pleased to hear that you wish to leave us. Perhaps we should escort you to the edges! You cause trouble when you are among us. It would be better if we were to help you find your home."

George did not answer. He stopped eating and looked into Gideon's eyes. George saw cunning and treachery in Gideon. Gideon glanced away. Staring Gideon down again did much for George's confidence.

Gideon lifted the horn from the table and stood. "I shall give further thought to this matter. Meanwhile, you will stay with the Spoils." He turned to one of the villagers sitting nearby and ordered, "Take George Severe to the Spoils and keep him there until I call for him."

Gideon left the Meeting Place. The villager stood next to George with his hand on his shoulder, inviting the captive to follow him.

Nineteen

Deliverance

TAMARA RESTED IN the tall grass of the Opens until much of the morning had passed. She stood, looking back at the troubled village. Nobody followed. She turned and walked toward the exposed ledge at the foothills. There was nobody ahead of her, either. Occasional glances behind her verified her good escape. During one of those glances, something grabbed her ankle and she tumbled to the ground. She rolled with the fall, trying to free herself until she recognized Cloud Walker.

"Stay low, woman."

"You know what I am called," Tamara said.

"*Tamara*, you stand so straight, you can be seen for miles."

"Nobody follows. I have watched." She sat on the ground. The grass stood near her chin.

"Have you seen George and that other woman?"

"George was captured. I have not seen *Annie*, but I think she escaped."

"We should go back for him. Do you know where they took him?"

"I know, but we cannot go back. We must tell the Ferryman."

"Let that crow, Annie, tell him," he said.

"George does not want us to help him."

"How do you know that?"

"I saw him after he was taken. I was going to untie him while his guard slept but he sent me away before I could get into the hut."

"It was because you are a woman. He would not send me away." Cloud Walker crouched and moved toward the village.

Tamara followed. "As you wish, but I know George wants us to go back to Wind Castle."

"We may not have enough time to go and return with help. You go to the Ferryman. I will try to release—"

Cloud Walker, come to me.

The Indian stopped mid-step and looked at Tamara. She said, "The Ferryman calls."

"All right," he said. "We'll do as he asked. But, be quick." Cloud Walker led the way and Tamara followed. The Indian set a fast pace that the native woman sustained. As their journey continued, Cloud Walker became less abrasive. "You travel well, Tamara. You are strong and you don't complain."

Their friendship was established that day. While they trekked side-by-side, Cloud Walker said, "I am an old man. I grew up in a time and place where men and women had their own tasks in life. Men never did the work of women and women never did the work of men. When we left Wind Castle, I thought you and Annie were meddling in the matters of men. But you have shown yourself worthy."

"You have been long in this Land, Cloud Walker. The Ferryman has great regard for you. Because he does, so do I. I did not wish to intrude on your work – I serve where I am asked to serve."

"You have served well. I am proud to say I know you."

Gideon walked into the Spoil's hut where George was kept and dismissed the sentry and the Spoil. George remained seated, leaning against the wall of the hut.

"I have come to offer you another opportunity to share your secrets, George Severe. If you do, you will be rewarded."

"I keep telling you, I don't know any secrets."

Gideon paced. "I have given much thought to our last conversation, George Severe, and I have decided that I do not believe you were traveling to the edges to find your land. Why have you returned to our village?"

George stood, his muscles sore from the abuse of the previous day. He looked down at Gideon, "That's a good question. Why *would* I return? There's nothing to attract me to this forsaken place."

"I will tell you why you have come," Gideon snapped. "You have come to steal my village away from me. You will spread your poison and try to become leader. You are just hoping I will be foolish enough to say something that will turn my people against me. I assure you, I will not."

"You're crazy, Gideon. I don't want to lead this place. Certainly not now that you and Telemachus have practically destroyed it."

"Any destruction brought here has been your doing, George Severe. I can save the village from the likes of you. You will see. I will lead us to power."

"Not likely. Look around you, Gideon. Think about the Land and how it was before you and Telemachus followed Jack LaRoche."

"Jack LaRoche helped us. He taught us how to fight – how to force others to serve us. We offered you hospitality and friendship and you gave us nothing but trouble in return."

"Your trouble began with your first raid. I was told that the Land resisted your ways even before I came. With Spoils doing your work, the waters stopped responding to your call. Now your sickness has spread and the waters do not respond to anyone's call. Waste lays all over the place – unconsumed by the Land. People get sick and many children have been born to this village."

"The births of our children are signs of our strength. What other village has been so productive?"

"You know as well as I do, that children are born in this Land only when the Land knows that death is coming. Your children reflect the Land's last effort to heal itself."

"Who told you that?"

262 | WIND CASTLE

"The Ferryman told me. Think about it! It makes sense. How many have died in your raids. How many of your villagers and Spoils were lost to sickness recently?"

George did not know that any had died from sickness, but he took the chance that some had, hoping Gideon would realize that the sickness was a result of the Land's rejection of their new ways.

George knew there *had* been sickness when he saw the expression on Gideon's face as he answered, "That is absurd, George Severe. If there has been sickness here, it was brought by the Spoils and you. It may be that you cursed the village when we sent you away."

"There's no curse on this village except that brought about by your greed for power. You're so blinded by it that you can't see what it's doing to your people. Think back, Gideon. Think how it was before you tried dominating your neighbors." Gideon opened his mouth but George quickly added, "Remember how beautiful your garden was? Remember how happy everyone was? You didn't need Spoils to serve you. The Land served you. It gave you anything you wanted – fruits and vegetables, flowers and trees. If you wanted water, you called and it came. You could have lived without food or water if you wanted because the Land gave you sustenance directly.

"It's still that way in the rest of the Land . . . but not here! Not in this corrupt village! I've been to Wind Castle and many places between. The Land thrives everywhere but here. Is that because of me, or is it because of you, Gideon? You and Telemachus and the dreadful things you learned from

Jack LaRoche."

Gideon said, "I can see I am unable to convince you to stop causing problems in my village. I have tired of this conversation. I will call for you next light. Then I will tell you your fate." He turned his back and stormed out of the hut.

Gideon walked into the Meeting Place and sat silently for a moment before he slapped the Unicorn's horn on the table and bellowed, "Some wine." When the keeper approached the table with a mug, Gideon snatched it away, spilling some of the wine, "Be careful, you incompetent. . . . There is hardly enough to quench my thirst. Bring another . . . and be quick about it, if you can do so without spilling."

The patrons of the Meeting Place were conspicuous by their silence. The leader looked around the room. Then he smiled and said, "Do not let my ill manner disturb you. Come! Everybody drink." He forced a laugh and called to the keeper, "A mug for all my friends. And forgive my earlier rudeness."

He emptied the second mug and left the Meeting Place.

Gideon had spent a restless night in his hut and quickly expelled his wife and son when their attendance to him grew bothersome. "Go be with other women and children and leave me to my concerns," he said. The two offered no argument and Gideon sat alone in his hut.

"Why did he have to come back? Unless I do something, George Severe will soon be brewing trouble. It is unfortunate he cannot see it would be better for him to stand by my side and teach me the secrets of his land. Then I could control these people – including those farmers who would rather try to force plants to grow than join in the raids."

Gideon rolled the Unicorn's horn between his hand and the top of the table. "But he will never help me. If he did, he might then betray me, as he wanted to do with Telemachus. I need a permanent solution – something to end George Severe's interference forever. It must appear to be the will of the people. Already, I have seen those who might follow him. But the farmers and some of the others will not resist if their neighbors call for action.

"I must show the people that he is responsible for all our troubles. Then, they will demand his execution. I need someone to help me – someone to blame if it should not go well." Gideon stopped rolling the horn and raised its point to his head, putting his Machiavellian mind to work.

Gideon sat at his table, clutching the horn over his chest. Before him was the first man to guard George after he was taken prisoner. "Thank you for coming to me in this difficult time, Dax. You are one of my most trusted friends."

"I am?" Dax straightened his posture.

"Quite so! There are few I would trust to watch the stranger. George Severe is very dangerous. I wish there was a way of convincing the villagers of that. He plans to destroy us and take the village, but he is too clever to show his true plans to the fools who would follow him."

"I could beat him until he confesses his treachery."

"He is too stubborn. We must discredit him. If we cannot do it with his own words—"

"We could make something up!"

Gideon smiled, "Yes, of course. You see it. You know what a danger he is. We must use any means of showing it. You are excellent at thought, Dax. But what could we say that . . . the people might fear George Severe if they thought he possessed some unusual and dangerous powers." Gideon tapped the point of the horn on his forehead. "If you were to pretend that he was able to put a spell on you . . . so that you would do violence to me . . . and if you pretended to perform this violence in the presence of many people . . . there would be no doubt. But how could we do this without actually hurting anyone? I am not one who enjoys pain and I certainly would not want you to suffer if someone unknowing was to come to my aid."

Dax thought for a moment, then suggested, "You could find another to stop me before I strike."

"Yes," Gideon said. "We could stage everything – the spell, the attack, and the rescue. Good planning. But what of the spell after I am rescued?"

"The touch of a friend and your wise words will bring me back to my senses and out of the spell."

"Yes, I believe it can be done. Congratulations, my friend. You are a valuable asset to our cause. I must include you in all my future plans." Gideon held his arm around Dax's shoulder and walked him to the door. "I will choose someone I can trust to play the part of rescuer. He will wear a red stone on a string around his neck so you can recognize him. Launch your attack when he is between us. Watch for my signal. The time will be soon. Bring the prisoner to the Meeting Place at midday and say nothing of this to anyone."

Gideon held something in his hand. "Thank you for coming to me in this difficult time, Lucius. You are one of my most trusted friends."

"I am glad to be here."

"I have a gift for you." Gideon extended his hand and offered Lucius a red stone suspended on a piece of twine.

"Thank you. It looks a valuable stone." The man placed the string over his head. The stone rested at his throat. "Why do you offer such a gift?"

"I believe a leader should always reward his friends. Friends are hard to hold when there is so much evil around us.

"Evil?"

"I have heard there are plans to do harm to me and any who would protect me."

Lucius grabbed the stone at his throat. "I assure you, Gideon, I am loyal to you."

Gideon waved his hands, "Of course! Of course. That is why I sent for you. I cannot always see what is happening. I need someone to watch out for me."

"You have nothing to fear as long as I am at your side."

"That is good to hear. I do not know why some people would want to harm me. But, if they do, it is good to know that you would see them punished. What do you consider a suitable punishment for someone plotting against their leader?"

"That would depend—"

"Their poisonous thoughts transcend the community like a festering wound. If evil people are allowed to spread their treacherous words, nobody will be safe in this village or anywhere in the Land. And, if they choose to do me harm, who will lead and protect our people?"

"They must be stopped. If anyone raises his hand to you, I will strike him down."

"You are a treasure, Lucius. I am wealthy indeed to have such a friend."

Dax relieved George's sentry in the Spoil's hut. George cringed as a chill passed along his spine. Dax said, "It is time for you to be judged."

George was bound and led on a rope by Dax to the village square. Gideon waited atop the steps outside the Meeting Place. A crowd had already gathered. The sentry stood George before the village leader.

Gideon mumbled to Lucius, "Be aware. This may be troublesome." He then spoke to George and the crowd. "Well, George Severe . . . it has been suggested that you have brought trouble to our village."

"I *told* you—" George felt a tug at the rope.

"It has also been said that you want to control this village."

"You know—" George tried to answer.

"You are also suspected of wanting to do harm to me and

certain others in this village."

"What harm can one—"

"SILENCE . . . until you have heard all that has been said about you." Gideon smiled when George stepped back. Two of the villagers held George fast. "It has further been said that you placed a curse on this village when we sent you away." The crowd mumbled. As the buzzing grew stronger, Gideon signaled to Dax. The sentry moaned as if he were being possessed while Lucius stepped between Gideon and the others.

George struggled with those who held him. He tried to dispute the accusations, "That's hogwash! You—"

Gideon raised his voice. "And it has also been said that *you* are the cause of the sickness which has come to our village."

"NO!" George cried. "That's a lie."

Just as George spoke, and more quickly than most of the crowd could follow, Dax lunged toward Gideon with a large cutting tool he had taken from his belt. Lucius drew a similar tool and thrust the blade deeply into the sentry's belly. There were fearful screams and cries from the crowd. Dax looked confused as he grasped Lucius's necklace and fell.

Lucius withdrew his tool, pulling with it the last fragment of Dax's life. George struggled and the crowd stepped back from the turmoil. Lucius moved toward George with murder in his eyes. Gideon yelled out, "STOP!" Lucius held his thrust and waved his tool close to George's throat.

Gideon walked to the fallen sentry and lifted his lifeless

head. The crowd hushed. The leader gently placed the victim's head on the ground and rested his own in his hands. He stood and paused, staring at the body. Then, he slowly walked over to George and said, "You are responsible for this."

George looked back at Gideon with furrowed brow. He could not believe what he had seen, nor could he respond to the incredible accusation. Gideon blamed him when he had been restrained throughout the incident.

"He was one of my best friends and you put a spell on him."

"No!"

"You cursed him and made him want to kill me."

A voice called out from the crowd, "Yes, he did! I saw it! Dax was acting very strange just before he tried to kill Gideon." Others in the crowd uttered their confirmation. The voice called out again, "He is dangerous."

"Quiet, all of you," Gideon said. "Let me think about this."

Lucius continued holding his tool at George's throat. He pleaded with Gideon, "Give me the pleasure of slicing through his neck."

"No," Gideon said. He pulled George's head down next to his face and said, "He was my friend, George Severe. You shall pay dearly for your crime." George tried answering but Gideon abruptly stepped back and ordered, "Put something in his mouth to silence his lies." He stepped further back and turned to the crowd, glancing across the faces and returning to George's face. "You will be staked for the night."

A voice in the crowd called, "No. Kill him!" Others agreed

and a wave of discontent rolled through the crowd.

Gideon said, "Next light, we will use you for sport. Take him away and stake him."

Two villagers led George along the perimeter of the square to the main way where they forced him to sit on the ground. During the walk, he managed to spit out the gag but said nothing – hoping to breathe comfortably for a while. The crowd, noticeably smaller, circled the prisoner and jeered. A man pushed through them carrying some heavy wood stakes. Another followed, hauling a clay spool of coarse coiled rope. The first man pounded the stakes into the ground at four points around the prisoner. George watched and said, "See what you're doing? Those stakes wouldn't last very long in the ground if the Land was as strong as it was before." He realized he had revealed his ability to speak again and tensed when one of the men cut a piece of rope and stuffed it into George's mouth.

A Spoil arrived with a crock of water and left it on the ground near the man who held the coil of rope. He placed the spool inside the crock. Some of the water spilled over the rim and George longed to quench his thirst. The villager said, "This will stretch the rope. It will shrink as it dries – cause you much pain." He turned to the Spoil. "Bring some salt so the ropes will burn him when they cut through his flesh."

When all four stakes were secure, George was stretched between them. The rope was taken from the water and used to bind George's hands and legs individually. Then, sections of rope were extended to the stakes where the ends were pulled tightly and secured. Onlookers kicked George and mocked him until late afternoon, when most tired of the sport and left him.

George watched his guard pacing at the side of the way. When the guard looked away, he dislodged the rope from his mouth. George felt more tension in his arms and legs as the cord dried. When the sky lost all light, he felt as if his joints would separate if he dared to relax his body. His constant resistance to the fetters exhausted him.

There was a stillness in the village, which told him most of the people had retired for the evening. He wondered how much more his bindings could shrink and how much longer he could resist. Then, he sensed a presence nearby. He tried looking around but could scarcely move his head without adding to the pain in his joints. He was sure someone was hiding in the shadows – watching him. He heard a thump near the place where his guard stood. Something fell to the ground.

"Who's there?" he asked. Nobody answered. "If any-body's there, please help me." His voice was weak. He heard his blood throbbing in his veins. There was no answer.

The ropes were now so tight that only his buttocks and head drooped to the ground. He closed his eyes and tried to rest while maintaining his grip on the ropes, holding his joints in place. He thought he heard some footsteps above his head. He tried speaking but was silenced by a heavy pressure bearing down on his mouth. He was at the edge of panic when he heard a whisper beside his head, "Be quiet, Sonny! . . . or you're gonna get us killed."

George nodded and felt a cautious release of the pressure over his mouth. He whispered, "Annie! How did you—"

"Shhh."

George felt tension at his arm as Annie cut the first rope. When it snapped, his arm and shoulder dropped to the ground. The other arm followed and soon his legs were also free. His body was so sore, he thought he could not move.

Annie helped him to his feet. He took the first of many painful steps. At the edge of the village, George said, "Am I glad to see you."

"Keep movin', Sonny. We got a long way ta go 'fore we can rest."

"Thanks for cutting me loose, but . . ."

"But what?"

"Weren't you the one who said nobody should play hero if someone got caught?"

"The difference b'tween me an' a *hero,* is that I know what I'm doin'. Now keep movin, or we'll both be stretched out back there."

TWENTY

Flight and Fire

CLOUD WALKER and Tamara arrived at Wind Castle to a clamor of curious villagers. In their absence, many of the stories about the troubles in the Land had circulated through the court. It was well known that George, Annie, Cloud Walker, and Tamara were on a quest to learn as much as possible about the troubles. The villagers gathered around them.

"What news of the troubled village?" several asked individually.

"Where are the strangers to the Land?" another asked. "Were you attacked?"

"What happened to George Severe and his little friend?"

Tamara tried answering them while walking, but the crowd was too large and the questions too many.

A few of the villagers cleared a path to the castle. The

people followed. A messenger met Cloud Walker and Tamara at the Inner Bailey and asked them to go to the hall.

"We must see the Ferryman," Cloud Walker said.

"He will come to you soon."

They were served wine and grains, which they consumed anxiously while people crowded into the hall.

The Ferryman walked down the stairs that led from the upper levels of the Heart. The crowd hushed as he made his way to the table. "Please forgive my delay. Simon held me in conversation and I had to adjust our course to avoid some high lands."

Cloud Walker said, "George has been captured. We have to go back right away."

The Ferryman said, "First, tell me all you learned of the village."

The two related their stories at the same time. Cloud Walker's glance at Tamara told her to wait until after he spoke. He told the Ferryman all the facts important to him concerning the village and the way the Land was reacting to the troubles there. The Thunderbird was an important part of his story. Tamara continued the tale with equal consideration to the damage to the Land, but added her account of George's imprisonment and her fear that Gideon would do him harm.

The crowd listened as the tales were told. When Cloud Walker and Tamara finished speaking, all eyes turned to the Ferryman. He did not respond immediately, but stood quietly, then answered, "I do not know exactly where George is, but I *do* know he is no longer in the village. Simon agrees. We have sensed George's presence and neither of us could do so when you went into the village. Hopefully, Annie is with him.

"Your descriptions about the way the Land is responding to the troubles explains why we could not sense your presence, or his, when you left the Opens. At first, we thought you might have been lost to the Land, but there were none of the other feelings which usually accompany death. Now, it is all very clear."

The Ferryman turned to all the listeners and spoke in a loud, clear voice. "Cloud Walker and Tamara have brought disturbing news about the troubled village. We do not know what those villagers will do next, but it is certain that we must prepare to confront this problem. Assaults on other villages will surely occur. I ask to meet with the trade leaders and those of you who are familiar with such circumstances as these." He turned to Cloud Walker and Tamara. "You have done well. Do not worry about your friend. I know he is free. I will send a messenger on a winged horse to search for him. George and Annie will be among us soon."

Gideon was sleeping in his hut when one of the villagers called to him urgently. The villager called twice again before Gideon answered, "Enter, and explain why you have disturbed me."

"You must come immediately," the breathless man said. "The stranger has escaped!"

"What?" Gideon roared. "Who was watching him?"

"His guard was laying unconscious beside the way. I was

walking along the way with a Spoil and we saw the ropes cut and the stranger gone. Who would have thought he could free himself?"

Gideon snapped, "He didn't free himself, fool. The other stranger must have returned – or the ugly woman who followed him." He raised his arms and pushed the villager out the door abruptly. "Form a hunting party – twenty or thirty in number – and have them assemble at the Meeting Place."

The villager left.

Over twenty people arrived at the Meeting Place. Gideon told them, "Gather weapons and supplies for a long hunt. The Ferryman instigated the visit from George Severe and his friend. They will return to Wind Castle. We will track and stop them."

The hunters left the Meeting Place, gathered their equipment, and moved toward the edge of the village, adding to their number as they walked. Thirty-four, Gideon included, assembled at the Opens to hunt for the strangers. Gideon stood at the point as two Unicorns watched from a distance. He hesitated. "George Severe must be captured and destroyed," he said. Then he stepped forward, followed by a mob, hungry for sport.

George walked beside Annie in the bright sunless morning. Exhilarated by a few hours sleep and the life force flowing up his legs, he walked casually, feeling less of the urgency he experienced while staked at the main way. He did not think about the Ferryman, or Cloud Walker and Tamara. Instead, he bathed in the warm feeling instilled by last night's dreams about Jane and Anastasia.

He turned to look back at the village. Below the rooftops, near the area where the Opens met the village, he saw some movement – many small, thin figures. "Annie, look."

"Seen 'em, Sonny. Keep movin' and they won't be a problem."

"Why am I doing this? I'm so stupid! I could be home right now, playing with Anastasia or going to a movie with Jane. But nooo. I had to go off and find out what this cloud is all about."

"No argument from me. I ain't the one who volunteered ta go back ta that danged village."

The day passed with George cursing himself as he struggled to stay ahead of their pursuers. They crossed the Opens to the hills where they lost ground when climbing and gained on the flats or descending. With dusk came fog that filled the space between the treetops and the ground, offering a respite from the chase. "It's pretty quiet back there, Annie. Do you think we lost them?"

"Doubt it, Sonny. They might o' stopped for the night. We probably ought ta do the same after we put a bit more distance b'tween us. My dogs is killin' me."

The dense fog made travel more difficult, and more treacherous if they were near the edges. George stopped on the crest of the hill and said, "We'd better stop and wait for daylight. Your feet are sore and we could walk right off the Land in this fog. I don't think we're near the edges, but it doesn't hurt to make sure."

"OK by me, Sonny. I'll cover our tracks a ways back. Then we can take turns sleepin'."

George stirred slightly, trying to avoid nodding off during his watch. A cool breeze swept most of the fog away and morning light tickled the sky above the trees. A sudden cry in the woods snapped George alert. He sat up quickly to see what was happening. Through the undergrowth, he saw two Unicorns looking toward him. In the foreground, he was sure he saw a hand pulling another's head down behind a rock. He knew they had been found and he looked around. He thought he saw another figure at one side. If they were not already surrounded, they soon would be.

He shook Annie and whispered, "Someone's coming, we have to get out of here."

Annie whispered back, "They seen us yet?"

"I think so."

"We'd best split up."

"OK. We'll meet at the next ridge."

"Pick yer path, Sonny. Are ya ready?"

"Yes."

"Go." Annie rolled and scurried into some nearby bushes.

George dashed toward a boulder. The hunters were not prepared for their quick movement and George crashed through one of them as he ran. The hunter was knocked senseless to the ground and George fled down the hill in powerful leaps. Each time his feet touched the ground he jumped again and practically flew down the mountainside. The force of the impact on his bones went unnoticed, as did the tearing of his flesh when he slid. All his energy and thought was on escaping.

His determination saved him from capture. The pain associated with his first movements became more obvious. Nevertheless, he ran – ran for his life. *For Heaven's sake! Get us out of here, pllleassse!* He tried avoiding the trees, but control of his descent slipped away. He plowed through some brush into a stubborn tree trunk, tripped over the heavy roots, and tumbled head over heels until his battered body came to rest near some boulders.

He was barely conscious. The ground stopped spinning in his head and he regained his sense of position. The hunters were not far behind. He rolled to face the ground and pushed up from the earth. *Help us! Somebody, please help us.* He leaned against one of the large rocks and twisted his feet in the soil, trying to catch his breath and gain strength.

The hunters pressed closer. He pushed himself away from the rock. His entire body protested but he forced himself to respond to the need for flight. He struggled up the next hill. His pursuers approached from behind and each side. A moment's pause to look back revealed some movement at the base of the hill. *Oh, please don't let them see me!* He pulled himself up the slope. With each effort, he thought his arms would separate from his shoulders and his legs would crumble. Yet he found the strength to continue. The Land helped him as well as it could, sending more energy through his legs.

Except for an occasional sound from one side or the other,

he thought he successfully remained ahead of his pursuers. The crest of the hill was just before him, but first he had to climb a steep section of ledge. There was no time to seek an easier path and there would be a risk in moving to one side or the other while the angry mob was near. So, he climbed the ledge. All he could see above the ledge was the cloud. Just a few more steps and he would be at the top of the hill where he could see better and choose a course that would evade the hunters. Then he would search for Annie.

Sweat and blood poured down his face, arms, and legs. His body wanted to quit, but he continued. If only someone could help them. He could not call out without risking detection. *Someone help us. Alden! Cloud Walker! Frothgarde! Tmron! Anybody! Please help us!* He struggled up the ledge and leaned over the top. Finally, he pulled one knee up and crawled up off the ledge to the flat ground.

He was about to rise from his hands and knees when he was struck in the face by someone's foot. His body was already so sore that he hardly felt the impact of the blow, which spread him flat on the ground. However, he was very much aware of a vicious kick in the stomach. Gasping did not draw any air into his lungs. As he struggled, he was lifted by his arms. He finally sucked in some air and his vision returned. Slumped in the clutches of two of the villagers, he looked up to the face of their leader.

"We are so glad we have found you, George Severe!" A hateful expression accompanied Gideon's sarcastic words.

George thought he heard Annie' voice. Then he saw her

flailing her arms back at the villager who held her off the ground by her waist.

George could hardly speak. He begged inaudibly, "Let us go."

Gideon responded with a blow to George's stomach.

Stop! I can't breathe! Please . . . somebody . . . somebody, please help us!

I come!

George looked around, trying to breathe again. Gideon said something that he could not hear through the ringing in his ears. He was confused. *What?*

I come, George Severe. Hold your strength.

Frothgarde?

I come.

Is it you, Frothga— George felt the pain of yet another blow from Gideon – this one across his face.

The earth rumbled and unusual sounds emanated from the woods across the clearing – the sounds of shrubs tearing from the ground, dirt thrashing about, and trees crackling and splitting. The hunters turned toward the din. Something very large rushed toward them through the forest. The two who held George let him drop. George focused on the edge of the clearing and saw Frothgarde charging out of the forest, flapping his wings and storming into the clearing. The villager holding Annie dropped her flat on the ground.

Had it not been such a serious situation, George would have thought Frothgarde's appearance rather comical. It was indeed a queer sight. An old Dragon, who had all he could do to walk a short distance without tiring, was attacking thirty-four armed men. His movement was clumsy. His wings were so tattered that they served better to distract the foe than to offer flight or draft. His flesh was wrinkled, cracked, and molting. Anyone who had ever seen a Dragon would not give this one a moment of serious consideration – especially in battle.

Annie stood and moved closer to George. "What in tarnation is that?"

The hunters had never seen a Dragon before. They had never seen any beast so large as this before. They scattered and it seemed that Frothgarde would be granted a quick, easy victory. George and Annie would be rescued. Except . . ..

Gideon called to the fleeing hunters, "Do not run! There is little to fear here. It is a Dragon. Remember what Norris told us? He said he saw a Dragon once before. And he said that he overpowered the beast."

The villagers checked their hurried retreat. Gideon stood in the clearing next to George. "Norris was but one man and we are many. And we have learned the ways of Jack LaRoche. Take up your weapons and destroy the beast." The leader grasped a crude spear from the ground and raised it toward the Dragon. Some hunters stepped out from behind trees.

Annie crouched near George. "You OK, Sonny?"

"Better . . . now that Frothgarde's here."

"You know that thing?"

"He's a friend." As Gideon moved closer to Frothgarde,

George called out, "Frothgarde! Watch out!"

The beast fiercely charged the hunters. Gideon and some others held their positions and launched their weapons. Gideon's spear and another's cutting tool lodged in the Dragon's aged hide. Frothgarde roared and continued his charge. The villagers in his path were thrown aside or crushed – but not without adding to Frothgarde's injuries by cutting and slashing at his flesh with their knives and spears as he passed.

The Dragon charged anything that moved. Some of the hunters distracted Frothgarde while others attacked from behind. He moved his tail wildly about as he chased the decoys. His tail proved deadly for the first few who did not expect the assault. They were cast aside and their bodies splattered against trees or rocks.

George slowly regained some strength after Annie dragged him from the thick of the battle. He leaned against a tree and twisted his feet into the ground to soak up the Land's energy. From that position, he watched the fighting. Eight bodies lay motionless at various places. A few of the injured rested behind trees.

Frothgarde endured many attacks, but George could not stand by and let his friend suffer so many injuries. He held onto a tree, while the dizziness slowly drained from his head. The earth covered his feet and the life force of the Land continued restoring him. He was not yet ready for battle, but he could warn the Dragon of impending dangers. One of the hunters objected to George's interference, but Annie saw him coming and discouraged him with a rock to the head.

George threw stones and sticks to protect Frothgarde. Annie helped George move about as necessary to avoid capture yet still inflict the greatest possible injury to the hunters.

Excretions of blood, mucus, and slime covered the Dragon's hide and his strength was waning. Nevertheless, he continued charging the foe. More than a dozen were dead and many were injured, but Gideon drove them to continue their assault. "The Dragon will falter. Look at his injuries. See him stumble."

Gideon dashed toward Frothgarde and threw a knife. "Fight on, my friends. The destruction of this beast . . . will be the greatest accomplishment . . . of any man in the Land – greater than the deeds of Jack LaRoche."

Frothgarde looked at George. *Run from here, George. I do not know how much longer I can continue.*

George stopped in his place. He had thought Frothgarde would prevail despite his injuries. It had not occurred to him that the Dragon might fail. *We can't leave you here alone.*

You must go. There is much risk here. You are no knight. You're outnumbered in this fight. We'll run, if you'll follow.

The Dragon fought as he projected his thoughts to George, *After I have taught these bothersome humans that they cannot attack my friends, I will follow. You must go now if I am to do this, for I may not succeed if the battle wages much longer.*

All right. We'll go. But we'll come back if you don't follow shortly. George turned from his friend. "Annie, let's go.

Frothgarde will hold them off 'til we're free."

They moved toward the edge of the clearing but were confronted by Gideon and two other villagers.

"Where are you going, George Severe?" Gideon asked. "It would be rude of you to leave our party so soon."

Annie stood between George and Gideon. "Party this, you snake-in-the-grass." She kicked Gideon's groin full force. Gideon crumbled breathless to the ground.

The others moved to each side of George. He did not wait for them to reach him before he struck the closer, nearly knocking him down. The other grabbed George's arm and arrested his escape. Annie jumped on the villager's back but was soon torn away by the man George had hit.

George wrestled with his opponent and avoided several of his blows while missing with many of his own. He thought his skill at fighting pitifully lacking. Nevertheless, he did all he could to fight the hunters.

Frothgarde puffed smoke and his charges grew more reckless. George, too, was more desperate in his efforts to escape. His recklessness contributed to his early success in keeping his attackers at bay.

Annie fought to free herself from one of the villagers.

Gideon recovered from Annie's earlier kick. He drew a curved knife from his belt and lunged toward George. The blade missed, but Gideon managed to wrestle George to the ground. The two men rolled, kicking and punching each other. Gideon finally plunged the weapon into George's side and George shrieked.

Frothgarde roared and flames exploded into the air — painful flames, deadly to anyone in their path. The Dragon lowered his head and spread the flames about the clearing, incinerating several of the hunters.

Gideon dropped his weapon and fled into the forest with the last of his mob. Frothgarde charged those who ran and roasted some. A few escaped with minor burns. Others ran into the forest with their clothes burning on their backs. Frothgarde chased them into the forest, blowing more fire after them.

George heard the sounds of the battle move away. He felt pain at his side and examined the wound. It was a sizable cut. He looked into the forest. *Frothgarde! Come back! You scared the hell out of them.*

Twenty-one
Dragon's Boon

"THAT'S A PRETTY nasty cut ya got there, Sonny. Better let me dress it with somethin' afore ya bleed ta death."

"I'll be all right," George said. "It hurts like hell, but I'll be fine. Where's Frothgarde?"

Annie tore some material from her shirt and folded it to form a pad, which she placed over his wound. "Hold that while I get somethin' ta tie it off. I don't know where that thing went and I don't much care. Not that I ain't grateful for his help, mind ya."

Frothgarde returned to the clearing. *Ohh! Ohh, George. I fear I have hurt myself. Ohh, I have never felt such pain before.*

Across the clearing, George saw the Dragon struggling to breathe while blood of various colors dribbled from his mouth.

"Frothgarde!" George tried standing.

"Easy does it, Sonny."

"Annie, help me up."

Annie supported George as he stood. "Frothgarde, what's the matter?"

I told you once before that I could no longer breathe flame. I should not have tried.

George asked, "Can we help you?"

The weary Dragon moved closer to George and Annie. A dozen weapons protruded from his hide. Large gashes penetrated the scales. Blood and mucus streamed from the wounds. Steady streams of fluids flowed from his mouth.

"He's really hurt, Annie."

"I can see that, Sonny. Worse than anythin' *I've* ever had ta deal with."

Frothgarde stopped walking near the center of the clearing. George walked over to him, holding his wounded side. Then, forgetting his own wound entirely, he rushed to the Dragon's side just as Frothgarde tottered and collapsed on his belly.

"Annie, help me pull out these spears and knives." They removed the remaining weapons. The Dragon winced as each weapon was withdrawn. "Maybe we can make some kind of poultice of dirt and water. That should stop the bleeding and help him heal."

"Looks like our time would be best spent doin' the same for you."

George did not listen. "There's no water for a mud pack,

so just press some of the earth onto his wounds."

Annie dug her hands into the ground but pulled away suddenly. George saw her hesitation. "Come on, Annie. He saved our lives."

"Tarnation," she said as she clenched her teeth and dug into the dirt.

Your effort is appreciated, George. But I fear you cannot save me.

"If we can only stop the bleeding."

You do not understand, my friend. I have done myself irreparable harm. It was the fire. . . . I never should have called the fire.

"What do you mean? What's wrong?" George was confused and unwilling to hear anything that cast doubt upon the Dragon's recovery.

It has been so long. Frothgarde lowered his head to the ground. Along with the wind he expelled came a sudden flow of blood. He spat the flow from his mouth and continued his thought, *So long since I have called the fire – centuries. My resistance to the flame left me long ago. I was quite surprised when the fire came. I did not think it possible.*

"Frothgarde, don't." George was frightened. The Dragon must live. "Hold on, Frothgarde. Annie, help me!"

There is no help for me now.

George's eyes were moist with tears. "Don't say that! You've got to hold on! I'll call to the Ferryman. There must be a doctor at Wind Castle."

No surgeon can help me. The Land heals, if healing is

possible.

"It *must* be possible."

"He's right, Sonny. There's nothin' we can do."

George was so preoccupied that he did not realize Annie heard Frothgarde's thoughts. "No. If you won't help me, then get out of the way." George pushed Annie aside. He reached down to the ground and gathered some earth to spread over the dying beast. "Feel it? Can you feel the energy? Move your feet into the soil. The healing powers will come."

Frothgarde closed his eyes. *I am tired, George. I must sleep.*

"No! Don't sleep. Don't give up." George cried and grew angry at the thought that the Dragon was surrendering. He shook the beast's head saying, "Don't give up, damn it. Hold on."

I have not lost yet. Some rest may strengthen me.

"Maybe you're right. Maybe you need some rest." He paused for a moment while he thought about the situation. "Yes, you rest and I'll treat your wounds. But I'll wake you if you seem troubled."

Yes, my friend. That would be very helpful. Frothgarde closed his eyes again.

George forgot having pushed Annie away. "Annie, get some dirt and press it on his wounds." Annie and George moved as much of the earth as possible to the Dragon's sides. Frothgarde's breathing was less labored and the flow of blood from his mouth subsided. "Oh, please save him." George continued checking the wounds and packing earth at the beast's sides.

He did all he could and Annie did whatever George asked. He sat before the Dragon's face and watched over him while he slept. Evening approached. The Dragon grew uncomfortable and blood and pus flowed out of his mouth. George called to him, "Frothgarde! Wake up! You're bleeding again."

Frothgarde opened his eyes. *You are still here. It is good to be with a friend when dying.*

George's vision clouded. "You're not dying. Hold on."

The Fates cannot be cheated. My time is about to end. He rolled to one side and cried out in pain, spitting more blood. His breathing was heavy and erratic. *You are a good friend to remain with me while I die.*

"Frothgarde!"

The Dragon interrupted him, *Be silent, please. There is something I must ask of you.*

George sat before the Dragon's face, resigned to the fact that nothing could save his friend. He reached to Frothgarde and touched his face to comfort the Dragon – and himself.

The beast sighed at the touch. *I am the last Dragon in this Land. You have the ability to preserve my race, George.*

"How?"

Do not speak. The sound hurts my head.

Annie stood beside George, insulated from the Land by her boots. "How what, Sonny?"

George shook his head. "Shh."

You have learned well the ways of passing your thoughts.

George nodded his compliance and the Dragon continued. *There is magic in the dying breath of a Dragon and it is my greatest wish that our race continue. You are my friend. Since I am about to die, I ask a boon of you.*

Ask it! George thought.

After my last breath has passed from me, you must take my teeth from my mouth. George squirmed at his request. Frothgarde explained, *By doing so, you can sustain the existence of Dragons in this Land. It will not be difficult. Most of my teeth are already loose. They will practically fall out after I die.*

After you have taken my teeth, wash them in a moving stream before the blood has dried. Then, you must sow some of them in the ground near some plants. Keep some of the teeth for sowing in another age or another land. But always keep one for yourself. A Dragon's tooth given in this way will always protect the receiver and any he chooses from harm by Dragons.

The teeth will remain in the ground until conditions are good for their growth and they become young Dragons. They will first find nourishment in the roots of the nearby plants, and then they will burrow out of the ground. Their natural instinct to eat will succumb to the forces of this Land and they will die if they leave it. They must be taught to continue eating. Then they will be able to visit your land and sustain themselves while there.

The Dragon sighed again and struggled with the pain that followed. Then he told George all he could expect to see while watching young Dragons grow and mature, including many secrets about Dragons.

George watched as his friend forcibly drew air into his exhausted body and exhaled putrid puffs of steam and smoke – the odor was one of burned and decaying flesh.

I'll do everything you asked, George thought. All was finished but the waiting and Frothgarde's last breath. George held his hand on the Dragon's nose in an effort to comfort him. A silent force passed between them.

"We ought ta be goin', Sonny"

"Not now," George said.

"There's nothin' we can do and that snake-in-the-grass could come back."

"He's a friend, and I'll stay with him as long as it takes."

"Ya shouldn't put yerself through this."

Frothgarde struggled and George grew anxious whenever his friend whimpered in pain. The Dragon strained to breathe and he raised his head. Each time his large head bowed, fluids gurgled out of his mouth. Finally, he stretched his head and neck up high. He sucked in the air and held onto it briefly before his head crashed to the ground. His last breath spilled over George and the earth with a final flow of blood and internal parts.

Frothgarde was dead. George sat in a pool of his friend's blood and cried out, "Noooo! Frothgarde. No!" Then he lowered his head. The Dragon's head had rolled to one side. His lips were parted and his tongue hung out between his teeth. His eyes were open and empty.

George could not overcome the ache in his heart. He could not move.

"Sonny, it's over."

George looked at Annie. All was quiet on the hilltop. *Before they dry.* The Dragon's spirit called to remind him. That was all he needed to move him to the distasteful task of removing the teeth from the mouth of his dead friend. George cringed as he peeled the loosest from the Dragon's gums. Some teeth were as large as his hand and many, as small as his fingertips.

"What in tarnation are ya doin' now?"

"What he asked me. I'm saving his teeth."

George removed his shirt and used it to contain the teeth. He used a rock and a stick, closing his eyes as he struck, to free the more stubborn teeth. When the gruesome task was done, he walked to the edge of the clearing, looked at the Dragon in the dark shadows one last time, then descended the hill in search of a stream. Annie followed.

The blood dripping from his shirt was beginning to congeal when he found a small brook. He followed the brook as it grew stronger and passed over a ledge. After surveying the ledge, he found a path, which took him to the base of the waterfall where a slow-moving pool invited him to a cleansing bath and shower. George waded into the pool, carrying the shirt filled with teeth. He walked under the splashing waters and the blood quickly washed from his body and clothes. The blood drifting downstream gradually thinned.

When the teeth were thoroughly washed, he waded out of

the pool. The first step out of the water and onto the earth sent warmth and energy up his legs. Then, placing the shirt with its magical seeds on a rock, he twisted his feet deeply into the soil and reclined. "Annie, will you watch the teeth for a while? I just want to rest for a few minutes."

"Sure, Sonny."

Sleep came quickly and soundly. George rested in absolute darkness, conscious of every living thing around him but unable to dream. He heard the flow of sap in the trees and the pumping hearts of animals nearby. He was an integral part of the Land. There was comfort . . . and hope. The pain from his wound left him, as did the overwhelming sense of loss that followed Frothgarde's death.

George felt something poking where his wound had been. He opened his eyes. "Annie? What are you doing?"

"Nothin'. Jes wakin' ya up is all. It's daylight an' we better get goin' in case yer buddies is still out there."

George sat up, saw the shirt that contained the Dragon's teeth, and was again touched by sadness – a peaceful sadness with a sense of a new beginning. He stood and stretched in the warm breeze. Then he lifted the shirt from the rock and climbed the hillside toward the place where Frothgarde was lost.

"Where ya goin'? This way!"

"I have to go back. There's something I have to do."

Annie followed him up the hill. "Tarnation, Sonny. Ya jes don't quit."

The clearing atop the hill offered no evidence of the earlier battle except the presence of several piles of white dust. One very large pile, George knew to be the remains of his friend. Gone were the festered wounds, the pain in his friend's eyes, the disheartening flow of fluid from his mouth. All that remained was the pure, white powder. Death was taken by the Land – removed from view and transformed to something less ominous, something ethereal that could float on a warm breeze and be carried away.

George didn't cry. It was not that he *could* not, but he felt no need for it. "He was a good friend, Annie."

"I know, Sonny. And so are you."

George looked at Annie. He knelt next to the large pile of powder and moved his fingers through the dust that was once Frothgarde. A sense of hope prevailed over all thoughts of loss. He leaned back on his legs, holding the sack of teeth in his lap. Then he looked around the clearing for a place suitable for new life.

A bed of mixed flowers and saplings flourished near the edge of the clearing. The brightness of the cloud above splashed over the bed, adding warmth to the location. What better place – near their sire and plenty of sweet roots to eat. George stood and walked to the flowerbed. He knelt by its edge and forced his finger into the soil. Then he opened the shirt and placed a tooth in the dirt. He did the same in five other places. He covered the finger holes and the task was completed. The other teeth would wait for another time and place.

George rose from the ground and looked again upon the remains of his friend before turning and walking into the forest and down the hillside. Annie followed silently.

TWENTY-TWO

Insurrection

SIXTEEN OF THE original thirty-four hunters gathered at the foot of the hill below the battle site. All agreed they should get as far away from the Dragon as possible but their flight was slowed by the need to assist the injured. Two died by morning when the survivors continued their retreat from the hills.

Gideon mumbled as they walked, "George Severe brings trouble wherever he goes. To have a Dragon come to his aid is unseemly for a stranger to the Land. Someone else is helping him – the Ferryman."

The other survivors followed without comment. Gideon stopped and turned to his friends. "They will not escape punishment." He pulled the Unicorn's horn from his belt and stroked it. "We will carry our raids to the gates of Wind Castle to avenge our friends. We will move with greater numbers. We will study the castle as Jack LaRoche taught us. Then we will crush them." Gideon smiled. He stroked the horn again and slipped it back under his belt.

When they broke out of the trees at the foothills, the Unicorns were waiting. Gideon stopped. Never before had they approached so near a group of people. "There are the beasts that warned George Severe of our approach."

Lucius said, "Fewer than us took the horn from one of their kind. They cannot harm us."

Gideon stooped to the ground and gathered some stones. "And they will not haunt us as they did Telemachus." He stood and charged them, throwing the stones as he ran.

The Unicorns instinctively fled beyond Gideon's throwing range then turned to watch the hunters. They followed Gideon's flight across the Opens. Gideon cursed, "They will not haunt me."

One of Gideon's friends said, "We are with you, Gideon."

Lucius said, "Do not fear. They will not come near you while we are by your side."

"I do not fear them," he snapped. "I fear nothing. They are annoying pests but they will not keep m— *us* from the greatness we will achieve when we have taken Wind Castle."

Two more hunters died during the trek across the Opens. The Unicorns were out of sight when the hunters approached the troubled village. Gideon stopped at the outskirts of the village and looked back over the Opens. "At last, they have gone . . . or do they wait behind the trees and bushes of the garden?"

He turned and led his battle-worn followers down the main way. The people watched as the hunters trudged past them. Some of the villagers counted – six, ten, eleven, twelve. Only twelve came back.

"Where are the others?" some cried, when they discovered that their husbands or sons or brothers were not among those who returned.

"Where is Nevin?"

"Jacob! Jacob!"

Gideon led the hunters inside the Meeting Place where they sat around three tables. The scrawny keeper and his patrons were gathered around a table at the opposite side of the room, actively engaged in conversation and speculation about something that rested on the table. Gideon scowled at the keeper. "Bring us wine and food."

The keeper left the attraction, looking back as he walked over to Gideon's table. He saw the scowl on Gideon's face and quickly prepared mugs of wine and delivered them with fruits and grains. Then he stood beside Gideon, awaiting further instructions.

The crowd at the distant table laughed and patted each other's backs. Gideon snapped, "Are you not able to control your patrons?"

The keeper immediately left his side and addressed the men at the other table. Gideon noticed some of them looking toward his table scornfully. He returned an angry stare and they turned away.

The keeper did not return to Gideon's table, but remained with the others. Gideon called to the man, but he did not answer. The conversations continued with renewed vigor and Gideon's anger boiled. He stood and walked over to the table and asked loudly over the conversation, "What is of such interest here that you cannot offer peace to those who have fought for this village?"

Everyone at the table was silent until a bold member of their number looked up to Gideon and answered, "We mean no disrespect, Gideon. We are simply amazed at the wonder of this plant which we have nurtured from a seed." He pointed to a potted plant at the center of the table and continued, "See for yourself! Where the Land has failed us, we have learned how to make things grow."

"It is a trivial matter," Gideon snapped.

Another answered, "But no! It is *not* a trivial matter! It is a great discovery!"

Gideon reached past the men who stood around the table and cast the plant off the table. The plant and its pot shattered against the nearby wall and crumbled to the floor as Gideon raged, "It *is* a trivial matter. Twenty-two of your friends are lost to the Land – beaten by George Severe, and his Dragon. *That* is of much greater concern than this worthless plant. They were your friends . . . and I saw them die at the hands of the beast – roasted by its fire, crushed under its feet, and snapped in two by its jaws. You should be more concerned with avenging their deaths."

Gideon turned and walked back to his table saying as he

turned, "Keeper, bring more wine to the brave hunters who fought so honorably." The men at the table remained speechless as the leader walked away.

The keeper immediately followed. After all were served again, he asked, "Can I be of further service?"

"Yes," Gideon mumbled. "Tell the villagers to assemble outside. I will speak to them after we have rested."

"Of course, Gideon. As you wish."

The keeper went to the opposite table. One of the patrons was picking up the pieces of the broken plant. The keeper said, "You had better leave it where it fell." The man accepted his advice. All except the keeper and the hunters left the room to call the villagers together. Outside, many had already assembled. Some were weeping, believing their loved-ones lost. Confirmation quickly passed from those who had been inside the Meeting Place and the weeping intensified. Word also spread of Gideon's maniacal assault on the potted plant.

Gideon walked through the doors of the Meeting Place followed by the other hunters. A hush rolled over the crowd as words announcing his presence passed from front to back. After the leader surveyed all who had gathered, he began, "I bear sorrowful news." Sighs passed through the crowd. "The brave men who stand behind me are all who remain of those who left to capture the villainous stranger, George Severe."

More cries followed as the leader spoke the news many had already guessed. Comfort was offered among themselves and the cries slowly subsided.

Gideon told them all that had happened. He mentioned

brave deeds of each of the deceased and told the crowd he witnessed each death, describing them with horror. "I promise you, the deaths of our friends and relatives will not go unavenged. Meet here in three days time and I will offer a plan to destroy George Severe and his Dragon."

George and Annie stood atop a hill overlooking the valley where the people of Wind Castle anxiously awaited his return. The dense clouds enveloped much of the castle, but its shadow made its presence known. George's spirit lifted immediately. He looked back toward the heights where he left the remains of his friend and protector. The dreaded battle flashed in his mind. Then he smiled.

"What are *you* grinnin' at?" Annie said.

He laughed aloud. "Remember when Frothgarde jumped out of the brush? What a sight."

"I'll say. Good thing he was on *our* side."

George's amusement waned as the details of the battle haunted his memory. "He was a good friend. I wish we could have helped him."

"He was beyond our help, Sonny."

George looked at Annie. "That's what *he* said . . . and you *heard* him!"

"What are ya talkin' about?"

"You heard him tell me there was nothing we could do."

"So?"

"Frothgarde couldn't talk. He could only pass his thoughts — and you heard them."

304 | WIND CASTLE

"Nonsense. That ain't natural."

"You say that about a lot of things up here. You heard him, Annie. You can't deny it. It was when you were pushing the dirt over his wounds."

"Who cares?"

"It's the Land. If you touch the Land, it's like closing a circuit. You should take off your shoes. You might find things go a lot easier."

"Ain't no way I'm gonna do that. This dirt ain't natural."

"Suit yourself." George hefted the sack, which he held by his side. He remembered Frothgarde's promise and imagined baby Dragons burrowing out of the soil. He looked back again, gazing through the clouds to his memories of Frothgarde.

"Let's go, Sonny."

George smiled and turned to slowly descend the hill that led into the valley and to Wind Castle. As they walked, Annie asked, "What do you feel when you walk on the ground like that?"

"It's a good feeling . . . warm, invigorating – like an electrical tickle."

"That ain't what I feel, Sonny. Whenever I touch that dirt, I feel like it's suckin' me down. Ain't no way I'm takin' these shoes off."

For many of the villagers, the plant Gideon destroyed was a symbol of hope – the first step on the road toward agricultural recovery. The gardens no longer supported the village and so, the raids on nearby villages had become necessary for survival. The growing opposition to Gideon, however, was not yet strong enough to challenge him.

Gideon stood before the villagers, three days after his return. His supporters had stirred the others before the meeting. They had asserted to the crowd that the massacre of twenty-two of their number must not go unpunished.

Gideon's expression was stoic as he climbed the steps of the Meeting Place. He looked over the crowd – motionless, setting a dramatic mood like a traveling preacher preparing to proclaim the blessings and damnations of Almighty God. When all were quiet, he raised his head. Slowly, purposefully, he cast cold eyes upon the crowd.

He started quietly. The people strained to hear him. "My friends. It pleases me that you have come to hear my words." He raised his voice slightly. "A ruthless enemy has taken the lives of many of your neighbors and families." Then quietly again, "If it would have been possible, I would have offered my life for theirs. But it was *not* possible. The destruction inflicted by the Dragon was so complete and so fast that I could do nothing but fight by their sides and hope our combined strength could subdue the beast."

Gideon raised his voice and pointed his hand to the crowd. "Know this, and know it well. That beast *can* be defeated. Do not believe that we have learned nothing from that terrible battle." His voice settled again. "But know, too, that only a fool would seek another confrontation with the beast intentionally. It is important that we know how to fight it and how to destroy it if we are given no alternative to fighting. With an adequate

306 | WIND CASTLE

force, we can destroy it.

"But the Dragon is not an intelligent beast. It is merely a tool of George Severe and the Ferryman. Destroy them and we will never have to fight the Dragon.

"You may ask, 'Why should we pursue this matter? Why not remain in our village? The Dragon will not attack us here!' I say it will. If I thought we could find peace by hiding, I would recommend it to you now. But think about this. Why did George Severe return to our village after he had been exiled? Why did the Dragon rend and incinerate so many of our friends? The beast was fast and strong. If it was the will of its master, it could have taken George Severe upon its back and fled from us. But that was *not* his wish. George Severe wanted to destroy us. That is why he returned to our village. And that is why he commanded the Dragon to use its fire against us.

"George Severe wants to destroy us because we did not want him in our village. And he will not be satisfied with the twenty-two he has already taken from us. I tell you this – George Severe is conspiring with the Ferryman to attack our village. And you can be sure the Dragon will be with them when they come. It may well be that there are other Dragons in their service, too!

"My friends, it is clear. We have no choice. We must learn to fight the Dragon so we can defend ourselves. But, most important, we must go to Wind Castle to stop the Ferryman and George Severe before they put an end to us all. We must capture them and then, for the sake of all those who have already been lost, we must kill them."

Many in the crowd shouted their agreement. Gideon raised his arms to quiet them before resuming. As the voices faded and all were quiet again, Gideon did not speak. His eyes were closed and all were still. With his arms still raised and his head low, he opened his eyes and looked about the throng of people. His arms slowly settled to his sides and he continued looking out over the crowd. Again, he began quietly and built up to a demanding challenge – naming each of the twenty-two lost villagers, crediting them with great acts of heroism. "I ask you, should our heroic friends and neighbors be forgotten?"

"No!" the people cried. "No!"

"No! No! No!" he repeated. "They should not be forgotten. Not the twenty-two. Not twelve. Not ten. Not six, or three, or two. Not even *one* should be forgotten." The crowd cheered. He continued, "And they shall NOT – if you will stand with me to avenge their deaths and protect the future of our village."

A voice called out, "What must we do, Gideon?"

"Yes. Tell us," said another.

The crowd cheered their support. Gideon paced before them as he spoke. His movement made the people more anxious, more angry. They were ready. But he pressed them further, arguing about the injustices of the Ferryman and the threats that he and George presented to them.

The voices called again.

"Kill the stranger."

"Kill the Ferryman."

"Kill the Dragon."

Gideon raised his arms until they stopped. "The Dragon

will not go to Wind Castle. It will stay in the forests of the hills." He continued pacing, though more slowly than before. "We know where it lives now, and we can avoid it when we travel to Wind Castle.

"We will go to Wind Castle and study it for a time. We will hide ourselves and watch the people as they leave the village to work in the fields, or mines, or forests. Then we will let our presence be known. They will wonder why we are there. Perhaps they will become fearful.

"We will harass small parties as they go to their work places. We will take their produce or undo what they accomplish each day. They will huddle in their village. We will enter it at night and raid their homes and take some Spoils. The people will go to the Ferryman to demand protection. But he cannot protect them because he does not know the secrets Jack LaRoche taught us. They will learn nothing from the stranger, George Severe. If he knew such secrets, he would not have been caught in our village.

"We will force our way inside the castle walls. Closer and closer we will come to the Ferryman and his followers and, eventually, . . . we will TAKE them." Gideon reached out as he said the last words and strangled the air. He twisted his fist adding, "And we will punish them." He smiled madly as the people raised clenched fists and cheered.

"Then," he quietly added after the cheers subsided, "we will take Wind Castle. We will take its treasures and learn its secrets and we will rule all the Land.

"Our lost friends will be avenged and our dreams for the

future will be fulfilled if you will march with me across the Opens and hills to Wind Castle." He raised the Unicorn's horn and shouted, "Who will follow me?"

The response was overwhelming. Gideon raised his arms to quiet the din. "I will choose one hundred to follow me, including ten or fifteen Spoils to serve the hunters. We will take more Spoils to help us from the villages we pass. We will leave next light." He stepped down from the platform at the Meeting Place and walked through the crowd toward the main way. Two of the men who were with him during the battle with the Dragon initiated a series of cheers as he passed. He kept his head straight as he walked toward his hut.

As one hundred men and women filed out of the village, two Unicorns watched from a distance, though not so distant that Gideon could not see them – and that they were following him.

TWENTY-THREE

Land Watch

GEORGE SET HIS sack on the table in his room while Annie and Alden sat beside him. "What do you have wrapped in your shirt?" the Ferryman asked.

George looked woefully at his shirt. "The Dragon's teeth."

"How did they come to you?"

"After he died . . . at his request."

"I sensed a great loss a short time ago, after your call for help. Around that time, I was sure I felt your presence, too, Annie. Did you remove your shoes?"

"I ain't never takin' these off hereabouts."

"The choice is yours," he said. The Ferryman looked warmly at George. "Tell me how the Dragon was lost to the Land."

George briefly told the leader everything he remembered

about the battle and the Dragon's last wishes. "This contains all the teeth except the six I planted."

The Ferryman said, "You were wise to limit your planting."

George nodded.

Alden asked, "Are you too tired to tell me about the troubled village?"

"It's changed since we left it . . ."

When George finished his story, the Ferryman said, "Rest now. I will tell the people what you have said."

Annie stood with Alden. "I'll be back after I get some shut-eye."

George stared at the entry for a time after they departed. He drank from his mug, set the mug on the table, and placed his hand on the sack of Dragon's teeth. He looked around the room and found two clay pitchers. He opened his shirt and poured the teeth carefully into the two containers. After placing his shirt over his back, he reached into the last pitcher and withdrew a handful of the smallest teeth, which he placed in his pocket.

The room was quiet and warm. Light passed through the covered window. George walked over to the stone bed. He rolled onto the bed and closed his eyes. The Torch Stone nearby dimmed.

As he walked down the stairs and across the courtyard to the hall, George noticed that some of the people followed him. He found a table and sat. The tabletop illuminated – its light glowing on the faces of those who surrounded the table.

He looked up at them curiously, wondering what they wanted. A Sasquatch, standing behind the first row of faces, spoke first. "What should be done are you thinking, George Severe? Of the people from the troubled village should we be fearful?"

"Why ask me?"

"Because you have been there!" another villager standing beside him answered. "You have seen what has happened and you probably know better than anyone what they intend."

"I don't know what their intentions are. But I do know that they don't listen to anything *I* have to say."

Yet another said, "*We* would listen. Tell us what should be done."

"I don't know what should be done. Ask Alden. He's your leader!"

"But, he offers no suggestions!"

"You're barking up the wrong tree," George answered. All the faces went blank. "I don't know your Land. I can't say what should be done." He wanted to add more – that, if he were in *his* land, Gideon would never get away with his actions. Someone would stand against him. But he did not say it out of consideration for Alden.

"But *somebody* has to tell us what to do! We do not know how to stop such things."

"Well, I'm not the one to say. Ask the Ferryman again. Please leave me alone."

Their faces crinkled with furrowed brows and downturned mouths, but they complied with his wishes and departed. He sat alone, watching the crowd disperse. Shortly, his attention was drawn to a mug of wine being placed on the table before him. The hand holding the mug belonged to Tamara and he smiled when he saw her face. He stood immediately and held her shoulders. "Tamara! It's good to see you again. I'm so glad you got out of there. How was your trip? Did you find Cloud Walker on the way, or did you meet him when you got back?"

The woman smiled. "Wait! I am forgetting your questions before I can answer them. I am pleased to see you. We were so worried that you would not come."

"Please sit down and tell me everything."

They had just taken their seats when Annie arrived, "Fancy meetin' you two here."

"Annie! Sit! You feeling better?"

"Amazin' what a bit o' rest will do for ya, Sonny."

"You are not such a good runner, George," Cloud Walker teased, "if you could not keep up with an aging Indian."

George turned to the approaching voice.

Annie answered, "Sit down, Old Man."

George shook his friend's hand. "I just ran the wrong way, that's all. It happens to the best of us." The two exchanged smiles. George and Cloud Walker sat at the table. "It's really great to see you two again."

Cloud Walker told him what had transpired since he left the troubled village. "So, here we are," Cloud Walker finished. "We are all safe again and ready to go on to other things."

George asked, "What other things?"

"Whatever we were doing before we went scouting, I guess!"

"I'm not so sure. I have a feeling Gideon isn't through with us yet. He's not one to give up – if he's still alive."

As George finished his sentence, a Faun approached the table and said, "If you will pardon my interruption, I am called Julian."

Annie looked at Julian from his cloven hooves to his horned head and rolled her eyes at George. George said, "Hello Julian."

"The Ferryman has asked me to escort you to his room. It is my good fortune to find you all together. Would you follow me?" Julian led them to the Ferryman's apartment where he excused himself and left them in the room.

Annie leaned toward George. "Don't they ever stop comin' up with weird critters in this place?"

The leader entered the room appearing weary and distraught. His greeting was solemn and he sat before speaking further. He drew from a mug of water and took a handful of grain. "I have spoken with the Ancient Counselor." He looked at each of the four and continued, "The people are concerned about the troubled village. Simon and I agree there is great risk to the Land in using the methods of those at the troubled village and fighting them. I do not know what to do." The Ferryman looked at George. "Jack LaRoche has brought a plague to our Land. I felt it when he first arrived. The Ancient Counselor felt it too . . . though more strongly."

"I know the plague he carried," Cloud Walker interrupted.

"The history of our land below is tainted by such people."

Annie said, "And Gideon's molded o' the same clay. He's a snake – the worst kind ta have power."

Cloud Walker continued, "Most wars in our land develop because of men just like Jack LaRoche and Gideon. They thrive on the excitement of battle, or lust for power. They must be burned out and destroyed."

"It is not the way of our Land to do such things." The Ferryman sat up straight.

George said, "It might not have been that way before, but it is now . . . at least at the troubled village. And it might have to be that way here, too, if you don't want the Land ruled by the likes of Gideon."

The Ferryman answered, "This Land is more than people. We have many different races and species. The Land has always given us what we needed and we never *wanted* more. Perhaps the Land itself has a way of suppressing such desires."

"Well, them desires is alive and well in Gideon's village," Annie added. "And they ain't gonna go away."

"Nevertheless," the Ferryman answered. "I am not prepared to use force – not yet."

"Do you have any ideas?" George asked.

"That is why I asked you to talk with me." He looked toward Tamara and said, "You have been silent, Tamara. You served Gideon and you saw what happened in the village when Jack LaRoche and Telemachus were there. Do you have any suggestions?"

"I do not know how to stop Gideon and those who follow

him. But I do know he will grow stronger. I have heard of Spoils who joined those villagers in raids and then continued because they enjoyed it."

"The ways of Jack LaRoche must not spread further. But, how can I stop it without jeopardizing the natural balance of the Land?"

George answered, "I'm not sure either, but you have to do *something*! If you don't, Gideon will walk all over you and turn Wind Castle into another troubled village. You know the people of Wind Castle are getting restless. They will follow you wherever you lead them, but they need to see where they are going."

"I have never seen the Land threatened in this way before. Any decision I make could have irreversible consequences," the Ferryman said.

"I don't envy you your decision," George responded.

"Well," Cloud Walker interrupted, "*I* won't stand by and let these coyotes walk all over us. If they come, I will fight them."

"Please hold, Cloud Walker, until there is no other way," the leader pleaded.

"As you wish, but the time may come when we must defend ourselves. It is better to *risk* the Land in defense of it than to give it up to ruin."

The Ferryman smiled and placed his hand on Cloud Walker's shoulder. Then he looked at Tamara, George, and Annie. "Your counsel is good. It is clear that I must do something, but I am still lost."

"I have a suggestion," George said.

"Please tell it!" the Ferryman said. Tamara and Cloud Walker leaned closer to the table.

"The people need to see that you are not just sitting around waiting for something to happen. If they have a role in the protection of the castle and the village, they'll feel less helpless. Maybe you need to send out a few scouting parties to watch for signs of advancement from the troubled village. Send some people out for a few days and send others when they return." George grew excited by his plan. "And you can have some people in positions not so far away, who could stand watch in shifts. That way, everybody gets to do something and they're not sitting around, letting their imaginations run wild."

"What do the watchers do if they see someone coming toward the castle?" the Ferryman asked.

"It depends on whether you decide to fight or step aside. But that doesn't matter right now. The important thing is that you get started. Show everyone that you're in charge. They'll assume you have further plans."

"Some of your terms are unusual to me, but I think I understand." A grateful smile came to the Ferryman's face and he looked at the others. "What do you think of that?"

"He's right," Cloud Walker said.

"It is a good beginning," Tamara added.

"It's the *least* ya should do," Annie nodded.

"I agree. I will let our plans be known to the Ancient Counselor. I will talk to the people next light. But now, it is very late and I am weary."

The four guests rose and bade the leader a good rest as

they walked out of his apartment. Cloud Walker and Tamara returned to their quarters, but George and Annie went to the hall to drink mead and eat fruit.

They sat at a table and talked about their meeting with the Ferryman until Annie said, "One o' them overgrowed chimps is comin' up b'hind ya." He turned and saw a wall of fur.

"Mlet I am called. Some words can we share?"

"Join us." George offered a seat opposite Annie.

"On quite an adventure you have been," the Sasquatch said as he sat.

"An adventure I could have done without," George answered.

"Away from Wind Castle I too have been. To learn whether any of my kind have been threatened was my wish."

"What did you find out?"

"Threatened no Sasquatch has been. But attack them in time the troubled village will. During my journey, some who claim to be your friends I met – Mrudg and Tmron and their families."

"Yes, they're friends. How are they?"

"When I left them well they were."

"How's Fleng, Tmron's daughter?"

"Well, she is."

"That's good. She had quite a way with Unicorns." The thought drew George away from the conversation to a vision of the young Sasquatch sitting in a clearing stroking a Unicorn colt.

Mlet brought him back to their discussion. "Coming here

to Wind Castle they were. Of your visit to the troubled village I told them. Concerned Tmron was. To the troubled village he went, your safety to assure. To the camp he will return. Watch the troubled village he will. If quiet all remains, here they will come."

"It'll be nice to see him again," George said. The mead made him feel drowsy. He rubbed his eyes and added, "It's strange that he should be doing this. The Ferryman is about to suggest the same thing in the morning. Between those sent by the Ferryman and the Sasquatch camp, we should have plenty of warning if Gideon decides to attack Wind Castle." He drew the last of his mead and begged the Sasquatch to excuse him.

Annie quickly followed, leaving Mlet alone at the table. When they left the hall, Annie said, "Whew! That one ain't seen a bath in a month o' Sundays."

The sky was pink with a low morning sun that pierced the thin clouds. The Ferryman walked to a balcony that overlooked the Inner Bailey, already filled with villagers. The surrounding rooftops, porches and parapets were also filled.

The Ferryman said, "My friends! We have heard from George Severe, Annie Strummond, Tamara, and Cloud Walker about the conditions at the troubled village. We have heard from the surveyors, who returned from the land below, about the raids that have taken place. We have heard from those who have escaped capture, of the violence of these raids. We have heard of the evil deeds of this . . . this . . . mercenary, Jack LaRoche, from the land below and how he has poisoned the minds of the leaders of the troubled village.

"I know many would like to fight, but we must consider the consequences. You have heard the words of the four who went there – the plants die, the water does not respond to the calling stones, waste lies upon the Land, and the Land gives no life to any who tread there.

"Such could be the fate of all the Land if we choose to fight. We must try to repel the evils of the troubled village by a method compatible with the ways of the Land. The Land is more powerful than any teachings brought to us from below and, as long as the good hold the helm, the Land will prosper.

"I am calling for volunteers to travel to the Opens between the troubled village and the hills that surround this valley. They will warn us if those from the troubled village approach. They will be relieved after ten days. Others will be asked to walk with workers to the mines and farms to keep watch and report unusual activity outside our valley.

"The villagers who attacked George ran in fright from the Dragon which protected him. They may not know that Frothgarde has gone from the Land and they may change their ways – or at the very least, perhaps they will think wisely before venturing to Wind Castle for fear of confronting the Dragon once again. If they continue their raids, we will take further action."

"What action?" one of the listeners called out.

"We will respond in ways which are in harmony with the Land. We must, or we will risk losing the Land itself."

"But what action *would* be compatible?"

"Yes, how do we know what to do?" another asked.

George pushed past those who blocked the corridors and stairs to stand by the Ferryman and show his support. The leader's response projected from the balcony, "Our plans will be revealed to you as troubles develop." The Ferryman's tone was firm. "Those who are willing to go with the first scouting group, please call out."

George finally reached the Ferryman's side and raised his hand saying, "I'll go!"

The Ferryman looked at George and smiled. Then he turned to the crowd and said, "I would be honored to have George Severe join a group of scouts but not the first, since I need his counsel in the ways of Jack LaRoche. George has already served us well and has earned a rest." Many of the listeners nodded. "Who among you will be the first?"

Several called out their names and many others followed. The Ferryman looked over the crowd. He raised his arms to quiet them. "Mordred and Duncan and Weldon and Tamara, take places in the hall and record those who will scout and those who will escort the farmers and miners. Prepare lists enough for two cycles of the moon." He smiled warmly at them as some turned toward the hall.

He called out to them one more time. "You are the Land Watch and you will quash the evil of the troubled village." He looked at George when he finished. Then he stepped away from the balcony and walked with George to the Heart.

As George and the Ferryman walked through the corridors of the Keep, the chatter of the crowd slowly faded away. Alden said, "Thank you for offering to scout again."

They came to one of the control rooms for the Heart and, once inside, the Ferryman walked to one of the windows and looked deeply into the warm, pulsing pit. George stood by his side and peered into the chamber below. The Ferryman spoke, "Looking into the Heart, it is difficult to see how the Land is distressed. But I can feel it – I can feel its resistance to the troubled village. I cannot bear to think that they would bring their poison to Wind Castle."

"If Gideon does come here, you may have to fight to protect the Heart. I know you're afraid that fighting will bring the same result as giving the Land over to Gideon, but you don't know that for sure. Do you?" The Ferryman shook his head slightly at George's question. George saw the response and continued, "Cloud Walker was right. It is better to take the chance than to let Gideon rule and destroy the Land."

"Perhaps. But I do not want to make that decision unless it is absolutely necessary."

"I don't blame you. Maybe Gideon won't come. Maybe he's had enough, but I have this terrible feeling that he won't be satisfied until he has *everything*."

The two were silent while the Ferryman adjusted some stones on the sills of the windows. "Do you remember when the Ancient Counselor suggested you could be Ferryman one day?"

"I remember."

"Would you like to begin learning?"

George hesitated.

The Ferryman quickly added, "There would be no obligation to you."

"I *am* curious about how things work here."

The Ferryman taught George the reactions of each of the control stones. "I will train many in these tasks before I choose a successor."

"I'm interested in the mechanics of these stones, but not very interested in becoming your next Ferryman. I have a family waiting for me below and I'm not about to forget them."

Twenty-four

Siege

THE SECOND scouting party assembled to discuss their departure planned for next light. A runner from the first party reported that the first party had met a band of Sasquatch who told them a large number of people from the troubled village were marching toward the hills. The Sasquatch and the scouts from the castle were going to take positions in the hills to monitor their progress.

The Ferryman dispatched the second party and asked the riders of the winged horses to carry messages between the scouts and the castle. He agreed to thin the cloud to facilitate their flight in the hills. He then called a meeting of advisors and influential members of the community.

George and Annie sat at a table in a large room with

six respected residents of the village. He knew a few of them by name and most by sight. They all waited anxiously for the Ferryman to arrive. Voices emanating from the corridor drew their attention to the room's entrance. Cloud Walker passed through the doorway, followed by the Ferryman.

Alden began, "Thank you all for coming. The news from the first scouts is distressing." Cloud Walker found a seat opposite George.

"There is great risk to the Land in fighting those from the troubled village, but a time may come when we have no alternative. To save the Land, we may have to accept that risk . . .." The Ferryman spoke at length about the need to use caution when considering their defensive measures. He reminded them of the Land's response to the ways of the troubled village and he painted a picture of Wind Castle without its plentiful farms and Torch Stones and the flow of life energy from the soil.

The assembly discussed all his points. They all understood the Ferryman's concerns, but they also feared the villagers marching toward them. Few at Wind Castle knew anything about fighting, but they wanted to be prepared to meet and stop the raiders. The Ferryman resisted the call for a violent defense.

"We must know where the raiders are at all times. The winged horses and their riders will help us in this matter. Runners will be used when the horses cannot fly.

"We will offer no resistance to the aggressors during their march. If they come to the valley, we will welcome them. Offer our friendship and our help. If they take a crock of fruit, give them two."

Some of those in the room shook their heads. "Please, hear me through!" the Ferryman begged. "If they take a farm, we will give them another. If they take a mine, we will help them work it. If they take a hut, we will leave another and offer it to them. We can help each other as we have in the past. And there will be plenty for all who want."

One stood to object. "We cannot forfeit all we have built."

"We understand your concern for the Land," another said more calmly. "But we must defend ourselves or be slaves to these troublemakers."

The Ferryman stood quietly, listening to each objection. Then, looking toward George, who had been quiet during the meeting, he asked, "And how say you, George? What would be the solution in your land?"

George stiffened as he tried to find words that would support the Ferryman but still convey his belief that Gideon would not be satisfied with tribute from the residents of Wind Castle. "There have been a lot of wars in my land," he said quietly. "Many times there were nations who thought it best to befriend their oppressors. Sometimes it worked, but usually . . . in the long run . . . it didn't."

"Almost always," Cloud Walker added.

The Ferryman looked at all in the room and continued, "I understand that it may be fruitless to welcome these raiders, but we must try. If we fail, then we will take a stronger position. That is why I spoke with Cloud Walker before we came here." George looked at his Indian friend curiously as the Ferryman revealed the subject of that earlier discussion. "Cloud Walker claims no great knowledge of fighting, but he said once before that he would not permit himself to be captured by the raiders without fighting.

"I have asked him to teach our villagers how to defend themselves. I ask you to understand that the things he will teach should never be considered for any reason other than to defend the Land against those who would destroy it. These things must never be used for aggressive purposes against others – or among ourselves."

"We understand."

"Let Cloud Walker teach us."

"Wait!" one in the group quelled the others' enthusiasm. "Ferryman, do you believe we would use these lessons against each other?"

The Ferryman answered, "It is a possibility. A *willingness* to fight usually follows the *ability* to fight. Conflicts among ourselves are likely to develop – the ways of the troubled village can be directed internally as well as to other villages. And when that occurs, the Land can be lost."

Everyone was silent. For the first time, they understood completely the magnitude of the risk they would take in learning to defend themselves. One of them responded with the suggestion, "Perhaps we should reconsider seeking the knowledge Cloud Walker would share."

The Ferryman smiled paternally. "We may not have to worry about it," he answered. "As I said earlier, this should be our last resort. Our first is to offer our friendship. If that is not accepted, we will simply avoid conflict – offer no resistance to their demands. If conditions reach this point, we will begin learning from Cloud Walker. And, if conditions become more serious, we will use what we learn."

Cloud Walker objected, "But we must begin now, if we're to be ready when the raiders get here!"

"*If*, my friend. *If* they come. I do not agree that the teaching must begin immediately. We will have time to learn as things develop."

Gideon and his raiders climbed cautiously through the dense underbrush of the rocky foothills. As the cloud closed over them and the Opens disappeared from view, they watched for signs of the Dragon.

Gideon's scouts returned and told him they were approaching a small village. "A good chance to take more Spoils," he said. "Our older Spoils will fight with us against the Ferryman in return for better treatment. The new Spoils can serve us while the others fight."

Gideon and Lucius peeked over a hill and saw the village. "This will not be difficult," Gideon said. "Assemble for the attack."

Lucius said, "Shouldn't we wait and watch them for a day? It is what Jack LaRoche taught us."

"Do you challenge me, Lucius?"

"No, I was only thinking—"

"I will do all the thinking," Gideon snapped. "We do not

have time to delay. We must get to Wind Castle quickly. Look. They are Fauns, Dwarves, humans, and a few Centaurs. The Centaurs may be difficult, but the rest will be easy. Tell the others to surround the village. Attack at my signal."

When the raiders were in place, Gideon waved his arm. The raiders shrieked a battle cry they had adopted and charged the village. Their victims stood in amazement and did not begin to flee until it was too late for all but the Centaurs.

The raiders swarmed into the village. The residents were knocked down, pushed aside, trampled, beaten, and herded into the center of the village. The raiders went into the huts, chased the frightened occupants outside, and took whatever they chose. Anyone who objected was instantly beaten.

Most Fauns huddled in fear. Some of the Dwarves and humans resisted with clubs and tools. The raiders subdued one of the defenders and beat him senseless and then continued beating him until he was lost to the Land. Resistance continued at various parts of the village until most defenders were subdued in the same way. Several villagers lay lifeless in pools of blood flowing from knife, spear, and ax wounds.

Gideon looked over his new captives and said, "So easy."

His complacency was short-lived, however. His failure to observe the village long enough before attacking was about to lead to disaster. A group of villagers, who had been working nearby, charged down from the ridge. Gideon's face was first white, then deep red when he saw woodsmen and miners penetrate his line of raiders. Many of the raiders were surrounded by villagers they had subdued on one side and the new defenders at their backs.

The defenders were no match for the skilled raiders, but they did cause heavy losses – the raiders suffering one death for every three lives taken. Many of the villagers escaped and fled to the hills.

When the battle was finished, the raiders held only twenty Spoils – many were injured and would be of little service until they recovered. Ten of the raiders had been killed and twelve were injured, Lucius among them. Gideon raged at his followers and the new Spoils. "How could such a small village nearly rout us?"

No one suggested that Gideon made a mistake by ordering the attack without adequately scouting the village. Lucius was too badly beaten to say anything, and the others never questioned him. The long silence brought about a change in Gideon's demeanor. His red face cooled and his angry expressions melted away.

"In the future, we will remember to guard our backs as we attack. Do not let this difficulty discourage you. Surprised as we might have been, we have conquered this village and we can do the same when we meet the Ferryman and George Severe. This difficulty only demonstrates that we cannot be beaten. We will avenge our families and friends whose lives were taken by George Severe and his Dragon. Gather the new Spoils and march with me to Wind Castle."

Gideon's speech was answered with cheers – less enthusiastic than those that followed the rally at their own village before their departure.

The injured and those who were unwilling to keep pace slowed the march. Eventually, the new Spoils learned that their attempts to impede the progress of the raiders would gain them nothing but physical abuse. They gave up their resistance and followed as directed. The injured, however, were not as easily hastened. Lucius and another raider were weakened by their injuries – the other died that night. Lucius recovered some the next day but continued slowing the raiders until Gideon decided to leave him behind. With the promise that he would catch up to them shortly, he ordered the raiders to continue the trek while he remained behind and saw to the comfort of his good friend, Lucius.

"We cannot leave another to serve you," Gideon said. "We need everyone who can fight and one of the new Spoils would only run away and leave you – or worse."

"I understand."

"Meet us at Wind Castle when you are better. If you are found . . ."

"I will say nothing."

Gideon stood and walked behind him. He stopped and looked back at his friend. Lucius lay helpless in the brush. Gideon moved his hand to the knife in his belt. He pulled the knife out and crept close to Lucius. Then, grasping Lucius' hair with one hand, he sliced his throat. After a gurgle and a brief convulsion, Lucius lay still.

Tmron and other Sasquatch scouts approached the plundered village while those who were killed were being lined on a hillside under a large oak tree. Tmron took a human body from six Dwarves and carried it up the last part of the hill. "Attacked, you were?"

One Dwarf answered, "Yes. Humans we do not know attacked us. These were lost to the Land, and they took others away. Half our village is following them."

Tmron rested the body beneath the tree. "A great nymph, this tree is, but on one side sick."

"The sickness points to where the attackers came. We noticed the brown leaves long ago but we did not understand the meaning. Then the leaves fell. Now, we know the tree foretold this attack. Perhaps, now that the attack is over, she will recover."

Tmron shook his head. "Follow Gideon, we must. To Wind Castle he goes, I sense."

"Yes, one of us heard their leader say it while she hid after the attack."

"After all are rested, join us you will?"

"I will gather all who can travel and we will try to catch the others who gave chase."

The Dwarf left the hillside to gather those who would march. Tmron dispatched another Sasquatch to Wind Castle with messages for the Ferryman. Then he looked up at the dying branches along one side of the tree. He bowed his head and held his hand to his brow.

The Ferryman stood and reached up to place his hand on

the shoulder of the Sasquatch messenger. "The raid at the hillside village is distressing, but you have also brought encouraging news. Return to Tmron and ask him to follow the raiders from afar. Ask him to send runners ahead to warn any villages in the raiders' path."

After the messenger left, Annie said, "Ain't a purty picture."

George asked, "Why are you encouraged by any of that?"

The Ferryman answered, "Because we know there are people in the Land who will assist us if called upon and they are led by your friend who is familiar with the ways of the raiders."

"Why were you so quiet after he told you about the tree?"

"It is the Mother Tree." The Ferryman paused and looked at Annie. "She is the oldest and strongest wood nymph in the Land. I felt her weakness, just as I felt the sickness of the troubled village. I do not know if she can recover."

Annie's shoulders shook for a moment under the Ferryman's stare. She looked at George.

George asked, "What happens if she doesn't recover?"

"I only know that she is an important part of the Land – almost as important as the Heart. She gives breath to the Land just as the Heart pumps its energy."

The Ferryman dissipated the cloud and presented the Land with a sun day to facilitate the movement of messengers.

Tmron's observers welcomed the sunlight but were forced to remain more distant from the raiders to avoid detection. As the raiders approached the camp of the castle scouts and the

Sasquatch camp, Tmron sent word for them to seek safety at Wind Castle or return with his messenger to follow the raiders.

The castle scouts sent their messenger to Wind Castle. She left the camp on her winged horse – dangerously near the marching raiders.

Under a clear night sky speckled with millions of bright stars, a miner led a bloodied winged horse into Wind Castle. The small, elf-like rider, pale from loss of blood, clung to the back of her faithful steed.

"The Ferryman," she mumbled in her delirium. "I must see the Ferryman."

A throng of villagers followed them. The Ferryman met the crowd at the Inner Bailey.

The miner said, "Never before have I seen such damage to living beings. I took a knife from the beast's haunch as carefully as I could . . ."

The animal snorted.

". . . and I did as much as I could to help the rider."

The Ferryman ordered, "Take her to the lower chambers of the Heart where she can rest and gain strength."

As the messenger was lowered to the ground, she awakened. She mumbled something and collapsed.

The Ferryman said, "It is too dangerous to leave the Land and sky exposed. Make her comfortable in the Heart. I will come to see her soon."

He left the courtyard and saw George in a corridor. "Please come with me, George. I must restore the cloud. It will be good for you to learn."

They went to the upper levels of the Heart and, searching through the open port, found a water supply on the land below. The Ferryman taught George which stones to manipulate to moor the Land.

"The stones responded nicely to your touch as you drew water up through the Heart. The cloud will slow those from the troubled village and offer cover to our friends."

George and the Ferryman went to the lower level to interview the messenger. She had recovered sufficiently to speak coherently. "The raiders are coming. Their path will lead them to Wind Castle. Some of our scouts have joined those who follow the raiders. The others are returning with a few from the Sasquatch camp."

"You have done well," the Ferryman's gentle voice drew a tired smile from his patient. "But you are so badly hurt that the Land cannot heal you quickly. You must remain here until you are better."

The Ferryman stood and spoke with George. "She will recover."

"It's getting worse with Gideon. He's not going to be satisfied with your welcome. Many of your followers could wind up just like her."

"Would you have me change the nature of the Land and risk its destruction to fight this man?"

"You're not going to have a choice."

"Perhaps later. But now, I do have a choice. I ask you to support my decision until it is clear that my methods will fail."

Cloud Walker entered the room. "Some of our scouts have returned along with some of the Sasquatch from Tmron's camp."

George, Cloud Walker, and the Ferryman met the scouting parties at the castle gates. As one of the Sasquatch approached, George said, "You look familiar."

"To you a greeting, George Severe." The female Sasquatch stood nearly a head taller than George and she smiled, revealing her large yellow teeth. "Remember do you, Fleng, daughter of Tmron?"

"Of course! But you're so . . . BIG. You've grown so much!"

They walked with the others to the hall where the Ferryman offered wine and fruits. Fleng was no longer the child he remembered. He thought back to the time she sat with the Unicorn by the pond. Then he thought about his own daughter. *How long have I been here? When did I lose track of the days? Why did I stop counting?*

Tmron and those who joined him in pursuit of the raiders closed on the aggressors under heavy cloud cover. A few Dwarves ventured close enough to hear conversations among the raiders. The dense cloud served its purpose. The pace of the march had slowed considerably.

Another full day passed before the raiders found their way to the foothills at the valley. A Faun who had moved close to the raiders' camp reported to Tmron, "Their leader asked some of their number to stay behind and follow at a distance."

Tmron sent a messenger to Wind Castle with the news that they would pursue the main party and monitor those who remained behind. In the morning, when Gideon resumed his march, Tmron and the others circumvented the raiders left behind and followed.

The messenger arrived at Wind Castle and Cloud Walker suggested that Tmron capture the lagging raiders so they could not assist Gideon later.

The Ferryman asked, "How can your task be completed without violence?"

George reminded him, "Tmron knows something about the ways of Jack LaRoche. The scouts, the Sasquatch, and those from the hillside village outnumber the lagging raiders *and* they're stronger!"

Cloud Walker added, "There will probably be very little fighting if Gideon isn't there to guide them. I can carry the message to Tmron and offer my help."

The Ferryman considered the suggestion and looked at George. George said, "He's right. I don't think anybody will do much fighting without Gideon's say so."

The Ferryman answered, "Do as you said, but take Tmron's messenger with you. I am sorry I cannot send a winged horse."

Cloud Walker and the messenger left the castle. The messenger led Cloud Walker toward Tmron. They watched for raiders and discussed Cloud Walker's plans for taking those who were left at the foothills. Cloud Walker suggested, "If we are discovered before finding Tmron, run in different directions. That way, one of us should reach Tmron with the message."

A short hour after leaving the castle, his suggestion was put to the test. Suddenly, three raiders appeared like ghosts out of the mist before them. The raiders walked toward them. Cloud Walker and the messenger ran. Two raiders pursued Cloud Walker and the other chased the messenger.

Cloud Walker was again shrewd and lucky in his escape. It happened that he was near the edge of the group that was approaching Wind Castle and he did not encounter anyone before him in his flight. Because of his method of changing direction while running, his pursuers were lost in the mist behind him. With no raiders ahead to hinder him, he remained free.

Cloud Walker found Tmron and checked their advance. He told them of his plan to capture the raiders left at the foothills and he convinced them of the likelihood of their success.

Tmron led the way back to the foothills and eventually found the small camp. Twenty Spoils huddled together, surrounded by almost as many raiders. A Dwarf advised Tmron, "Most there were taken from our village. They will help us if we fight."

Tmron whispered, "Around this camp hide. On our signal be seen by standing."

When all were in place, Tmron and Cloud Walker approached the raiders. Cloud Walker called out to them, "Where is your leader?"

Some of the raiders stood and moved toward them. Tmron gave his signal and the Sasquatch, scouts, and mountain villagers stepped into view.

The raiders looked around them and at their Spoils. One raider said, "Stay seated and quiet, Spoils." Then he answered Cloud Walker. "Our leader is not with us."

"Who speaks for you when he is away?" Cloud Walker asked.

The one who had answered accepted the role of spokesman. "I can speak as well as any here. What do you want of us?"

"To talk," Cloud Walker answered as he advanced toward the self-appointed spokesman. "Our friends tell us that someone attacked their village. Have you seen anyone who might have done such a thing?"

The spokesman signaled the raiders and they all stood. He presented a feigned expression of surprise. "No! We have not se—"

The spokesman suddenly folded over after a kick in the groin issued by Cloud Walker. Some of the raiders moved to assist their friend when those who had been watching from the perimeter of the camp closed in on them. As the raiders rallied to receive the attack, the Spoils stood and advanced on them. The spokesman rolled breathlessly on the ground with his hands cupped between his legs.

One of the raiders drew a weapon from his belt and stretched his arm back, ready to throw. Tmron's friend, Mrudg, caught his hand and clutched it and the weapon, casually crushing both. While the raider wailed in agony, the blade fell from its handle to the ground. The raider dropped to his knees while reaching up with his healthy hand to the arm that Mrudg still held in his crushing grasp.

The other raiders abandoned their defensive posture after seeing themselves entangled by attackers and Spoils and hearing their friend's bloodcurdling screams.

Cloud Walker asked Mrudg to release the injured raider. The raider dropped to the ground wailing and grasping his forearm. By then, the spokesman regained his ability to speak. "What do you want with us?"

Cloud Walker stood triumphantly above him and looked around at the other raiders. "Take your knives and tools from your belts and place them on the ground."

Some of the raiders delayed, at first. "Must all your arms be crushed?" The raiders did as they were told.

"We don't *want* anything to do with you," Cloud Walker said. "But you have forced yourself on us. Now, you will come with us as prisoners"

Cloud Walker asked some of the Dwarves to collect the weapons and bind the raiders. Then, they followed a circuitous route back to Wind Castle.

In the time it took Cloud Walker and Tmron to circumvent the main raiding party and return to Wind Castle, Gideon had come across some villagers and taken their wares, proclaiming that anyone who ventures from the castle village must pay a fee to Gideon.

Cloud Walker and George were unable to convince the Ferryman that he should not try to win friendship with the raiders. In the days that followed, the cloud was lifted to its usual level and the villagers tried to function as they always had – except for the need to pay tribute to Gideon.

Gideon first accepted this as a victory. However, he soon demanded more than the tribute they offered and took anything the villagers had when they passed him. If they had nothing, he beat them. The community responded by withdrawing into the village.

TWENTY-FIVE
Last Counsel

ALDEN SAT quietly while a delegation of local villagers complained about Gideon and his raiders. Their complaints were directed randomly at the Ferryman and each other. The Ferryman moved his attention to those who spoke loudest or stood most prominently before him.

"The more we give them, the more they want!"

"They cannot be satisfied!"

"Refuse them!"

"They come into the village at night when we sleep. They beat us and take what they choose. We are not safe within our own homes!"

"We must retaliate! It is the only way."

The Ferryman stood, "The Land could be lost if we follow their wa—"

"We lose it n—"

"Let me speak." the Ferryman insisted. "Already, we confine prisoners taken by Cloud Walker and Tmron at the foothills. It is not good. Should we fight and imprison all these raiders? And for how long? Will the Land refuse us then as it has Gideon and his followers? We are tempted to fight, but we may suffer more later if we do."

The Ferryman looked at blank faces. His appeal was not working. He sighed and dropped his shoulders. "I will consult with the Ancient Counselor again. He may know of such a problem in the past, if his memory does not fail him. Go now, and I will make a decision afterward."

The Ferryman stood beside his table until all had gone. He hesitated before leaving the room. Then, he walked to the lowest level of the Heart where Simon clung to life. Alden sat at the table where the Ancient Counselor rested, wrapped in his heavy robe, its cowl hiding his head. Simon struggled for each shallow breath.

"Simon, I do not know what to do." The Ferryman looked at his own hands as he spoke. "My decision could destroy this Land forever. If I let Gideon control the Land, the Heart would reject his touch and soon the Land would die. If I fight him, the Heart might soon shudder at *my* touch. That, I could not bear. The Land means so much to me." He wept. He held his breath and swallowed before exhaling. Then he wiped tears from his eyes and mucus from his nose. He smiled at his mentor saying, "I pray you hear me, Simon. I see so little awareness in your eyes these last days. You taught me so well to love this Land. Does my love for it make me too hesitant to protect it?"

He sighed and leaned against a stone wall behind him. He rolled his head back to the stone, closed his eyes, and rested until his head rolled forward, keeping him from a deeper sleep. The Ancient Counselor moved his hand. Alden grasped his friend's hand and looked into the darkness under the cowl. The clouded, half-blind eyes were barely visible.

The Ferryman walked to his friend's side and gently pulled back the heavy hood. Simon's condition was much worse than when George had last seen him. The Ferryman looked upon his friend's sunken features – skin so lacking in substance that blood vessels, bone, and tendon seemed hideous growths upon his head; ears drawn into his skull; thin wisps of hair barely holding onto his scalp; the head supported by a neck so thin he could nearly see through it in the light cast from the Heart; and those lost, sunken eyes with lids that could no longer close.

The Ancient Counselor moved his hand again and reached toward his mouth. "Wa . . ."

"Water?" the Ferryman asked. Simon nodded weakly. "I will be but a moment." The Ferryman stepped out to a cor- ridor where he drew some water from a fountain. He carried the water to his friend and he lifted the mug to Simon's lips, which quivered as they touched the liquid. A small portion was sipped from the mug. "I will keep it here if you want more."

The Ancient Counselor feebly turned his head to the sound of Alden's voice and spoke, "Ssit . . . and listen." His words were slow and garbled, but deliberate. "I hhha," he coughed. It was a cough that wrenched his whole body, and he sat convulsing for a moment. "Little time . . . no time . . . no time."

The Ferryman waited.

"Beware," the Ancient Counselor continued, "of strangers in the village. Not those from mmbelow . . . others . . . from this Land. Watch for them. They will come." He signaled for more water.

"Yes, Simon," the Ferryman answered as he brought the mug of water to his lips. "I will watch for them."

Simon continued slowly, "George . . . Cloud Walker . . . good choices. As are others . . . but these two . . . would be best if . . . if . . ."

"Would you do better to send your thoughts?" the Ferryman asked.

"Too difficult now . . . and others might receive." He sucked slow, hoarse breaths of air. "Each must be at peace . . . in his own world before . . . beefffore he can lead ours. They must find their peace . . . before you can choose . . . from them. If you cannot wait, then you mmmusst choose . . . from our Land."

The Ferryman nodded as he held his friend's hand.

"But you are yet young . . . and . . . and if you keep yourself from harm . . . you can wait until they find their peace. You can wait . . . but you must not risk yourself. If you are lll . . . llossst to the Land, there is nobody to guide it.

"If you do not ch-choose, you must . . . you must begin . . . to teach. If the best Ferryman cannot be found . . . *someone* must guide the Land. Maybe more than one. Do not risk your-self . . . and teach."

The Ferryman offered him another sip of water. "You should save your strength, Simon."

"No time . . . I cannot. Listen."

"I am here to listen."

"The troubled village. When the siege is over, . . . it must be abandoned . . . until the Land can heal itself. The village is an open wound that will be long in healing. Annie . . . can help. Try to . . . make her see.

"You will discover the ways of ending the siege. Have faith in . . . in yourself and in the Land . . . and in your friends." He sucked in some air and coughed. Mucus, spotted with blood, hung on his lip and below his nose. The Ferryman wiped it away and offered more water, which was taken in small quantity.

"Soon . . . I will be lost to the Land," the Ancient Counselor said. Alden leaned over his friend and gently hugged his skeletal form. Simon touched his arm.

"I do not fear this death," the Ancient Counselor said as the Ferryman released his embrace. "I have lived many years and I have served the Land as well as I could."

"You have served the Land as well as any Ancient Counselor or Ferryman before you. And probably better than any that will follow. I love you, Simon. I can think of no greater honor than to have served with you."

The Ancient Counselor smiled painfully. "Beware of strangers in the village. You know who belongs and who does not . . . beware." He was quiet for a moment. Then he stretched his painful smile. "Remember? . . . Remember when you were first lllearnning to guide the Land? How fffrrustrated you became if you missed the course. You were so eager to please me. . . . You have not changed, my friend. You work so hard . . . to please. So hard. We shared many . . . adventures. Be careful . . . watch for strangers.

"Seek advice from George, . . . Cloud Walker, . . . the Sasquatch you spoke of, . . . listen and decide. The two from below must be settled. Choose one if he finds peace . . . ffinds peace. Show her . . . Annie belongs to the Land . . . a mother does not leave her child.

"Alden, do not worry! You will learn . . . you are doing well. With practice you will guide the Land. Just touch the stones gently and use your will." Simon's conversation drifted to and from other times. The Ferryman held his hand as he babbled.

Simon was quiet for a moment and his breathing slowed. "It is time . . . my friend . . . mmy friend, you . . . must go . . . before I breathe my last. . . . Hold me? Hold me once more before you leave?"

The Ferryman sat beside him, weeping as he hugged his dying friend. Simon relaxed. He patted Alden's arm and whispered, "Gggo now. You are always . . . in my heart."

Alden kissed the fragile head of the Ancient Counselor and walked out of the room, looking back for a brief moment before passing through the portal. He walked a few steps down the corridor and collapsed. He struggled to sit up and lean against the wall. At the sound of a groan, he looked back through tear-clouded eyes. A sudden flash of light was followed by a puff of smoke and a hot odor of burned flesh. The ground rumbled and something surged through the Heart.

It was evening when the villagers and the raiders felt the rumble at their feet. Those inside the castle and the village looked to each other and then to the Keep for an explanation. Bolts of lightning surged from the Keep and stretched to the sky, eventually dissipating in the clouds above the castle. Many screamed and ran. They crowded each other as they approached the gateway, shoving and crying in their haste to leave the Inner Bailey – shoving more at each new lightning bolt.

Knowing the Ferryman was often at the Heart, George and Cloud Walker rushed to the chambers. They found him, weeping on the ground.

George said, "Cloud Walker, see to Alden." He ran into Simon's chamber and saw nothing but scorched stone and white powder. He returned and said, "There's nothing we can do in there. Help me get Alden to his room."

The Ferryman told George and Cloud Walker the Ancient Counselor was lost to the Land. He drank some wine in his room and told them why he had gone to see Simon.

Cloud Walker offered the same advice given before. "The people of Wind Castle must stand against Gideon."

George said, "You know about the troubles outside the

village – and inside the village at night. The trouble will eventually find a way into the castle. I agree with all your reasons for wanting to resolve this peaceably, but it's just not working. We have to defend ourselves. If you wait any longer to train your people, it'll be too late."

The Ferryman took a deep breath. Then, he reached over the table and held the hands of George and Cloud Walker. "I am grieved by the loss of my friend and by your words. I know you speak truly." He stood and turned away from them. Cloud Walker looked at George. George shrugged. Then the Ferryman said, "We will begin. We will learn to defend Wind Castle and the Heart."

Gideon saw the flash from his camp outside the village as he awaited the return of a small party he had sent to harass the villagers. All the raiders stood and watched the lightning display and pressed Gideon for an explanation. Some wanted to flee. A few did, but Gideon persuaded most to wait. He paced about the camp, rejecting all other inquiries until the raiding party returned.

"What happened at Wind Castle? How went your raid?"

"We did no raid because of the storm and the quake. The village was in turmoil. At first, everyone rushed out of the castle. Then, after the storm subsided, they crowded back into the courtyard. We followed, hoping to learn about the disruption."

"Do not hold from me. What was the cause?"

"The Ferryman appeared on a balcony looking haggard –

maybe injured and weak. He said the Ancient Counselor was lost to the Land."

"The Ancient Counselor lost?"

"The villagers were horrified and they asked who would guide the Ferryman. The Ferryman told them there would be no counselor until he chooses a new Ferryman."

Gideon smiled.

"The villagers shouted questions and demands. It was then that one of them recognized us. We were forced to flee and, had it not been for the confusion in the village, we would not have escaped."

"Intriguing," Gideon said. "The Ferryman will be a lesser obstacle without the Ancient Counselor's influence."

The Ferryman announced his new plan at the balcony after the spies had fled. Just as he had called upon the residents of Wind Castle and the village to serve as scouts, he called upon them to stand and be selected for combative training, which was to be provided by Cloud Walker and Tmron.

As before, there were more volunteers than needed. The Indian and the Sasquatch were selective in creating their small army – Cloud Walker called them *Warriors*. Tmron did not care what they called themselves.

After his plans were set in motion, the Ferryman retired to his room with George. George told him, as they walked together, "You made the right decision."

The Ferryman said, "The castle guard must be small and

manageable. It must be abolished after the trouble has ended. The ways of Jack LaRoche must not take root in the Land again."

George remained in the Ferryman's room. Alden related some of his adventures with Simon. "Learning how to man-euver the Land was the most exciting thing I had done – not for the skill I developed, but for Simon's teaching. I loved the Land long before I was chosen to be Ferryman and Simon saw that. It was as much a part of me then as it is now. I pray it will recover from what we do."

"It will."

"Why do you have such faith, George?"

"I don't know. I just *assume* everything will turn out all right."

The Ferryman nodded and closed his eyes. "Thank you. I must rest now. Please leave me."

George stopped at the entry for a moment and looked back. "I'm sorry about Simon."

The Ferryman nodded.

As Cloud Walker and Tmron taught the basic techniques of fighting to their band of defenders, Gideon stood outside the village planning his next attack. "The loss of the Ancient Counselor is most fortunate. They will be too concerned about their loss to prevent us from taking Wind Castle."

Some of the raiders nodded while others drank wine and gambled with goods they had stolen.

"We will intensify our attacks on the village and entice the

Ferryman to a place where he can be taken. With the Ancient Counselor lost, and the Ferryman captured, Wind Castle will be ours."

That evening, after dispatching two raiding parties to the village, Gideon walked alone at the perimeter of the camp. In the dusky haze, two Unicorns stood before him – watching. He made a quick move toward them, calling out, "Away with you! Leave us!" But they did not move, so he bent down and took a stone from the ground. He wound back and hurled the stone toward them yelling madly, "Away! Away! Away, away!"

Two of his followers responded to his cries. "What has upset you?"

He cursed, "Unicorns . . ." He pointed to the place where he had thrown the rock. "Over there!" His friends saw nothing but the encroaching darkness.

TWENTY-SIX

Plans and Preparations

"DON'T WALK away when somebody hits you!" Cloud Walker called to one of his recruits who had turned his back after being struck on the chin by a mock raider. "If you turn your back, he'll hit you again or maybe stick you with his knife. Always watch your enemy! If you have to step back, do it facing him. If you figure you're going to trip unless you turn, turn fast – so fast that he won't have time to get you. You've got to watch out for yourself!"

Cloud Walker took a position opposite the mock raider to demonstrate. He asked the opponent to attack him while he retreated by moving around the opponent and stepping from side to side or directly backward without looking where he placed his feet. Then, when he found himself backed against some onlookers, he swiftly spun along while watching the attacker.

Nearby, Tmron showed some others how to stalk an opponent and how advantageous the element of surprise could be. His lesson, too, was that they should be ever vigilant – never stop watching because those who stop watching can be surprised and defeated easily.

Cloud Walker and Tmron had agreed that size was not the most important quality of their Warriors. They looked at the outstanding abilities of each species. The Sasquatch were large and powerful, but clumsy at times. Fauns were quick but, once caught, could do little to affect their own escape. Dwarves were short and strong. They moved quickly, but not very fast or very far. Centaurs were very fast and powerful, but were easily trapped in confined spaces. Several of the other fairy-like creatures were better suited as messengers or watches – except those who possessed knowledge of magic or illusion.

The emphasis was placed on defensive maneuvers. The leaders would direct aggressive actions. George, Annie, Tmron, and Cloud Walker met with the chosen leaders as their defensive training continued. George said, "Remember what happened when Cloud Walker assaulted the spokesman for the raiders at the foothills. One good surprise kick and the battle was all but won."

"Ya gotta intimidate the sons o' bitches," Annie said.

Cloud Walker said, "If you're outnumbered and have nowhere to go, attack their leader or the biggest one among them. Put them down, and the others will follow."

The Ferryman did not speak of the training taking

place in Wind Castle when talking to George about the siege and the attacks in the village. Occasionally, George told him that things were going well, but the leader usually accepted George's comments and then quickly changed the subject.

George knew the Ferryman's struggle. He shared it – the Ferryman's love for the Land and the need to defend it while disdaining the methods of the insurgents. A meteorologist who had lived comfortably all his life was hardly qualified to train others in combat, but there were few others in the Land who could. So, he accepted his role. He taught all he knew and everything he learned while watching Annie, Tmron, and Cloud Walker.

Because of the harassment from the raiders, none of the villagers dared venture out of the village and, more and more, they sought shelter within the castle. They became easily agitated and their demands for action came more frequently.

When the Ferryman discussed these matters with George, George said, "It's easier to demand action and complain about conditions than it is to *do* something. Stick to your plan. Don't fight until you have to. The more training the Warriors get, the better they'll be."

Gideon assembled his raiders and said, "You have done well. We control all movement outside the castle and the village. You have been rewarded with Spoils and riches from the village, but we must remember why we came here. We came to avenge our friends who were killed by the Dragon. We came to destroy George Severe and the Ferryman. The time has come for a large-scale raid on the village. Such a raid will draw the Ferryman out of Wind Castle to a place where we can capture him.

"We have controlled this village since coming here. All that remains is to take the castle. When it is done, we shall share the reward. Our friends will be avenged. We will rule the Land and you will want for nothing."

The raiders cheered. After Gideon ordered his followers to prepare for the attack, his new confidante asked, "Is this wise? They have greater numbers. We could be trapped inside."

"Do not be concerned about their numbers, Cedric. They have shown that they do not know how to resist us. It is time to stop our play and take what we seek."

The small lean raider persisted, "What of the Unicorns that follow us?"

"The horn I hold shows them what will happen if they approach us. I am not so easily distressed as Telemachus."

"And George Severe?"

Gideon snapped, "George Severe is no threat. If he knew the secrets of Jack LaRoche, he would have used them by now. And we have seen nothing of his Dragon – not that it matters. We are ready."

"Are you su—"

Gideon's face reddened and tightened as he moved close to Cedric. He mumbled through clenched teeth, "Offer no further objections – unless you want to join the Ferryman and share his fate."

The darkness exploded with yelps and screeches, the battle cries of the raiders. The raiders attacked every household in their paths. George ran to the courtyard and up the gate tower to the parapet where he saw the Ferryman looking down upon the village.

The battle cries continued in the distance, punctuated by screams of horror. Shadows advanced on the bridge. The Torch Stones illuminated the retreating villagers, melting the shadows and casting their distorted brethren over the ground toward the castle walls. The shadows grew larger as their terrified sources approached the gates. George followed the Ferryman down the stairs of the tower and into the courtyard where they met Cloud Walker. The Ferryman said, "Assemble your Warriors at the gate. George will stay by my side."

Cloud Walker ordered the Warriors to the gates against a throng of villagers rushing into the court. The Ferryman asked the Warriors to move out of the gates against the crowd and work their way toward the battle cries. Tmron took the lead and broke a path for the Warriors to follow. George and the Ferryman went up the tower to the parapet to observe as much as possible.

Small circles of light from the raiders' torches moved randomly from hut to hut. A few fires cast red glows over the buildings. The battle cries advanced, preceded by the fearful cries of fleeing villagers. The Ferryman asked, "Why do they do that? Every time the raiders attack, they raise their voices in those horrible screams."

"Intimidation. Some call it psychological warfare. They

scream to make us nervous."

"There is more. It becomes more frenzied as the attack continues. Their screams grow more ferocious with each victory – like they cannot be satisfied."

"They never *will* be satisfied – especially Gideon. He's intoxicated by power and he loves the chase."

The defenders reached the Bridge-Over-Nothing as the battle cries subsided. When they pushed into the village, the battle cries were gone – all that could be heard was the panic of the villagers pressing toward the castle and the lamentations of those who had seen their friends and families assaulted or taken prisoner. The Warriors moved toward the village gate.

Atop the castle wall the Ferryman said, "I believe the attack is over. We must go to comfort and heal the villagers."

George followed the Ferryman to the courtyard and watched him become enraged as they saw the fear and physical injuries of the villagers. Unlike the first to arrive, these had been beaten, wounded, and burned. "Are you all right, Alden?"

"This . . . this is not right." The Ferryman huffed and clenched his fists. "It is the worst attack yet. Gideon has brought the ways of Jack LaRoche to Wind Castle."

"Worse will come."

"We cannot let him attack us again." The Ferryman asked, "Can we oppose the raiders successfully?"

George answered, "If we surprise them and, if we can divide the raiders' camp into smaller groups. But the rest of your villagers would have to help if called upon. They're not trained, but with overwhelming numbers, they could succeed if the Warriors fail."

"Thank you, George. I will offer Gideon one opportunity to abandon his siege. If he chooses to continue his assault, I will order an attack."

Cloud Walker and Tmron returned just in time to hear the Ferryman's last words. They reported the things they saw in the village and asked the Ferryman to repeat his conversation with George. Upon hearing all that was discussed, each proclaimed his endorsement of the Ferryman's decision. They returned to the Warriors to prepare them for the likely confrontation while George and Alden remained among the frightened villagers.

Annie and Tamara were busy helping the injured villagers in the Great Hall. George found them and told them about the Ferryman's decision.

"It's about time," Annie said. "I's jes gettin' ready ta whomp his head with a two by four. Some folks ya gotta do that ta get their attention."

Tamara remained crouched quietly beside her patient.

George asked, "Is something wrong, Tamara?"

"I am afraid. I have seen what happens to those who resist Gideon and his friends."

"You'll see a lot worse, Dearie, if that snake ain't stopped."

Tamara nodded as George said, "Annie's right."

George, Annie, and Tamara stood beside the Ferryman as he spoke to the villagers and asked for a volunteer to take a message to Gideon at first light. "There is a risk. The messenger might not return – you could be captured and detained, beaten, or even lost to the Land. But it is important that the message be carried."

Several individuals stepped forward. One voice came from the middle of the crowd, but George did not see who spoke. He was curious about the owner of that voice and asked the Ferryman to call him forward. The voice spoke again, but George still could not find its source. He looked dumbfounded at the Ferryman.

The Ferryman smiled. "Show yourself."

A strange shape formed before George.

Annie stepped back. "What in blazes?"

The shape became a shadow of a small man. George saw a youthful face gradually develop out of the shadow.

"George. Annie. This is Zane. He is a Phantom – one of only twenty in all the Land."

George was amazed at the figure, which acknowledged him. He wanted to ask about this being who was so human in appearance, but the Ferryman spoke too quickly. "Do you wish to be the messenger?"

"Yes," Zane answered.

"You are young, but probably best suited." The Ferryman turned to George and explained, "Phantoms have a unique ability to blend into a crowd – to disguise themselves or hide in such a way that they cannot be seen." He then turned back to Zane and continued, "But they can be sensed in other ways. The raiders have lost their communion with the Land.

BRIAN HAMMAR | 361

For that reason I believe you will be safe, Zane. But you could be hurt if I am wrong."

"I am aware of the risk."

"Walk with me and we will talk about the message you will deliver." The Ferryman asked George to walk with them and to add his comments.

"You are to go to this man called Gideon and tell him that the Ferryman wishes to speak with him. Tell him I will meet him at a place between the village and his camp. He is to know and understand that the villagers will not harm him during our consultation. Tell him that next light will be a sun day and we can meet when the sun shines above the hills. Ask him to offer a response to my request and to include any conditions that would satisfy concerns about his safety.

"George, do you have anything to add?"

"Alden, you should know better than to trust Gideon. You can't go out there by yourself. Who will lead the Land if you get captured? Let somebody else go!"

"I appreciate your concern, my friend, but this must be done. I must try to help him find reason before we resort to his methods."

"You're not the only one who can do it!"

"Perhaps not. But I am the only one who *should*. If you try to meet with him, he will kill you immediately. Anyone else from Wind Castle would most probably be poorly received. It is my responsibility to end this trouble."

George silently conceded to the Ferryman. He looked down to the ground, trying to think of something more to say.

His concern was obvious.

"Fear not. I will take no other risk."

"I shall deliver your message, Ferryman," the Phantom said.

"My heart is with you, Zane. Go now. The darkness will serve you well. When you return, come to my room immediately."

Gideon congratulated his raiders for their successful raid and passed wine to all. "Cedric, sit and drink with me. You have been a great help since Lucius was wounded."

Cedric took a mug of wine and sat on a stone beside Gideon. "I do not understand why he has not healed and returned to us."

"He was badly injured. I hope he was not captured."

Zane suddenly appeared. Gideon leapt from his seat. "Who are you?" Gideon demanded. "How did you come to be among us?"

"I am Zane," the Phantom answered. "I was sent by the Ferryman to —"

"Take him," Gideon commanded. Cedric grabbed the Phantom before he faded away. "Where is he?" Gideon asked.

"I hold him!" Cedric said while other raiders gathered around. "But I cannot *see* him!"

"Hold what you have," Gideon looked at the vacant space near Cedric's clutched hands and said with a sinister smile, "Show yourself." There was no response. "Show yourself now or I will tell my friend to rip your arm off."

Zane slowly reappeared. The watching raiders buzzed their amazement. Gideon said, "You are wise to do as I command. Why have you come to my camp?"

After the Phantom delivered his message, Gideon asked, "What does the Ferryman plan for this meeting? Does he think he can capture me?"

Zane did not answer. Gideon took Zane's hair in his hand and twisted his head while thrusting his fist into Zane's stomach. "Answer, messenger."

Trying to speak while gasping for breath, he answered, "The Ferryman is honorable . . . he offers no harm, and he trusts that you will not harm *him* during the consultation."

"Why should I believe you?"

"I speak the truth, and you must release me to return your answer."

Gideon released Zane's hair. "Perhaps you do."

Gideon stepped away from his prisoner. "Cedric, we should talk about this. Come with me, but don't release your grip until others hold him firm."

Two raiders grasped Zane's arms. Gideon mumbled to Cedric well away from Zane. "This is our opportunity to lure the Ferryman to a place where we can capture him."

"Are you sure he doesn't mean to do you harm?"

"The meeting was his suggestion." Gideon looked at the Phantom while speaking to Cedric. "No, the Ferryman is too long in our Land. He knows nothing of the ways of the land below. Capturing me would not occur to him."

Cedric answered, "But what of George Severe? He

might have—"

"Why must you argue with me in these matters? George Severe knows nothing of the ways of Jack LaRoche. He is useless."

Gideon returned to the Phantom. "I require certain conditions."

"The Ferryman will allow some conditions."

"Tell the Ferryman I will meet him. Each of us will be accompanied by only two others. I will meet him when the day is brightest. I will listen to his words, but I will kill him if I am ever in danger. I will know if he is planning a deception." Gideon struck Zane again in the stomach saying, "Go, now. And do not return here."

The Phantom gasped for breath as the raiders released him. Slowly, he regained his composure and stood, bending forward slightly, holding his arms to his stomach.

Gideon said, "Leave now, before I decide to beat you until you are lost to the Land."

Zane stood upright and disappeared.

Gideon squinted and his raiders marveled as the Phantom faded from sight. Then there was a hush. Suddenly, Gideon doubled over from an unseen blow to his midriff. Then another of the party fell aside as Zane scrambled away from the camp. "That was from Zane to you, Gideon, in return for your welcome," he called out. "Do not be concerned. I shall deliver your message. The Ferryman is honorable. He will accept your conditions. Just be sure there is no treachery on *your* part." His voice drifted away as Gideon recovered from the blow.

Gideon said, "When I have finished with the Ferryman, I will find Zane and kill him." He called to one of his followers and said, "Go to the foothills. Find those we left behind. The Ferryman must see greater numbers watching our meeting. The Spoils from Wind Castle and the hillside village will add to the effect as well."

After his messenger left, Gideon addressed his raiders. "We must prepare to meet the Ferryman. While he speaks with me, some of you will be inside the village and at the gates of the castle. You will secure the gateways. Some others will follow the Ferryman to the valley to be certain he cannot return to Wind Castle. If I do not capture the Ferryman during the meeting, then they will capture or kill him as he returns. Gather what you need and prepare for victory next light."

The raiders cheered and moved about the camp, making preparations – sharpening knives, packing personal goods or those stolen in earlier raids, and piling their weapons for easy access.

After the crowd dispersed, Cedric said, "Your plan to attack the village and castle while the Ferryman is outside sounds good. But, forgive me for asking – my only concern is your safety – are you not concerned the Ferryman might have some power he might use to capture you?"

"If the Ferryman had such power, he would have used it long ago. He is doing exactly what I want him to do. By accepting my conditions, he will have no help once he walks beyond the village gate. Accepting the delay I requested will give our rear guard time to cross the valley. The Ferryman will then see our numbers. He will have to surrender or be taken by force."

TWENTY-SEVEN

Unicorns' Peace

THE FERRYMAN thanked Zane for delivering his message to Gideon. "But you should not have struck him, Zane. He might have reneged on his agreement to meet me."

"I am sorry, Ferryman. But, I gave him less than he gave me and he knows it was my own doing."

"Sounds ta me like Red got a taste o' his own," Annie said. "Serves 'im right."

Cloud Walker nodded and George smiled.

Alden smiled, too. "It is done. Cloud Walker and Tmron, see that the Warriors are well-rested. Then, take your rest. If this meeting does not succeed, we may be quite exhausted by this time next light. I will go to the Heart at first light to remove the cloud. I will take George and Tmron as my escorts. Cloud Walker will lead the Warriors if necessary."

"Yer fergettin' someone, ain't ya?"

"Cloud Walker and *Annie* will lead the Warriors."

George reclined on the stone bed in his room. The glow from the Torch Stone cast distorted shadows across the uneven stone ceiling. The usual warmth from the bed could not drive away the chill in his back. He rolled to his side and tucked his knees into his arms but could not warm himself. He sat up, rocking in place, his arms wrapped over his weak stomach.

Eventually, the chill subsided and George rolled back down on the bed. Sleep came sporadically at first but finally grasped him so tightly that he dreamed he could not awaken.

"You up yet, Sonny?"

The voice sounded familiar but George was not compelled to answer.

"Hey, Blondie! Up an' at 'em. We got lots ta do."

George rolled to his back and opened his eyes. Someone stood over him, saying something and . . . shaking him.

"C'mon, c'mon. Let's get to it."

"Wha . . . what? Annie!"

"That's right, Sonny. Rise an' shine."

"I'm up. OK, I'm up." George sat on the edge of the bed and tried to shake some consciousness into his head.

"You look like hell, Sonny. Rough night?"

"You might say that. I had one of those feelings again."

"Not—"

"Like something bad is going to happen."

"Tarnation."

The Ferryman called from the corridor, "Have you awakened, George?"

"Yes. Come in."

"Ah! Annie! Cloud Walker is looking for you. George! Are you ill?"

Annie said, "He's had one o' them feelin's o' his. If I was you, I'd listen ta what he has ta say. I'll go see what the Injun needs." Annie walked out of the room.

George said, "Are you sure you want to go through with this meeting?"

The Ferryman answered, "I have to try."

"Annie's right. You should listen to me about this. I have a way of—"

"I know, George. But our fate could be equally unsettled if we choose another path."

George looked at the Ferryman. He wanted him to explain.

"Come. It is time to greet the sun."

George and the Ferryman went to the Heart. Alden let him adjust the controlling stones to dissipate the cloud. At mid-morning, they walked among those villagers who had refused to return to their huts. The Ferryman said, "I want to send a messenger on a winged horse to survey Gideon's camp and the surrounding area before our meeting. Clearly, there is no room to run and fly here."

George said, "Good idea! I'll find a rider. There should be

room outside the walls."

George and the Ferryman watched the winged horse rise above the castle walls into a deep blue sky streaked with high wispy clouds. Just before the time had come for the Ferryman to leave the protection of Wind Castle, the rider returned, her steed snorting and sweating as it held its wings out to let its body cool.

"All is well in the valley," the ethereal elf-like rider said. "And, wondrous to see, there are two Unicorns near the camp."

George said, "They haven't been far from the horn since Telemachus took it."

The Ferryman told the rider, "Continue surveying the valley and warn me if you see any sign of treachery."

George said, "More than that, if you see anything, come down and get Alden away as quickly as you can."

"That will not be necessary, George."

"It *is* necessary. I know Gideon."

"But—"

"You know I'm right. You're taking too much risk as it is." George looked at the rider. "Will you come for him?"

The rider nodded to George, bowing to the Ferryman as she backed away.

Gideon's runner returned from his search for the rear guard in the foothills. "They are nowhere to be found."

Gideon quickly grasped the messenger's throat. "What?"

The messenger gurgled, "I ggg searched everywhere. Ggg They are ggggone." He grabbed Gideon's arms and patted his chest while standing on the tips of his toes.

Gideon released his grip. The messenger dropped to the flats of his feet, gasping. Gideon said, "It seems we chose some cowards to join our quest. They will be punished when we return. And when we have tired of their punishment, they will be killed."

Annie, Cloud Walker, Tmron, and several of their Warriors arrived to escort the Ferryman out of the village. The Ferryman silently led the way, apparently lost in his consideration of the impending meeting with Gideon. George walked beside him – equally anxious.

The Ferryman hesitated as they walked past the gates and again after passing the Bridge-Over-Nothing.

He stopped short of the village gate and said, "There are strangers in our village and at the gates of Wind Castle. Do not look about at this moment. The Ancient Counselor warned me of this before he was lost to the Land. I believe they mean to cause harm to us or to the village while we are gone."

Annie blurted out in a muffled voice, "I tol' ya not ta trust that snake."

George said, "Gideon will have other plans for our meeting. We'd better call this off . . . unless we can turn the tables in some way."

"I am not prepared to abandon the meeting yet. What is meant by your words? How can we turn the tables?"

Annie answered, "He means get *them* 'fore they get you"

George continued, "You know they're here. *Do* something about it!"

The Ferryman paused for a moment. George, Tmron, Annie, and Cloud Walker waited. The leader looked at Cloud Walker and asked, "Are you certain our Warriors can defend Wind Castle?"

"They have a lot to learn. They're not very aggressive. But I think they can beat the raiders if we lead them well."

The Ferryman looked at each of his friends. "Then now is the time to defend the village. Tmron, you know many from the troubled village and can recognize them. You must remain here. Lead our Warriors with Cloud Walker and Annie while I meet with Gideon. Go to the gates and the bridge and the end of the way and wait for the raiders to reveal themselves. Then fight them, if you must, and capture them."

Tmron objected, "By your side who will stand when Gideon you meet?"

"George will be with me."

Tmron looked around and saw his daughter. "With you Fleng will go. Strong she is and much protection she can offer."

"It is not necessary," the Ferryman responded.

"Alden," George interrupted. "Don't take any more un-necessary risks. Gideon said you could have two with you."

The Ferryman looked at George. "Simon said the same. Very well."

Tmron called Fleng and told her to accompany the Ferryman.

The Ferryman said, "When you have captured all the raiders in the village, place a signal at the top of the gate tower."

George said, "Better yet, place a signal there regardless of your success – stationary if you're still fighting and wave it when it's over."

The Ferryman nodded and wished them good fortune. Then he, George, and Fleng walked out of the village.

The sun warmed the valley and all the vegetation reached up to it. Every color was changed and the valley seemed a different place. It happened every sun day. This time, however, there was a shadow of concern that could not be completely cast aside.

The Ferryman, George Severe, and Fleng walked away from the security of Wind Castle. Shortly after they left, they heard isolated shouts and cries from different parts of the village. The three stopped for a moment and turned to look back. A winged horse gained flight and moved across the sky toward Gideon's camp.

They continued walking. A wide line of raiders and Spoils stood nearly a mile away. Three figures approached. The Ferryman said, "They have many Warriors, George."

"It's not too late to change your mind."

Alden shook his head.

George looked back at the gate tower. "No signal yet."

They stopped midway between the village and the line of raiders. Gideon and his friends walked toward them, stopping short of striking distance. Gideon looked at Fleng and sneered at George. "Ferryman, you have requested this meeting and I have come. What is it that you wish to say?"

"I asked to meet you in the hope of understanding your reasons for attacking our village and other villages in the Land."

"I attack because I *choose* to. I need no other reason."

"It is not good that you do this. It is not good for the Land, or the villages you attack, or for you."

Gideon smirked and answered, "It is good if I say it is good. You have the power to control the magic in Wind Castle. That magic should be in other hands now – my hands. I am prepared to take it if you will not give it freely."

"There is no great magic in Wind Castle," the Ferryman answered calmly. "The magic is throughout the Land, and you can never wield it in the shadow of Jack LaRoche."

"We shall see, Ferryman. I have many with me who will do as I say. If I tell them to go into your village and take what they choose, they will do it. If I tell them to kill those who live within, they will do it. If I tell them to take Wind Castle, they will do that, too. Before the light is lost, you will serve as my Spoil. The treatment you receive will depend upon the difficulty you cause."

"Your followers are not as loyal as you believe. The ways of Jack LaRoche have no place here. Think about the changes in your village since you followed his ways. The Land—"

Gideon interrupted, "The plague upon my village was brought by this stranger to the Land who stands beside you, or perhaps at your hand. When I take Wind Castle, I shall cast the plague upon *you*."

The Ferryman remained unshaken. "There was no plague cast upon your village. The undoing of your village was at *your* hands and those of Telemachus and Jack LaRoche."

Gideon tried to respond but the Ferryman raised his voice slightly and continued, "And you are not going to take Wind Castle."

"We shall see, Ferryman. Look at those who follow me." He waved his arm behind him. "And there are others in the hills waiting for my call."

"There are no others," the Ferryman retorted. "Tmron and Cloud Walker captured them and took them to Wind Castle. They cannot help you."

Gideon stuttered, "You captured a small number of cowards who claimed to be my followers. They were unimportant. I have many more hidden among the trees in the hills." Gideon's tone was obviously less confident.

The Ferryman pointed to the sky where the winged horse flew. "If you did have others in the hills, I would know despite the forests."

Gideon looked back and shouted in anger, "I told you I would have Wind Castle before the day is ended and I *shall* have it. You will not return to your castle, Ferryman."

George interrupted, "Oh? What treachery have you planned, Gideon?"

"Be quiet, stranger."

George would not be silenced. "Could it be that you planned to take the gates and streets of the village and castle?"

Gideon's face turned crimson. "I did not come to talk to you."

The Ferryman continued, "We saw your followers waiting by the castle gates and along the bridge and at the village gate. By now, they have been taken."

Gideon's face tightened. The sides of his head pulsed at the grinding of his teeth. His eyes squinted.

"George and Cloud Walker taught us the *secrets* of their land. Tmron taught the secrets you learned from Jack LaRoche." Without having looked back at the castle, the Ferryman added, "If there is a signal at the gate tower, your followers have already been taken."

Gideon looked at the tower and blurted, "I will have Wind Castle this day and you will regret the trouble you have caused, Ferryman." He looked at his escorts and barked, "Take them."

The two drew knives from their belts while Gideon reached toward the Ferryman. George and Fleng stepped between them. Fleng brushed Gideon aside and arrested the charge of the other two. George waved his arms at the winged horse until Gideon knocked him down with a blow to the side of his head.

George fell and rolled in a stupor on the ground. Images scrambled in his brain. He heard Fleng yelp. One of Gideon's escorts flew over George. George could not tell if he ever hit the ground. He rolled to his knees, trying to join the fight. Gideon drew his knife, threatening the Ferryman. George stumbled toward Gideon, intending to disarm him. Disoriented as he was, he knocked the knife from Gideon's hand before falling to the ground again.

George saw the winged horse approach. He directed his thoughts to the sky, *Save the Ferryman.*

Gideon stood over George. "This is the last time you will interfere." He thrust his foot toward George's face. George deflected the kick with his hands. Gideon tumbled over him and George rolled aside, jumping to his feet. George thought the ground spun as he stood.

Another yelp from Fleng. George saw her fall, bleeding at her arms and legs. One of the raiders stood beside her, ready to thrust his knife. George did not know what to do - ward Gideon's next attack, reach down for a rock to throw, or throw himself at Fleng's attacker. If he reached for the rock, he might be too dizzy to stand and throw it. He did not know exactly where Gideon was but he might do just as well to move away from him as to stand and receive his attack. He plowed into Fleng's attacker before the knife reached her.

Fleng crawled toward George and her assailant. George and the raider rolled side to side, George groping for the hand that held the knife, the raider keeping it away from him while searching for the chance to use it. Another roll brought them closer to Fleng. She reached the raider's hand and crushed it in her grip. Bones cracked and crumbled until there was nothing left but a bloody stub stuck to the knife handle, the assailant screaming throughout.

George stood on shaky legs. The winged horse had landed. George saw a crowd of people running toward them from Wind Castle. He turned and saw another crowd closing from the valley. The winged horse trotted toward the Ferryman but Alden held his place. Gideon and his last escort closed on the Ferryman. *Go, Alden. Before it's too late*, George thought as he ran toward Gideon.

I cannot leave you here.

You must. This is going to be a full-scale battle any minute and you can't be in the middle of it. GO!

But—

Go back!

The Ferryman turned toward the winged horse but Gideon kept him from mounting. George knocked the other raider aside. Gideon swung his knife at the Ferryman but missed, striking the winged horse instead. The horse reared up and kicked Gideon away. The Ferryman leapt to the horse's back, behind the elfin rider. Gideon grabbed its wing and thrust his knife wildly at the Ferryman's leg and the horse's side.

George caught Gideon's arm. He twisted it and slammed it to his knee until Gideon released the knife. The winged horse found sufficient clear ground and took to the air. The other raider jumped on George's back, forcing him to release Gideon.

George twisted, trying to dislodge the raider – a task better accomplished when Gideon punched George in the stomach. George collapsed, sending the raider rolling close enough to Fleng to be caught in her grasp. Gideon kicked George in the side. He stood over George, huffing. "It is over, George Severe. Now you will die."

Gideon scrambled for his knife. George struggled with the little air he could hold in his lungs. He found the strength to throw himself at Gideon, wrestling him to the ground. He regained his feet before Gideon and kicked him. Then he recovered Gideon's knife and smashed it with a rock.

George heard the calls of the crowd rushing from Wind Castle and the battle cry of the raiders. *No. Stay back – everyone.* George looked toward Gideon and ducked as the heavy end of the Unicorn's horn crashed on his back and shoulders. The sky flashed white and his ears rang. He could not breathe. He rolled with each of Gideon's kicks.

"I said it is over, George Severe. I still have the magic of this horn and it has the power to strike you down."

No. Another kick. *No. Stop.* Another kick. *Please.* Another blow toward his head. A bright flash. Ringing. *Help me. Somebody, help me.*

George felt the ground rumbling – different from the onrushing crowds. In fact, *that* rumble seemed to slow. The new one sounded like . . . *galloping*?

Another kick. George rolled and looked up through bloody eyes. Gideon stood over him with the Unicorn's horn raised over his head, its pointed end directed at George. *Please help me.*

George raised his arm to deflect the impending blow. He looked up past his arm. Gideon's motion and words were suddenly interrupted and his abdomen exploded as a long red horn protruded from it. Gideon lowered his hands, his face twisted in pain and amazement. He rose into the air, impaled on a young Unicorn's horn while clutching the one taken from its dame. With a twist of its neck, the young Unicorn withdrew its horn and let Gideon fall to the ground in a crackling thud. The second Unicorn, older and stronger, trotted around the combatants, warding the approaching throngs.

One raider crawled away, nursing his crushed hand. Fleng released the other from her grip. He rolled away from her and lay still, watching the trotting Unicorn.

George lowered his arm, wiped blood from his face, and spit blood through loose teeth. He fought against a gray tunnel that threatened to engulf his consciousness. He pressed against the ground. His vision cleared. Somehow, his feet found their places and he stood, fighting the dizziness.

The large Unicorn slowed its pace while the other stood over Gideon. George took a step closer. The young Unicorn looked at the horn in Gideon's hand then back at George. George felt compelled to offer his approval. He nodded. The Unicorn lowered its head, took his mother's horn in his teeth, and tried pulling it out of Gideon's grip.

Beaten and near death, Gideon would not release the horn – as if it were all that held him to life. The Unicorn withdrew and looked at George again.

The Warriors and raiders had slowed their charges when the Unicorns intervened. The slower runners of each party caught up with their friends. George was the only individual of the two delegations standing. He took another step toward Gideon. "Release the horn, Gideon." George coughed and spit more blood. He saw only a glimmer of life in Gideon's glazed eyes as the raider turned his head to one side.

Cedric called out from the midst of the raiders. "He

has stricken Gideon and readies to kill him. Save Gideon." He resumed his charge, followed by the remaining raiders, which incited the Warriors to do the same. In seconds they would clash and the battle would rage.

George watched Gideon's face as he stepped on his arm. Gideon's chin and neck were stiff with stubbornness and his throat swelled with futile attempts to swallow. George stepped harder until Gideon's hand opened, releasing the horn. Gideon convulsed briefly before blood flowed out of his mouth, nose and ears. Then he lay still.

George shook his head. He looked around and realized he was about to be overwhelmed by the converging adversaries. He reached down for the horn, intending to give it to the young Unicorn. As soon as he touched the horn, he saw the bright flash he had seen each time Gideon struck him with it, but this time, the flash did not end. The ground trembled and the brightness grew, lifting him into the sky. The Land, the battle, and his pain seemed to fall away. The cool white energy surged through him. He felt invigorated . . . POWERFUL. He was certain he was invincible.

George looked down at the raiders and Warriors, ready to clash. Some looked at him and stopped their charge. Others had not noticed the growing conflagration where George stood and they continued their attack. He felt detached from everything, recognizing nothing but knowing that something down there irritated him. "STOP!" George yelled. He felt his feet stretch to the ground while a shaft of bright light rose to his head in the sky. He pointed the horn to the narrowing space between the converging fighters and a bolt of lightning tore into the Land.

Something flew by him and another bolt of lightning blasted through the sky – barely missing the Ferryman on the winged horse. "STOP, I SAY!" The winged horse landed behind the line of Warriors.

George.

He looked around for the source of the sound in his head.

Hear me, George Severe.

He looked around again. Creatures stood looking at him. Some lay on the ground – one of them larger than the others. Something moved toward the large creature. "STOP!" A small bolt arrested the movement.

Hear me, George.

"WHO CALLS?"

Your friend, Alden, calls.

"FRIEND?" He looked at all the frozen creatures. One of them moved and he pointed the horn.

"Hold, George! It is I – Alden, Ferryman for the Land, and your friend."

George held the power back, but continued pointing the horn at Alden.

"Many of your friends are here. Look! There is Cloud Walker."

George looked at Cloud Walker and back at Alden. There was something familiar about the two creatures.

"You remember him, do you not? And there is Tmron."

George looked at the large creature standing beside a crater in the soil.

"Here is Annie! Certainly you remember her."

There was an odd creature where the Ferryman pointed. It was not the same as the others – more like a tree at times. He squinted and thought he saw a face within the leaves – not very pleasant.

"Tarnation, Sonny. Will ya put that danged thing down an' come back ta earth? Or whatever this place is supposed ta be."

George lowered the horn. That voice was familiar.

The Ferryman called out. "There is Fleng, lying on the ground."

George looked at the large creature. "She's hurt, George. Let us help her."

Tmron moved toward his daughter but jumped back when another bolt crashed into the crater. George looked at the injured Sasquatch. "FLENG?" He stretched his arm and the horn toward her. Tmron tried going to her but Cloud Walker and Alden convinced him to wait. George released a cool shaft of light, which enveloped Fleng.

"No, Blondie," Annie said.

The shaft of light remained steady.

"She's your friend, Sonny. . . . George, don't!"

The light faded to pink and slowly extinguished. When George lowered the horn, Fleng was healed and the blood, which matted her fur, was gone.

"George," the Ferryman said.

George looked at him.

"Think of who you are, George. Think of what you believe. Think of your friends and your family."

384 | WIND CASTLE

George recognized him. He knew he was his friend. His hand felt cold. He looked at the horn and back at the Ferryman. Then, he looked around him. *Tmron? Cloud Walker? Fleng.* Then he saw a short, wiry woman and remembered what he thought the first time he met her, *Even if she were a man, she'd be ugly.* "ANNIE?" A strange aura surrounded her and her appearance wavered.

He looked at the two Unicorns and again at the horn he held. He pointed it at the blood-drenched Unicorn. Cool white light fell over the young beast, purging the blood from its horn, head, and neck. The light faded. George extended the horn to the Unicorn but something told him to hold short. He thought he would lose something if he extended further.

It is hard to let it go, George. You must choose.

George knew the Ferryman's mental voice. He looked at the horn.

The power feels good, comfortable . . . intoxicating. Only you can decide whether you will control the power or allow it to control you.

He looked at the Unicorn.

Do what you believe.

George extended the horn and the Unicorn took it in its mouth. Suddenly, George felt as if all his blood drained from his body. He felt oppressed by the pull of gravity. He could not speak but looked at the Unicorn, pleading with his eyes. The Unicorn bowed to him.

The Ferryman then spoke to the raiders with a strong voice, which carried over the distance between. "Hear me, all of you from the troubled village. Gideon is lost to the Land. He was lost before this day – lost in the ways of Jack LaRoche and Telemachus. There is no reason for those ways to continue in this Land. We have lived in peace through most of our history. You were never in want until you followed the ways of the stranger. You can find the ways of the Land again if you are willing to try.

"We offer you no harm if you choose to cast aside the new ways you have learned. If you do not, we must stop you before you do great harm to the Land. Gideon knew we could stop him before he died. He knew that we captured those you left at the hills. He knew that we stopped those who were sent into our village and to the gates of Wind Castle. His last hope was to destroy us, thinking he would then control the Land.

"The strangers to our Land have taught us many secrets. We know all the secrets you learned from Jack LaRoche and we can defend the Land if we must, but it is no better for the Land to use these ways for this purpose than it is to use them for your purpose. Our Land is a very fragile place. Even the Mother Tree is sickened. There are forces here that are easily upset – as you have learned in your own village. The plague on your village will spread throughout the Land if you continue to follow the teachings of Jack LaRoche."

The Ferryman paused. George's memory and awareness returned. He looked at the Ferryman and at the raiders who looked among themselves. The Ferryman continued, "Unbind your captives and let them walk to our village. You too, can come to us, if you will cast away your weapons." He waited for a moment but none of the raiders moved. George felt the quiet tension. "Do it now!" Finally, a few dropped their tools and weapons to the ground. Others turned and untied some Dwarves and Fauns.

The young Unicorn raised his head with the horn in his teeth. He trotted to his father and both circled George and the Ferryman before trotting away, taking a path around the line of raiders and toward the hills. The raiders watched silently until they felt the Unicorns were safely away. Spoils and raiders walked toward the Ferryman and the Warriors who stood behind him.

George *felt* the Ferryman's anxiety drain away. Alden said to him, "We will fight no more." Then he turned to Cloud Walker. "What of the events in the village?"

Cloud Walker reported, "The castle and village are ours, but many were killed or injured on both sides."

"Such was not unexpected. I knew how many young had been born to the village. The Land foretold our losses."

The raiders and their Spoils assembled before the Ferryman. "You should not return to your village except to find your families and move away. You may rest at Wind Castle and leave whenever you choose. If you leave, find another village that will have you, or build a new village. Your homes are lost to the Land and will be long in recovery."

As the last of the raiders joined their friends, one youth remained at a distance. The Ferryman asked, "Who stands there?"

George had been trying to reconcile all that happened to

him when the Ferryman's question drew his attention. He looked at the youth. "It looks like Elias, Gideon's son."

The Ferryman called to him but he did not respond. The boy looked at those who watched him. Slowly, he withdrew his weapon from a rope belt and dropped it to the ground. Then, he turned and walked toward the foothills.

George asked, "Do you want me to bring him back to Wind Castle?"

The Ferryman answered, "We should not take him against his will." He and George watched the boy walk away as the others moved toward the village. In the distance, two Unicorns trotted across the valley floor. The Ferryman continued watching them as he said to George, "Perhaps he will find his peace as the Unicorns found theirs – after much time has passed."

Twenty-eight

Choices

THE SUN BEAT down on the castle village. Many who had called so forcefully for action were not very pleased with its consequences. The dead residents were taken to a place of peace near the Heart or out of the village to places they had loved when alive. The villagers helped the raiders carry their dead out of the village to the place where Gideon lay. The dead decayed to white powder by next light.

The injured were taken to the chambers around the Heart where their recovery was quick. The Ferryman released the earlier captives on their oaths that they no longer raid their neighbors. He repeated his instructions that they were not to return to the troubled village except to find their families. If they did not want to leave Wind Castle, they would be welcomed there. Few chose to remain, however – better to begin anew elsewhere.

The first to leave Wind Castle after the fighting were the Dwarves, Fauns, and Sasquatch of the hillside village. Some left saying the Ferryman had been too generous with the raiders. They wanted greater punishment for those who had taken the lives of so many of their friends, but they accepted his judgment. Tmron, Fleng, and the remaining Sasquatch built a small village outside Wind Castle.

The raiders and their first Spoils departed shortly after the mountain villagers. The Spoils returned to their own homes after finding their families in the troubled village. Some of the raiders went to other villages. Many who had no families in the troubled village, started a new community in the hills overlooking the valley of Wind Castle.

The Ferryman had dispatched some winged horses and their riders to the troubled village to report the results of Gideon's insurrection. The messengers returned and reported that Gideon's remaining supporters were few. Once the frenzy of vengeance had subsided, the dissent of the trade and craft leaders had grown. Some villagers as well as most of the Spoils had already left to begin new lives, confident that they could find new homes beyond Gideon's grasp after his expected return. The greatest factor in establishing the influence of the trades and crafts had been Gideon's destruction of the potted plant in his rage after his return from the battle with the Dragon. The villagers realized there could be no light for them if they continued following Gideon.

Despite Cloud Walker's recommendation that a force

should remain ready to defend the castle, the Ferryman called his villagers together and disbanded the Warriors – thanking those who served.

The Ferryman walked with George along the corridor leading to George's room. "The messengers told me that those who had not yet left the troubled village will seek a suitable garden and pool of water in the Opens and build a new village."

George said, "You were right about their reluctance to follow Gideon. I wish they'd stood up to him sooner."

"Most important, they finally chose the ways of the Land on their own. They were ready to leave the troubled village even before they learned of Gideon's defeat."

In George's room, the Ferryman said, "I have spoken long with Cloud Walker. He has no interest in leading this Land."

"He seems more comfortable on his own. Although, he did well leading the Warriors."

"He told me he is going to the troubled village to consult with the Great Wakinyjan."

"The Griffin? His Thunderbird?"

"Yes. The Ancient Counselor told me Cloud Walker would not be happy here until he found peace in his own land. I passed these words to Cloud Walker and he said he would like to return to his family after seeing the Thunderbird."

"I'm surprised. I didn't think he'd ever go back after hearing the stories his son, Phillip, told me."

"You should not be surprised. He has been unsettled since you told him about the pride in his son's heart. He took the name Cloud Walker, despite its intended mockery, to share in that pride. Until then, we knew him as Iron Bull. He will go home and find peace. Then, he will return."

George sat at his table for a few moments after the Ferryman left, wondering why he had not thought about home. Guilt crowded his mind as he thought about Jane and Anastasia. He rose from his seat and went to the warm stone bed where he reclined and gazed blankly at the ceiling, trying to see his wife and baby through the stone. Weariness soon overcame him and he slept restlessly. Jane called for him in his sleep and Anastasia reached out to him. As his dream progressed, they called out less frequently. He tried calling back – to tell them he heard them and would return. But they did not respond.

His vision of his wife and daughter faded, replaced by a view of a large dark cloud. A Dragon flew around the cloud, past a castle and toward some hills. The sky blackened and there was a flash of lightning. The Dragon was a black shadow in the distance. With the next flash, the shadow became a Griffin, flying in the storm. George watched its flight until it landed atop a gold dome. In a street below stood a dark form noble and respectful, apparently worshiping the beast. A flash of lightning revealed Cloud Walker's face.

In the darkness that followed, the form changed. It became smaller and the appearance of reverence was replaced by something else – wonder. A boy – George many years ago – looked up to the roiling clouds of a rushing storm. Someone called to him. Briskly, a hand reached out and pulled the boy away. George was pulled through the darkness to a cool, damp, foreboding place. Noise and turmoil followed and the next thing he knew, he looked down into a dark pit. A woman struggled in rushing water. Another person tried helping her, but alas, she disappeared in the darkness. George cried out in his sleep, "Mamma, Mamma!" There was no answer.

George twisted on his bed. As the dream passed, he rested for a short time. More dreams followed. Most presented pictures of Jane and Anastasia. He tried reaching out to them, but they did not see him. Occasionally, they spoke of him. His one-year-old daughter spoke? Whenever he heard them he called back, *I'm here! I'm over here!* Again there was no response. The images drifted away and his dreams were gone.

George woke before daylight and left his room. He walked to the courtyard and up the tower stairs to the parapet of Wind Castle where he looked over the valley toward the hills. There was greater peace in the hills than in his dreams. He looked at the pond outside the village. The shadows were beginning to find greater definition. He saw a small figure standing at the edge. "Annie?"

The Ferryman surprised him by answering as he stepped beside George, "Yes. She has stood there every morning since the battle."

"She's been acting very strange lately. *Everybody* has."

"Many witnessed your battle with Gideon and what

occurred afterward. When you first came here, you were just a stranger. Now that you have been revealed, you are seen with awe, admiration, and a sense of fear. It is only natural that so many would look upon you differently. It will pass in time. Annie, on the other hand, is at the edge of making the most difficult decision she has ever faced."

"What do you mean?"

"It is a decision she must make on her own."

"What—"

"We cannot interfere. You will know the instant she has chosen."

George and the Ferryman watched quietly from the parapet. George thought about his dreams, the power he felt when he held the horn, and the Ferryman's suggestion that some looked upon him with fear. The Ferryman interrupted his thoughts. "You are troubled, George?"

"Yes, I am," he answered. "I miss home. I want to return to my land. I can't bear to be away any longer."

"I had hoped you would stay with us. But, like Cloud Walker, you shall never rest here until you have found peace below. Perhaps you can leave with Cloud Walker – or shortly afterward."

George held back tears. Finally, he bowed his head, "This Land is such a fabulous place. Part of me doesn't want to leave, but, right now, I can't bear to stay. I have to get home."

"It is indeed understandable. You have experienced much and the time has come for you go back to your land. Fear not, my friend. This does not prevent you from returning."

The sky was pink and the village below them stirred. The Ferryman placed his hand on George's shoulder. They retreated to the hall where they ate quietly together. As the hall began to crowd, they went to the Heart where the Ferryman instructed George.

George said, "You still want to teach me, knowing I want to leave?"

"It costs me nothing and I enjoy teaching you."

"What can I do in return?"

"You have done enough for me and for the Land. However, if it would please you, teach me more about the weather in the land below and how you were able to find this Land."

"If you don't want to be discovered, you'll have to maneuver in a manner more in line with normal weather behavior. There are satellites that survey the Earth and pass pictures to observers. You have to be careful about the areas you choose for sun days. . . ."

They instructed each other and studied together throughout the day. Both enjoyed the lessons, but to a much greater extent, they enjoyed the company.

George paced in his room. He thought he might be feeling the approach of something awful, but the feeling was different – like the *awful* would be mixed with good. He left his room and walked to the Great Hall. The hall was deserted and dark, except for the Torch Stones, which illuminated as he approached them. He went to the gate tower and climbed to the parapet. It, too, was deserted. He saw nothing in the darkness of the village and valley outside the castle. Still uneasy, he returned to his room and slept.

George rested quietly through most of the night, teased by the start of a dream, which did not become established until nearly dawn. He saw a small dark figure, standing at the edge of a pond. The figure slowly waded into the water. He shared the chill of the water as he followed the figure to an island. He stood in the cool water as the figure stood motionless on the island. At length, the figure moved to the center of the small island and stooped to remove a shoe. Standing on one leg, the figure turned and looked at George.

Suddenly, George awoke and sat up on his bed. "ANNIE, NO!" As his feet reached the floor, he felt the ground gently rumble. He ran out of his room. All the corridor Torch Stones were bright – even before he approached them. The entire castle suddenly came awake. George ran through the court and up to the parapet where the Ferryman stood. George looked at the pond. A kaleidoscopic-glow emanated from the island. He looked at the Ferryman.

Alden smiled, "She has chosen."

"No!" George said as he ran back down the tower steps toward the pond outside the village. The villagers, milling about in response to the rumbling, did not slow him. He ran over the mud at the shore and through the shallow water with high steps until the depth slowed him. Then he ran through the water pushing it behind him with his hands.

He stopped at the island shore, knee-deep in water, and peered into the variegated light. He stepped out of the water, close to the source of light, and saw a tree – shaped much like a Mulberry tree, but different. Beside the berries and leaves common to that species, it bore flowers, nuts, cones, and needles. The tree was strong and healthy in appearance. The thick trunk was protected by sturdy bark and at the root were two handmade leather shoes.

"Oh, Annie." George dropped to his knees and sat back on his feet, shaking his head. "I'm so sorry."

Ain't nothin' ta be sorry about, Sonny.

George lifted his head. "Annie! You're still here?"

Course I'm still here. Do I look like I can walk away?

George offered a meek smile. "No.. . . Are you all right?"

Never felt better! How do I look?

"You look . . . beautiful."

What?

"There's no other word to describe you. Annie Strummond, you look beautiful!"

Well, I'll be.

"How did this happen?"

I don't know how. All I know is what I did an' how I felt – ever since we came here. All this time, I been fightin' against this place. But, when I seen what happened to you when ya picked up that horn, I knowed I couldn't fight much longer. It's jes too strong, Sonny. So, I finally took off ma shoes.

"But you didn't have to fight much longer. We're going back! The Ferryman will let us go whenever we want."

Hardly matters now. I don't think this is somethin' I can

change – even if I wanted to.

George shook his head. "Oh, Annie."

Don't ya go poo-pooin' me, Sonny.

"But—"

No buts. I said I ain't never felt better an' I meant it. This is where I'm gonna stay.

George thought about the crusty, weather-beaten little woman he met at the outfitters. He would never win this argument. "What does it feel like?"

Feels purty good mostly. Ever'thin' in this Land seems ta be talkin' ta me – stuff I ain't never heard afore, some good, some not so good. I can feel the warmth an' comfort o' that there castle for the first time. I can feel the sickness in that village we was at. Oh, an' I can feel them Dragon's teeth ya planted a stirrin'.

"Really? They're hatching?"

An' gnawin' at them flowers near 'bouts.

George remained with Annie throughout the day, oblivious to the crowd that surrounded them. Annie's shoes became small piles of white powder. Eventually, George and Annie grew weary.

You go rest now, Sonny. When you're ready, go back to yer family.

George stood and walked off the island. He looked back at her, then turned and waded past the onlookers.

The time passed quickly for George. He learned and taught as much as he could. The village had recovered from the siege and life returned to what it once was. Cloud Walker had returned from his pilgrimage to the Thunderbird and reported that the village was deserted, except for the Great Wakinyjan. He marveled at the new tree that adorned the island and proclaimed great respect for the woman he once barely tolerated.

The Ferryman told Cloud Walker they were approaching the place where he had stepped onto the Land. "Do you want to return now?"

Cloud Walker closed his eyes and nodded. He and the Ferryman planned his departure.

George guided the Land with Alden's instruction by turning and adjusting the stones along a shelf overlooking the Heart chamber. "Where are we going?"

The Ferryman said, "Cloud Walker calls it *Harney Peak*."

I know that place. That's where I met Cloud Walker's son."

"You could go with him, George. But there is another mountain closer to the seacoast which may better serve you — although the mooring is difficult because of the need to avoid certain structures near its peak."

George agreed. "If it's faster, I'll wait."

The Land approached Harney Peak and Cloud Walker prepared to leave Wind Castle and go to the edges where he could walk off the Land to the earth below. The Ferryman told him how to find his way through the dense fog. The last time Cloud Walker had left the Land, it was without guidance and quite unintentional. "You were fortunate you did not fall from the edges. You will lose memory of this Land just as you did after your last visit, but you will probably regain it more quickly. Those who have traveled between lands many times have better retention of their memories of this Land.

"George will probably not remember the Land as quickly as you. Try to find him and wait for him to decide whether he will return with you. I know you will return, but it might be more difficult for George. Help him, but do not try to influence his decision. Answer his questions and help him through his doubts until he is sure he will be at peace with his choice."

Cloud Walker agreed and, although the Ferryman had offered an escort of surveyors, he left the castle alone.

George and the Ferryman were at the Heart during the mooring. George heard the bell toll and felt a slight shift in the ground below him as the Land held its mooring. He felt a loss as soon as Cloud Walker stepped off the Land. After another toll, the Land drifted away.

George prepared for his own departure. He was in his apartment realizing he had nothing to pack — except the Dragon's teeth. The Ferryman was with him, discussing their lessons and thanking George for all he had done.

"I'm not so sure I want to leave."

Alden said, "You can never guide the Land if you are not at peace with your own world."

George nodded and looked at the clay crocks holding the Dragon's teeth. "My land is no place for Dragons. Can I leave these with you?"

Alden nodded. George gave his friend the two crocks full

of teeth. As Alden accepted them, George placed his hands in his pockets and felt the small teeth he had kept. Remembering Frothgarde's suggestion that anyone who possessed the teeth when freely given would never need fear a Dragon, he kept those in his pocket. Then he reminded the Ferryman of Frothgarde's instructions concerning the teeth and the young Dragons.

George hesitated. He wanted to ask one last question. The subject had only been touched once since his battle with Gideon – his transformation when he took the Unicorn's horn. The Ferryman had only alluded to it when discussing the new behavior of the villagers toward George. "What happened when I took . . ."

"Ah!" Alden reached up and placed his hands on George's shoulders. George felt his penetrating gaze. "The horn of the Unicorn." The Ferryman squeezed George's upper arms, then stepped back, holding his gaze. "I wondered if you would ask or if you already knew."

"All this time, I've denied its magic. Gideon and Telemachus were right. It did hold magic and power."

"No, George. It wasn't the horn. The magic is in you. Simon and I knew it the moment you touched the Land – just as we knew Annie could become the Mother Tree when we saw her. The horn only showed you the way."

"But—"

"Do not deny yourself, George. The power and magic are in you. And you chose to control it over being lost to it. You did so when you gave the horn to the young Unicorn. You have shown that the power is well-placed."

"What should I—"

"I cannot answer questions that *you* must resolve. Find your answers within – just as you did when you held the horn."

George lowered his head and nodded.

The Ferryman reminded him, "After you return to your land, your memories of Wind Castle and this Land will be lost for a short time. We believe it results from the loss of energy from our soil – a shock to your system most noticeable in those who have not been here very long. It will be more difficult for you to find us again since you have taught me how to follow the natural course of the weather. When you seek the Land, call to me with your thoughts and dreams, and I will guide you to it. Listen for the toll."

George thanked him and left Wind Castle. He walked across the Bridge-Over-Nothing and looked back at the parapet. A small figure watched him. He waved and said to himself, "Goodbye, Tamara. Thank you."

He stopped at the pond to say goodbye to Annie. The glow of her transformation had waned, but her beauty was no less magnificent.

Take care o' yerself, Sonny.

George choked. He couldn't say what he wanted. "You know, Annie, the Ferryman says that you're the new Mother Tree for the Land.

Jes 'cause I call you Sonny don't mean you can start callin' me Mother.

George smiled. "All right. But could you call me—"

Clam up, Sonny. I got one more thing ta say afore ya go. You remember the time with that Ancient feller when they tol' ya why they had ta raise that cloud?

"Yes?"

Them people ya was workin' for – they ain't no good. Ya oughtta know by now that I'm pretty good at readin' folks. If they're int'rested in helpin' ya find this place, they want it for somethin'. I'd say it's a pretty good idea to ferget as much as ya can about this place as far as them folks is concerned.

"Don't worry. It took Cloud Walker two years to remember anything after his first trip."

Well, when things start ta come back to ya, jes try ta be careful 'bout who's around at the time.

"I will, Annie. It's not going to be the same without you."

Annie did not respond.

George blinked back tears. "Goodbye, Annie." He turned and walked away.

George.

George stopped and turned back.

I'm gonna miss you, too.

TWENTY-NINE

Home

SEAN YOUNG AND Tony Catrone were recording their latest weather observations atop Mount Washington when two of their instruments failed. They had been monitoring a cold front as it dropped down on New England from Canada. Although Mount Washington had already received some snow this fall, the new front promised to deliver measurable precipitation to the lowlands as well. When Sean had noticed a dense echo in the west, moving toward them, he had been certain the observatory would be clobbered.

The storm cloud hovered about the observatory. Tony speculated that the mast holding the failed equipment might have broken loose again. Sean doubted that, since the winds were exceptionally weak, compared to those normally recorded at the highest point in New England.

Sean said, "I'm going out to take a look."

"They're not critical. We can use the backups."

"I know, but I want to check it out anyway so we can call in for repairs." Sean took a parka from a hook near the door and stepped out into the cold autumn air. At three in the afternoon, the sky was unusually dark. Sean ducked his head unnecessarily to pass under the low clouds. The light of day passed along the horizon below the awesome cloud hovering above.

Someone stumbled toward him. He quickly moved toward the stranger who was obviously in need of some assistance. The stranger wore a heavy, hooded cloak or robe that hid his features. He stretched his hands toward Sean. Sean asked, "Where did you come from? Who *are* you?" The stranger collapsed into his arms.

A telephone rang inside the Severe home. Jane Severe fumbled with her house key. It finally went into the lock and turned. She pushed the door open and ran to the phone that hung on the kitchen wall. The ringing stopped. Nevertheless, she quickly lifted the receiver and answered, "Hello?" There was no response – just a tone telling her she was too late. "Oh darn!" she said as she slammed the receiver onto its cradle.

She rubbed her knee, which she had hit on the storm door before she found her key. Then the phone rang again. She immediately lifted the receiver while massaging her injured knee. "Hello? . . . Yes, this is Jane Severe. . . . Is this some sort of joke? . . . Are you sure? Is he OK?" Jane sat on a stool beside the kitchen counter. "When did this happen, and where?" She sat erect and nearly stood. "Yesterday? And you're calling me now? . . . I'm sorry. I've been at work. . . . Can I talk to him? . . . Why not? . . . When can I see him? . . . No. I'm driving up tonight. If he's not awake, at least I'll know for sure it's him. Are there places to stay up there? . . . What's your number? I'll call you after I've checked in. . . . OK. Thank you for calling. . . . Yes. Goodbye."

Jane slowly rested the receiver on its cradle and looked at the pad where she had been writing during her conversation. She lifted the receiver and pressed the buttons for directory assistance. "Bretton Woods, please. . . . Community Hospital." She followed the numbers already written on her pad one by one with a pencil and wrote a checkmark at the end.

She called the number. "Dr. Thompson, please. . . . Dr. Thompson? . . . This is Jane Severe. Did you just call me?" Tears flooded her eyes. "No, no, doctor. It's just been so long. I practically gave up hope. . . . I'm sorry I doubted you, doctor. I'll see you later. . . . Thank you."

Jane sat quietly at the kitchen table, wiping away her tears and blowing her nose into a small tissue and then into a few more. She lifted the receiver again and dialed. "Hello, Ma? . . . Listen, Ma. I just got a call. George is alive! . . . Yes, they found him up on Mount Washington. . . . They don't know for sure. They say he passed out just as they found him. . . . They got his wallet. It was all beat up, but they were able to read everything. . . . Oh, I hope so, Ma." She cried again. "I'm driving up as soon as I pick up Anastasia. . . . No, I'm taking her with me. . . . Yes, I'm sure, Ma. I'll call you as soon as I find out anything. . . . OK, Ma. Goodbye!"

George thought he was dreaming. A large man, at least it seemed like a man, had wrapped a heavy cloak over him and told him it was to keep him warm. He argued that he was not cold. The man insisted that he take the cloak and some awkward leather shoes, which he told him to wear as soon as he stepped onto the cold stone. Then the man faded away. Later, he heard a voice. It told him to listen for the bells when he wanted to return.

He remembered stepping onto a ledge that was so cold that he lost all thought of the voice. He quickly placed his feet into the crude shoes and stepped about nervously. Then he heard a bell toll and he wanted to run back to where he had been, but a dense fog surrounded him and he could not see. The fog was less dense at one horizon. He walked in that direction. Soon, he saw someone moving. He stretched out his hands toward him but could not remember whether he had ever found him. He remembered being cold and thought he had heard conversations.

Then, he was warm again, but so exhausted. All he wanted was to sleep. He ignored the calls to him. None of the voices were familiar and he felt so warm and comfortable in his sleep. Eventually, he became aware that he was in a bed – a bed with sheets and a warm wool blanket. It was a strange sensation, although he did not understand why it should be strange. He often slept with blankets clutched around his neck.

Someone mumbled. He strained to understand the words.

"Look, I know this is hard on you, but we've been paying his salary all this time and I think we have a right to know where he's been."

"You paid his salary because you were afraid I'd go public when you gave up the search."

The wool blanket itched his neck and he wanted to scratch but he could not move his left hand. It seemed to be caught on something. The mumbling continued. The voices seemed familiar. He felt as if someone was watching him. That itch. He tried again to move his left hand then thought to scratch with his right hand instead.

"He moved, Mamma! He moved his hand!"

Who was that? The voice was very close to him and it came just after he scratched himself.

"Just a minute!"

One of the mumblers. *Jane?* The familiar voice softened as she finished her sentence to the other mumbler. "Just give us some time, Mark. Then you can have all the time you need. All right?"

"OK, you can have some time together. But I've got a whole bunch of questions and my superiors won't wait very long."

George felt something push his left arm. "Hey, Mister!" Another poke followed that strange voice beside him.

"Be careful, dear. I'm coming." The familiar voice proclaimed. "Thanks. We'll see you later."

"Maybe I should stay just a bit longer," Mark said.

"You promised!"

"OK, OK."

That annoying poke again, but he could not move his left arm to push it away. George turned his head and slowly opened his eyes. Before he could focus, he heard that voice again. "He's awake, Mamma! He's awake!" George turned his head and saw a little girl looking up to his high hospital bed, poking his arm, and asking, "Hey, Mister! Are you my papa? Huh? Are you my papa, Mister?"

George was confused by the question and he looked around the room for assistance. Finally, he saw Jane standing at the foot of his bed waving back to his boss, Mark Waxman as he left the room. "Yes, Anastasia. That's your papa."

George looked back at the girl. Then he looked again at Jane with that same confused countenance. "Welcome back, George," she said. He recognized Jane, but he was very confused. Anastasia is just a baby. Who is this little girl standing beside him? Jane called her *Anastasia*. But this was much more than a baby. She was a beautiful young girl with silky blonde hair and bright-blue, inquisitive eyes. He looked at each again. "It's been a while, George," Jane added.

"How . . ." George could hardly speak. His mouth was dry and he thought he had forgotten *how* to speak.

Jane answered the unspoken question, "Over five years, George. Do you remember anything?"

George panicked. Five years? This news was too much for him to understand. Gone? Gone where? Five years? Why couldn't he remember? Tears welled up in his eyes and he shook his head.

"All right, all right George. Don't get excited," Jane said. "Take it easy now. Anastasia, go get Dr. Thompson. Everything's going to be fine, George. Just take it easy. Take it easy." She stroked his head, trying to comfort him.

George gradually accepted his situation but was unable to remember anything about the last five years. Mark Waxman questioned him before he left the hospital. He reminded George about his expedition up the mountain near Durango and he told him they found everyone caught in the avalanche except George and the guide, Annie Strummond. George told him Annie would not return. He did not know how he knew it, but *that* was one thing he knew for sure. The interview ended with George promising to visit Walter Reed Hospital for some additional testing.

Dr. Thompson completed his final examination of George. "You've recovered from most of your injuries but I still can't explain this blackening of your feet. It's not unusual to see this in frostbite cases, but there's no other evidence of frostbite – no tissue damage, the skin isn't broken, you can wiggle everything just fine. It's not a dye. In fact, they look more like they've been burned."

George said, "I don't remember being burned."

"Your memory loss is the only thing that still worries me. There seems to be no physical reason for it. Could be a psychological shock of some kind. See how things go. Call us in a few weeks, or see your own doctor. No reason you can't go home now."

"Thanks, Doc." George was glad to be leaving the hospital but not so happy about having no recollection about the last five years of his life.

Jane gave George some new clothes and carried his other personal belongings in a box provided by the hospital. They returned home – Jane, George, and the daughter he had never really known. He smiled more and more as he came to know her. She was a most garrulous child. She told him all about the school she attended and he learned much about the other children in her class. Jane told him how proud Anastasia was when she went into the school and told them that her father had been found. The child spent many hours sitting with her father, talking about the events of each day.

Years ago, Jane had taken all George's research material and stored it in boxes in their basement. George did not think to ask for it. In fact, he did not want to think about *anything* that might have taken him away from his family for such a long time.

George enjoyed the weeks of rest promised by Mark Waxman before he was to report to Walter Reed Hospital. He dreaded the need to travel there, but he pushed it from his mind. Nothing would interfere with his reunion with his wife and the opportunity to get to know his daughter.

One day, Anastasia was curiously digging into the box that her mother had carried home from the hospital. She found her father's wallet and the Dragon's teeth. When she asked George what they were, he could not tell her. Although he felt something when he saw them, he could not remember. He placed them in a small dish atop his bureau, hoping someday he would remember their significance. Then, to draw his daughter's attention away from her questions, he led her out to their back yard.

She told him she enjoyed being pushed on the swing and George was eager to please her. He pushed and pushed, carefully but firmly. She pumped her legs to go higher while calling to her father, "Higher, Papa! Higher! I want to touch the clouds. Just like you, Papa. I want to touch the clouds."

George suddenly stopped pushing and sat in the swing beside her.

Anastasia asked, "Why did you stop?"

He did not hear her. He was thinking about the clouds. Something about them haunted him.

Anastasia stopped pumping her legs and her swing slowly stopped. Then she jumped off the swing and walked over to her father. "Do you want *me* to push *you*?

Again, he did not hear.

The child tugged at his arm, "C'mon, Papa! I want to touch the clouds."

George came back. "What?"

"I want to touch the clouds! Are you OK, Papa?"

"Yes, Darlin'. What did you say?"

"Just like you, Papa. I want to touch the clouds."

"What do you mean, just like me?"

"Mamma said you were chasing clouds. Whenever my friends told me about their papas, I asked Mamma about you and she always said you were chasing clouds. I like clouds too, Papa. They're so white and puffy and pretty. I'd like to fly up in the clouds . . . and maybe live there. Do you think I could, Papa? Do you think someone could live in the clouds?"

George looked strangely at his daughter and pondered her question. He was beginning to slip away into another world of thought when she tugged at him again. "Well, Papa?"

"Well what?" George asked.

"Do you think someone could live up there?"

"I don't know, Sweetie. I don't know." He looked up to the sky and wondered.

His wondering was cut short by another tug. "C'mon, Papa. Push me!"

George dropped his eyes and answered, "OK, Sweetie. I'm gonna push you as high as a rocket." Anastasia giggled as he placed her on the seat and pushed.

So begins the tale of
Anastasia's Quest for
Wind Castle

GLOSSARY

ALDEN: Ferryman of the Land (150 years old +/-)

ALEXANDER: A resident of the Troubled Village

ANCIENT COUNSELOR: Former Ferryman retired from active leadership - Simon

ANNIE: also AJ Strummond - A crusty mountain guide hired by Mark Waxman to lead the expedition to the Land of Wind Castle

ARISTEIDES: A Centaur at the Troubled Village

ARTHUR: Background character, King Arthur; Gwydion

TONY CATRONE: A weather technician assigned to the Mount Washington observatory

CEDRIC: A confidant of Gideon

CLOUD WALKER: also Thomas "Iron Bull" Gravely - Sioux Indian believed to have traveled to a floating land in the sky

DAX: A resident of the Troubled Village

DUNCAN: A volunteer for the Land Watch at Wind Castle

ELIAS: Son of Gideon and Hilda

ELKE: Nurse at the Troubled Village

FAT DANNY: An acquaintance of Ben Kniep and Josh Windale

FERRYMAN: Suzerain of the Land, Alden

FLENG: A Sasquatch youth, Tmron's daughter

TOM FRANKLIN: Outfitter outside Durango, Colorado

FROTHGARDE: A very old Dragon in the Land

GIDEON: Telemachus' red-haired lieutenant

PHILLIP GRAVELY: Sioux Indian, son of Cloud Walker

GWYDION: Background character, King Arthur

HAP SAAD: Home village of Tamara and other Spoils; last village before the foothills

HILDA: Wife of Gideon and mother of Elias

IVAN: A resident of the Troubled Village

JACOB: A resident of the Troubled Village

JEWEL: A fairy-like creature who rides winged horses

JULIAN: A Faun at Wind Castle

BEN KNIEP: A Colorado Rescuer

JACK LAROCHE: A mercenary who escaped from a Montana prison work detail and accidentally fled to the Land, killed in a fall from the Land to a farm in Tennessee. While in the Land, he was a mentor of Telemachus and Gideon.

STAN MASZEWSKI: George Severe's expedition assistant sent by Mark Waxman to make all arrangements.

MEETING PLACE: A large stone building at the square in the

Troubled Village, much like a pub

MLET: A Sasquatch at Wind Castle

MORDRED: A volunteer for the Land Watch at Wind Castle

MOTHER TREE: A large oak Wood Nymph, sickened by the troubles in the Land

MRUDG: A Sasquatch friend of Tmron

NEVIN: A resident of the Troubled Village

NORRIS: A resident of the Troubled Village

PETER: A hunched servant in the Great Hall at Wind Castle

ROLLABEE: A nocturnal animal indigenous to the Land, crocodile-like underneath, furred back. Moves by arching its back, taking its tail in its mouth, and using its legs to roll. Makes a chirping sound.

SCRAGG: A Sasquatch at the Troubled Village and cousin to Tmron

ANASTASIA SEVERE: George Severe's daughter born at 9 lb., 2 oz. approximately one year before the expedition

GEORGE SEVERE: A Meteorologist obsessed by his discovery of a strange cloud that does not follow standard weather patterns

JANE SEVERE: Accountant wife of George Severe and mother of Anastasia Severe

SIMON: Ancient Counselor at Wind Castle

SLANTED FOREST: Area of gravitational distortion in the Land

SPOILS: Captives (servants) in the Troubled Village (spoils of war)

SURVEYORS: Individuals of the Land who explore the land below when the Land is moored

SWEETROOT: Red-leafed plant with edible, bulbous roots (tubers)

TAMARA: A Spoil in the Troubled Village

TELEMACHUS: Leader of the Troubled Village

THADDAEOUS: Brother of Telemachus in the Troubled Village

TMRON: A Sasquatch at the Troubled Village

TORCH STONES: Self-illuminating stone material mined and set where light is needed. They sense the need for light and brighten when approached.

TROUBLED VILLAGE: First village in the Land visited by George and Annie

WAKINYJAN: Thunderbird and/or Griffin

MARK WAXMAN: George Severe's employer who financed George's research and the expedition

WELDON: A volunteer for the Land Watch at Wind Castle

JOSH WINDALE: A Colorado Rescuer

SEAN YOUNG: a weather technician assigned to the Mount Washington observatory

ZANE: A Phantom messenger at Wind Castle

ABOUT THE AUTHOR

Brian Hammar was born in Lowell Massachusetts. An Engineer and Pilot by training, he sought some other means of satisfying his creative aspirations. He had always been intrigued by the flight of passing clouds. Long before he took the controls of an aircraft, he flew among the clouds in his dreams. Mythology was also of great interest. The imaginative explanations that the classical writers offered for the development of the world stimulated his creative and technical curiosity. Legends and folklore of the North American Indians nurtured a similar fascination.

Brian lives with his wife in New Hampshire. He has two grown children and two grandchildren.

www.ingramcontent.com/pod-product-compliance
Lightning Source LLC
Chambersburg PA
CBHW080857020726
47502CB00008B/2267